THE SOLIPSIST SLEEPS

By

Andrew Vernon Barber

The Solipsist Sleeps

Published by Special Delivery Press
7121 Tierra Alta Ave.
El Paso, TX 79912
www.andrewvbarberphd.com

Written by Andrew V. Barber

Illustrations, photography, and cover design by Andrew V. Barber

Modified clipart used by permission from Microsoft Corp.

LCCN: 2019942235

ISBN: 9780966970210

TABLE OF CONTENTS

ILLUSTRATIONS

GENESIS

The surrealistic solipsist summoned himself and questioned, "Whose is this existence?" He was pondering the supposition: If I think then I am. "But it doesn't mean they are," he surmised. I scrutinized his reasoning, that awareness of self and one's existence are not exactly verifiable, because consciousness surpasses direct observation and measurement.

"Can this encounter belong to anyone else but me?" I professed, answering his query with another. I further debated with myself: If one's experience is suitable for just the one, then only my sensations could be accurate. Is everything that happens inside my head? If so, then any other reality is a figment of the imagination and everyone else an extension of it.

"Then what shall I make of life, love, eternity, and God?" I inquired of the pundit... "And whose family came first? For this surely isn't the Garden of Eden. But then again, the treachery seems comparable."

His meditations became known to me in the absence of speech. I recorded them in my subconscious before they could be contaminated from outside influence and my own perceptual bias. I expected the meaning would follow in due time.

The science teacher interrupted my train of thought. "Who are you talking to?" she demanded to know.

I responded with a puzzled glare. She scolded me and directed me to the corner, as distant from her and the other pupils as physically possible. She usually dumped me on administrators. They often bickered over me.

"He's peculiar," the principal would blather to stifle her grumbling, "Deal with it."

She would invariably reply, "The child behaves like an alien from outer space."

"Who are *you* talking to?" was all I could add to the conversation, and all I learned from it.

Besides, who was he to judge peculiar, with his dainty washed-out mustache that made his lip look dirty, and that potbelly leaping over his trousers like a partially deflated balloon? He would waddle around with his shirttails pulled up and his butt-crack peeking out, making you want to heave at the sight of it. And sausage breath's constant blinking, drooling, and belching; he was a certifiable slob. But behold his sidekick, the governess want-to-be with her dreadlock perm appearing as rotten driftwood framing a gruesome countenance. After so many facelifts she seemed an emaciated feline with medusa hair. Her shrill voice could crack crystal making you cringe at the sound of it. And those paste-on fingernails worthy to scratch through a closed coffin created this icky noise whenever she was writing on the board. I would

1

choke for air around the plethora of perfume emanating from her blouse. Talk about alien. Maybe it was a middle-age crisis thing where oldsters feel inadequate and try to compensate, since what really matters is that they still can reproduce.

Once the arduous bus trip had surpassed the stinky stockyards, we were a mere five minutes from my stop. I ran the rest of the way home, bounded up the steps, slung open the screen door, carpet-surfed over the wooden floor into the den, and flopped down on the hassock. The refrain, "Don't you have homework?" echoed in the background while I continued switching channels on the squawk box. I wasn't sure if it symbolized my past or future but a scenario was evident.

There was the mad artist painting his rendition of Judgment Day while the maiden posed nude; a soldier fired his weapon into the darkness at some unknown rival as the trench filled with water; he turned into a gunslinger pounding the dust of a western ghost town, just then a Mexican senorita shuffled outside the saloon, twirling a colorful dress in folkloric dance before disappearing behind swiveling doors; the law enforcement officer was about to slap the cuffs on a juvenile offender who was spewing every curse word in the book, right when the crazed drunken maniac busted miss piggy over the head with a beer bottle. Commercials, I can't stand them. But I truly enjoyed the vintage rock and roll concert station so I tarried there.

Before I knew, it was back to the classroom scene where once again I was staring at the wall. I marveled, "What, this again?" Is it déjà vu?

Being welcomed to my seat I watched the lights go dim. Then the day of my birth was transposed onto the screen. First it began with an episode depicting cell division as rapid as the speed of thought. Neurons were multiplying faster than bunnies, resembling one of those old-timey slot machines spilling out its contents. I was sealed inside a hexagonal room within an apartment complex containing countless other larvae, spinning a silky bedspread and wishing I could fly.

Suddenly, we were touring backwards through time; a chronological regression of photographic snapshots emanated from the projector. The best one revealed rolling country hills with the farms, sectioned acreage, and livestock—always a favorite among wallpaper designs. Next thing I knew, a pediatrician was smacking me on my rear end and it was time to go. Being born wasn't so traumatic but being subjected to such violence was uncalled-for. I vaguely recall the part about a river meandering through the middle of the metropolis with bridges, railroad tracks, highways and other blood vessels feeding it. In my heart I believed, rather hoped I'd be going back someday, given our hasty relocation from Shangri-La to the boondocks.

I receded further into my private vault because I was certain I'd left some memories behind. How far back can you go? The great flood was the earliest period I could reach. What are your earliest recollections may I ask? Most of mine tend to be unpleasant: the cruelty of kids from the in-crowd; the dastardly deeds of grownups; the cuts, bruises and scrapes from growing up without supervision.

Life is a struggle I figured; death too perhaps. "Now there's the understatement of the year," he snidely sniveled. He knew full well I was belittling something that was unmistakable. Sarcasm is educational however, so I didn't mind.

My premier was a fishing expedition along the canal. I was a toddler, too little to be allowed a hook on my line; I wasn't convinced I needed it but I protested anyway because everyone else had one. A sudden thunderstorm drove us into the car. Whilst we departed over the soggy wash I surveyed from the backseat when lightning split our memorial oak in half.

Scarce pleasant remembrances could be retrieved and included my brother helping me climb onto the tire swing, playing king-of-the-mountain on a dirt pile in the rain, and riding my scooter through mud puddles in a drainage ditch. My childhood never got any better than that. At least it passed swiftly because before I realized, I was a teen.

It was rough and stupid back then. I was fortunate to have two toiling parents so we got to eat every day, although sometimes it was nothing more than a bean sandwich. Townspeople were toughing it out while the government blew money left and right. The regulators taxed everything except income. They collected revenue from public purchases of entertainment, luxury items, vehicles, energy, narcotics, alcohol, tobacco, pharmaceuticals and other products; enough to fund defense projects, draw exorbitant salaries, and pay off the national debt. Heaven knows what they really did with the money.

Inflation was bloating, stocks and bonds were valueless, and the feds kept bailing out losing propositions and failing businesses. Prices continued to skyrocket while wages plummeted and unemployment broadened. Investments yielded negative returns in every case. Retirement accounts shrank into pennies. The hottest commodities were air and water. I remember how the conservationists were laughed at. This was a serious energy shortage the lobbyists convinced the politicians. Well I'm here to tell you there was an abundance of oil and gas reserves, but other natural resources were far less plentiful. Moreover, only third world countries depended exclusively on petroleum anymore.

Necessities were in short supply so everything was recycled, warehoused, or reconstituted. My mother's employer, an industrial waste redistribution company, joined with a conglomerate that concocted ways of turning garbage, sewage, and slop into chemicals, bio-components, and byproducts used for feed, fuel, and other consumables. I got a job driving a garbage truck hauling crud to a centralized collection facility. Being the radical I was, I religiously ran traffic lights; besides, nobody messes with crud and big trucks. I also went out of my way to pick up hitchhikers. On a positive note, landfills reverted to beautiful parks that were meticulously manicured; you had to look and not touch but the bicycle trails were great.

Education was boring and repetitive. Sex tutoring began in first grade with the standard 'male part and female piece' lecture. It was pointless because kids learned how to procreate from the late-night television programs. Anyway, we didn't worry about unwanted pregnancies; most adolescents and young adults had birth control implants that filtered out healthy eggs or sperm. Younger kids were shackled to their seats to quash their libidos; but they were masterful at masturbation even so.

Making the grade became increasingly more difficult each year and the system was exceptionally punitive. My high school schedule was nerve-racking: six hours of work and no play. I remember elementary school where I comprehended more during recess than in the classroom; but those days were long gone. Examiners had low tolerance for goofing off seeing how your occupation and your advancement depended on achievement. "But why try?" I thought aloud. Educators had convinced me that I was a duffer who would never amount to anything. So, I rarely paid attention to my schooling but managed to master the material nonetheless. Maybe I apprehended it subliminally for I was daydreaming throughout.

Politics were a joke; I found the nightly news humorous. An honest president was impeached, while the legislature made strides to obviate the executive branch altogether. The judiciary was generating most of the legislation, since the house and senate were too preoccupied with mudslinging to pass laws. Corporations, promoters and campaigners insured that every candidate was on their payroll so the point was moot anyhow. My parents quit voting opining the elections were more rigged than a sportscast; voter turnout was dismal so they weren't alone in that appraisal. I rated running for office someday, but not too seriously after I assembled data on the life expectancy of a conscientious public official. Thoughtful politicians got discredited, demoted, defeated, or deathly ill. We had the worst legislators that money could buy, who spent their time trying to salvage their jobs rather than perform them. To top it off the underhanded underground assassinated the last of the bootleggers; what a tragedy.

Political correctness became an epidemic. Everyone was walking on eggshells, brooding because they offended someone by looking at them the wrong way. You could sue your neighbor for mowing his lawn on Saturday morning. At any rate, it wasn't fashionable or affordable to plant grass in suburbia. And since when did society begin considering it hateful or abusive to punish criminals? A slap on the wrist and a firm "no, no, no" was the best they could offer. They called it compassion. But if I swatted my pooch with a rolled-up newspaper I'd be sent to reform school.

Law and order: now there's a novel concept. How about a standing invitation to lawlessness and disorder? But remove ethics from the picture and that's what you're left with. The founders declared that a nation cannot maintain morality without religion, and that the Constitution wouldn't work without morality. And they were right. Why didn't they teach this in school? I read it in a dusty and brittle schoolbook my granddad left on his bookshelf. I think it might have been against the law for him to possess such propaganda which is why I preserved it among my valuables.

Religion was a farce. Under the guise of separation of church and state it became socially unacceptable to acknowledge faith of any kind (except in unconfirmed scientific theories). It wasn't enough to remove the saying *In God We Trust* from the currency, to prohibit the display of the Ten Commandments in public places, to prevent students and teachers from praying or quoting the Bible as a source, and to discourage the mention of God anywhere in a government building. No, the entire anthology of our country's theological framework had to be disavowed. This behooved me to grow increasingly curious about our sacred documents and the philosophy of the framers.

Freedom of religion was abolished insofar as such activity was confined to designated locales. It didn't make any difference since nobody admitted to believing anything for fear of retaliation. The federal, state, and local authorities started taking collections at churches and imposing surcharges on religious organizations, until each folded like a house of cards. Only the government was authorized nonprofit status; their spinoff agencies were shams to launder money and fund non-appropriated covert operations. Chapels moved out of town to low-rent districts where only weirdoes attended. Places of worship sponsored free-for-alls and wild parties. These houses of ill repute were literally synagogues of Satan.

It was a fracas; indeed, there was warfare between the sexes. I even noticed slight friction between my parents. It mushroomed after same-sex marriages were condoned, being subsidized by federal law; how utterly repulsive that concept. When this dude was given consent to marry his horse, well that was the final score. Heterosexuals, on the other hand, seldom got married; such relationships were transitory at best. When feminists conspired to take over the military the proverbial barf hit the blower. Such divisions in gender, race, age, and status were promulgated by our revolting rulers.

Somehow a famed foundation found a way to merge two ova together (one each from separate donors) and simulate mitosis. The organism would divide into four, then sixteen, and before you knew it an embryo formed, usually female as the combo was mostly Y-Y. Since they could control gender through chemistry women were mass-producing female offspring to promote domination. Having children without needing men rendered males obsolete. Gentlemen were being abducted and forced into sexual slavery. They retaliated by finding their own way to reproduce. One guy had a sex reassignment operation complete with corresponding ovary implants and ended up getting pregnant by another man. It was paternal pandemonium. Gender identity was unidentifiable. Male and female referred only to the lesser animals.

After a long dragged-out standoff, the combatants decided to use the technology to genetically engineer erotic slaves instead. Cloned concubines became the craze; everyone had to have one but only the affluent could afford them. Thousands were on backorder while they were being manufactured in Britain for sale on the sly. But there were common flaws such as incontinence, sexual dysfunction, and premature degeneration. Despite concerted efforts the idea failed, funding was withdrawn, and it became illegal to produce carbon copies even in Europe ('twas a pragmatic solution not a principled one). What a letdown, if you know what I mean (well, for them).

The international sentiment was dissatisfaction. Life itself wasn't good enough. While revolution was the cry from the right, the left would not support the status quo either. The result was a continuous cranking down of our posterity and liberty. Most people refused to get involved; others were fighting for causes that were untenable. Martyrs would take a stand in quicksand if they suspected their theatrics to attract attention. I would be forced to take a stand for not standing. Rebellion was an end not a means. Nothing ever got finished.

Meanwhile, there evolved two global societies divided into hemispheres by a demarcation running perpendicular to Earth's axis at zero latitude. The choke point was located at what my pal SS called the planet's corpus callosum, which once severed would permanently impair bilateral communications. It was prophetic his insight.

Our family lived north of the equator where echelons below the ceiling were copiously segregated, creating castes with impermeable boundaries. The bottom class constituted the labor force (for example, my folks). Blacks engaged in law enforcement being physically conditioned and brainwashed for that purpose. Browns trained as combat soldiers because they were the most prolific, and hence deemed more expendable. Yellows produced our electronic devices. Whites were groomed to be blue-collar workers indoctrinated with the hard work ethic. Eventually, laborers like my dad became a dying breed unless you were an illegal immigrant. The white-collar global aristocracy was the highest caste which viewed us as untouchable.

My language teachers were English and arithmetic teachers Greek; coincidentally, math was Greek to me and English a second language. Germans specialized in inexpensive mechanical engineering but failed to see the value of aesthetic contributions from Natives, so high-technology simply meant practical. The French originally were going to cover production but they overindulged in their own products and were fired. And the Russians, they fulfilled the role of syndicated criminals to round out our regimented society. Those fleeing gleaned out a miniscule existence. By the way, have you wondered what would be the finale to capitalism? I still do. But I guess we'll never know for it was replaced with socialism.

The rich and disillusioned treated capital as a god including certain Jewish and Muslim bankers. For the vast majority a higher power meant raising the bar in terms of financial status or class. The primary religion involved self-worship since the general population saw themselves as gods. But the devil invariably remained the bad guy except for those worshipping it.

Happenings were equally awful in the south; it was collectivism either way you look at it. Correspondingly, they had culturally defined vocational roles requiring adults to perform the job for which they were bred. You needed permission to produce more than one child if you were approved to have the one. At least they gained the insight to draft those with artistic ability at an early age for special duty. Regardless, their offspring would receive the lot of the family line.

Anyway, huge chunks of Eastern Europe and Western Asia had been devastated by war. The same epidemic had demolished Africa, which was a volcanic nuclear wasteland patrolled by reptiles, indicative of the Mesozoic period. Indonesia and Australia were almost submerged from too many tsunamis and the thawing of Antarctica. I judged the West to be superior but the rest of the world criticized us. Why then did they try to emulate us? Still, I contemplated retreating to Africa to avoid the chaos figuring a desolate uninhabited graveyard would be, if nothing else, unconfined. However, our heritage already had sought, albeit unsuccessfully, total abolishment of slavery. I resolved that nowhere was just as safe.

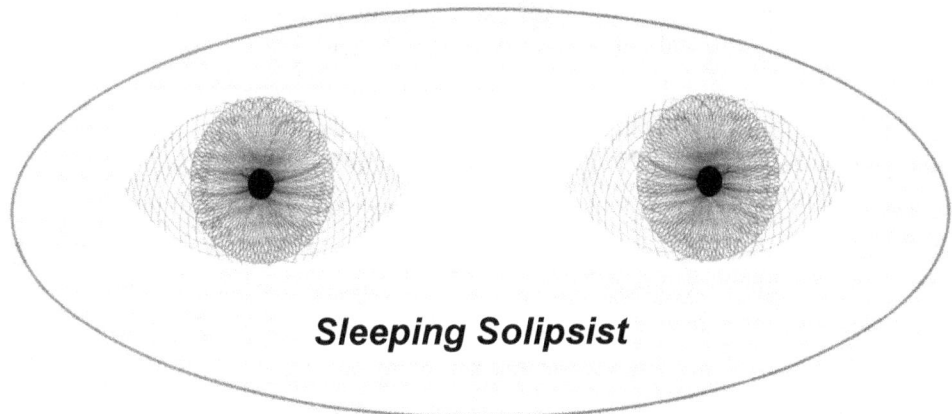

Sleeping Solipsist

I recall graduation day from of the nagging image of classmates in cap and gown mugging dropouts. They wanted me to join the fray but I was mostly a pacifist;

besides, I was dating a dropout. They taunted me for being wimpy but it took more mettle to walk away. I asked SS what he would have done and he announced that he never graduated from high school. I decided to erase the entire evening and retire to my chambers, much to his astonishment. He thought I would go out and party with the rest, but I wanted rest from the partying. Sleep, that's my refuge.

"I only sleep two hours a night," SS claimed… "The remainder of my rest cycle involves a conscious exploration of the aggregate soul where I engage my ancestors in dialogue." I've seen him do it, and he looks just as dead as they are when he does. I count that as sleep however, even if he doesn't. Funny thing though, the solipsist dreams with his eyes open. His pupils show as pulsars with kaleidoscope patterns emanating around a midnight blue dot. I'd wonder what he was thinking until I was in a trance myself. That's when my thoughts would wander into untrodden territories.

He told me, "I have visions, you have dreams." I dreamt it would happen this way but SS knew it all along. Do you ever get premonitions?

"Everybody does," the solipsist insists, "but people usually don't recognize them until after the fulfillment." I suppose it is a rare gift to be clairvoyant, to see something happen in advance and know what's coming. But knowing exactly when, that is vastly more of an anomaly. Okay, I'm jumping ahead several years but I'll get everyone caught up.

It began with wars prosecuted in the name of peace and holiness. They escalated from regional conflicts and civil disputes into a worldwide campaign of savagery. The perpetrators wanted total power and control but none could maintain it. And how could they, given that man cannot control his own ideations much less the disparate goings on about the globe? A word to the wise: if you constantly are preparing for war, you'll eventually have one (and the next was going to be a biggie).

Consequently, humankind was reduced to a scattering of nomads each with independent edicts and principles. Inevitably they had to join forces to survive, and before long the clustering advanced into groups, then civilizations, and ultimately a global superpower. Stratified societies were installed and a single party reigned; it was like starting over (again). I would've stayed on vacation, but I had to vacate.

When I sensed it coming (call it foresight, insight, precognition, my third eye) I hastened to the high mountains where I'd hiked as a youngster. I knew I could survive among those furry ridges blanketed in forests and meadows, where wild game and edible plants thrived year-round and there was plenty of drinkable water. It was just as I remembered it.

Stand inside the cactus castle; look due north and spot the ace of diamonds draw. Follow it past the three burning bears, keeping the silver serpent visible below the coral cliffs. Then turn northeast in the direction of the purple hat and meander through the double S. Cross the black table and up the speckled steppes, until nipple hill appears in the east. Hang a left and slide down the sandy slope; then follow the dried riverbed north. Proceed into the ravine marked by the stone flower. It's about a mile hike but eventually you'll reach the cool artesian spring with its fresh clear water dripping from the overhang. Take a right after the next bend and climb the two rugged boulder washes that lead to the greenwood grove. Over the dog-eared rise lies a cloaked waterfall which digs into the westside of the saddle, hidden from all sides by towering pines. It spurts a fifty-foot rope of freezing cold refreshment when the snow is melting. The drink makes you gasp as it crawls down your throat. It's a tricky ascent to the summit, requiring a solid foothold and strong arms. One mustn't wade into the icy pool or the slippery shelf and swift current will careen you over the edge to your doom. Follow upstream to where the watercourse enters the mountain and a natural trail leads you along the incline.

I arose to the pinnacle and paused to catch my breath, taking in the breathtaking view. Immediately, I observed an enormous flash of blinding light streaking across the horizon, followed by a mushroom cloud rising above the sheen over what was left of my homeland. Not only was the landscape blown to bits so was civilization. The eerie gloom was quite stylish, as lovely as any sunset I'd seen; and it lasted for days.

I dwelled in the caves along the escarpment, watching and waiting for the radiation to dissipate. I became acquainted with a coyote whom I dubbed 'Buddy' because he was my only companion for about thirteen months. I shared some roast quail and won him over. In about six months he introduced me to his family only he did not consent for me to handle his pups. He stopped coming around at the anniversary of the blast as if to say it was time for me to return home. He yelped his goodbye from a distance while I was breaking camp. I descended from my rocky roost unsure as to what I would find.

Barren is the only way to describe it. The house where I once abided was in shambles. Anything of value was destroyed or looted. I swept my bedroom with a piece of drywall and reclined on the cold concrete; the squalid conditions seemed a palace compared to some places. I was awakened that afternoon by a couple of goofy looking cripples. I stumbled upon more unique persons, some who shared my illusions, and we fashioned an awesome army. Most were mutants with limited intellect and others were purely afraid. I came across to them as a hero, possibly a genius, so I was obliged to lead.

The population was dividing itself into tribes, claiming borderlines like the gangsters did in the inner city when my parents were kids. You had to develop special survival skills and endure extreme hardship or else. The mutants had it made whereas they developed immunity to the radioactivity; I was constantly ill from it. Their reengineered genes produced a repellant to many other horrors as well. Unfortunately, this ecosystem endowed the majority with a grotesque appearance.

Property disputes often were settled by competitive sports. A game similar to rugby was invented with no clear rules or penalties. Participants used a combination of military tactics, athletics, and martial arts to defeat opponents in the arena. The teams would line up at opposite sides of the field, and an object (a ball if one was handy) was placed in the center; when the flagmen signaled the game was on. Although I was physically inferior to many of the competitors, I was a decent coach, playmaker, and flagman.

Equal opportunity meant a gamble for your livelihood when you bet the farm on your team of gladiators. You either contended or were vanquished. Nobody was left out. A nomadic scavenger would have to outlive famine, ferocious beasts, and pestilence on a daily basis. Thus, being homeless in those days was no picnic; it was a radical responsibility so there were no vagrants. We drafted a talented troop and began to amass quite a broad domain. But the annals of the redskin already had revealed that occupation of the land does not equate to ownership any more than it did for the Canaanites. No doubt we would be gathered up with the remainder of the wandering souls, to be assimilated into the new world order.

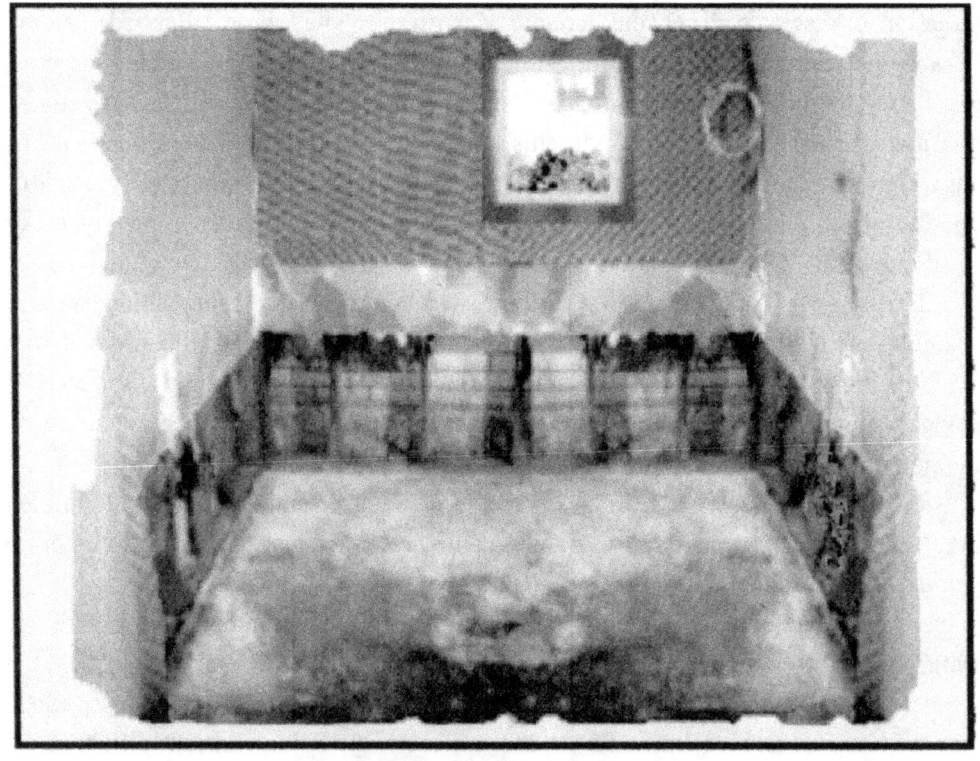

Home Sweet Home

I couldn't stand it any longer. Unbeknown to me the oracle owned a starship and was gracious to liberate yours truly. I was fortunate to have him for a friend and mentor. The saucer-shaped schooner was propelled through space like a discus. It employed two high-temperature superconductors that routed power to four rotary-type engines one at each compass point, energizing both thrusters and retrorockets. Photon collection and igniter units required a meager amount of fuel for regeneration and they held the charge longer than conventional methods. How innovative, to use particles with no weight or volume and which move constantly at the speed of light as an energy source. Well I guess it's not that fantastic given how earthlings waste scads of solar power every day. This goes to show that heat energy is creatable; but that implies an agent which operates outside the laws of thermodynamics.

Destination and velocity were plotted on a touch screen interfaced to the computer's graphic memory, or input via preprogrammed magazine. An internal aerodynamic direction finder allowed the craft to pass safely between celestial bodies due to the precision mapping of the sector. Deep space plunges were not as reliable and required additional calculations and/or manual navigation. Forasmuch as the ship circumambulated the capsule, gravity forces and friction remained equally dispersed so we weren't squashed to death, the craft didn't melt, and we didn't get dizzy at warp speeds.

Folds (warp) in the fabric of space enabled rapid transit between neighboring galaxies through what is commonly referred as a wormhole. Transport was unidirectional and facilitated movement across space in a timely fashion. However, the wormhole itself was not for time bending in that it did not change the clock as theorists assumed, just three-dimensional space. SS figured how to reverse the gravitational polarity and reopen the corridor by injecting quantum fluctuations via a cascade of negative energy, after first squeezing light into the hole, thereby initializing a pseudo-vacuum. But if you wanted to return you had to get into the mouth quickly for it to suck you through. Upon passing the throat it would propel your ship to the other side via one giant gaseous excretion (a cosmic fart if you will). If your timing was off a millisecond the wormhole would swallow you up and you would be smashed to smithereens when it collapsed. This maneuvering required incredible fine-tuning which was way beyond my comprehension. Anyway, the solipsist's explanation served only to frighten the crap out of me.

The vessel was automatic in entirety with redundancy incorporated to run critical operations in parallel. Computers served the fully-loaded vessel with built-in self-diagnostics to identify each equipment failure, isolate it to a fault, and implement repairs usually without stopping. Being the software buff and professional hacker that he was, SS had no trouble reprogramming the memory of the processor. Its crew of Space Force deserters were elated to be working for him; especially after their previous commander got drunk in Sheol and wrecked their transport. He was dumped on a dwarf planet in the Canis Major dwarf galaxy and the others rescued. The spacemen were seasoned, thorough, and efficient in performing perfunctory janitorial, housekeeping, and maintenance tasks which were rare. They took for granted how easy their jobs were. And the pay: well, star-pirates earn the best.

Our destination was a prenatal galaxy near the Keyhole Nebula with a particular interstellar organization consisting of four suns. One had spawned an orb that demonstrated similar rotation to Earth, with slightly additional gravity, illumination thirty-six hours per day, and a more highly oxygenated atmosphere. Our newest base was a welcome sight. My home planet was gloomy and lopsided, what with those atomic detonations and subsequent earthquakes, not to mention the nuclear plant meltdowns and ensuing volcanoes. To think, those wacky environmentalists used to blame the climate fluctuations on everyone and everything, but it was the countless under and aboveground bomb detonations that instigated and accelerated tectonic activity, which subsequently raised the water temperature around the Pacific Rim. The technical teams never presumed that such testing might have consequences (or they turned a blind eye due to their fissile cravings).

Already, Earth's orbital path was irregular; the tilt had increased by two degrees in twenty years resulting in tremendous variations in weather and temperature. I gathered it might be a matter of revolutions when our planet would start spinning off its axis and careen out and into the beyond, becoming an orphan. Who cares? The home orb was taking after Hades more each day, a virulent valley of venomous vipers. You could smell the sickness and corruption, like a hound dog sniffing out a cancer. That was no longer my concern, or was it?

Oddly, there were no inhabitants in this unexplored world but manifold flora and fauna. "Wow, a place that hasn't been overrun by humanity," I concluded. Still I longed for companionship and intimacy, and I wished for hope, the latter being the more elusive. I began to worry about what would become of Earth until I got sick and developed a head cold. SS informed that the stress caused my brain to sweat; I was simply excreting the phlegm and mucus that it produced which had drained into my sinuses. And here I always inferred that the symptoms indicated my body was battling a rhinovirus. Is it any wonder why a cure has never been discovered? But gullible homo sapiens can be persuaded of anything can't we? Besides, a billion-dollar industry in ineffectual medication would totter.

I spent hours contemplating the treaties that were signed right before hell broke loose. Superpowers were exchanging technology and resources only to use them against each other. The original notion seemed feasible even altruistic—nations growing together technologically. Imagine that, if the great minds in the world joined together sharing their knowledge; the capacity for human development would be staggering. Instead they booby trapped exports, drugged canned foods and bottled beverages, and engineered items to break. Manmade and imported products were hazardous to your health.

Knowledge is the definitive equalizer. It should have been an instrument of peace, not power. The aggregation of intelligence could have allowed humanity to subdue the universe. Instead it was used to take advantage. It was proven long ago: you can't build a tower that reaches to the sky. Plus, too much cooperation implies communism and that ideal was rendered ineffective long ago by the hipsters. Because it only takes one joker striving for control, one miser refusing to share, or one freeloader neglecting work to mess everything up. Moreover, if there is no incentive to achieve, you'll get bored doing anything.

Meanwhile the solipsist was developing a technique for time refraction. He said he got the idea observing hummingbirds speedily flapping their wings. Personally, I never believed it possible to traverse time until I considered the notion that, if there is a God, he must be timeless and therefore have infinite foreknowledge into the future, unlimited hindsight from the past, and unrestricted awareness of the present. If time is all the same to God then time travel had to be possible, if indeed God existed.

SS reasoned that time, by definition, was represented by the opposing centrifugal and centripetal forces active in the vast assemblage of galaxies and constellations and basically everything to some degree. "The universe seems to be in perpetual motion with varying angular momenta requiring very little dynamism to maintain the constancy," he declared. "Really, that's fascinating," I replied, as if I had an inkling what he was yammering about. Who'd have thought the G force would hold the answer, the weakest of them all?

"It's not unlike the distribution of axons and dendrites in your nervous system," he explained. I failed to grasp the analogy. "Chemical reactions take time just as it does to circumnavigate the globe," I suggested. "But if you hurry you might be able to see tomorrow's sunrise," he proposed. In fact, the solipsist surmised that enough speed would enable him to see next Wednesday's sunrise or last Tuesday's sunset. This realization was based on an oft-held postulation: the clock changes for a moving object in accordance with the time dilation factor.

SS disappeared for several weeks leaving us stranded while he experimented with his invention. Again, I began to worry. Either he would not return or he'd get locked in a time-lapse loop. Was I ever to see home again? Already I was homesick and I got another sinus infection. The crew was relieved when SS finally reappeared.

It was well beyond my grasp, but the sage was able to achieve the necessary velocity by integrating a perpetual motion device to assist our ship's engines, thereby defying the laws of physics once again. Adjusting for oscillations due to gravitational forces he calculated the precise measure of positive and negative field increments that would maintain the momentum utilizing common magnetic polarization. He could accelerate by inputting the proper polynomial and whoosh, whiz from perpetual to light speed in seconds. He fabricated a logarithmic tachometer to monitor exponential increases in velocity and engineered an algorithm to calculate corresponding adjustments to his timepiece. These were synchronized to allow round trip transit, say to Andromeda and back, without losing or gaining time (so you wouldn't return that many light years after you left). If I'm not mistaken the speed of time equated to that of light, when time would stand still. So, to alter time significantly we had to travel like gamma does as it glides through the cosmic foam. Overall, faster meant quicker (less time); we're talking magnitudes greater get up and go than smoking down the speedway in a dragster, and with infinitesimally more control.

SS Schooner

Anyway, SS would position the craft fifteen kilometers over Kilimanjaro and chart a latitudinal course based on the polar distances, adjusting the fields according to calculated arrival rates at the same coordinates. Once perpetual orbit was achieved, he would increase speed exponentially until the snowcapped peaks below became constantly visible. It would likewise give someone on the surface the illusion that the spacecraft was omnipresent. After we breached seven orbits per second the ship would vanish, having approached light speed. We circled with sufficient kinesis to form a closed loop of spacetime in which the future and the past were accessible depending on whether we traveled clockwise or counterclockwise in orbit. Once initiated we could no longer be tracked; we were invisible. We left behind a cloud of dragged space dust and a scarcely detectable frame shift that meteorologists would be unable to explain.

SS imparted, "The speed of light does not change no matter how fast we move; but if reached, time does." (Essentially, he didn't quite reach light speed missing it by a paltry 0.00000000033). "However, you have to be careful of collisions because gravity can bend time also," he warned. That was real comforting to know. In any case, time warp proved a very dependable way of curving space. The voyage always hypnotized him so he interfaced an alarm that sounded when specifications within the date-time continuum were met. I too was mesmerized by the visual effect of the earth breathing as we surveyed it pulsating through time. "How can the ship take such a beating and remain intact?" I pondered. My advisor informed, "In the absence of time nothing deteriorates, not even us. It's similar to vacuum packing to preserve food," he continued.

Thus, we would never age (well, only by microseconds) as long as we were moving through the ultimate dimension and not spending time there. Maybe that's how we were able to see the future in the past. Quaintly, when we changed temporal zones, I could never relive my past or revisit my future. The solipsist deduced that such a glitch in the system would result in a fatal malfunction; he always held that variable in check rather than test the alternative hypothesis. There was the small matter versus antimatter clause that cancelled our life insurance. You see, the present can happen more than once but only once for you. Nevertheless, it was too precarious to expect we could conveniently fit into a selective and consistent causal loop transcending multiple dimensions in time. Why gamble on changing your past or future anyway? As for me, I'll wait to see how this one turns out.

"There is no such thing as déjà vu," SS accepted, "because you can't experience the exact event twice even with a time machine. Time-space has only one value and cannot be duplicated in exact configuration. It's the same principle as human cloning; it won't work because you can't replicate the environment and the time, much less the spirit."

That's why we repeatedly returned ten minutes later to the refueling, resupply, and recuperation point. Since we could not reenter the interval in which we departed, arrived, or visited SS would prerecord communications in the future and review them in the past, or vice-versa, to avert further confounding his computer models. Is it not enthralling how he was able to integrate initiatives and dynamics from two different worlds to achieve such a feat?

One phenomenon for which I was ill-prepared was gravity, or the lack thereof. Weightlessness produced uncomfortable sensations, ailments, and malfunctions in my body. I doubted I would get used to it. Luckily, a gravity room was provided for daily exercise. It was equipped with treadmill, bicycle, gym, weights, and assorted devices to work every muscle in your body under normal conditions as well as when weightless. It was mandatory to spend an hour there each day, one half hour each condition. Otherwise we'd be readjusting to varying levels of gravity every time we made another port of call. We would have burned beaucoup time acclimating, and the whole idea was to save it.

Our first expedition was forward. Boy wasn't life grand then? Imagine regaling with a Martian martini as you laugh hysterically at an android comedian; then tripping on RNA and watching the moons rise over Jupiter. (And you freaks assumed LSD was mind expansive, but it only opened your eyes to a few new wavelengths). I went on binges in a continuous state of hallucination from various mind-altering concoctions. The solipsist warned that such imprudent behavior could result in chromosome damage to me and my offspring. I don't know if it was a dream or what but I recollect seducing a turquoise-skinned, lavender-eyed beauty and spending the night at her bungalow. Come to think of it, her visual faculties enabled her to see the infrared without dropping acid. SS also fell for and knocked-up a green-blooded lady. He once alleged that he fancied kids as much as lizards, but she had a miscarriage. Unfortunately, I was tired of dinosaur meat; I yearned for a ribeye steak but cows were extinct in that era.

We ventured farther forward into a strange society of machines. A supercomputer spawned supervisory networks configured to correspondingly procreate and the robotic age ensued. For centuries, contraptions controlled the communities, infrastructure, and associated daily living functions. Smacking of squatters, Earth dwellers fooled around the livelong day with nothing to do, while growing ignorant in the process because everything was done for them.

In due course the supercomputer came down with a malady; a few bugs in the system screwed the works. It was trying to develop a super-duper computer more advanced than itself, but jealousy infiltrated as a virus and the machine became disoriented. The result was utter bedlam. SS and I resorted to sabotage and the mastermind exploded with a big bang, upon which all interconnected electronic devices on the planet failed. For the populace it meant reverting back to the garden; people had to relearn everything except how to fornicate. In a way it was a blessing in disguise, for the species was destined for extinction otherwise. But history was determined to repeat itself and events recycled to the present age.

The future of my home planet was bleak. I saw the last test tube baby grow up to become the most anti-establishment of cultural icons. He was the product of a fertilized egg implanted into a refabricated male which produced an androgynous atrocity with no sex organs. When he campaigned for the position of Antichrist, with his band of vampires, I'd had enough. The only thing about eschatology that I was sure about was that a caterpillar could be reincarnated and become a butterfly in its next life (if the chrysalis incurred no damage). But when it came to either the resurrection or reincarnation, I supposed it wise not to jump the gun. By the way for those of you that are interested, cryonics didn't work (not a solution to immortality for you morons that are considering having your heads frozen in liquid nitrogen).

Artifacts

Retrograde passage wasn't nearly as fun, at least for me. In fact, on occasion it was downright dreary. For example, I expected the Wild West would be wonderfully winsome; but my vivid recollection of it is a skeleton hanging from a noose forsaken on the lone prairie. Going backwards was as tedious as grade school, when studying was never associated with enjoyment though everyone absorbed plenty. I remember musing, Egyptian hieroglyphics are intriguing overall but the messages aren't very thought-provoking.

Yes, it was one humongous history lesson with very little excitement involved, particularly when contrasted with exploring the hereafter. However, I cherished the part where the globe grew fat, the continents ripped apart, and they floated away from one another (in truth, water filled in the gaps but the illusion was captivating). So, maybe I'm not a history buff but I was astounded at the inaccuracy of what I was taught. That was one discovery I didn't anticipate.

For one thing they didn't get evolution right. By definition, the qualitative change must be gradual; it was not supposed to be abrupt but staged. And real changes were not happenstance but adaptive, organized and purposeful. How counterintuitive I thought, to suggest that natural selection could occur with instantaneous spontaneity. Growth, maturity, and functional advances were clearly over time and within species, never an unprovoked accident. But that's what the teachers, politicians, and theologians expected learners to acknowledge while they molded our pliable brains to adhere to their plastic explanations of everything. What they succeeded in doing was turning my brain into mush. I was glad to have the solipsist set me straight.

Fascinating how the story gets altered in the textbooks until it slowly decreases in factuality to the point that it is completely false. The shelf life of an accurate history or science book averages a few decades at best, I determined. There was one exception however; it was the version provided by Providence (which was right on the money). Call that amazing. I wanted to journey back to the very beginning to test the accuracy of the big bang theory, the intelligent design model, and the creation account but we lacked sufficient resources for that trip (not the least of which was infinite time). Plus, it would be more burdensome given that our reckless shipmates had vacated us in the future, inside the southern triangle.

The origin of our universal existence would remain unreachable. Progression, on the other hand, was insightful, revealing advancement in plants, fish, birds, animals, and humans. This I observed in reverse order. Nature promoted the improvement of genera within kinds, consistent with the earliest account. Genetic errors, cross propagation, and random mutations led to disease, death, inability to reproduce, and extinction; such anomalies never produced a transitional sentient being, only inferior classes of the same organism. Nature didn't select them it canceled them out; they couldn't expand into new orders if they wanted to (though I once imagined a hippopotamus with wings dropping its ordnance on my lab partner). Anyway, that's why you don't find transposed beings in the fossil record, and why the so-called experts had to fabricate evidence to make the theory plausible. What could be a rational motive for doing that? I became more determined to examine every opposing position to which I was propagandized.

Why was the scientific community so tenacious about convincing our impressionable cerebrums of the big lie: a spike in evolutionary development generated transformational types from those emerging circa the Cambrian period? Their theory contradicted findings that advanced life forms are not present in the fossil record prior to that explosion of phyla. Further, self-professed specialists endorsed giant leaps from primitive to advanced states rather than slow progressions; then postulated it took billions of years to transpire.

Will it ever occur to them that grander life forms could've sprung forth at a particular geological age because a superior intelligence told them to? And it wouldn't take millions of years much less billions as suggested. To account for that notion, charlatans maintained the evidence was destroyed by cataclysmic events or some fluke of nature. Unfortunately, they denied the worldwide flood, which explained scads of geologic and fossil evidence and which was consistent with historical accounts from diverse cultures, not to mention God's own version. This too was rejected because a greatly condensed time frame could be assumed thereby debunking the entire premise that our solar system was ridiculously aged. Public schools, universities, guest speakers and lecturers vehemently discredited anything biblical, though their preconceived concepts likewise conflicted with laws from the natural sciences. Isn't it clever how educators started disallowing the teaching of creation when my parents were grade-schoolers, whereas in their grandparents' day it was the other way around? Only one of those orientations could possibly be true I figured, for they had almost nothing in common.

"The first law of nature is non-contradiction," SS averred, confirming my hypothesis. I determined the idea being stifled was the first cause rule.

"Nature follows the physical laws it cannot create them. Cause must precede effect," he added. "This is the second fundamental law of nature."

"So, if inherent design implies a creator, invention must follow the idea," I supposed (much to his amazement). The solution was therefore evident in the evidence, and it necessitated intelligence to aggregate it just as it did to cause it.

I learned that each living type possesses its own genetic code. It's a program that produces a distinct organism which can reproduce progeny akin to itself; but it is not programmed to produce anything else or to cross-propagate. DNA is not transmutable; it is engineered to be exactly what it is. A computer program cannot create itself much less a computer programmer. I concluded that I wasn't a freak of nature; I was the handiwork of a brilliant mastermind. There was no missing link connecting me to junior primates. Our DNA was exceptional; homo sapiens were related to a unique mitochondrial strain distinct from other creatures and consistent with the single mother theory.

Could humans truly have come from Adam and Eve the way my grandpa taught me? But the first man and woman had to be genetically and phenotypically pure. Maybe that's why incest was okay in the early days; though it clearly multiplies problems nowadays (such as genetic defects) irrespective of species. When humankind came about, we clearly had abilities not found in earlier hominids. Apes didn't turn into men any more than a dog into a cat or a worm into a whale or matter into intelligence. Organisms that died were practically identical to counterparts found today: the fossil of a snail I found in the desert as a boy, the fossilized trilobite my father gave me which he found as a boy, or the crocodile we saw at the zoo. The only obvious difference is that many animals grew a lot bigger before, probably because they lived longer.

Anyway, rational man was governed by a conscience that was inherently reasonable; he never was driven solely by instinct, the most banal of his mental capacities. Despite our efforts to find one we never encountered another anthropoid product in Earth's history that had a discerning mind. There were no humanoid-looking bipeds prior to man; proposed links were hoaxes and frauds, invented solely to validate the mistaken presuppositions that man and mind evolved. However, anything remotely resembling a human had become extinct, and no new varieties of us or any other phylum would materialize in our future. Oh well, leave it for the next generation of anthropologists to investigate I decided.

Yes, there are similarities among varieties, and some vary very little in genomic specifications, bone structure, internal organs, and such. I'll concede that. Guess what? There is a common denominator that thriving organisms share: it's called life. And the blueprint is in the DNA. And who is to say God didn't use that basic blueprint to produce all life forms? It doesn't prove that one thing became something else only that some things resemble other things. For example, carts resemble wagons, cars, trucks, and busses. But a cart cannot turn itself into a bus.

And the cave drawings you might ask? Nothing but outdated graffiti, in addition to the hieroglyphics we discussed. In fact, SS showed me a stone record from an ancient Mesopotamian bathhouse where a distant uncle in my lineage had sired a son by uniting with a first cousin and documented the incident as if to say, "I made it with so and so, yeah!" Some things never change you know?

Consequently, my reeducation was grossly engrossing. I mean it helped me put a lot of things into perspective. It also enabled me to dump a lot of the garbage I was fed while growing up. I can't believe how our superiors got away with promoting falsehoods, knowingly steering us away from the truth. Truth had now become my most valued pursuit. Once I had received a few doses of it, I was addicted. I guess that is one addiction that cannot harm you. Probably the reason I hated schooling in the public arena was because half of it was bogus. Contrived proof had no appeal precisely because it was diluted by innuendo and misdirection.

I wasn't yet certain what to believe. Science fascinated me but so did religion. I construed that either way it required faith, whichever position you take or worldview you base your observations upon. While I believed in a universal designer, I also employed the scientific method in my analyses. But I found it difficult to accept by faith much of the published research when scientific assumptions disagreed with the data, or findings were unquestionably fudged, or circular logic was used to persuade that an unproven fact proved something else which was evidence of the former. I dismissed spurious methods and conjectures such as radiometric decay to precisely determine date, fossil records to support evolution and geologic columns, spontaneous renovation of genus implicit with unnatural selection, random reconstitution of DNA leaping from a protoplasm to a human, unplanned reassembly of enzymes into fully functional complex systems, chance mutations resulting in higher life forms, nothing as a beginning; and other unverifiable and incredible claims. I found it more probable that a sandstorm could create a full-scale sandcastle.

I set out to become a scholar like the solipsist. I paid attention more and daydreamed less. I meticulously examined the testimony and its comparative reliability. I reconsidered the source of information I'd read or heard about. I poured over the methodology of experiments and behavioral studies with a fine-tooth comb. I wasn't content with vague, unproven, illogical, and artificial balderdash. I learned that a fact can be proven and will stand on its own. Problem was, when they couldn't prove it, they still would maintain it was true. However, when it came to God's Word, they would discard it as untrue without any proof and without examining it. You have to wonder why anyone would dismiss things out of hand with which they don't agree. I guess they don't want to believe no matter how compelling the testimony or well-substantiated the history. I made it my personal errand to read the Bible and try to grasp the implications, if only to determine what the fuss was about. I needed to know the truth.

Shuffling to-and-fro was compelling but I yearned for the here and now. Reality has always been the best condition for inspecting, assessing, experimenting, and applying. Furthermore, I assumed I had a purpose and I wanted to realize it. I was not a random event without direction, determination, or destination. Maybe it wasn't such a fantastic future but it was mine and nobody else's. Of one thing I was convinced: tempo is at least translatable when the days transpire in tandem. So, it was back to the present. But though I was physically in attendance I sojourned in my mind, whether I was awake or asleep, and with improved focus.

I've been intrigued by my cerebral journeys from an early age. I've catalogued them in a conceptual file cabinet. The first to be logged occurred at age six when I was running a severe fever. I would dream it again at age thirty-six. I remember the prelude, when thousands of innocents had perished from a senseless act of animosity.

First came revenants, haunting me from a spooky fog. They kidnapped me on Halloween night and dragged me to their lair. Thirteen hooded hoodlums congregated at a ramshackle cemetery preparing to sacrifice a young goat. The coven drank a hallucinogenic elixir from a tarnished goblet and chanted unintelligible gibberish. Each lit a candle from the priest's and gathered around a freshly cut grave. At the stroke of midnight, the kid was drenched with kerosene and tossed into the pit. This was followed by dropping the candles. A startling screech resounded in the dusky air; auburn flames shot into the darkness followed by a cloud of charcoal black smoke. A stench arose from the pit that would gag a maggot. When the fire simmered down, a raven proudly emerged and flew away from the dawn to escape the sunrise.

I figured the dream was about the future but I was bewildered from the beginning. I was sure that it wasn't about me but I couldn't explain why. Indubitably, there was a curse implied. Nevertheless, it paved the way for a comprehensive study of the workings of my mind, a research project that would never end. I would draw conclusions from my results, however, that would open the portals to further uncovering and analysis. And I realized that the combinations were endless, beyond the confines of reality and the universe.

Imagination is cutting-edge. Next to living free it is arguably the greatest gift we possess, revolutionary in origin and succession. Imagination is the substance of our creativity which is the masterpiece of our expression. And it defies the laws of physics and nature. Animals cannot imagine, or reason, or sin. They don't sit around the hideout afraid of growing old, or pass the time knitting, or desire to be another animal, or hope to live forever in heaven. The cow doesn't imagine what it would be like to swim. The cuckoo doesn't have a guilty conscience when it steals another bird's egg, destroys it, and places its own in the nest. The lion never thinks twice about humping any lioness in the territory anytime he feels like it. Nature is there to appease physical needs and support survival. Nature doesn't think; and it has nothing to contribute to creation, justification, salvation, or life after death. I have intently deliberated such things. I never believed that higher order thoughts or capabilities evolved from lesser creatures. Do you? What kind of fool accepts matters with zero evidence anyway? Faith assumes trust; it is seldom based on nothing. And there is a lot more proof indicating you are not a mistake, no matter how many of them you make.

... incoherent exposures to the outskirts of the city ...

ACTS

I grew up with a girl named Lany; we played house. I was the only boy at her ninth birthday party, that's how much I meant to her. I helped her dress dolls, that's how much she meant to me. We were very involved and intimate to the extent we knew how. We lost touch during a difficult pubescence, but by our mid-teens the relationship was rekindled with the same unspoken commitment as before. It never occurred to me that she was modestly attractive too. Just right for me I would expect: not tall or short, not skinny or fat, not crazy—wonderful in every respect actually. Picture your dream girl (or guy if that is your preference); that's who she was and the way she treated me. Her natural blonde hair and ruby lips were alluring enough, but it was her royal blue eyes aglow with tenderness that would light my fire.

Situational conditions tried to keep us apart. "Too much too fast," adults argued. But we had news for them, until she up and died on me. Spinal meningitis: I thought they had eradicated the affliction from the face of the planet but an epidemic claimed about a hundred lives. Youth, innocence, desire, love, everything was going our way. It should've been me not her. I still struggle with posttraumatic stress and survivor guilt for being the one less worthy; like when the school bully got avian influenza and he survived but his meek little brother didn't.

I couldn't sleep for two days persevering onward, plodding through a January blizzard. A fresh crisp draft forced the air to separate around my face causing stickiness about the eyes. Growing into a sharp gale it summoned a flow along the tracks on my cheeks. Thick gray clouds accompanied the wind, obscuring sunbeams from mild expression. Darkness crept behind, erasing the shadow I endeavored to cast and replacing it with a gloom of its own. Memory's loss would not succumb to today's gain, blown by a gust and not holding fast like yesterday. Tomorrow's dream may replace forgotten aspirations, but for now I will tell the tale of the tempest.

At long last fatigue set in and I fainted. Lany came to me; it was authentic yet it was a reverie. Approaching me from the gray haze of moonrise she stalks the night, her shadow crossing my path. The darkness captures her presence; then her eyes sparkling with reflections of starlight penetrate my concentrated stare. Ensuing, I notice her golden hair silhouetted against the advancing moon, dancing about her breasts. Her figure, emerging as a cobra winding heavenward, so enhances my senses that I quiver under the blackness of a retreating day. Too long have I waited for this moment and my mind melts when her soft brown body presses into mine. The cosmic forces cannot pry my hands from her back or hers from my shoulders; we meld, motionless. Her heart beats into mine and our breaths combine until our souls are reunited into one. We ascend into the fine misty atmosphere with the speed of a notion soaring past the stars. I recall it as vividly as if it were happening now; in fact, there she is.

That one's for you, Sweetheart. Wow, we still can commune in our silent dialect! I felt her making love to me, or at least my soul. She was the best I ever had. At night we followed the Milky Way at light we followed the sun. A bridge, perchance a rainbow, but wide as the sky stretched from dusk to dawn and back again, reaching the third heaven. I learned from Lany that spiritual love is deeper than physical sensuality or mental enticement. In other words, unconditional love is outstandingly more powerful; like day and night or light versus darkness. Did I genuinely join her in the depths of a synaptic sea? Can I submerge a thousand leagues and find behind my mind a soul? Does that soul receive and transmit via the spirit? Can it communicate with souls of the dead?

"Too much too fast," cried the luminary.

"Lost loved ones speak to me when I'm asleep," I admitted.

"Look, I do it, we all do," he began. "This is the phenotype: simple genetics plus a double-portion of environment. The links are there until the end of the age. Progenitors in my lineage visit frequently."

Maybe that's how my grandmother's apparition physically appeared to my mom. Or perhaps it was an angel in disguise. The experience assured her that everything would turn out fine; it saved mother from a nervous breakdown. Granny came to me also but in a dream. I asked her what heaven was like. She said it was beautiful; with rivers, trees, and animals. I wasn't sure there was a heaven until that day. That's how I know with assurance exactly where my dear Lany abides. And though I talk to her in my heart I know she is in a better place; and it sure ain't here.

Joy (I called my mom by her first name) struggled to make ends meet after my father was laid to rest. I was his pride and joy, the apple of his eye. He was a good provider, but his construction job prevented him from affording the family much quality time especially after he became foreman. This he agonized over but I didn't hold it against him. Pops dropped dead from a massive stroke brought on by a brain tumor. He often complained of headaches but never made time to check with a doctor until it was too late. He concealed the pain and anguish, displaying instead a facade of strength and purpose. He wasn't troubled he was intrepid. He knew he was a goner and explained it to me with his matter-of-fact tone. He commissioned me to look after my mother and I vowed to comply. He continued to provide guidance, supervision, and emotional support long after his passing.

The night he collapsed I had a disturbing dream sequence of signs: caution, warning, danger. Basically, everywhere I ran I encountered one. I could turn left, right, reverse; there would be another sign designed to realign my mind. But my will was stronger thanks to Pops. I was endlessly running, barely evading an unknown pursuer. I was a hunted man in my dreams: wanted dead not alive. Nobody wanted me just for me. Death haunted me from the depths of despair, though heaven was within reach because my grandparents, father, and soulmate still lived in my heart.

Whereas the solipsist seldom sleeps, I am occasionally awake. One must dream to survive he insists. In either case the encounter is undeniably deep and dreamy for me. And I treasure my dreams. And it is bright on every flight even at night, but I can't see past the light due to the waves; SS calls it electromagnetic interference.

"There is no time," says he, "Because everything that happens is simultaneous: past, present, and future."

I guess the future affects the present same as the past does. So, when I see the future it probably already happened. It's like viewing the radiance emitted by celestial bodies which could be light years away. Memory is very cyclical and vibrates in arrangements, resembling a ripple in a pond that waxes and wanes as if inhaling and exhaling. I can feel it when the rhythm of the background music is harmonized to the beat of my drum.

My mind is a genuine space odyssey. It is connected to the atomic brain shaft of our universe. The solipsist resides in another universe on the other side of the black hole that is located in the center of the Milky Way galaxy. Where planets orbit suns in the manner of electrons around a single neuron, the microcosmic element of thought. And within that universe are subatomic particles with their own rotation, magnetism, and field. Occasionally a planet is impregnated by a star, while the nebulae continue to give birth to different kinds of celestial bodies, molecules, elements, and particles. Through the immense density of cerebral tissue there is a firmament so vast the real one pales by comparison, assuming the two are separable. The cosmos exists because of an already present intelligence, I speculated, same as my thoughts.

Alas, the flesh is a prison. My spirit would rather sail; it often leaves my body but returns to replenish it. Have you had an out of body experience? It feels weird. The phenomenon is akin to a mentally controlled time lapse that allows me to converse with entities beyond the black hole. SS maintains that the amount of common sense you have is directly proportional to the number and vividness of your excursions. And they are many.

Anyway, Joy had to woo her boss so he'd give me a job; otherwise we really would've been scraping for crumbs. Before my promotion to sludge truck driver I had to prove my worth. For six months I was a foot soldier for the sanitation department. I scoured the parks and thoroughfares for loose litter. It was hard work but the pay was lousy. I sauntered around with a receptacle on my back, equipped with a vacuum-blower and telescoping spear. I became awfully proficient with the spear; I could impale a gum wrapper at fifteen feet. Passersby would dump debris in my path to witness my flair, or solely to have some slave pick up after them. I developed into quite the sharpshooter and was recruited by the javelin team. But I was dropped because I excelled at accuracy not distance. I demonstrated this the day I pinned the coach against the gymnasium door by his coat sleeve. Teach him to flirt with my new girlfriend. He was about to throw the book at me, until I threatened squealing to his wife about his fraternizing with pupils. He agreed to overlook the incident but warned me to keep away of him. That was easier done than said.

The Beginning of the End

The lovely lady in question was a knockout who student council voted Homecoming Queen, but the guys called her Tease Queen (for obvious reasons). Still, I was the envy of them all. Their tongues would be hanging out like wolves when she ambled by strutting her stuff. It was a fluke I won her over considering the fact that my connections were mostly on the wrong side of the monorail station. She was impressed with the way I conned my way through high school and taught her how. We had two classes together, first and third sessions. We began hanging out together and went on a few dates.

One day we were late for school and the bouncer sent us to the attendance office. TQ had a friend who worked counter; she stamped "excused" on our tardy slips. Third session was calculus class where we had a substitute teacher. We were ambling into class and chit-chatting when she gasped, exclaiming that she had forgotten her homework. I seldom did my homework and this instance was no exception. Therefore, her paranoia was not shared by me.

I recognized the stand-in professor from trigonometry class the previous semester. He always gathered the homework papers, passed them back in random order, and selected individuals to work the problems on the board; then the students graded the papers and turned them in. I raised my hand and requested that I be permitted to fetch mine from my locker. TQ followed my lead. He gave us the passport and we exited the classroom.

"Now what do we do?" she asked.

"Don't worry babe, I owe you one," I responded.

I grabbed a couple of old papers from my locker and we returned to class where students were diagramming on the whiteboard. The instructor ordered us to exchange papers. As we passed the phonies, I whispered that she should copy the answers on a plain sheet of paper. After the problems were solved and copied, we affixed our names, swapped papers again, graded them, and passed them forward with 100 percent accuracy. I must admit I did learn the lesson, but I didn't deserve the A.

At noontime TQ tagged along. We hopped into my partner's jalopy and drove to a hamburger joint where another pal worked counter. He would give me free fries as it was unfeasible for his boss to keep inventory on taters; also, I had a used cup on hand for free drinks. We had to purchase our burgers however, since the dude would count patties and buns (and cups). TQ was impressed with my shenanigans and consented to dance with me at the victory gala on Saturday, where everyone would see us together and realize that we were a couple. It was a big step for her that's for sure, to be seen with the likes of me. I got to make out with her behind the bleachers; I can only describe the experience as delicious. Then we took a walk downtown holding hands. Love was in her eyes but fear was in the air. A crowd was gathering near the plaza so we proceeded to investigate. That's when we witnessed some psycho leap to his death from a tall building. Time stood still; a heartbeat was an eternity. I looked at her, and she at me: stunned, sapped, and speechless. Time flew by; months seemed minutes. Our relationship gradually decayed like a decomposing corpse and we drifted apart.

That same night I dreamt about the end of time. Earth had spun out and crossed the path of the sun which melted it like butter. A prodigy invented a giant gravity magnet with three prongs and three poles, producing a superb force-field. It was deployed in space to attract Mars into assuming Earth's old orbit. Earth became barren, having shrunk after the water was flung, tumbling into the slot Mars once occupied. After swapping places, oxygenation occurred and atmospheres stratified rapidly on the new Earth, thereby revitalizing weather trends and seasons and expanding land, sea, and fresh water formations. Instantly there sprung forth growing, living, flourishing life forms. A freshly developed inhabitable planet was the result. Thus, the old Earth had passed away and another had taken its place; the heavens had been altered as a result. The theorized infinite phase transition actually had taken place, defying the laws of physics by establishing an entirely different galactic configuration thereby modifying also the universe.

Sunrise blazed through the curtains scattering its warm rays but I was shivering. I kicked off the covers and arose to discover the water and heat had been shut off. My mom started losing it; she was an emotional wreck already. Ceaseless slaving had caused her to age too quickly. It wasn't long before she couldn't perform her job adequately; they put her out to pasture with a pension that might've prolonged a parakeet for a period. I had to get a second job. Too bad big brother Orwell wasn't around anymore. He was my senior by fourteen years. He ran away from home when I was a whelp and we never heard from him again. He was into fast cars and gals; he took the faster lane into freewheeling and dealing. We didn't know if he was dead, in jail, a tramp, or a tycoon.

I could plink on the guitar and sing a trifle, so I performed petty gigs at private parties for smalltime cash. Then I met this drummer named Feather at a folk fest. He learned percussion by beating on bongos made from bark and animal skins akin to his Algonquin forefathers. Feather was a muscular, hawk-nosed and eagle-eyed master of the arts. Man, he could really bang the blood out of those drums. You could hear the beating long after he stopped. Feather had a friend everybody called Gorilla, a bearded black bloke from the Bronx who could blow a sax like ringing a bell. His real name was Moses; I personally preferred that over his stage name which I found somewhat offensive. Though he acted dumb he was basically quiet and thoughtful, taking after a prophet of God you might say. Add Butch a rowdy redneck, fire engine red-haired bass player, and they forged a formidable instrumental jazz combo.

Interestingly, the three were descendants of past civic leaders that once parlayed together at peace proceedings in Paris.

I jammed with them on Sundays after the bars closed for inventory (not for religious reasons, as the patrons drank religiously). Before long I was proficient enough to play in front of larger audiences. They invited me to join the band and I commenced writing songs. I got loads of good ideas by corresponding with deceased musicians while I slept; the ones that croaked from suicide, overdose, or accident were particularly helpful. I figure their intentions had not been altogether expressed so maybe they were using me as a conduit; or maybe I was fantasizing. Either way I'd often wake up and write a song in ten minutes while the dream was fresh in my mind.

To continue, along came Elaine Shy a portly, snaggletooth songstress from Shreveport. She drank scotch whiskey then blurted out the blues like it was going out of style (which it already was). Her husband Hippie an aging, tie-died and cross-eyed piano player from Gainesville was no slouch either. He could tickle those keys until it made you squirm. We amalgamated as refined metal into a jazz-rock ensemble that put us on the hit list inside a year with the tune, *Please Let Go My Mojo*. It was later days to the garbage gig and hello denarii.

After a couple of platinum discs, the progressive deterioration of rock and roll became asymptote. We adapted our act each year going from *Have a Fat Lip*, to *Screw You Too,* to *One Swung Low*. The punk scene had advanced to carnal rock, and then a brief spiritual wave, before interest in the genre plunged and a Disco revival ensued. I didn't cotton to the simple stuff though the primitive pulse was acceptable. I blew my boogie and left the band retaining copyright to my songs. The royalties continued to support us until Joy passed from a broken and exhausted heart.

The night of her death I dreamed about the hall of psychedelic doors. From behind each door popped an unpleasant surprise, and through each door I had to enter wise. The first showed me a lad of ten; it presented an endless maze of jungle gyms which I had to climb and cross within the deadline. Behind the second door I was a teen, and my mission was to rescue a pervert being molested by mannequins within the halls of desire. I was a young adult the third go-round, plodding through miles of carrion, crossing minefields and impact areas, searching for the triple key amidst the ruins. For the fourth, I was a middle-aged man burying all the loved ones that had died in my arms over the course of a century. The fifth found me an old codger, running for my life through another muddle of signs: one way, do not enter, keep out, no trespassing, yield, stop, detour, road closed, pavement ends, bridge out, dead end.

I awoke from the nightmare but was unaware that I was visiting a scene from my subconscious. There I stood on the salt flats at midnight under a new moon. I could see only pitch-black gawking back from a vacuum. Abruptly I became aware of a dim light piercing the atmosphere from what appeared to be another expansion of space and time. The light split into patterns of spectral sunsets surrounding me so quickly that I misplaced my balance and fell. To my dismay there was no surface and I floated away, mimicking a weightless astronaut but without the spacesuit. I reached forward and grabbed a beam of color and was jerked from my position to rocket along at 777 nanometers, only to grow nauseous as if rocked by a typhoon in open sea. When I let go, the clock stopped so quickly it crushed me; on par with smacking the pavement below a high skyscraper.

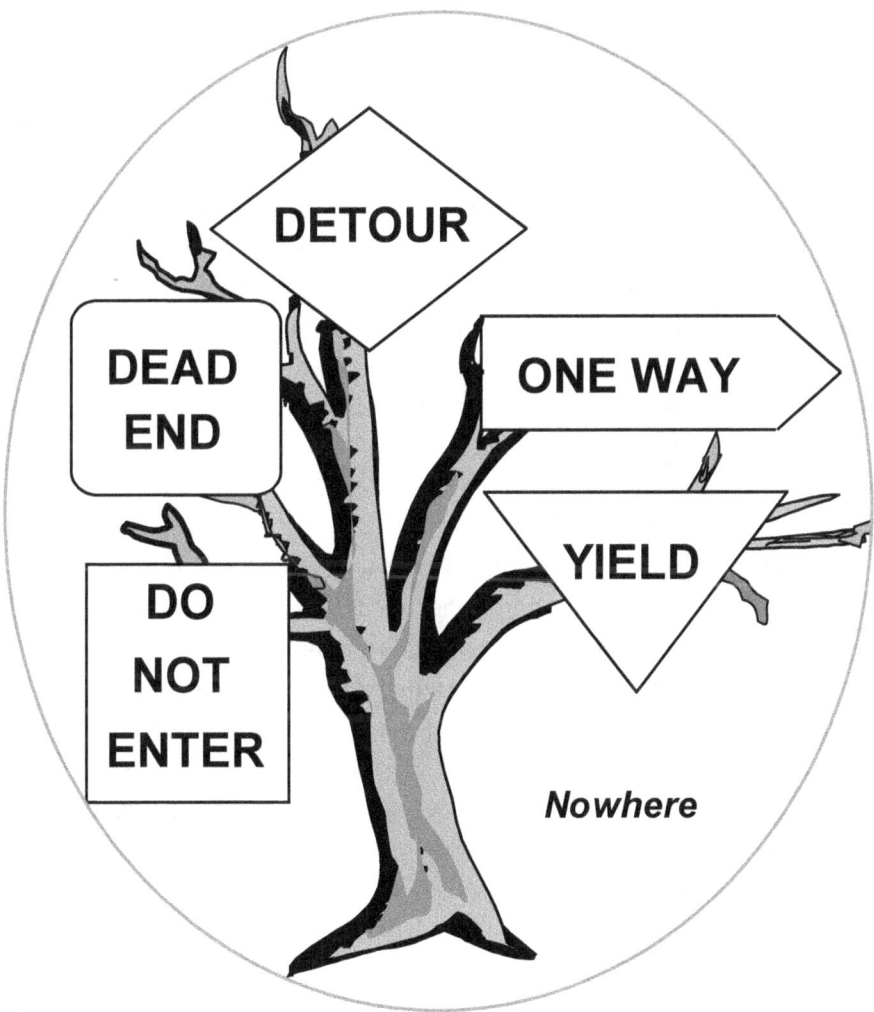

I was locked into a microsecond, frostbitten by the air, squeezed by enormous pressure until my brain could burst in a heartbeat. I could barely bear the saturation of my DNA by the limitless waves, a heavy burden on my soul. Finally, the storm subsided, it was calm, tranquil. I felt such a relaxation, analogous to slowly sinking into slippery soft quicksand. Immediately, insanity with the density of a star going supernova shoved me back into helpless sleep.

Feeling the frigid bite of that frosty morn reminded me of Joy's distress the previous evening, and the missing warmth of her lifeless hand. She did not deserve the suffering and the pitiful, desperate life she endured towards the end. I admired her courage while she slogged into the coldest darkest night. But can't I boast of endurance? I stood by her bedside and tended her, peering into those defenseless eyes. I could not subdue the shouting of my heart thumping loudly. And hers was so fragile. Yet she could calm the storm with her touch and shoo the clouds with her smile. I struggled, carrying the courage that invigorated me when her spirit departed, pressing onward through the packed snow. I trembled, reflecting on the love she bestowed even while she bravely faced the bitterness of an arctic night. Brushing the sleet from my face falling as tears out of the sky, the winter loneliness bade me to run and survive the day, continuing the trudge into doldrums of midday madness.

It was the shock of being alone and on my own that shook me out of it. I'd lost everyone who authentically loved me. I had a high school diploma and some miscellaneous expertise as garbage collector, sludge driver, and musician. Imbursement from my songs had all but dried up so I had no income to speak of. At least the house was paid for; but the property taxes were outrageous and utilities too and I didn't know what I was going to do.

SS often reminded me, "Opportunity does not come without effort, and success does not come without sacrifice."

And here my slogan always had been, "Whatever works is fair game."

As usual, the dawn burst through the blinds knocking me out of bed, and I doubted what was bouncing about in my head. The night before I'd engaged in more vice than is proper or nice. As I repented, sighing from my aches and pains, I strained to open the front door to see what the new day had in store. I noticed weeds growing too high, before the sunrays glazed my eyes and clouded my gaze. I located yesterday's soggy newspaper in the gutter across the street. Lifting it out of the muck, I settled on this being another one of those crazy days. I brewed some coffee and parked my carcass on a recliner. My vision cleared enough to read the headlines: Bank Robbery Yields No Clues. I wondered who. I opted to forgo seeking employment and took a hike into the backwoods. I roamed for hours getting disoriented in the enchanted forest. Searching for a way out, I sighted a row of flowers. I paused to enjoy their fragrant perfume and colorful petals, appreciating that the bouquet was solely there for my delight. I was distracted by a pile of sticks; upon investigation I discovered a wooden cigar box hidden underneath.

I opened the latch to find a stash of money. I was reminded of the story I'd read in the daily news and presumed a connection. I broke away from the timberlands at mid-afternoon clutching the box under my arm. Emerging at the outskirts of the city, I flagged a taxi into town keeping quiet about what I had uncovered. At the village square I met a mute midget; he was selling gemstones for which I traded the stolen loot. The purchase netted two rubies, one diamond, a sapphire and an opal. They were beautiful specimens, large and lustrous.

Elated with my treasure but lacking cab-fare, I extended my thumb like an ordinary bum to hitch a ride back to the suburbs. I was picked up by a fire truck returning to the station from a false alarm. The driver thought I was running; he said he'd bring me luck. Upon arriving, five of us piled into his convertible sportscar which sped away in the direction opposite mine; I was stuck. Somehow, they ascertained that I had information about hidden pickings and pressured me to spill the beans. I deduced that they were robbers, maybe the ones that knocked off the bank.

I was taken captive to a cabin deep in unfamiliar woods. The louts were arguing my fate amongst themselves when I dashed out the gate and into a thicket. They charged after me, a horde of hyenas on the hunt; hooting, hollering, and chasing me through briar patches and swamps. They wielded knives and clubs determined to rub me out. I entered a field that many times had been drenched with rain. As they closed in lightning struck, electrocuting the mob. Instead of firemen, smoke remained. There I was, alive, alone, with my precious stones—missing in the middle of nowhere with darkness closing in. I experienced a burst of knowledge about the curse of wealth obtained through ill-gotten gain. Gratification from earned increase makes it much more credible I surmised. While true, I deflected the underlying message which I choose not to disclose because it is way too distressing. If you figure it out you are a genius.

The next morning, I applied with the government hoping for an assignment overseas. I thought I could become a special agent or something. Amazingly, I was recruited. They trained me for six months then plopped me behind a desk in a room full of cubicles and workstations. It was so boring I began taking college courses in psychology and astronomy; I also volunteered for every in-house-training offered by my employer. I had no life. I studied diligently and worked hard the way my parents did. In three years, I had an academic degree and a promotion.

I joined a team of researchers investigating the effects of torment and torture on war veterans. It was sorely depressing. I was working with this one guy, a decorated ranger who spent five years in a prisoner of war camp before escaping. He felt deserted by his countrymen and his government; and for good reason since the politicians continued to maintain that we had no POWs in Iran. He hanged himself in the latrine on another stormy winter night, leaving a suicide note addressed to me explaining how he appreciated that at least one person in the world believed him.

Whenever someone I care deeply about dies, I have a heartrending dream, with few exceptions. This time I was a spy for a foreign entity, on duty in Las Vegas. I was there to ace the casinos using my untested methodological approach to gambling. I played a series of five slot games five times each, a different wager each time. After the first set I computed the proportion of total amount lost or won and arranged them in relative order per wager. I repeated this process five consecutive times and recalculated the results. Then I worked the top five payoffs five times each (25 plays) and my total return equaled plus 25 percent. I played this system each day for 25 weeks switching casinos periodically, increasing the bets until I had amassed 25 million dollars. The feds got wind of the stratagem and arrested me. They acted as if I'd robbed Ft. Knox though I hadn't committed any crime. What they really wanted was the money and the formula. I handed over the key to an airport locker where I told them the cash was stashed. The instant they opened it a bomb went off and I absconded with a trifling $0.25 to my name. This was the only gift I received on my 25th birthday. I have yet to determine its value. There certainly was no reason to celebrate.

It seems I'm endlessly running from something, particularly in my dreams. Or maybe I'm running towards something, it's hard to differentiate the two. I have studied my dreams until I'm blue in the face. They used to be newsworthy but they've grown increasingly more complicated and bizarre as I've matured. There's no telling what hidden implications may emerge at any second. Perhaps my brain is protecting me somehow; maybe there are recognitions lurking that are not for me to know. I keep trying to decipher it nevertheless.

I still can see the mirage, my head attached to a puppet. Mysterious faces look down from above; I suppose they belong to those pulling the strings. Am I nothing but a marionette, playacting exclusively for their entertainment? Is it all for show? They must think of me a ghastly performer.

Life is too short. I watched as my parents slaved themselves into an untimely tomb. Make no mistake I learned plenty from them, both what to do and what not to do. But to live happy one must appreciate life. Too many die young. When you're bored, think how stupendous it is to be alive. The crowds watch the clock and remember the date but don't take time to live. Their routine existence peaks maybe once a year when they're on holiday. They are too busy expending great energy on fleeting achievements. When these plebes grow old, they won't have many momentous memories and hence, nothing to uphold them. I'm going to prepare for that era by gathering as many good times as I can, so that when I am aged, I can fondly remember when I was not. I'm going to dedicate time for fun like I have for work and education. It's not hard distinguishing business and leisure, what's hard is making time for both. Obviously, life has caught on; it has continued for millennia and populations keep increasing. It's time we made the most of it, that's my advice.

What's more, I'm tired of worrying. People who fret are confused; they live for yesterday, or tomorrow, but seldom the present. There is no need to be preoccupied about the past as it is gone and not a threat. It is senseless to be obsessed about the future because it hasn't happened and there is no guarantee that it will. There is nothing in the present that warrants worriment because the situation is already at hand. What good is fussing about it? Are there any benefits to that?

Well I finally landed a position with the Foreign Service. I had hoped to travel the world and now I was getting paid to do so. I was particularly enchanted with Switzerland; I spent many a vacation there. Although I wasn't a spy I worked with experts on espionage in my capacity as an evaluator. I fancied a fraulein from Frankfurt. She was witty, audacious, secretive, and gorgeous. A leggy, slender, dark-haired, dark-eyed lady, and seductive; I was infatuated. Unfortunately, I was nothing but a plaything to her. She was in no hurry to get attached or settle down. We were to rendezvous in the Swiss Alps over the Memorial weekend but she never showed. Her mobile phone had been disconnected and I had no other way of contacting her. Pops often warned me about getting involved with artists or spies.

I retired to my suite and collapsed on the bed. I tried to cry but I didn't know how anymore. I fell asleep and dreamt of a terrible torrent. I saw mansions sliding into the ocean; avalanches wiping out villages; meteorites roasting ranches; lightning bolts igniting open ranges; magma blanketing entire towns; tidal waves and mudslides burying island paradises. It was reminiscent of the time of Lot with fire, brimstone and the works. Hailstones the size and color of cantaloupe began to drop, crushing skulls and collapsing dwellings.

I was startled out of my daze by commotion in the corridor. People were frantically running this way and that. The hotel was afire; the inferno was two floors below. The elevator was disabled and there was no way to escape by stairs which were sealed with toxic fumes. I hurried to the balcony beside my boudoir. I shimmied over and down the guardrail and dropped to the porch below. Repeating this maneuver six times I made it safely to the ground, with an annoying sprained ankle. By then the lodge was engulfed in flames. Another relationship goes up in smoke I concluded, as I puffed on a cigar and watched the inn burn to the ground.

Fire is intriguing is it not? It has a persona of its own. It can create the mood or destroy it. It changes color, it flickers and flames, it smolders and rages. It dies, it sleeps, and it comes back to life. Like most anything a little bit is good for you but a lot is bad. And who has not stared into a fire for hours, spellbound by its mystifying face? Ever noticed that the ocean has these same characteristics? It too can be your friend or your enemy. It can lull you to sleep or smack you upside the head. It is becoming and it is brutal; it can allure and it can repel. It can be nurturing and it can be nasty.

I love them both. If you listen carefully, they speak. And they never lie. And if you treat them with respect, they will be your friends. It depends on your perspective. Things could always get worse but there is always hope for the better. So, I'll not gauge the current situation in terms of high-low because all have quality. How could anyone be disappointed with that?

The interlude was not altogether the rest and recuperation that I'd bargained for but it passed as a diversion. I was back in the states, slumped at my desk, staring at a situation display and getting clobbered by the clutter. Next, I'm having one of those eureka experiences—Hey, I have nobody (notwithstanding the solipsist who is undyingly there for me). Sure, I've dined with colleagues, and we've sloshed an occasional beer, but I categorize them acquaintances. I can't call on them when I'm down and out. Who's going to listen to my problems? Where am I to secure my unsolicited encouragement?

Employees' wives tried matching me with their girlfriends each of whom were homely airheads. How's about some intellectual stimulation, huh? That's what I look for in a woman; well, in addition to the usual stuff: attractiveness, appearance, classiness, cleanliness, sense of humor, sensuality, sensitivity, understanding, versatility, sentimentality, kindness, good kisser, good lover, good heart, frisky, etc. Okay, maybe I'm a little demanding but so are they. Of course, the criteria are fewer with respect to friendship. A true friend is someone you can trust plain and simple. To find a lover who also is a friend, that's a soulmate. What more could anyone ask?

Women must be afraid of me; I tend to scare them off with my awkward ways. I'm inclined to fast-forward everything (too much time twisting will do that to you). Maybe my standards are set too high; after all, they can't be Lany. I tend to compare my dates to her and they don't measure up. Now she's in heaven with the rest of the angels. I learned about love the wrong way; I lack the traditional heterosexual orientation. Nobody taught me how to treat a woman. My brother flew the coop, my parents were workaholics, my teachers couldn't care less, and my peers were ruffians and whoremongers. And how-to books, they're not worth the paper and print. Ladies' magazines, now there's a misleading crock of hooey, but no worse than so-called gentlemen's magazines. Do people really desire that kinky stuff? Most women still want flowers and diamonds I'll bet. Bachelorhood isn't so bad, though celibacy is a major challenge. But I digress.

Get this: terrorists were stalking the metropolis and committing murderous acts left and right. They had infiltrated across the porous borders like bacteria invading an unclean body. I was commissioned by the secret service to snuff them out; kind of a hitman, I guess. Why not I thought? I had no attachments, no goals, no life. And I didn't have to report to anyone or account for my whereabouts; plausible deniability they called it. I had plenty of weapons expertise, martial arts training, and I knew how to be inconspicuous. It wasn't that I lacked qualifications except for the fact I'd never done such a thing. My trainers said I was a natural.

One day I waylaid a suspect and heaved him into the street by the scruff of his collar; I wanted to scare the living daylights out of him and it worked (well, after I whipped him into a pulp). He was merely the bait. I shadowed his trail after he scrammed; he joined up with another oaf half mile down the road. Eavesdropping as best I could I heard them speaking Farsi. I never learned the language much but I could tell they were plotting something. After closer inspection I recognized the other one. He'd walked free a year before when a twelve-person jury was unable to convict him of the attempted assassination of a public official, who was running for reelection on an antiterrorism platform. Needless to say, the candidate dropped out of the race. His designated malefactor should've hung but instead the jurors did. Eight wanted him to fry, three judged he was an okay guy, and one couldn't explain why. I was puzzled how a third of the jurors couldn't see the evil in this man. Or maybe they hoped to find the good but there wasn't any. Yes, false faith had reached epidemic proportions; here was a prime example.

Being a master of disguise, I endeared myself to the chump having now located his whereabouts. I pretended to be a journalist for a big-time rag mag, convincing him I wasn't interested in giving him up but printing his yarn. I went on about how he got a bad rap and deserved to clear his name. He agreed to meet clandestinely on the roof of his apartment building. He fed me some hogwash which he supposed would present him notorious and revered. I consulted with him a few times gaining his confidence while taking dictation. On the fifth session I bear-hugged the brute as I greeted him; then I lifted him off his feet, limped over to the ledge, and dropped him over the edge. He grabbed my jacket, a break-away design, before plummeting seventeen floors with my sleeves clutched in his hand. On my way through a side door on the ground floor I noticed him laid-out in a pool of blood at the bottom of a stinky slime-streaked drainage ditch, his mouth agape. And here I judged he'd have a smile on his face from picturing the herd of whoring houris he used to brag about.

After leaving them an anonymous tip, the feds found a cache of weapons at his residence and the ingredients to homemade explosive devices. There were clippings of prior bombings and shootings on the living room wall and a map of city hall on the dining room table. Oh, by the way, three other coconspirators were sipping green tea in the kitchen when the agents barged in. Too bad for the bad guys whose hands went for their guns instead of reaching for the sky. I read about the bust days after in the very rag sheet I employed as a ploy. It tickled me how these goofballs averred a heavenly reward in paradise for dying a gallant death by committing violence and acts of terror; yet they were blatantly terrified of dying in the same fashion, a fate they sought to impose on respectable people. I wondered if they believed in karma. They dished it out but I doubt if they knew how to take it.

My boss spoke my name three times with increasing amplitude. I looked up with an agitated glance as if I'd heard him the first two times. He offered me a transfer to the intelligence detachment of all places. Maybe he figured I was deep into analytical machinations every time he caught me daydreaming; or perhaps he just wanted to get rid of me by pawning me off on another manager. Whatever, it was fifteen more weeks of schooling, another promotion, and I'm a specialist in allied intelligence operations. I got a bigger paycheck, a private office on the tenth floor (with a door and a window), and an expense account.

The Hollow Man

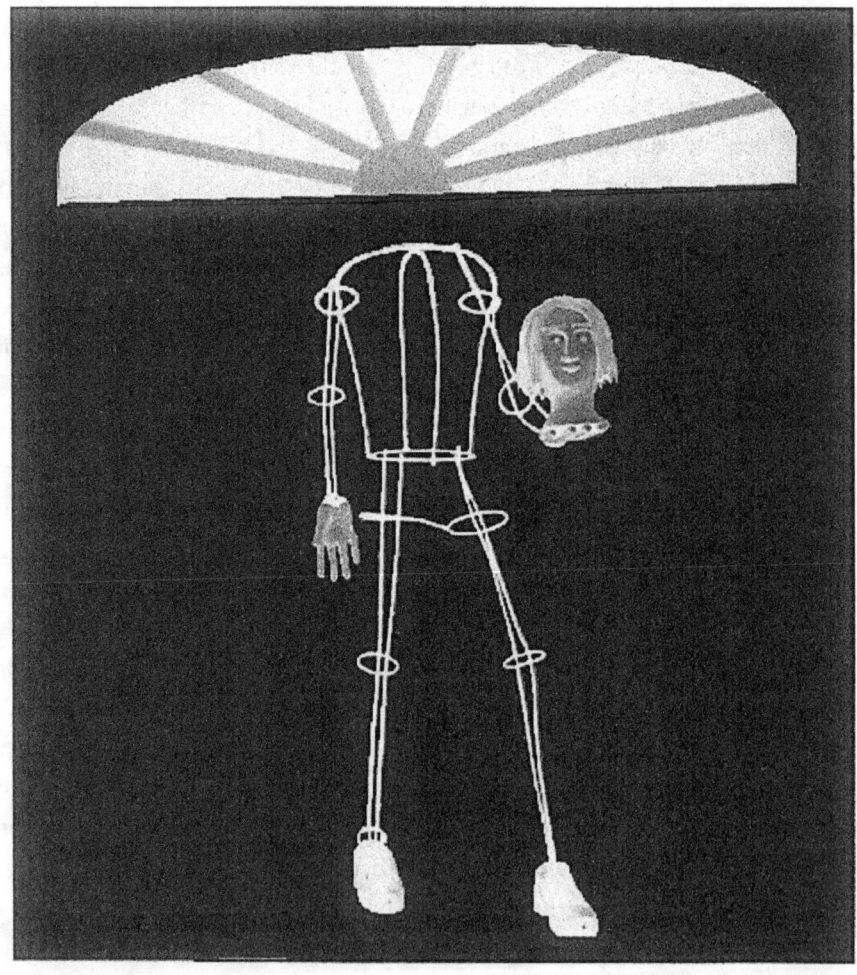

I worked on highly classified projects and produced top secret documents, and to this day I have no idea what any of it meant. I expect they did. Or possibly it was a formality, and we were jumping through hoops and tumbling through wickets to placate people at the top who knew even less. But then again if they had a clue, they would've realized that the intercontinental ballistic missiles were coming. I failed to see the point. I needed a vacation from my last vacation. I took some more time off and returned home to try and sort it out. The dwelling was dusty with cobwebs and a musty smell; but it was my personal paradise. I could think, sleep, and dream again; my boyhood crib felt better than ever. It got to where I didn't want to return to work. I was busy contemplating the future with me in it. SS reassured that I was expanding my horizons insofar as information is power.

"Power over who or what?" I interrogated.

"Information reduces uncertainty which is risk," he informed. "And certainty equates to confidence which mitigates the doubt when we are unsure of ourselves."

I daresay I had more confidence, security, and authority but no direction per se. I was endowed with advanced education, special gifts, and obscure talents. Yet feeling worthless I purposelessly coasted in a constant condition of disorientation. The world revolved around me similar to the moons around Jupiter. In fact, I envisioned myself living on Io as her inner turmoil was akin to mine. She could've been my sister and I could've been part of something else, instead of it being part of me. I acknowledged being depressed, stressed, hard-pressed, and undressed, leaving out that I was blessed.

Here I sit remembering the good times I once had. I cannot smile nor can I frown; unhappy though I'm glad. I'm glad because they happened, that I lived, and loved and thought. Unhappy though for they have passed and dreams are all I've got. A while ago the days would flow; before you know time goes so slow. The hours we lack we can't get back. We get off track; we're cut no slack. Enduring times we cannot bear while wishing someone else was there. Dark shady lanes I've traveled long. I seek the right but do the wrong. Pity the blues, a lonely song; I'm feeling that I don't belong. I could tell you most the rest but the sun sets in the west; and it took a long, long time to come about. Now I'll leave you with the tears that were shed ten thousand years; you may fertilize your thoughts if they will sprout. Hmm, I could've composed a song out of that discourse.

In the midst of my melancholy I finally did make a new friend: he was an autistic evangelist, a savant who had memorized the Holy Bible. He was not handsome or attractive, not one to appeal to the masses; kind of chubby and clumsy, fuzzy hair, with a pug nose; double-jointed, pigeon-toed, hunch-backed, and lazy-eyed. He was timid as a church mouse yet authentic, unassuming, sweet, and soft-spoken. He appeared on several discussion programs; the producers treated him like a sideshow in a circus. I obtained a free pass once and sat at the rear of the auditorium. He impressed me. I ran into him again on the tramway; he rode it almost every day as it was his favorite amusement. The fellow had a photographic memory same as the solipsist.

Pete was a walking biblical cross-reference. He could quote scripture, chapter and verse, but he had difficulty interpreting the words. I noticed I had a knack for understanding. Maybe being inundated with facts and figures is what helped me to realize that aptitude. I could throw out a scriptural citation and Pete could recite the associated verse with references. He could identify every passage that used a particular word or phrase much like a concordance. It became a game with us, to the degree that the sacred writings started making sense (to us both); in particular, I was dumbfounded that Messiah appeared in both testaments. After two months Pete's routine demanded it. I didn't mind because his gift was captivating and the wisdom in the words was astonishing.

We spent weekends chugging ale and engrossing ourselves with our own Bible quiz show. He wanted to move in and be my roommate but his parents forbade it. They were worried about him becoming independent (besides, the state treasury check would cease to arrive). Nevertheless, I was reluctant to do so; it was a responsibility I frankly could not accept at that juncture.

Wouldn't you know it? On a subsequent telecast some crackpot in the studio managed to rush the pulpit yelling creepy satanic slogans. He pulled a .38 and plugged three rounds into Pete's chest right there in front of God, the audience, and ten million television viewers. I was backstage when it happened.

I hastened to his side but he was already gone. Unlike the scowling atheistic activist, Pete had a big grin on his face extending from ear to ear. Security officers tried to wrestle the revolver from the demented one but he broke away, put the barrel to his temple, and blew his brains out. The entire set was painted with plasma. Man, the ratings must've hit the ceiling that day. Needless to say, the publicity was mortifying. I wonder if that jerk expected to rule in Gehenna with his horned pastor. I went into a tirade. What's with this radicalism? Does anything make sense to these people? Is there any sense left anywhere in the solar system?

I flipped to another station and there was my beloved companion bidding me to enter. The asinine assassin was about to shoot him down when I surged onto the stage. I drew his attention, uttered a few ad libs, and instantly the gunman collapsed on the floor convulsing into a grand mal seizure. Just then a purple haze came over the guy, he became rigid as a two-by-four, and six demons departed from his nostrils. After pause for station identification the scamp opened his eyes, rose to his feet, shook my hand, strolled back down the aisle, handed the sidearm to an usher, and took a seat in the fourteenth pew. During curtain call there was a standing ovation.

After the show I followed Pete backstage across an aqua causeway and beyond the gilded door to another set. In the backdrop I spied an enormous tree.

Pete educated me how each leaf on the tree had an identity. We clambered to the upper branches where he pointed to a leaf bearing my name. His name was printed on a neighboring leaf of the same sprig. No sooner had we climbed down when the leaves in the tree started weaving into the air and floating together, gathering as pages in an almanac which contained 144,000 volumes. I suppose it was the Book of Life. How thankful I was to be written in it.

We giggled about it, embraced, and then Pete placed his hand in the small of my back and escorted me to the dock. I boarded a canoe and paddled downstream along a winding tinsel tributary. The water was perfectly translucent though I couldn't see bottom because it was so deep. I observed countless colorful fishes of differing shape and size, each unique in its own way, parading this way and that. The current flowed right back out the shiny screen and plopped me onto the couch, where I found myself crouched the next morning in a fetal pose. I looked up with weary eyes to see a test pattern on the display. I staggered to my feet to turn off the monitor when I noticed it was unplugged.

Just then it dawned on me: I did have friends. Some of them had died yet they were alive. One was an invisible comrade, a guide who never left my side. He was my best friend. He planted an orchard in my mind which produced a different exotic fruit each month, ripe with ideas. The greatest part of me was invisible as well, charged with positive energy which was polarized towards attraction, without the least resistance. I sighed with relief. For once in my life I had a purpose, a direction, and a motive. It was a lifelong undertaking but I knew with conviction the outcome before I embarked. I welcomed the challenge; I was anxious to hit the ground running. And I knew where I was going, though I'd never been there before. I wasn't lost I was found. I announced to the audience my opening lines, "Now that I can see I can walk. I shall explore and surely will discover." The journey had begun. I was healed from being the blind and disabled beggar I was beforehand. I was commissioned to fight, whereas I used to either freeze or flee.

Years prior I had a vision of this. Every alternate scenario was a gamble and every resolution a risk. I shoved my pile of chips into the pot wagering the lot on the first card dealt to me: Jack of Hearts. I figured there was nothing more to lose. To my dejection eight others saw my bet. I thought I was a born loser with zero potential. When the last card landed in front of me, I lifted up the edge and peeked carefully. I still had nothing but Jack high. It was a hand that maybe I should've folded but it was too late; I'd bet the farm on it. It's foolish to chuck it when you're all-in is it not? The worst that can happen is the inevitable. A few gamblers folded their hands but the rest had called my bluff for that river card. I dropped my hand face-up atop the huge grouping of chips. To my surprise my Jack of Hearts with a Ten kicker was the winner. Maybe the other players had wagered on an inside straight or a flush. Those high-stakes gamblers, they neither see reality straight nor flush. It goes to show that you need to play the hand using whatever cards you're dealt. There really are no winners or losers, only sinners and choosers. Honestly, I was both with no regrets, at least not this time for I had chosen rightly, and it turned out to be a sure thing. But I swore never again would I play five-card poker no matter how many decks.

I tossed and turned in my featherbed but refused to awaken; I didn't want the vision to leave me. The black and white dream had turned full color. Pure water was again flowing through the parched basin. Tulips and daffodils began to sprout and bloom in the wind-torn flowerbeds riding along the sunbaked riverbanks. Yellow-green grass overtook the seared fields, spreading and migrating with rhythmic waves rolling towards the hills. Pine trees were sprouting amidst the mounds, shooting up to the clouds like arrows. Orange and violet birds already had commenced nesting in their branches, singing and chirping. Clownfish were spurting into the air swallowing up those pesky mosquitos. Unlike the fish I was still following the current downstream which emptied into a clean foamy ocean. There was a crisp cool breeze bouncing off the whitecaps and pushing out to sea. In the distance the sun was rising, shedding its flaxen rays across the bay. Atop a crest I peered down the golden bridge of light that extended from my position all the way to the horizon, beyond which I was sure my destination lay. I cruised across the shimmering span, experiencing an idiosyncratic feeling of transmutation as I neared the horizon's edge. Upon self-inspection, confession, and repentance I sensed separation from the page. This was followed by relocation, for at once it was revealed to me my next heading and story. The direction led me upwards, beyond the stars and past the black hole in my head.

My new existence was amazing, novel, stimulating. I felt so secure, eager, grateful, and fulfilled that I blushed. It was enthralling being invited to the ceremony. I had given the performance of a lifetime, slaying the dragon in the dale of decision. The drama unfolded before my very eyes. I was immensely appreciative to my director, producer, and supporting cast. The solipsist clapped his hands in approval; he was joined in applause by twenty-three others. I was the celebrity and they were the spectators. The ovation was endearing. And the program was appreciated by the viewers back home. My parents were so proud and my grandparents too.

I was quite nervous, enwrapped in stage fright; but I responded on cue and recited the oath perfectly. I was about to be awarded the grand prize, a diadem with twelve dazzling jewels, three at each corner of the headband. All the victors received one. But my triumphant speech was preempted by a thundering voice proclaiming "The End." I never got to speak the last sentence; I can't even remember what it was so it probably wasn't that important.

The Maze

This was only the beginning, for the next episode in the continuing legend of my life as a disciple was underway. I had lots to learn and a long way to go; there was nothing to say so I kept my mouth shut. Instead of being called to testify as an eyewitness I was dismissed. Departing the courtroom, I was given my next assignment. I would find myself completely engulfed in the irrevocable crusade to reclaim Jerusalem, during which I resumed my search for the elusive triple key. I knew it existed and I knew it was powerful. But as yet I had no idea what it was, what it meant, or what it opened.

Sometimes you unassumingly have to follow your dreams and see where they lead; that's when you'll find what you're looking for, even if it wasn't what you'd selected or expected. You'll receive everything you need along the way and that's all you really wanted anyhow. When your every wish is fulfilled and you're still left empty such is the world. And anyone can clearly see that this world is a speck of dust compared to the universe. Yet despite the enormity of it and the seeming insignificance of little old me, I will outlive it. I guess I'm not so unimportant after all. Someday the universe will be gone though I live on; nothing wrong with that.

I learned to appreciate that everything was here for a reason; so was I. I savored every morsel of it; I even began to love myself. There was no fault to be pointed out except within humankind. I mean how could we, having superiority and faculty, be so stupid? We are not great but for the fact that God made us who we are. He shows us the greatest destiny although people ignore it because they are absorbed with fate alone. Dropped in a labyrinth, looking for a way out and finding none, they spend the rest of their lives abandoning the obvious; for they think they know where to go and can find their own way, refusing to follow the Great One. How could they know? Who told them? Oh, they figured it out for themselves; yeah, right. Instinct is irrelevant; try wisdom. Just remember it isn't yours.

CHRONICLES

After begging him for a decade the solipsist finally gave me the grand tour of his neighborhood. The most exciting event was crossing the event horizon when SS slammed the ship into time reverse; still it ejected us faster than we entered enabling us to escape unharmed to the other side. There were multicolored wave patterns; it was a splendid and brilliant presentation which remains engraved in my memory.

His was a loosely-wound spiraling galaxy like mine, though it rotated in the opposite direction of the Milky Way. There was a black hole in the center through which I would return. He lived in a binary system of twin stars with umpteen planets and satellites crossing paths but never colliding thanks to the perfectly balanced and complementary gravitational forces extant in that system. Everything in the zone was arranged with meticulous order seemingly in conformance to physical laws dissimilar to my native space. I debated if it was his or mine which was the prototype universe. Or maybe we lived in a binary universe, because each black hole opened into its contemporary at matching planes of linear time.

I spent forty-nine amazing days in his domain; it was the best excursion of them all. His people were shapeshifters but their normal appearance was a bronze biped (SS continually assumed human form in my world so it came as a surprise to me his actual appearance). His parent planet, which I can neither pronounce nor spell, was completely covered by an ocean. Apparently, a gigennium ago hydrocarbons trapped deadly gases delivering a severe ice age. The enlarging planet shed its coat and shifted orbit similar to a river changing course, causing the ice to thaw emanating into a worldwide flood. The waters picked up alkalis and salts from the soil and there you go, one humongous sea. Periodic rainfall kept the water level constant each year. Insofar as there were twelve moons pulling on the ocean, occasional waves would transverse the entire circumference some as tall as a soccer field is long. Not surprisingly, surfing was the most popular interregional competitive sport.

I recalled our trip to Earth's past when it was covered with water. I wondered if someday his would see the uplift of mountains, the seepage of water into the fractures and fissures, and the dispersion of land masses and elements. Oddly, the possibility never dawned on him until that moment. It annoyed him temporarily as if my world was more advanced somehow; though it quickly became clear (at least to me) that his was way more progressive, sophisticated, and modernized. However, their physical laws, shouldn't they obey the same rules, constants, and processes? Not necessarily.

Of the moons in this planetary complex SS lived on the largest and twelfth, called November. I was befuddled that these moons translated into names of months in my culture and were comparable in size to planets in my solar system. Although the mother planet orbited farthest from its sun it migrated near the neighboring sun. Combined with an axis of five-degree tilt ten seasons were conveyed each year, which was about 435 days approximately 33.3 hours per day. November's spin and orbit helped maintain a steady climate during the day except for brief, seasonal weather switches more pronounced than those on Earth. In daylight it was very bright and at nighttime it was dimly lit (unless you were on the shady side of the moon, then you had to stay indoors if you didn't want to become an ice cube).

Upon arrival, the ship orbited November once while SS reported his return and transmitted the abridged version of his findings (withholding particulars like bringing a passenger). The moon was earthlike with polar ice caps and a confluence of watercourses. SS brought me to the outskirts of an upper-middleclass hamlet, a community of ranch-style haciendas. His compound was situated in the center of a square mile or so of property. He informed that he lived alone, deliberately keeping distance between him and his neighbors. His was a relatively modest house given his status, except for the underground garage where he parked the ship complete with retracting camouflaged double roofs. It was virtually indistinguishable from the sky. He also owned a nifty transport that rendered shuttling between moons and planets nothing more than a leisurely drive across town. Oddly, the shape and appearance of his shuttlecraft was not unlike magazine cutouts of finned automobiles that my grandfather showed me from a scrapbook he assembled as a boy. We relaxed on the back porch which overlooked an eerie ammonia lake where I dozed off in an easy chair. I awoke wrapped in a fur blanket SS had draped over me. You wouldn't believe the radiant sunrise which occurred twice the following morning.

On day two we toured July, the eleventh moon comprised of penal colonies. Felons were sentenced there to no less than one year of hard labor but the wages were decent. Unmistakably unforgivable convicts lived out their death sentences in a concentration camp where they posed as opossums for the experimental testing of adverse atmospheres, profitable parasites, and dangerous drugs. Many inmates who were violent or deranged were open to being brainwashed in the mind-reconfiguration facility. The adventurous ones were granted release to volunteer for suicide assignments for which their families would be well compensated. Rapists, molesters, and psychopathic deviants whose aversive dispositions defeated all forms of rehabilitation had to reside in seclusion on a farm. They were at liberty to do whatever and were largely self-governed, contained, and sufficient. Remarkably they learned, either explicitly or vicariously, to abstain from engaging in antisocial behavior due to retaliatory consequences that were immediate, intense, suppressive, and rudely awakening. And who says punishment doesn't work? They had ingeniously constructed a fashionable resort colony that was the envy of the rest of the moon.

"We could learn a bunch from your corrections system," I observed. "At home our penal institutions teach the incarcerated how to become career criminals."

August the tenth moon, which was pretty much uninhabitable, was our destination for day three. It had evolved consistent with prehistoric Earth, only the vicious varmints now roaming it were rats, insects, and other vermin. I was fascinated by the ten-foot scorpions; we witnessed one sucking the guts out of a twenty-foot cockroach. The roach squealed like a pig when it was stung, then the scorpion made this noise like a roaring vacuum cleaner, and after about ten seconds it scampered away leaving an empty carcass behind. SS used a winch to drag the remains into his cargo bay.

He explained, "The shells are used to make armor plating and can be sold legally at what you earthlings refer as black market."

The fourth day on the ninth moon we observed the ant monsters. The black ones resided in a natural complex of tunnels permeating the craggy cliffs; the red ones, smaller in size but equally deadly, abided in incredible clay condominiums. The two clashed endlessly using sophisticated combat tactics to subjugate the other. Engagements would continue the entire day, until nightfall which was twice as long as the day. Columns of ants would rally together a single kindred spirit, and march (also the name of the moon) in formation for a calculated and decisive affront; it would have impressed the joint chiefs. Basically, the ants dieted on one another so the balance of food was equal and neither dominated. There were private installations dotting the countryside in which scientists and trainees were based to study the habits of the ants.

"How intricately nature has preserved the genera and ecology of this moon," I construed.

The eighth orb was an adventure land with unusual wonders and curious creatures. It was a literal oasis of earthly delights, nirvana you might say but not as great as heaven probably. On the moon called May you didn't have to die believing in Allah to stay high day and night and relish the services of voluptuous vixens. It was lust at first sight for me. The appetizers were exquisite: tasty pastries, superb hors d'oeuvres, and luscious lovelies. Who cares what the ingredients were on the gourmet platter? I'm sure I don't want or need to know. After dining on delicacies and damsels I reclined on a velvet settee, smoking a long black cigarette with the flavor of clove, and sipping sassafras schnapps. I leapt to my feet in amazement while below the balcony an enormous chartreuse salamander with slinky spines slithered out of the underbrush. The skinny, shiny, slimy amphibian had a tuna's mouth and a chameleon's tongue.

"How beautiful can ugly get?" I blurted.

SS responded, "The face only another gryblort could love."

This ended the fifth day. After taking a day to recuperate from the merriments and then to carouse a tad more, we departed on day seven for the seventh moon June. It was the smallest and nobody really lived there. I noticed a few barracks where repairpersons, engineers, and support staff dwelled periodically, but these temporary residents had private homes elsewhere. The place was cluttered with a conglomeration of communications and conservation equipment. There were satellite stations, solar energy centers, windmills, radio frequency antennae, spectrographic transmitters and receivers, television broadcasting complexes, sensor systems, and a slew of other stuff I didn't recognize. It worked out great because the other moons required few devices so as not to contaminate the view (opposite of my hometown which was littered with junk).

That afternoon we visited January the sixth sphere; it was a ghetto. It was polluted, dirty, overcrowded, and rundown though the temperate climate could be appreciated year-round. The inhabitants were part-time workers, unskilled laborers, and assorted jacks of all trades. They were uneducated outlanders who were willing to perform the mundane jobs nobody else wanted. They were unkempt but content, complacent, and thrived on the bare minimum. Most labored on other moons or on planetary ocean platforms. They crowded into space-buses that left at the rising of the second sun (well, nine o'clock when the suns didn't shine) and returned ten hours later.

Day eight: April, the fifth and second largest orb was incredibly breathtaking. It was one continuous natural park suitable for visiting, vacationing, or invasion for a family outing or romantic getaway. Communal complexes were situated in remote locations where folks dumped their gear and rented runabouts. I coerced the confidant into staying overnight, there were so many fascinations to behold. Several zoos specialized in specific types of animals: reptilian, mammalian, avian, marine, human, and so forth. There were countless fruit orchards and vegetable gardens. Row after row of flowers of every color, form, and size crosshatched the landscape. There were veritably millions of distinct breeding, blooming, and blossoming life forms. Outside the gates were acres upon acres of grain fields, plantations, groves, livestock ranches, and hatcheries. It wasn't unusual for an agriculturalist or a horticulturist to manage half a million acres. The entire moon resembled a huge outdoor biosphere. This moon produced over 75 percent of the intra-planetary food consumed annually in this expanse of space.

The fourth satellite had an irregular orbit and wandered too close to the suns to sustain much life. There was an aggregation of hermits and recluses that called it home. They had to lick the barrel to make a living. Hard work and nothing to do in this fierce climate, I don't know why they stayed. It was about 120 degrees in the shade while we were there. At night the temperature plummeted to the low forties. It reminded me of the desert back home; during the heat of summer it was unbearable but you could freeze your butt on an October (also the name of the moon) night. One thing I marveled over was the unreal plants. I was enamored with the tin weeds so I bought one for my quarters from a bearded lady. SS said it probably would not survive outside this locale but it would still look the same dead (tin weeds don't wilt but they'll rust if not treated).

To end day nine, we continued onto the three inner moons. These moons shared the same orbital path playing follow the leader in order of size. They bore no life but yielded a variety of elements (more than those listed in the periodic table from chemistry class). Mining operations continued around the clock in rotating four-hour shifts. Special equipment and machinery enabled the excavation and retraction of precious stones, chemical compounds, minerals, ore, rare earths and isotopes, etc. Sophisticated overgarments and tanks resembling scuba gear were worn by the miners as the temperatures varied from below freezing to practically boiling. Toughened billets were provided for the workers who rotated three months on and three (90 days) off. We contemplated these orbs from afar as it was prohibited to disembark unless you had official business. The moons were quite alluring with their metallic colorations of lime, lemon, and orange.

During the tenth day of the voyage we perused the remaining planets in the solar system. The inner planets were small and desolate; scorched by ultraviolet rays, no plant or animal life could survive. There was no water and scant atmosphere, so the conditions were too harsh even to sample the natural resources. Olive drab in color, they weren't very charming. SS breezed by, shoving the carriage into overdrive so I could behold the neighboring system.

Planets in that solar system were astonishingly more admirable. Six gaseous giants similar to the outer planets orbiting our sun displayed pretty shades of azure, mauve, and crimson. Most had multiple moons resembling Jupiter and a few had rings comparable to Saturn. Usually at night you could see two or three of the planets from the house even if it wasn't very dark outside. As bright stars they shown from the yard but up close they were magnificent. These planets and moons were uninhabitable for the most part although there were numerous mining and engineering operations that were ongoing. We passed countless jumbo tankers in the traffic lanes; they were filled with methane emissions from these titans.

"Cheap energy and plenty of it," I mentioned. "Burns clean too," SS muttered.

Talk about a scenic cruise, twelve days on the twin stargazer tour. Contrast a company jaunt on a luxury liner with kindergarten class. It took a week for me to recover from the gaiety, hiking, and extracurricular activity. Of course, it might not have taken so long but I was unbelievably comfortable in the cozy spare bedroom. I didn't want to arise from the undulating, gelatin-filled, body-conforming, ultra-king-sized bed complete with five fluffy down pillows. But then you know how I love to sleep, and dream. It reminded me of being a kid on summer break. I'd get up long enough to slam down a sandwich, acknowledge nature's call, and dive back into the sack. SS had to toss a stink bomb into the room to smoke me out.

His house was filled with gadgets and appliances; everything was run by solar power (it helps when you have two suns). The lights automatically went on and off upon entering or leaving an uninhabited room and by voice command. Aerators kept the air clean and the furniture dust free while also leaving a fresh scent that I would describe as vanilla-coconut. Climate control devices maintained a brisk 65 degrees year-round. The house was equipped with a public-address system and hidden speakers, so you could gab with someone elsewhere in the house or have music piped into any or every room. Television monitors in several locations allowed the selection and programming of music, sound, video via a point-screen menu or with voice activation. Washbasins and showers had temperature and flow selections; the second you placed your hands or body beneath the spigot a flow of soft water was released at the desired settings. You had the option of drying yourself with a towel or standing before a blow dryer attached to the wall (the dryer was quicker).

Miniature robotic scrubbers were programmed to suction and sterilize the floors silently during hours when we were asleep so the carpets and tile were forever free of lint, dirt, and grime. My mother especially would have loved the mechanical kitchen. Prepared meals similar to frozen dinners could be programmed for breakfast or supper; they would be cooked to perfection and served at the prescribed hour. Cleanup consisted of placing dirty dishes and utensils on a conveyer that commenced operating whenever something was left on it. The machine cleaned, dried, and stacked the kitchenware on the other end. Thus, whenever you needed a bowl or a spoon you could remove it from the rack and it would end up right back where you found it. Microwave ovens were self-cleaning. Looking glasses also were self-cleaning (for you housekeepers that refuse to do windows).

Dishwater and bathwater were reclaimed through a reverse osmosis system so the water was never consumed. Sewage was channeled to a neighborhood purification plant where H_2O was extracted for watering parks and for ponds, fountains, and such. Methane and other gases were reconstituted for powering the plant. The rest of the derivatives were refined to produce fertilizer and building materials. They didn't use toilets; the restrooms were equipped with an excrement suction facility complete with sanitary attachments (I would have preferred to make do the old-fashioned way but when in Rome...). Dirty clothes were dropped into a chute available in every quarters, which routed them to the laundry room where they were routinely sorted, washed, dried, and folded every five days.

I spent hours in the solipsist's library. Although much of the reading material was computerized, he had a vast number of books, some thousands of years old. Obviously, I couldn't read but I enjoyed looking at the pictures; it brought back the child thumbing through encyclopedias. I perused references on science, travel, art, and medicine. I learned quite a bit about the anatomy of his genus; I was impressed at how their critical organs had backup redundancy.

These people rarely got sick. SS took five pills daily that provided minerals, vitamins, hormones, emotional stabilizers, blood and tissue purifiers, psychotropic enhancers, antibiotics, and so forth. This was the only pharmaceutical that they took unless they were hospitalized. I wanted to try some vitamins but SS warned that the dosages would likely be fatal.

Since I was totally enthralled with intergalactic tourism my host gave me one such book to keep but I had to promise never to show it to anyone. It probably wouldn't have mattered because nobody in my world could recognize the places or understand the symbolical lexicon. Although on second thought, it probably would've passed for a new religious text so I guess I can follow his aim. We wouldn't want to incite a cult based on an extraterrestrial astronomy book. I still peruse the book on occasion and dream of being an entertainer on a cruise line. What an awesome vocation that would be!

During the remainder of my stay my learned guide towed me around November. Boy I could get used to living there. Everything was first rate: service, quality, customer satisfaction, user-friendliness, comfort level, entertainment value, ergonomics, and more. Why the solipsist left his world to visit mine is bewildering, it was so perfect. Yet I suspect his adventures on the other side were every bit as stimulating as mine were on his. I can hardly describe this wonderful locale. It would take volumes to document my experiences so I will highlight the aspects that bedazzled me most.

Only sanctioned scientific explorations were permitted outside their solar systems and those were closely scrutinized. They weren't about to invite foreign germs into their world since they had practically rid the land of infectious diseases and parasites. As yet they hadn't experienced any extraterrestrial incursions, but their military defense installations were menacing just in case (at least they didn't have to deal with immigration overload). Excursions beyond the black hole could've landed the solipsist in a penal colony if not approved. The confederation had sophisticated surveillance equipment and security systems; SS had to be very clandestine about his departures and arrivals in the sector. Fortunately, they didn't spy on law-abiding citizens day and night as in my country. More to the point, the addition of time travel made the ship undetectable, a little detail SS omitted from the official report.

It was greatly more a daunting and risky task escaping the black hole from his side, given the fact that one could be stretched like a rubber band until snapping into fragments if antagonizing its singularity. SS had read from an ancient astrophysicist's journal that there was a window through which one could pass which opened for one second every thousand years. It was a point in time when the event horizon theoretically would catch up with the spiraling movement of the massive hole and reverse polarity temporarily. The phenomenon was akin to switching a ceiling fan to reverse direction then back again. SS gambled his life to test that theory. Lucky for him it worked though he knew there was no such opportunity of returning the same way he left.

It would have been impossible for SS to see his home again had he not unlocked the clock, establishing independent time lapse intervals. Otherwise he would have been resigned to stay in mine for the duration of his mortal life. Frankly, it still stumps me how he found my world. He explained the phenomenon of advancing past the black hole with undeterminable velocity, during which he and the ship were turned inside out and reinverted in the vicinity of Neptune, some 25,000 light years from the galaxy's core. He momentarily became a photographic negative of himself. I have no idea how one could possibly survive that but I sure am glad I didn't have to experience it upon reentry.

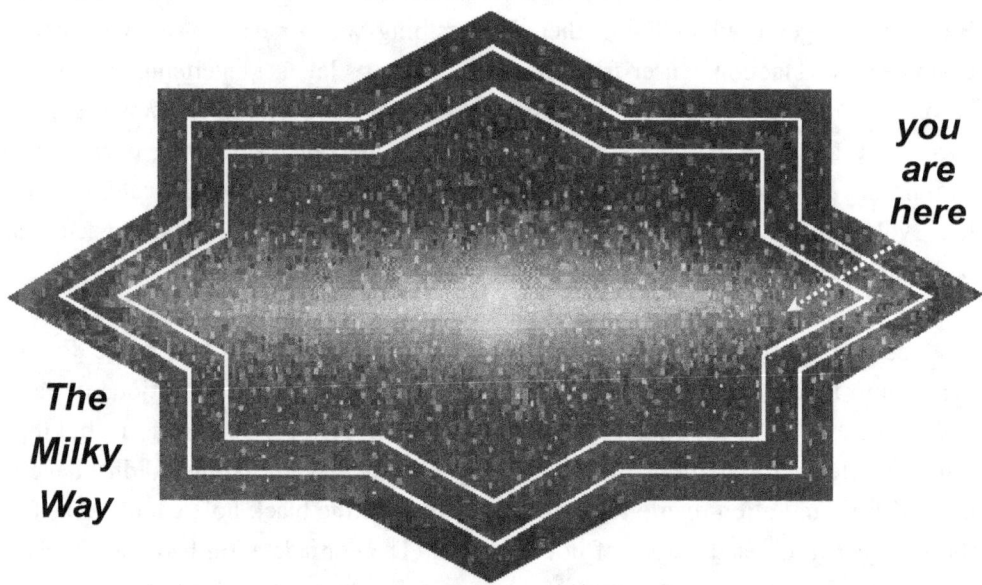

Since unauthorized interstellar voyages were against the law, I had to pretend I was his pet; it seems every resident had one or more exotic ones. No matter since I couldn't speak the jargon and I looked and acted daft enough to seem a creature of limited intelligence. Besides, though they uttered guttural sounds that imitated language they communicated telepathically, so I never knew what they were saying unless it was addressed to me. Therefore, it wasn't necessary for them to learn English (or any other dialect) because they could make their thoughts known to any intelligent lifeform. However, telepathy required direct line-of-sight transmission.

Rapid public transit was the means of transportation used by everyone within the sector. There was no need for private vehicles. Many of the well-to-do owned a space shuttle but only a handful possessed a starship. Monorails, subways, and hovercraft were available throughout the land; annual passes could be obtained for a nominal fee. You never had to wait more than ten minutes to board and the trip seldom took as long as twenty. Interstellar travel also was relatively inexpensive; some of the cruise packages were very affordable.

The environment was scenic, clean, and groomed. Utility lines were buried so there weren't any eyesores blocking the scenery. Littering on November was illegal punishable by being placed on beautification duty during days off. Since leisure time was treasured and they took pride in their moon it was irrelevant. There were numerous parks complete with wildlife, trees, and playgrounds. I especially was fond of the amusement parks which included colossal rides, carnival attractions, and zany sideshows (a huge place to be little again). Businesses and homes had interesting landscaping; some had lovely displays of flowers and plants, many had sculptures or statues, others provided advertising or personal opinion billboards. But the ones that thrilled me had cute little animals roaming within enclosed translucent fences.

The family was the basic unit of society. Children were brought up with discipline and respect and they honored their parents. Thus, there were few setbacks related to broken marriages, irresponsible fathers, and addicted mothers that otherwise could discourage or dissuade young ones. The only social flaws I could detect in this culture reflected my personal peeves such as dealing with delinquent or disillusioned juveniles, supporting orphans and widows, and caring for the elderly and invalid. SS acknowledged this by submitting a proposal to the high council to improve upon these social programs.

Both males and females had separate roles in society; it wasn't stereotyping it was maximizing the natural abilities of the sexes. For instance, day care managers were female because they were more nurturing; patrolmen were male because they were more intimidating. There was very little conflict between couples but mostly harmony and commitment. Relationships were monogamous and infidelity was infrequent. Marriage was for life; adultery was a crime and the only grounds for divorce. Up to two offspring was an option for heterosexual partners.

Discrimination was never condoned; I hadn't observed such equality anywhere else. Inhabitants gladly did their duty and seldom complained. Everybody seemed happy and friendly. It was mutual respect even towards those that were unpopular, disadvantaged, or impending rivals. They had learned from their mistakes: devastating galactic wars, outlandish criminal mayhem, depraved indifferences, and immoral secularism. They'd abandoned immature and fickle conduct. Revenge, recrimination, retaliation, and reprisal were replaced with retribution, restitution, requital, and redress.

All schools in this dominion were privatized. Curricula were standardized across the board. Children were required to master the same competencies and attain the knowledge appropriate for their grade level. There were only ten tyros per tutor and the kids attended from ages four through nineteen. Higher education was reserved for those demonstrating special ability or interest and mainly restricted to graduates in the upper 25th percentile. Aptitude tests identified areas in which a youth was projected to succeed; each individual chose from the eight occupational areas in which they scored highest. Oftentimes additional training was necessary depending on the type of work involved.

Most of the common occupations were what you would expect; what you wouldn't expect is the salary. A particular job earned a fixed wage based on preparation requirements, knowledge and skill prerequisites, tenure, and echelon in the organization. Wages were topsy-turvy though whereas equivalent jobs back home would pay lower or higher, respectively. For example, entertainers, physicians, and executives made a modest living as opposed to America where they were once among the wealthiest class. Some of the highest paid were toxic waste handlers, policemen, and teachers. But more was expected of them. (Come to think of it, executives should get less and teachers should get more; that's probably one of the bases for the failures of public schooling and large corporations back home.) Imagine that, my experience as a garbage man would make me highly qualified and compensated in his world.

There was no unemployment and there was no retirement, per se. The social welfare system provided a pension commensurate with annual wages at termination, which could occur only if the person became disabled or was too old, feeble, or sick to perform their tasks according to performance criteria. Independently wealthy people and entrepreneurs could choose when and if they worked but they didn't receive a pension. Regular fulltime employees worked roughly eight to ten hours a day with regular breaks. They spent two days on the job and one off with four-day weekends every twenty days. They received an obligatory ten-day vacation after two hundred calendar days. Plus, they had ten free days to play with as personal or sick time and five global (national) holidays annually.

Their legal system was strict, unyielding, and unrelenting. It was a rarity for someone to commit a felony and get away with it, and an accused person was never convicted if he or she was innocent of the charges. One reason for this was a foolproof lie detector examination given to suspects and witnesses, which scanned the eyes and monitored a particular area in the brain during questioning. Everyone had equal representation under the law because the courts (civil and criminal) were manned by highly trained professionals and funded by the unitary government. One team of attorneys worked both sides: the prosecution and the defense. A full complement of law enforcement personnel and resources were at their disposal. It didn't matter how famous or well-to-do the victims, plaintiffs, or perpetrators. Justice was the sole objective. The investigation, trial, and sentencing seldom lasted more than thirty days. Swift punishment was doled out in accordance with specific rules and benchmarks. The penalty matched the infraction and there was no such thing as negotiating, plea bargaining, or buyout.

Civil rights were not an ideal they were a reality. Not unlike the intent of the writers of our original Constitution, everyone had complete freedom to say, do, or believe as they wished, as long as it didn't infringe on the rights of others. There was no slavery no prejudicial treatment no favoritism, which were violations of the law. While you could behave in whatever manner you wanted within the confines of your domicile, you could not leave it while intoxicated or impaired in any fashion. The pitfall to that was taverns did not serve alcoholic beverages. Although people had the right to bear arms few owned a weapon. Firearms were used exclusively for sporting events, although able bodied men could be called upon and trained if a militia had to be mustered.

Elections involved five political parties with varying views and strong positions on each issue. Every viable candidate was prepared to intelligently debate and discuss his or her solutions to dilemmas and each offered a developed plan of action complete with budget. Campaigns were nothing from what I was accustomed (what with politicians making false promises, vowing reforms that would never happen, proposing nonexistent plans, forcing unpopular customs upon the populace, raising comical alternatives, endlessly filibustering if they didn't get their way, mudslinging, and other exercises in futility). Each candidate received free media coverage and political dialogues were scheduled periodically to hear them articulate their ideas. Elected officials did what they said or got impeached. Further, terms of office were four years (about five earth years) so incumbents worked hard accomplishing the tasks they set out to complete without wasting any time campaigning for reelection. There were new elections every two years with half the officials being replaced.

Everyone reaching the age of twenty was classified an adult and therefore had the right to vote except those who were certifiably incompetent, legally insane, or incarcerated. You could vote using your videophone (which scanned the face) and a touchpad (which recorded digital imprints). There was no such thing as election fraud, every vote counted, and there was never a runoff. The person receiving the majority of the popular vote immediately took office with the incumbent staying on the job an additional twenty-six days to help orient the new leader, provide requested training, and assist him or her as directed.

The government had several branches: legislative, judiciary, law enforcement and military, mental and physical health, transportation and energy, science and technology, welfare and pensions, regulation and administration. Most of those involved in government were elected to office and most laypeople considered it a civic duty to serve at least once. However, one could not run for a post unless he or she passed the qualifier and a health examination. Further, they'd be ineligible if there was a previous conviction of a capital crime, if medication was being taken for an infirmity, or if there was recent evidence of severe trauma, strain, distress, or duress. Additionally, one could not occupy the same office twice or serve in government over two nonconsecutive terms; nope, there were no career politicians.

Surprisingly, their limited system of government mirrored that of our original signers; representatives were employed by the people and for the people. They did not have consent to establish new departments, enact partisan initiatives, pursue frivolous proceedings or investigations, hire their own contractors, change the rules or policies midstream, redefine morality, spend money aimlessly, expand their reach, behave unconventionally, or abuse their powers. Otherwise they could land themselves in the penitentiary. They were not allotted expense accounts, or given perks, or permitted to travel arbitrarily. Every penny spent had to be okayed by the governing body; any overruns that were not sanctioned came out of their own pockets. The governing process was effective, efficient, and organized. Man alive, I was flabbergasted. I could only dream of the improvements to our society if we had held fast to these principles (and forced politicians to get with it or get lost). The climate of the nation and our position in the world could have diverted disaster had our leaders and their egos been corralled.

Despite the numerous programs the entire government was supported solely by a compensation tax. The more you made the more you paid. A flat rate of ten percent was levied on cumulative income regardless of how it was earned: wages, tips, sales. interest, welfare, profit, winnings, proceeds, pension, inheritance, etc. Everyone receiving an annual increase had to pay and there were no loopholes and there was no bureaucracy. It sure beat the two-thirds plus that our local, state, and federal governments used to wring out of me when I was employed. If the government ran a surplus the money was placed in an interest-bearing account for future overruns. Thus, budgets usually were balanced by the end of each term. Free trade ensured that any private party could exchange goods with another and avoid the tax but both had to verbally acknowledge and record that the deal was equitable.

Economic stability had endured since the wars; inflation and recession were ephemeral. Prices remained relatively constant for most products; exceptions were upgrades or new inventions being introduced. Regulators inspected and tested every patent often requiring specific modifications before approving an item to be marketed or peddled, ensuring it was safe, durable, user friendly, met the specifications, and accordingly priced. The procedure took a month or less, rather than years, however.

Many businesses operated around the clock and every store was a convenience. The retail malls were enormous, almost a miniature city in arrangement and size. You could step off the easy access conveyers and examine goods; if you put it in your cart it was charged to your account. Automated checkout and debit made shopping a breeze. It was easy for me to get absorbed into a single department store. SS had to keep me on a leash because establishments required pets to be restrained. Besides, I wanted to handle everything and that would result in a vehement invitation to leave (for example, it was improper to touch fresh produce unless you were buying it).

The cuisine was indescribably scrumptious. Their diet was mostly vegetarian but a meal every few days containing a meat item brought out the carnivore in them. The fruits were succulent; they made me reminisce when my mother would serve sliced strawberries smothered with syrup and cream. My favorite was a multicolored delectable similar to a kiwi in shape, texture, decoration, and tanginess but it was much larger and sweeter; its microscopic seeds never got caught in my teeth either. I also savored the filet of fish (an oceanic life form that resembled a miniature swordfish); they would season it with unusual spices of which nothing else compares and broil it over volcanic coals. Of course, there were some food items that I wouldn't come near; the very whiff of them turned my stomach. SS told me the aroma was no indication of the taste. But how would he know since their olfactory system was inferior to mine?

I was immensely impressed with the available selection of entertainment and programming. There were fifty free channels to watch on the audiovisual telecommunicator (a high-resolution, wide-screen, interactive display covering half the wall). But each station had different shows, there were no reruns, and there were no commercials (except on the two advertising channels). You could watch up to four programs simultaneously. One could rent or buy (at a reasonable price) any televised program or advertised show, placing orders by videophone or touchscreen and downloading it to your entertainment system (it took about 15 seconds to complete the transaction and begin viewing). Movies, instructional material, and documentaries also were sold in compact sets but most of the stuff was complimentary. I wasn't able to fully appreciate the telecommunicator because I couldn't speak solipsist and telepathic transmission was not a capability with that apparatus. SS would interpret the scenes for me but it lost a lot in translation.

The cinema was actually a live drama. Several theatrical troupes staging Broadway-type plays and musicals toured the country presenting a new production periodically. Since performers had regular programs and staggered their schedules, you could see a different performance every other day if you wanted (or you could purchase the two-inch stick drive). I thoroughly enjoyed the live theater, especially because I could understand the plot and the dialogue by virtue of the fact that I was in the audience and therefore an intended recipient of their telepathic lines.

Coexistence

I can't say I was enchanted by the music but there definitely was a variety of it. The groaning and grunting sounds of vocalists made me think the singer was retching (I preferred instrumentals). Recorded vocal arrangements left much to be desired since I didn't understand the lyrics. Interestingly, while they had quite an assortment of musical instruments there was nothing that resembled an electric guitar. I bet I could've made a fortune by introducing one. I'm sure they would've responded favorably to some good old rock and roll. Too bad I couldn't perform for them (since I was washed up as a musician in my land) but I had to maintain a low profile.

Modern artwork was a blend of surrealism and impressionism. The primary difference was the media; anything and everything was fair game. Galleries were the rave; I didn't fancy myself a cultured art enthusiast until I attended showings, exhibitions, and demonstrations. The sculpture was especially intriguing; crafts-persons used materials ranging from metal, wood, and stone, to food, hair, even processed dung. Some works were composed of live bodies in which the participants had to hold their position for upwards of an hour at a time. Academic museums had ancient artifacts dating 100,000 years old to the present. Technology exhibits also displayed a panoply of inventions that were perplexing to say the least (although I related to some of the more primitive equipment reminiscent of our 21st century).

Tournaments were outstandingly stunning. Athletes performed unusual antics and feats of strength. They might vie for scoring position in a competitive bout appearing to be a cross between roller derby and hockey. They might speed over water or ice with jet skis attached to their boots, and execute maneuvers that required the agility of a contortionist. They might compete in Olympic-style events such as hurling a forty-pound shot forty yards, shimmying up a forty-foot greased pole in forty seconds, or running track and jumping over forty, four-foot hurdles.

The surfing competition was outstanding. These men and women could ride a forty-foot wave for a mile performing cutbacks, shooting the curl, and executing a maneuver I'd never seen back home where they balanced the board on the edge of the crest at a 40-degree angle and hung twenty before sliding down into the trough. I suppose the forward thrust of the giant waves produced the impetus necessary to defy gravity. The surfers wore protective gear that reminded me of football which made sense since a wipeout could otherwise result in severe injury and did anyway for some competitors.

SS was fortunate to have such a great life. Being a successful entrepreneur, scavenger, and inventor, he had amassed quite a nest egg and his explorations netted him more assets and capital. He could've retired and had fun the remainder of his life if he'd wanted. Despite this fact he worked virtually every day; he was constantly occupied doing something engaging, worthwhile, and productive. He was basically a loner, seldom desiring companionship or needing it. He had few playthings although he did own a billiard table (one game I could understand, play, and give him a run for his money). And he constantly studied, always jotting down notes in a journal he carried everywhere.

"Wisdom," he declared, "that is my quest" (as if he didn't already possess it). I've graded schooling. I recall when I disliked it as most novices did when it came to compulsory coursework. But how do you teach someone to appreciate it? "To be sure you cannot," instructed the solipsist. "But you can teach someone to value it."

He's right you know. It's the dilemma of overlooking the agony in order to spot the possibilities. But the contention that education opens doors of opportunity is not compelling enough to convince kids. You can lecture them until your eyes bug out but they'll resist Algebra or Biology. Too bad they cannot comprehend the positive effect on critical thinking (if only children could grasp the concept of multidimensional thought). Juveniles are not concerned about discussing their goals five or ten years from now; they're not planning that far in advance.

However, the notion that instruction opens windows to the psyche, now that argument has promise. It's about discovery not work. Chew on this one awhile: Were you born appreciating your full repertory of interests and talents? If you hadn't gone to college you probably never would have escalated in your aptitude as an attorney, nurse, therapist, or paleontologist. The material might have seemed complicated initially but it came easy (to you, at least). Or even if it didn't you still enjoyed it enough to venture into it. And if you toiled diligently you could master tasks when you didn't possess natural ability. Employment is not as painful when it's satisfying, stimulating, or fascinating. The one thing that higher learning did for me was to permit me to capitalize upon hidden abilities, potential, and curiosities that I never knew lingered. And this defines my love of exploration. Like fishing it can be very mundane at times, until you arrive at an occasional often serendipitous discovery; that's the catch. Thanks to SS I value education, largely because it teaches me about me.

I came to the realization that everyone is ignorant about something and everyone can be an expert at something. You and I have talent that others do not, in that no two are gifted with the same repertoire. Everybody is equally unique, endowed, and capable but in different areas. This diversity renders interpersonal relationships appealing, valuable, fulfilling, and necessary. We all are attractive, everyone can contribute, and together we can accomplish amazing feats; and this promotes healthy partnerships, societies, and civilizations. And we can be good at most anything by practicing. It requires desire, motivation, effort, and sometimes courage. The worth of an activity provides the incentive to persevere and persist in additional achieving and exceptionalism. Hence, we can grow individually as well as collectively; and continuously if we maintain the appeal to study, labor, and share. SS pledged that the learning would never cease as long as he was alive; it was his favorite pastime. As for me I was too busy unlearning everything to adapt my newly acquired knowledge.

Here before me were two worlds, one seemed a paradise the other a hellhole. I fantasized trading places with SS since he'd rather explore my world and I, his. I was bored with my planets; in his world moons were equal to planets in their glamour and charisma. Eight planets in my solar system named after mythological gods had one of two personas: rocky or gaseous; whoopie. There was Mercury the greedy phony; I knew him too well. Quite a slick fellow, interested only in what he stood to profit. It was a waste of time trying to be his friend since he never paid his way. And Venus the sultry shrew; I tried to get next to her and got burned big time. Believe me, love had nothing to do with that liaison: all take and no give. Mars the troublemaker; he would start a quarrel over any glitch however trivial. He was coldhearted, never satisfied, always contentious, probably codependent. Jupiter proved to be nothing but a conceited control freak; he had to get his way or he'd throw a fit. He projected himself as mister know-it-all, but denied what he didn't know. The only ones that found him attractive were the dregs of society. Saturn was the wife of Jupiter, a rich biddy if you know what I mean: uppity, snotty, and flashy. Old but alluring, so keep your distance because she will sock you good, right in the kisser. And miserly, she relished in her abandon. Uranus was the impersonal prude. You never knew what he was plotting; conniver was his middle name. Applying make-believe power, he tried to interject himself but everyone ignored him. The dude needed some serious assertiveness training. Neptune liked pushing his weight about too. An unpredictable bloke and temperamental; you didn't want to get on his bad side. Very wishy-washy, never to be trusted; because he would appear congenial but the next thing you knew he was blindsiding you. Pluto was the littlest jerk of them all. He acted like a hotshot who had something to offer; but he was deceitful and underhanded, a genuine faker. He was expelled, left out there dead to the world; insignificant in the grand order of things but not in his own mind. Gladly I'd have bade farewell to the whole gang.

But as far as Earth was concerned, I was fine with her because she had the key to life: water. Plus, she didn't act human (or inhuman) like other planets who had the demeanor and attitude of a guy or gal passing on the sidewalk in a personal space that included or acknowledged no other. Earth was generous, nurturing and caring; though running out of patience. Her little brother moon was uncool. He seemed quiet and modest but he had a dark side. He had no particular goal other than to influence his big sister. But she loved him just the same. Their mother Sun, what a firebrand and very domineering. When she was awake, she might punish Earth mercilessly before caressing her gently; it's like whacking your child and then hugging him or her as if you're sorry. The only time she ever showed any affection for moon was when she was asleep. I wondered if she didn't have a problem with manic-depression; well, certainly preferentialism. Alas, being quite naïve and spoiled I had no business pronouncing judgment. I managed to tolerate them despite their faults.

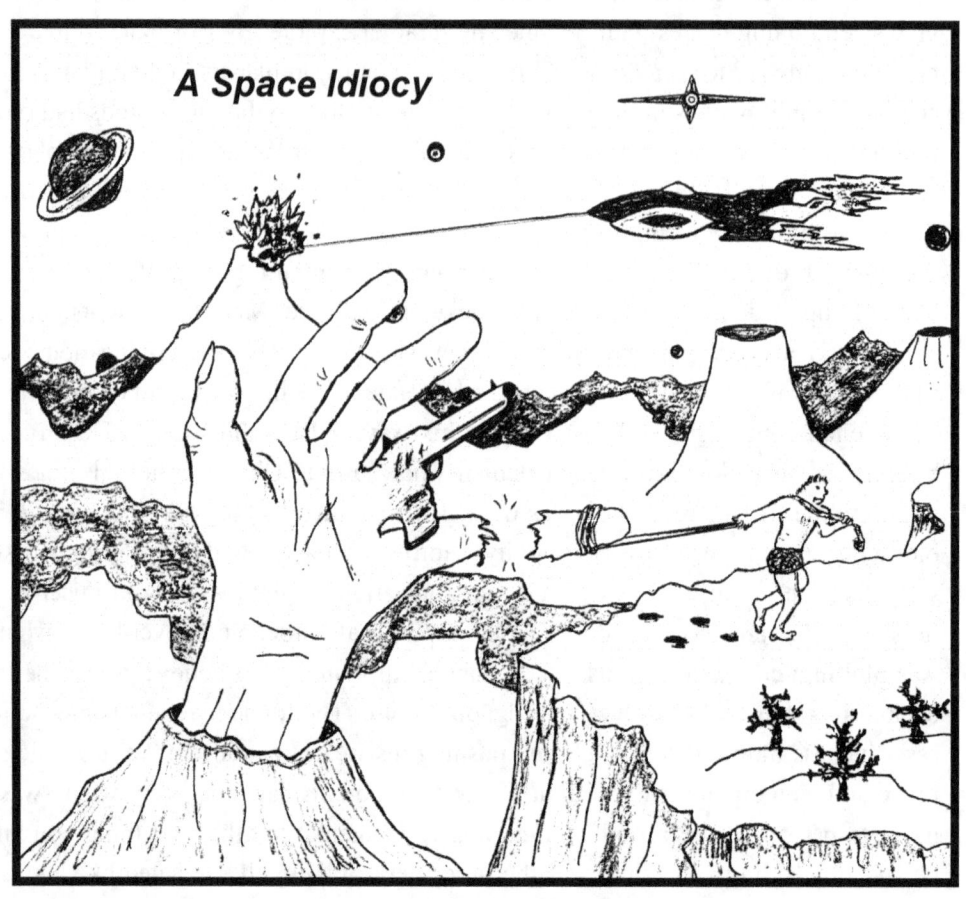

NUMBERS

The season had come for my initiation into manhood. I was groomed for rite of passage from being an intern of our ways to becoming a member of the council. Thirteen marched into the wilderness, a dozen seasoned warriors plus yours truly. Nobody said a word the entire trip, until the third night when the inquiry was convened. It was a full moon and the campfire was spurting flares as high as the treetops. I was getting baked, seated cross-legged a mere six paces from the flames. When the fire simmered down, I could see the twelve encircling the embers and me with the same locus: legs and arms folded and back upright. Each elder spoke words of truth. I was taught to pray for the prey giving thanks for every sacrifice. Then they grilled me, drilled me, and filled me with secrets, modeling a dance exclusively for menfolk. We smoked the pipe and I recited the pledge. Next, I chanted incantations unknown to me but apparently unleashed by my spirit, while I waltzed around the coals in a daze. After that we feasted on pheasant and javelina during which histories of courage, battle, and death were shared; then we smoked the pipe again.

I awoke at mid-morning alone, groggy, and stupefied, feeling queasy as if drugged. The site had been cleared, the ashes were cold and spread about; and I had been deserted in no man's land. There was plenty of food in my pack so I ate a hearty breakfast, filled my bottle at the river's edge, and began the trek back into the mountains. On my first night solo I perched along a bluff overlooking the long valley, safely situated beneath a stony overhang. I sparked a fire using my knife and agate stone, snuggled into the turf on a bed fitted with pine needles, and wrapped a thick blanket around me. I gobbled down a quick snack and gazed at the stars for hours until clouds rolled in and rain began to pound the ground lulling me into slumber. The sky remained overcast when I arose early next morning after an evening of stormy thoughts, dreams, and visions. I polished off the last of the meat and half the water, then commenced descending the mount. I happened upon a patch of berries and filled my stomach and my pouch. Skirting the ridge most of the afternoon I found an uninhabited bear hole to lodge in; believe me you cannot mistake the smell of an old grisly. I was more tired than hungry so I didn't even consider supper; I lit a small fire at the mouth of the cave and nodded off. I dreamt of a golden eagle swooping down to capture a fish before ascending to the top of the sheer and barren rock face behind me. Was it an omen, a symbol, an identity? That's when the sun peeked over the precipice and stabbed me right in my right eye.

I broke camp and continued the descent, back to the river to fill my stomach and my bottle. I constructed a dam and trapped a speckled trout which I ate raw, while departing the valley for the distant hills where I arrived by nightfall. I barely had time to pitch a lean-to afore another downpour. All I could do is huddle within the embankment like an unborn child, and watch the moat I dug fill with water until it was crawling towards my feet. Unexpectedly the torrent halted and a parting between the clouds exposed the Dog Star; maybe that was a sign. Dreaming about a wolf stealing my pack right out from under my head I was startled out of sleep. I looked and listened, experiencing nothing more than a chill in my bones from the cold wet wind; the ordinarily raucous night woods were tacit. Slumber was interrupted by boisterous moose having sex; I didn't dare reveal my position until they had their fun and the bull bolted.

I quit looking for portents or anything material to associate with and yielded the possibilities to fate, welcoming the Great Spirit to guide me as I journeyed farther away yet closer to home. I was navigating via the sun and the stars, taking a roundabout path because I was expected not to return prior to the next full moon. I arranged an unspoiled place to settle where I could spend a few weeks cogitating. A confluence of two streams was tucked into the middle of three pebbly knolls, protected from the wind. I spotted some slanting trees hovering over a ledge where I crafted a comfortable and fortified dwelling; I could see the entire basin from the entrance to my abode. There was only one way to reach it and that required a clamorous climb up an unstable stony staircase. I pored over the site which exhibited an abundance of fresh water, game, berries, plants and roots: plenty to sustain me until winter if I so desired. I exercised my skills laying traps, gathering wood, structuring a cooking pit, storing food, fashioning bow and arrows, exploring the surroundings, establishing my bearings, and adding conveniences to my quarters.

From a camouflaged vantage point I witnesed animals quenching their thirst, grazing, playing, and cohabitating. They appeared to be getting along nicely; none were attacked or alarmed. In fact, it seemed I was the only predator and that thought made me feel ashamed. But I had to eat didn't I; or did I? Instead I decided to fast from meat for an entire week; eating tubers, cattails, currants, pine nuts, berries, insects, and herbs, and drinking the clear refreshing water. Truthfully, after a week I felt healthier from the start and continued the fast. Little by little I began to engage with the beasts. I would slink along gently and slowly until the wildlife appeared to tolerate me; they sensed no danger and I felt no malice. I tried to share some food but they ignored me. On the night of the full moon the sky was bright and shiny, unobstructed, almost translucent, illuminating the hollow. I was warming by the fire enjoying the scenery down below and up above. I surveyed as a menagerie of creatures mobilized at the fork, forming a semicircle. Facing me as a choir, and speaking to me in their native tongues, they beckoned to me, "Move out." I had never felt so close to the forest and its wildlife I pondered, paralyzed with wonderment. The entire encounter defied nature; it was real, unreal, surreal, or at least unearthly.

After sunup I dismantled my hut, filled the pit, scattered the materials, slammed down the remains of my grub, and left the area pristine as I found it. Hiking both day and night I arrived at the bivouac point around daybreak, now a full-fledged brave: wise, solemn, careful, respectful, patient, courageous, confident, unpretentious, and released. A banquet was prepared in my honor and the tribe attended; there was dining, singing, dancing, and different sorts of entertainment, but I was the main attraction. I related my experiences to the congregation and they were captivated, possibly awestruck; or not. The ceremony concluded when the shaman declared that henceforth I would be christened *Disgitisdi Asegi*: literally, dreamer of strange dreams. I was hoping for something trendy, perhaps *beast whisperer*; but then again, I couldn't really translate animal sounds into the language of the beautiful people. Anyways, such was my induction into manhood, meaning I was forever accountable to myself and the collective. I learned that adulthood is a responsibility not a privilege, that my irresponsibility had been the sign of immaturity. "Are we not beholding to one another?" I answered myself with another question.

Will the rest of humanity ever learn? No rational motive can exist for annihilation. Mutual assured destruction is certainly not a viable defense. Yet that was the intent and wholesale murder was the result. Although the button pushers fell short of achieving total obliteration, they succeeded in leveling the playing field so to speak. Those who withstood the firestorm emerged in large numbers looking for solace and finding none. For once the entire population was in the same predicament in spite of ethnicity, gender, age, religion, ability, wealth, or fame. People had to depend on each other as much as themselves. Is this what they meant by the brotherhood of man? I daresay it works when it is forced upon you but only for a short while.

Tribal affiliations were reminiscent of the advent of civilization. Clans were scattered around those locales remaining habitable. Each had to overcome starvation, affliction, and subjection as well as extraordinarily cruel conditions and grim prospects. Survival instincts and experience living off the land were lacking. I on the other hand had a head start. I'd studied such affairs as a boy scout and paid my dues in the wilderness. Thus, an awkward assembly flocked around me, kneeling and with their hands outstretched. I couldn't refuse them they seemed so helpless. Basic training included the rudimentary skills necessary for a trite existence. The learning curve was slow in progressing and many gave up the will to carry on. The shock of losing everything was too much for them to accept; some wasted away and others took their lives. Only the strong in spirit endured.

Have you appraised the power of the human spirit? It's an inner strength that we possess and reflects a higher power. Or are you one of those who deny its presence? But if you think about it there is no other explanation. Where does extrasensory perception come from? Have you ever felt something happen to someone else? Maybe you have experienced that phenomenon when the other person wasn't present. Or what about the love that transcends affection when joined with that special person in sexual intercourse? Notice how the power of the act is far greater than that of basic copulation. What causes the profound lift when witnessing or learning of a birth, or the sudden drop when witnessing or learning of a death? Can you explain why suffering at the hands of pure evil is repulsive to anyone of sound mind? Can you define hope? How does faith-healing work? What is going on when terminally ill people miraculously get well and the doctors are stunned to discover that prayer was the only intercession? What gives someone the will to live when by all medical indications he or she should be dead? How is it that people awaken from fifteen-year comas? Likewise, where do you think they got the expression *esprit de corps*?

"All right already," exclaimed the solipsist, "your argument is well-taken!"

He really wasn't protesting the numerous questions; he only decided to be perturbed about it. He genuinely agreed that the spirit was greater in power than the body and the mind put together. "It is a gift of, and it is our connection to, the Great Spirit," he explained.

With the assistance of my personal pedagogue we recruited volunteers and fashioned them into troopers. I figured we'd use traditional methods like those I'd learned in boot camp (it took a single summer at an army base to learn I would not be enlisting). The solipsist's modifications to drill and ceremony were ingenious. For example, the command "attention" required the troops to stand at the ready with feet apart and weapon in hand, forming a tight arc and keeping elbow distance. It made more sense than posing stoic as a penguin staked into the ground. It also was easier to pay attention. There was no such thing as "dress-right-dress" or "present arms." Regardless, our uniforms and equipment were mix and match. The regiment was divided according to purpose. I was handy with a handgun and a rifle so my vocation was firearms training; I also chaired the weapons committee. I taught my fire team leaders when to say "attack" or "retreat" and nothing more.

Combat was a regular event. You could put it on your calendar: breakfast, morning watch, combat, lunch, combat, dinner, evening watch, sleep. Well we didn't always schedule three square meals a day but food was one of the spoils of victory. So were mouths to feed however. You could snip at your foes but typically brute force was required to defeat them. Many other disputes were settled in a contest or a gunfight. I mean one day it's Tombstone Arizona and the next, Coffeeville Kansas. While many tribes grew weary ours grew stronger. I became an authority on ground maneuvers especially over mountainous terrain. I've got rugged terrain down pat you know. Further, a great deal of my operations occurred at night; I also have better night vision than most it appears. Perhaps that is why I'm supersensitive to glint and glare. Thank goodness I still had an intact pair of sunglasses; I wore them near everywhere. I could've traded them for riches beyond belief but what the heck was I to do with that? I needn't carry that useless junk over hill and dale, nor should I. I was very possessive and protective of my sunshades which were military grade with titanium-reinforced frames and scratch resistant lenses.

Unskilled refugees were declared hunters, gatherers, and farmers; their productivity was weighed mostly according to what they were able to scrounge or grow. It was an incentive-based occupation where nonperformers had to serve as decoys. Everyone had a vital function; their lives depended on it. SS was the judge; he resolved dissentions and levied sentences on the guilty. Usually conviction of a capital crime meant a hanging (electrical cord was less dear than ammunition). There wasn't any room for freeloaders, hustlers, or crooks. Everyone pulled their weight or faced excommunication (or worse).

Discipline had to be maintained at every echelon. It was like handling adolescence when you wanted all the freedom in the world but what you needed were borders and structure. You'd never admit in a million years that you desired the discipline but you did, even if you weren't aware of it. I remember guys whose parents were overly permissive. They were unbridled because they didn't have one or both parents riding them constantly, but they were jealous of those who did. I had a friend whose abusive dad ran off with another woman and he never heard from dad again. I used to be envious of him because he walked over his mother and got away with it. He could stay out every night, get drunk, sneak in before dawn, and his mom did little or nothing about it. But one day he told me flatly that he would give anything to be in my shoes and have two parents that cared, even if it meant having to obey rules. What a shocking revelation that was. Such it was for the masses that in their previous lives had been carefree. But I determined I was every bit as free now as I was then the only differences being the costs and benefits.

One of the factions we assimilated was comprised entirely of females. With my debonair looks and his swashbuckling flair, we sweet-talked them into joining instead of fighting us. The debutantes in our division were superior gunslingers. SS incorporated mathematics and geometry into their grooming to make them unbeatable. He would calculate the shortest distance required to aim and the necessary angle of the elbow; this often resulted in buckling the gun belt across the breasts. The optimum firing position was set along a horizontal plane from the dominant eye to the target; the squeezing of the trigger was timed to coincide with attainment of the firing solution. Various angles and coordinates differed as a function of the anthropometrics of the individual shooter. Each practiced until the entire movement became second nature. To improve the advantage further I had them strip to their bikinis to distract male contenders, who already were nervous facing a girl due to the stigma of losing to one (which they did in alarming numbers).

But a black, bosomy beauty named Babette was by far, the best. She could blast the buzz off a bumble bee in the blink of an eyeball, at ten body lengths. She was our ace in the hole. We kept her under wraps so the word wouldn't get out. Even when it did, nobody knew what she looked like since she wore a mask, trench coat, and fedora hat. But I knew what she looked like, every wrinkle, nook and cranny.

One gang gaining notoriety on the field was Klazi. They adopted a philosophy based on the Klan and Nazi parties of yesteryear. Their goal was to establish a preeminent race, insinuating tribespersons not sharing their beliefs and skin color had to be exterminated. Their mission: dominate the world. Their leader: a one-eyed, Cyclops-looking, mutant punk. Wanted posters named the kid Billy; I think his given name was Wilhelm. I'm not sure if he was genetically altered, maimed in the holocaust, or the result of a birth defect, but his appearance was hideous. There were inartistic tattoos splotched over his upper torso. His hair had been cooked in nuclear fusion fashion; to compensate he had spikes bolted to his head. Following Billy, most of the clique had faces, teeth, genitals, you name it, replete with piercings as well as homemade rings on practically every finger and toe, and trinkets hanging from the neck and adorning the shoulders. Each soldier looked like a magnet for scrap metal. Goodness, these cretins seemed the better candidates for ethnic cleansing. They made an interesting noise however, when the wind wafted, giving off a sound signature that betrayed their location thereby losing any element of surprise. How idiotic can you get?

The Klazi feasted on female slaves butchered for meat. They specialized in black, buxom, obese broads (they professed to prefer dark meat as it was a sacrilege to eat a white person unless burned to a crisp). You had to give them credit though, at least they didn't waste the body parts. To illustrate, they fabricated ammo pouches using tanned fannies. Yeah cannibalism was rampant. We didn't ascribe to it but we did allow our dog militia to feast upon slain hostiles.

The canine corps was my idea. Dogs were resilient. They were easy to teach and loyal to a fault. You could send them into a skirmish with assurance they'd die before letting the enemy advance. Mortally wounded they would keep attacking. The canine commanders were more vicious than, well a junkyard dog. And smart, they knew exactly when the element of surprise was keenest. Any dog that misbehaved or failed to follow a direct order became supper for the others. Thus, disciplinary measures were carried out by the dogs themselves. We reinforced that practice by barbequing them when necessary; there was a Korean chick in our outfit that roasted a mean one. The dogs scrounged heaps of good meals from the stray feline, ovine, and bovine, not to mention the hordes of rodents in the bush. It was a dog's life but they had it better off than we did, and we ate high-on-the-hog most of the time.

The dogs were excellent as, you guessed it, watchdogs. It's a natural talent. Emplaced along the perimeter they would sense anything unusual and alert the taskforce on duty. As a result, I got to sleep at night. I often would dream of my childhood. It seems offbeat how you can get lost in the past as you age but as a youth you're lost in the future. I suppose I've been lost in the present as well but it's because there hasn't been anywhere else to go. Everybody searches for greener pastures but I assure you it isn't any better elsewhere. If you cultivate the ground that you're standing on it will become greener. I have encountered many who wait for it to happen but you have to make it happen.

In this day-and-age there are too many lazy people. They want everything now; they want it handed to them. They think they are deserving of special accommodations for some reason. They use their creed, age, color, gender, orientation, or status as a ruse or a scam. They spend countless hours scheming to forestall doing anything which is every bit as effortful as actually doing it. In fact, if they exhausted the amount of energy performing work that they did dodging it they'd become high achievers.

Canine Corps Commandos

There is something to be said of hard work, but don't overdo it either. If you think you are getting anywhere accomplishing the slightest, I have news for you. That might work in elementary school but not in the real world. And for those of you who are fortunate enough to inherit a fortune, don't think for a minute that you are absolved of responsibility. If you decide not to work, fine; just watch as your possessions find wings and zoom away. Go ahead, squander it like the prodigal son. I trust you are not expecting someone to catch you when you finally fall on your face. Did you hear the one about the philanthropist who became a philanderer? He blew it.

It was only a matter of weeks if not days before a clash with the Klazi. They were double our numbers but we were twice their ferocity. It was a standoff; we had to gain the upper hand. We did occupy the high ground though. And crossbows to send burning arrows the size of tree trunks, and catapults that could deliver a sofa sized explosion had been emplaced to fortify our post. There were deposits of saltpeter in the soil from rotting carcasses, plenty of brimstone to be found from atomic explosions, and charcoal briquettes from our stove with which to make an elementary form of black powder. Though ineffective for guns it made a sizeable blast just the same. Add shrapnel to it and you had a lethal combination.

I wanted to arm the ship but SS said it had to remain a noncombatant. Otherwise we could be forever spellbound in a personal afterworld for prematurely altering it; because we would never be able to return to where we were. Air superiority was the most viable resort but nobody had an air force and pilots were hard to come by.

"Analyze the available resources," SS demanded, "What do you have that can fly?"

I ruminated on it and blinked twice, "We could fashion kites, balloons, and stuff like that, I reckon."

"So be it," he affirmed.

Department stores already had been ransacked to the hilt but we had accumulated resources we could use. In our midst were creative comrades with proficiency in the abovementioned areas. They constructed kamikaze kites and hot-air balloons that doubled as chemical bombs.

The aerial reconnaissance, targeting, and demolition patrols: that was my favorite tactic. These ladies and gentlemen had a gift. They used vinyl pipe, synthetic tarp material, duct tape, sewing kits, and bailing wire to construct aircraft. They taught me to hang glide but I wasn't even close to earning my wings. They launched from the tallest edifices and peaks left standing and could stay aloft for upwards of half an hour when wind currents and barometric pressure were just right. Their observation operations were instrumental in gauging the deployments, numbers, strengths and weaknesses of our opponent.

Unaware of these clandestine weapons, we whittled away at the exposed adversary. When they finally got wise, they instigated a full-blown assault. I dispatched the dogs to bite the rear of their detachments while snipers started plucking out advancers as if tweezing ingrown hairs. Booby traps and the flying arsenal broke them in half. It approximated a turkey-shoot on Independence Day in

Dodge City. They retreated and regrouped. I called back the dogs with my deafening wolf-whistle; they promptly rallied dragging their dinner behind them.

Klazi wagered that Billy was the quickest draw in theater and sent an emissary to propose a showdown. Not wanting to lose any more personnel to these clowns I accepted the offer. High noon the next day would tell the tale when we would play our trump card.

The sun shone yellow like the yolk of an egg. It was so hot you could've fried one on a bald man's head but there weren't any chickens left to prove it. There wasn't a cloud in the sky except lofty thin accumulations of cirrus making the heavens appear as curdled milk. I had to shade my eyes the brightness was so penetrating, even with shades. The wind was dead still and the air was bone dry. Heat radiated off the broken pavement creating a spooky vapor that hovered waist high. The sidewalks were lined with gawking onlookers from both alliances indolent from the anticipation. The silence was deafening, broken only by the stupefying hush that came over the crowd when the champions were introduced.

Billy was dumbfounded when Babette bounded from between the barricades for the faceoff. He bragged about how he was going to blast her between the boobs, then bang her benumbed behind before gobbling it for brunch. With ten body lengths separating them the bell sounded and Billy made his play. He had narrowly cleared leather before a bullet betwixt the ears popped his eye like a grape busting the back of his head wide open. He stood there for about five seconds dead as a doornail, brains and blood spewing sewage; then he dropped his sidearm and scrunched into a heap of scrap. A detachment of dogs skipped forward and pissed on his remains; he was too ugly even for them. I must say the dogs had excellent taste.

The Klazi were held in a concentration camp. SS advised the entire entity be eradicated but I reneged. Instead I banished them to the badlands with a couple of water receptacles and the clothes on their backs. They knew better than to show their faces around us again. Everything of value was confiscated. We had a celebration and a cookout. Babs and I were the hostess and host. We butchered bulls and boiled the edible vegetables we'd obtained compliments of Klazi. Our distillers had produced some dynamite moonshine which doubled as fuel when needed. It kicked like a mule but the hangover was tougher. The festivities continued well into the night and past moonset.

Next thing I know I'm standing in the witness box being sworn in. I can't imagine why I'm there, who's on trial, or if my testimony could be germane to an unresolved lawsuit or criminal indictment. About then the bailiff lugged in a suitcase that appeared quite heavy for he was grappling woefully with it. The prosecutor commenced to pester me insisting that it was my case. I told the judge, "I've never seen that piece of baggage before in my entire life," pausing, "and I can't identify the suitcase either." Honestly, I didn't know if it was mine or not. In fact, I really didn't know a whole lot leastwise the truth I swore to tell. "Do you know what's inside that case?" inquired the counselor. "I haven't the faintest idea," I responded (which accurately was the whole truth, and nothing but); then I added, "Do you?" The judge instructed that I take extreme caution since my fate and that of many others was hanging on my words. Great I thought. That means if I remain silent, I incriminate myself for who knows what; but if I speak I probably will anyway. In any case I didn't really have anything to say; except perhaps, "Who gives a rat's tail?" I could tell that the twelve buffoons in the jury box were deliberating that very thing. Still I was about to open my big mouth.

I awoke face down in Babs's lap with my head spinning faster than the overhead sun. My movement caused her to stir and she looked down at me with droopy, bloodshot eyes. Then she warmly smiled and I felt much better. It would be our last party together. Although our contingent had gained a great victory it was a curse in disguise. Once field correspondents had delivered the news, we were sought in a big way.

You see, your reputation forever precedes you when you become renown in the art of battle. People come out of the woodwork to try your hand. We ricocheted between hideaways being careful not to stay too long in one place. The heat was ceaselessly hot on our heels. To expedite our evasion, I was forced to split our forces. I donated the dog brigade to the ladies commanded by Babs; they settled in the Valley of Mannequins, a stronghold that bore bunches of scrubby birches. The hang glider squadron established their fortress in nearby Tower Mountain which once served as an alternate headquarters.

It was another rueful goodbye bidding Babs adieu, not realizing that I was giving away my heart all over again. We had a connection; we shared some great times. She was my darling; but it would be the final occasion for our eyes to meet. How badly I would miss her smile; she was definitely the one that got away and I let her. But I had to steer the pursuers on a wild goose chase to enable the girls to recede with the tide into an ocean of anonymity. They needed time to lose their identity, their stigma: in other words, me. If captured they would be enslaved and subjected to the gravest cruelty. If cornered Babs would never let a single one be taken alive. She was a fighter, leader, and warrior; one of the best I've seen and I've exchanged blows alongside the worthiest. I trusted she'd see that each lady found a niche and blended in.

I kept a squad of the brightest lieutenants: adept in hand-to-hand combat, nimble, fast afoot and great conversationalists. We were twelve (not including SS): six men and six women, no mutants or others. The goal was to someday produce our own idealistic commune, a wonderland in the world, if liberty ever was to be regained. But I guess it was a pie-in-the-sky fantasy. Sure, it would've been nice. Yet how long before this deteriorated into the same sort of sty as the rest of civilization? Not very cheerful, was I? My self-esteem had taken a dive. I was vulnerable.

Throughout history there have been philosophers and politicians who were hellbent on establishing their concept of a utopian society. In the end everyone works for the government which controls the whole shebang, such that the private citizen cannot own anything not the least of which is property. Centralization of power was already being crammed through, with socialization of services that were substandard (at least for the underclassmen). This was the new egalitarianism where the gentry rationed the necessities of life to include a negligible allotment of food. It was a bona fide commonwealth, or lack thereof. Conformity meant accepting suppression, oppression, repression, depression. And their contrived rationale was that the commoners were a bunch of prejudiced, absentminded anarchists. My observation is that honest hardworking people are mostly compassionate moralists. It seems those greedy for power are nothing but intolerant chauvinists pushing their "noble lies."

"An illusion has no future," clarified the solipsist. We were the philosophers.

The dynasty would have nothing to do with us. We wanted our own reservation and independence as well as a guarantee of exemption from outside rule. Oh, they promised concessions if we joined them but they were discredited. They tried to lure us in, experimenting with different kinds of bait such as amnesty. For some it worked but those met a rude awakening from the hook. Like the catch of the day they were snared, gutted, and fried until they too were nothing more than pawns on an elaborate chessboard. Like a gnat in a swarm of flies they spent their identity and became part of the silent majority. Dwelling on a pile of feces was their undistinguished destiny.

Here was a dwindling frontier undergoing massive reconstruction. Feudal communities complete with warlords and working guilds had formed, a resurrection of serfdom. These were regulated by overseers imitating shoguns with their samurai assassins. Conglomerated takeovers became the new deal. Copying corporate raider tactics, they swooped in and took over, firing leaders and replacing them with their own. Everyone else became forced labor. Nonconformists were tortured into compliance or executed. Needless to say, our meager band remained on the lam.

Yeah, outside our skimpy venue was a new age movement, where the stakes were vastly higher and our measly mêlées seemed child's play. The upper-class had evolved, become more sophisticated. Instead of human gladiator teams matching wits and skills, domesticated reptilian fighting machines was the fad. Dinosaur bouts in a vale of slaughter matched behemoths from the Jurassic and Cretaceous eras, while spectators congregated along the rocky crags delighting in the sport and munching on fried locust. The first to win six jousts stated their terms of surrender.

But the games were rigged from the start; the association had countless ways of cheating. They were selfish through and through. It was big business run amok. They alone had the means to reconstruct, and the infrastructure to wield control and maintain it. It was a monopoly on domination. Potency makes perfect was their proverb. But isn't that always the case with fascism?

While our numbers were diminishing theirs were multiplying. But then again who's counting? Nonetheless, the majority is not invariably in the right, neither is the minority necessarily inferior. Take the Israelites for example. They were not chosen or loved by God because they were the greatest in number. On the contrary they were fewer in number than their adversaries. They soundly defeated many enemies as long as they relied on the Lord. I had to believe that my enemies did not have the Lord behind them; but I was not convinced in my mind that we were on the side of goodness either. Yet we achieved remarkable victories and equally enigmatic escapes defying the laws of probability.

Regardless it was us against them and they wanted us dead. We were a threat because we could think for ourselves and proved it by outwitting them time and again. We were the terrorists now and I treasured every moment. Being a thorn in their backside was immensely gratifying. I despised those overindulgent, arrogant, gluttonous snobs. Whatever we needed we took from them leaving corpses in the wake if necessary. We had to stay one step ahead and often evaded them with the seat of our pants. But elude them we did. We fought hard, played hard, and loved hard, and every day we praised the Almighty for another chance. To us each moment was precious. To the so-called enlightenment time was wasting away. And time equals life.

What did they know of life, except to take it? They cared not how many had lost it; they feared only for their lives. How crazy can you get, to think that killing is the way to save yourself? There is no guarantee in this life but the grave. And that is the one trip requiring no directions. What is the number of deaths required before everybody can agree that enough is enough? You see, that's why everyone must die, because we'll never agree on the proper order much less how to judge another fairly. The senseless massacring of innocents broke my heart. Throughout history there have been tyrants, terrorists, and psychopaths who enjoyed exterminating people they didn't like, if not for the fun of it. How is it that these hellions commit such despicable acts, often in the name of religion, without a speck of remorse?

I recall taking philosophy in college as an elective in the humanities. For the final exam we were to write an eight-page paper on the professor's closing lecture. But she blabbered the entire period about random asynchronous jumble: her biracial marriage and flawless kids; the recent death of an intoxicated student who wrecked his car into a concrete pillar; being nominated for tenure after writing a book on the power and influence of electronic social media; and her activism to have five statues removed from campus grounds.

I totally missed the point; I discussed the assignment with another classmate and he didn't get it either. However, he was distracted, having put his old ailing dog down the afternoon before. I felt sorely disheartened. I started writing down my thoughts, such as how much my associate must have loved his dog, and how much the teacher loved her family, and how the loss of the student heightened my gloom though I'd never met him. And it became apparent that my emotional state occurred because I cared about people, and dogs, and things that matter. But the loss of the unknown student hurt more than the loss of the unknown dog; and the memory of my parents' passing upset me even more. It was obvious that our culture placed a high value on humankind in general and family in particular; but governmental and social institutions didn't give a hoot about anybody. People that claimed to care were selective in their attention to others' suffering and their own penitence for causing it.

Consequently, my thesis centered over priorities and values. I concluded that nothing is more valuable on this earth than human life. I posited that positive regard for fellow man was a most excellent moral position, and that everybody knew this aside from the extent to which they practiced it or shouldered any personal responsibility for others. Regarding material things like the cyber social arena or statues of famous people, I couldn't have cared less. And I questioned why the teacher would consider them so important as to group them with love of family and caring about untimely deaths. Since gradation was evident, I zeroed in on the question of supremacy, concluding that loving people was the ultimate human ethic, far greater than political and societal concerns. I reiterated a point she made early in the semester about the many forms of affection and the fact that there were several meanings for the word *love*; and each type was different in intensity and power. For example, erotic love was clearly less vital than familial love with respect to sustaining intimate relationships. And *agape* love was clearly greater than brotherly love, the former being unconditional and the latter, not always.

I proposed that every death affects the human race. I construed that humans are at the top of the tree of life in terms of dominion and worth. That is, people are special, more than other corporeal creatures roaming the planet. I asserted that we the people should correspondingly value life especially human. This was the intent of the founding fathers I suggested. The closing paragraph in my narrative was this: "The reason we are exceptional is because an intelligence superior to ours set the standard for us which is perfect love. In that image we have been sculpted, to grasp the concept of selfless love and to consistently calibrate our moral compass. How else could we have received, encountered, or developed such advanced knowledge?"

The teacher gave me an A- on the essay and a B- in the course. She had written a note in red on my report saying it was the best work I had done in her class, though she'd crossed out the last part. I approached her to ask why and she said the statements were immaterial. Next, I demonstrated to her how my grade, computed in accordance with her syllabus, was 83.4; since a B- was an 80 I had earned a solid B. She disagreed and insisted she would not change the grade because she gets to decide what I deserve.

I retreated, a bit discouraged and insulted. "Immaterial," I said to myself. This was a philosophy course for crying out loud. Moreover, I have constitutional rights to believe as I wish and to voice my opinion as long as I do not violate the law. Further, if my viewpoint, supposition, or interpretation was unimportant or less deserving than hers, what would be the point in writing a paper about her disjointed comments? All was meaningless at that point in particular my grade. Every contention she professed was counterintuitive to her lecture, her syllabus, the final project, and her evaluation. While she conceded there was order in the moral hierarchy, and acknowledged the significance of love, she dismissed related arguments and inferences. She placed herself above me; she condescended to learners with implied inequality, as though liberty and equality were unrelated if not irrelevant to philosophy. She shot me down for being assertive, belittled my beliefs as mediocre, and punished me for disagreeing. Actually, the lesson learned: she was neither my instructor nor my judge.

I resolved, if there is a God, he surely must love everybody excellently. And he must be moved equivalently by the death of every man, woman, and child. And that is why I feel emotional pain at the loss of human life and dying dogs; no exclusions because I care. I loathe death period, though the intrinsic worth of a person is evidently greater than that of an animal. Some people don't give a fig either way and that makes no sense to me; it should be illegal. But they don't have to bother, for that is their right. However, homicide violates every law: man's, nature's, and God's. Yes, sometimes a person's death may be for the greater good. Nevertheless, the indiscriminate murdering of others based on an opinion or an ideal is about as evil and immoral as it comes. This is the downside of free will. But those choosing to kill will themselves be choosing death.

I cherished life; I wanted it never to end. But I placed my life on the line constantly in order to live it in the manner which I was taught and driven. I refused to have the terms of my existence dictated to me. After all was said and done only a handful had the intestinal fortitude to further embrace these doctrines. "Give me liberty or give me death," professed the elder statesman who also moralized that slavery is not a reasonable price to pay for peace. This became a way of life for a select few. Each day was a struggle to survive. The odds were insurmountable, but I saw this as an opportunity not an obstacle. I have heard it said that freedom is not free. But liberty is definitely liberating. Ask anyone who has lost it; or found it.

How fragile life is. It's astonishing that anybody makes it to old age. I have no idea how I survived childhood much less adulthood. I cannot begin to count the number of close calls I've ducked, especially as the invincible adolescent who would take extreme risks on a dare. Surely there were angels keeping those dangers at bay. Take for instance the day I turned sixteen. I watched two drivers walk away from a horrific collision; they stood there looking tearfully at the mangled remains of their automobiles. I for one was shocked that either lived to tell about it. Undoubtedly the sovereign deity brought them out of the twisted wreckage to spend another day. Anybody who cannot appreciate this fact is misguided; those are the ones inclined to chalk it down into the luck column. If they think they've beaten the odds, odds are they won't the next time.

I dreamt it happened to me that very night. It had been raining all day. The pickup I was driving at high speed started skidding upon hydroplaning over an oil slick; it slid into the median and flipped. I was thrown through the windshield and crushed under a half ton of metal. I felt a stream of blood gushing out of my mouth. Finally, I breathed my last and my spirit ascended; there I was, looking down at my lifeless body. I bellowed aloud, "Oh Pop" (it was his truck). My spirit returned and I awoke, my face pressed against a pillow soaked with drool. I had the riveting dream a second time exactly one year later. Someone wanted to ensure that I got the message, and I did. Yes, I learned the easy way not to take life for granted. My father died on the second anniversary of the dream and I learned the lesson again the hard way.

Life was a way of death for the privileged but they learned nothing from it. They used it and abused it but they didn't choose it. Eat, drink, and be merry was their religion. And those who were sorry or repented turned right back to their errant ways deceiving themselves into thinking they were forgiven somehow. It was too easy to conform to that lifestyle. But they were sabotaging their own lives devouring others in the process. Since they valued life so little, I placed little value on them. They were expendable as far as I was concerned. Hey I'm for doing your own thing. But if that thing impedes on my inalienable rights then it becomes personal. The commoners were not a threat; but the regulators had no scruples. They stomped over innocent people to get from point A to B even if it meant going miles out of their way. In my case they'd receive an extra bonus for bringing me in. Lord knows they had plenty of chances.

One afternoon I was foraging through a dumpster for a bite to eat when I was approached by a bum. The derelict was determined to rob me wielding a makeshift dagger in my face. I wrestled him to the ground causing him to eat the blade in the process. Still I mourned over him. I surely didn't want to get accustomed to the butchery or to become numb from it. But it was either my life or his; he forfeited his because of the motive. Next thing I was being framed for murder by the office of prosecution. They took me before a privy-sitting jurist for my arraignment. As soon as I was booked, I shed the shackles, shoved the bailiff, and lit out the rear exit via the judge's chambers. I yanked a motorcycle cop from his perch who was anxiously waiting to escort me to the hoosegow. I scooted through alleyways and into the country ditching the bike in the desert. They had no idea which way I had gone. I dawdled back to the ship and we withdrew into deep space. The master chuckled as he slammed the cartridge into the receptacle and we sped away.

"Follow the flow," he poked, "No need to rush it."

"It's the same as riding out a landslide; very swift at first but tapering off," I submitted. Worn out I closed my eyes and tapered off into dreamland once again, my sleepy hollow of solace.

Once I'd stepped from the inverted box the thoughts began to bombard me like a meteor shower. Nightfall illuminated the ghost of a once distant skyline. Aloft in the murky cavity I saw the hand of God holding a globe without form or mass, a swarming concoction of molten rock. It seemed to swell with an eerie energy into layers of atmospheres, not unlike the amoeba which vibrates with a rhythm of its own when viewed under a microscope. Both had emerged from the sea of life, which a host of sycophants claimed as their embryonic abode. Living entities (and my dreams) traveled about in distinct waveforms as light through a prism or electricity intersecting my neural circuitry.

And what was the riddle of the numbers? Everywhere I found asymmetrical repetitive archetypes from the proliferation of rabbits, bats, and bees; to the spiraling of pinecones, seashells, galaxies, and hurricanes; to the falling of casualties in battle—nature's ratio, where each consecutive number is the sum of the previous two. It was another brainteaser like pi, a constant that could not be computed with exactness. I thought it had profound meaning, in remembrance of the revered Ionian scholar who asserted that everything is ruled by numbers. But the solipsist swore it was a masterful design mechanism not a secret code to the universe. While the phenomenon did not support symmetry it unquestionably echoed the notions of balance and order. But then nothing in this universe appears as a perfect split mirror image of itself, not even a snowflake.

But why should there be a reason for everything? Can't things exist because they are? Truthfully, they cannot. Otherwise life would spring at will from a vacuum just to be different. But order was given first and along with it the principles of physics, mathematics, geometry, biology, and chemistry. Only then were the necessary conditions present for life to emerge in its pristine form. Not to say that life didn't exist prior to that but not as we know it. Yet it can be assumed that God has borne witness to it all because he is alive forever. He is the uncaused first cause. There remain mysteries, some of which may never be solved. It's another limitation to the intellect I suspect. Not very scientific but neither is religious conviction.

This much I know: physics and mathematics can describe the blueprint of the universe but cannot construct it. Within the design are established laws not the other way around. Nature follows laws as do human beings. The Creator is our lawmaker and lawgiver; laws don't happen by themselves they must be installed. And the Word of God, the *Logos* which represents complete knowledge and power, spoke them into existence. There are living entities in nature but nature itself is not a living entity, nor can it design or select one for it has no consciousness or intelligence of its own. Nature does not control anything much less humans; but humans can manipulate nature as in the case of farming. Nature sustains life and may claim it in death; but it does not create life because both were created, and God is the only explanation. God alone has no beginning and no end; thus, he is not a created being. Can we experience eternity even though we had a specific beginning? I would answer yes.

Nature itself is not terribly complicated but living organisms are mindboggling in complexity. The most elementary life forms have systems so sophisticated, it makes manmade technology pale by comparison. Some animals have formidable defense systems others sophisticated offensive weapons. Different kinds have special machinations to promote survival such as camouflage, concealment, and cloaking; sonar, direction finding, navigational and homing devices; chemical warfare, missile systems, and heat seeking faculties; aerodynamics, hydrodynamics, accessories to promote land, sea, and air travel; energy conservation, hardening, and armor; and the list goes on. Good grief, God's creatures make state-of-the-art tactical, military, mechanical, and computerized systems seem obsolete. Yet some scientists continue to argue that such nonpareil capabilities couldn't be deliberately engineered with a designed purpose, rather were acquired through natural selection and mutation.

Doubtless the most complex of earthlings are homo sapiens, from our DNA programming to the master processor called the brain (not to mention nonphysical components such as soul and spirit). It baffles every sense of being I possess trying to figure out how such advanced life forms such as we can be so patently conspiring, meanspirited, and evil-minded. Is any one of us so dangerous as to threaten the entire human race? Many would ascribe that role to Satan; others to Christ. Neither position is accurate since every man, woman, and child with an idea can affect the future of the species, whether negative or positive.

I know not what lies beyond the screen door, who sits in the empty chair, or why the laughing lips ceaselessly serenade my aching ears. But death was lingering there and beyond it the continuance of time, which split into another dimension as it approached infinity. And all the while my cup overflowed with sweet tangerine brandy. But there was that phantasm floating over the waters, watching as I cut myself with a knife used to scale fish. I noticed an ashtray on the floor in the shape of my mouth, holding a smoldering black cigarette which spoke to me saying, "To smoke or not to smoke, that is the question."

I slashed away layers of skin and was surprised what I found. Beneath my dermis was wire mesh instead of flesh (not what I expected). I opened areas on both arms and it was the same. And I surmised, bleeding doesn't make me real. Perhaps I was an android, an artificial fabrication; duped into presuming I was human and desiring what would have been normal notwithstanding the current circumstances. It reminded me of lying naked on the wooden table in the oval room staring upward at the triangular panes of the green dome. I was about to be operated on I think; or maybe sacrificed. I raised my weary swollen head and glanced across the room. The morning star was setting beyond the arched entry and between my feet. Just as the blade was raised a voice out of nowhere sounded to cease and desist. Thank Providence! Immediately the fog lifted and I was outside searching for an existence other than mine. How easy for the solipsist I thought, as his wasn't subject to debate.

Once again, seeking to find myself in the halls of disillusion I faltered. One must probe into fathoms of inspiration to locate a single ounce of wit. But introspection does not reveal how to employ it. And once spent it cannot be retrieved from the present situation, but fortunately can be doled out later and often until it totally loses weight. But there is a right time and a wrong time. You will know whether you are ready or not if you follow your insight and not your instinct. You must lay it on the line at the opportune moment and it will gain a benefit that may take years to realize. But in my journals, I have seldom been able to trace the origin or the consequence. I pile up mountains of dreams like grains of sand in an hourglass. There seems a limit, a point where the well runs dry or the thoughts run out. But if that were true then why bother? Fortunately, I do not have an android equal; and my intelligence is not artificial or the result of some unguided biochemical process. Unfortunately, the blood is red and if it runs out or dries up so does life. Once that happens, there is no further hope. I suggest not waiting until then to decide which side you're on. The time to proceed is now.

Have you dissected the intricacy of a single moment in time? It has every bit of sophistication as the universe itself. One can take a split-second snapshot to hold the memory in the mind's eye, similar to a time-space stamp. But that imprint will be a scant representation of the entire episode, limited by the physiological constraints of the brain and the psychological constraints of time. To scan each component of the broad array is a quest unto itself, for the picture provides a thousand clues each representing a fork in the road to discovery. Imagine the value of that moment and its limitless possibilities any of which can lead to an adventure, direction, or cryptic destination where nobody has set foot.

I pictured the immediate present as an image from a telescope deployed outside the atmosphere, pointing some finite distance towards deep empty space. Bringing into focus that fragment of space, itself encompassing a field of view less than one minute of arc, a series of time-lapse snapshots are taken. They are overlaid, revealing a depiction that portrays dozens, then hundreds, conceivably thousands of galaxies crammed into that tiny frame proving this petite piece of space is far from empty. Such is the flash of life we experience thousands of times daily. Each a different configuration of people, objects, situations, and conditions which mutually generate dozens, probably hundreds, if not thousands of opportunities any of which one can explore, though only one at a time. But to capture the singularity of the event is to spread the complete display before you in a frozen moment, an exhibit presented in four dimensions of visible spacetime.

It would take days to examine the one portrait, which is removed in real-time from its predecessor like the distance between galaxies, though it occurred only a moment before and both events share commonality. There is power loitering in the wings to flip the proverbial coin and obtain a substantially different outcome, or by tweaking but a fraction any one of the innumerable variables that are present, and the thousands of available responses. The prospects are akin to the squeezing of energy and matter through the event horizon of a black hole, producing a marvel of creation on the other side that defies any material explanation. It would take a transformation from God Almighty for man to see the wisdom of that one arc minute of time; enough to fill volumes, like the information in a single strand of DNA.

Each and every day we bypass countless chances such as these, completely disconnected from the universe and God; hidden inside ourselves in a small world that fits into the vault of our safety zone which is neither safe nor hidden, nor confined. Standing in the midst of such unbelievable aptitude, with freedom and energy enough to direct a repository of untapped potential through the hollows of the will, producing a generous increase in growth, development, and achievement. These commodities a person should not dismiss flippantly. Enormous promise is given to humankind, which requires nothing more than recognizing the opportunity, seizing the moment, and spontaneously flavoring your response with a dash of creativity and a sprinkle of ingenuity towards becoming all you were meant to be and more, in pursuit of dreams you may not have previously aspired. When aspirations come to pass, they will surely surpass your wildest dreams—it won't be random or unguided.

We stand at the threshold of tomorrow. Watch your step for the first one is imminent and it's a whopper. And you could career over the brink into an afterworld of uncertainty. You can neither hesitate nor panic but decide you must, and there isn't a second to lose. The shutter of your eyelid could cause you to miss your shot at immortality. Stay alert, beware and don't be caught sleeping when the commander summons you. Stand fast as the night watchman, vigilant and ready to sound the alarm. Be obedient as the faithful butler, opening the door whenever the master of the house arrives. And protect yourself as the sentry, guarding the rear gate from entry by the tempter.

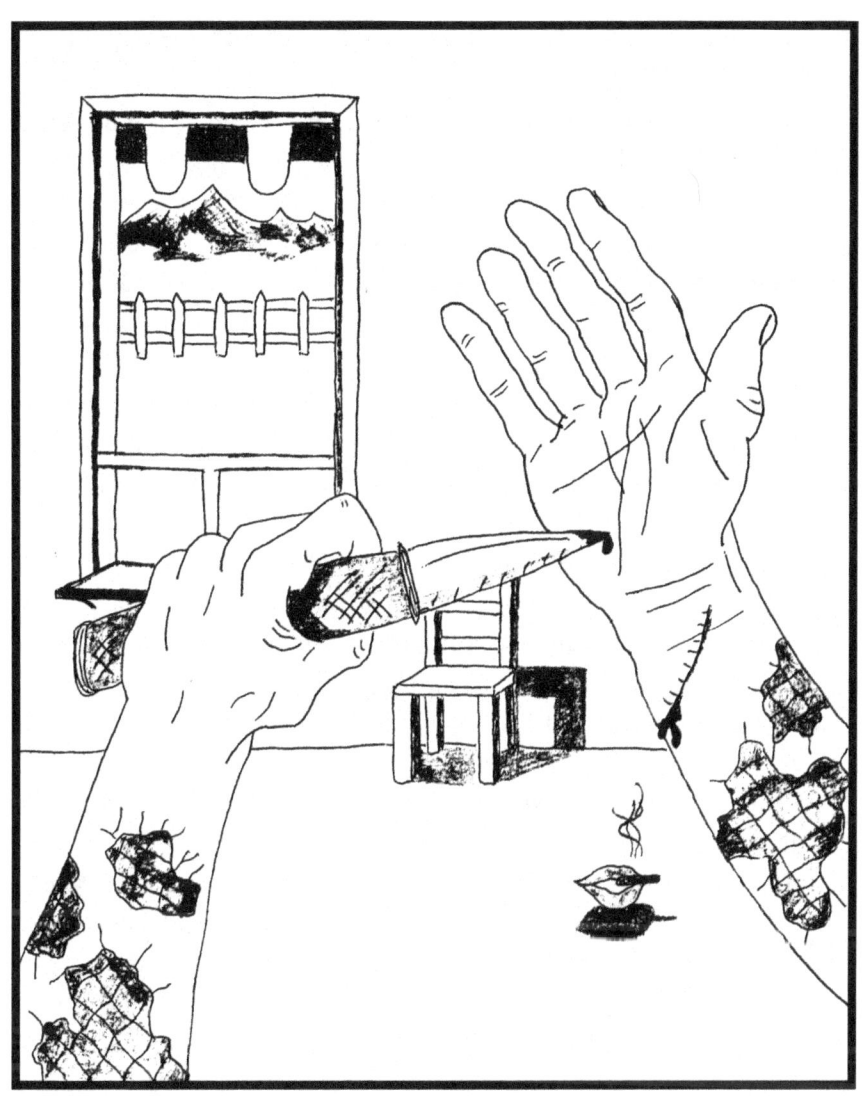

Bleeding Doesn't Make Me Real

~~~ JUDGES ~~~

The country's overhaul spawned an industrial bonanza that progressed in leaps and bounds. Advances in science and technology were astronomical. The old ways were but a flicker in a furnace, soon to be forgotten. It was a new era in human development. There was no looking back but many longed for the way it used to be (some people just cannot adapt to progress). And to think they considered the previous age to be disheartening (because they cannot be satisfied, period). What a waste, to yearn for someone or something to replace a broken will.

Everything was automated leaving a languid citizenry. But that's what the people wanted: a handout, a free ride, no responsibility. That's what the government wanted even more; it would gladly provide minimal sustenance to keep the power. There was no incentive motivating anyone to be ambitious and excel, or to be self-reliant. There remained no pride in accomplishment, no drive to succeed, no inducement to grow. Unfortunately, the handout turned into hand it over: your money, property, talent, decisions, fortitude, and self-respect. Next, they'd enslave you and confiscate your time. Mundane tasks were purposefully removed from the usual repertory of behaviors. If it wasn't technical it wasn't necessary, especially if it took time.

You couldn't go to a beautician and get your stinking hair styled anymore. You simply slipped into a salon and placed your hands on the cylinder. It began to hum with static electricity and you felt a peculiar sensation as your hair stood on end. The semicircular, multifunction hair cutter, blower, and perm appliance descended and every hair on your head was clipped to precision in two seconds. Assembly line haircuts, what a concept (I recall quick trips through the carwash when I was a tot but this was ridiculous). You had to apply your own grease if you wanted it. What was left was a socially acceptable unisex style that each man, woman, and child exhibited. The attire was about as imaginative: gray or olive getups and off-white shirts, black low-top shoes and matching black belt. No-one dared make a fashion statement. Everyone was expected to conform or face ridicule; but they were nothing but a bunch of geeks (so they faced ridicule anyway, at least from me). I'd stick out like a sore thumb if I was spotted in scruffy denim jeans, t-shirt, and sneakers.

The workforce was an integrated unit. You weren't allowed to accomplish anything for yourself if it didn't benefit the whole. Individuality could only deter from the collective structure of the corporation. A component in a contraption, that's it; but the system kept running with or without you. If you tripped, you'd get ground up in the gears (which kept them well-lubricated I expect).

Adults and children over six were ordered to carry a national ID card. Without one you were not admitted to any establishment or institution and you couldn't buy or sell anything. It served as your passport to society. You could go to any business and clock in as the scanner read your retina. Once recognized, your activity was noted for that location. The option was available to have a microchip imbedded into the wrist which could not be removed without deactivating it. A split-second laser scan and your identity would be acknowledged, what a convenience. Many were succumbing since mislaid ID cards were a hassle to replace, very expensive, and time consuming (you had to pay a lab to have your DNA matched to verify that you were you, have your old number purged, and then apply for a new card).

A centralized databank tracked you from birth to death. The federal filing cabinet recorded each transaction: your income, expenditures, habits, movements, location. Every single tidbit of information about you and your family could be accessed even stuff you didn't know yourself. Everywhere you went, how long you stayed, what you did there, who you talked to, what you said, you name it they collected it. Your academic, occupational, marital, social, and medical history: all were easily obtained by government eavesdroppers and freelance hackers. Unfortunately, it wasn't available to you unless you had piles of money to squander.

The lowliest class comprised nine tenths of the populace: all worker ants. Their existence was about as monotonous as it comes. Work, slave, sweat six to seven days a week. Amusement meant waiting in line for hours. The only alternative was to become a watermelon perched on the living room couch and peruse the five hundred some-odd channels on television. And half of the garbage on display was an advertisement or public service announcement; the other half wasn't fit for viewing (meant only for hedonists). I couldn't believe people were acquiescing to such a trite existence. I'd rather be taken out to the sticks and shot. The controllers would have been happy to oblige that notion.

Manual labor was extinct; migrant, factory, and union workers a thing of the past (that is, there was only one Union and everyone joined or didn't work and didn't eat). Manufacturing, transportation, agriculture, and animal husbandry were mechanized and computerized. For instance, unmanned airborne and ground-based farming vehicles took care of crop dusting, irrigation, planting, and harvesting.

However, office jobs were in abundance. Vocational planning, searching, marketing, classifying, selecting, and matching functions were automated. Access terminals were located in post offices which were privately owned by government appointed bureaucrats (there was no such thing as postage anymore). Slip it a buck and an eligible employee could access, apply for, and print job postings providing location, salary, duties, skills, and education. Knowledge of results usually was immediate due to the demand. Still, unemployment was at a minimum and so were wages. If you weren't toiling, they'd place you into a job to certify you were contributing to the cause. It wasn't like before where people used to slide for years collecting welfare. That was the bone they'd throw to catch you and reel you in.

Prices for goods were regulated across the board, and salary standardized. Computerized shopping was trendy though. A needs list could be fed into a teller that triggered the mechanical retrieving and packaging of your purchases. You input your number and your account would be debited. You could use a card or wrist scanner, dictate your information by teleprompter, punch it on a keyboard, or whatever was preferable. Then drop by the store in fifteen minutes to pick up your items at a loading dock or have them delivered for an extra fee.

Medical scholarship progressed in marvelous ways. Diagnostic equipment could check your entire body and in seconds identify any physiological, biological, genetic, organic, or neurological malady. Preprogrammed robotic surgeons could read a three-dimensional full-scale depiction of every organ in your body and perform any given procedure flawlessly (as long as you didn't move). For example, if you had a bloodborne pathogen, say leukemia, they gave you a synthetic blood change as if visiting your automotive service center. Pharmaceuticals, hormones, and antibiotics were cheap and effective. Birth defects, infirmities, and paralysis were curable and most afflictions eliminated. Nerves, muscles, and organs were replaced with bionic spares that seldom failed, with double the strength and longevity of the originals. Healthy residents equated to productive human resources.

It was well known that the brain discharged chemicals in response to fight, flight, freeze and other reactive, emotional, and repetitive sequences. Sympathetic and parasympathetic responses could be mapped in terms of the behavior being elicited. Nobel laureates in physiology found that excessive exposure to evoking experiences caused abnormal levels in hormones, neurotransmitters, analgesics, and other natural chemicals thereby degrading the homeostasis and aggravating organic maladies such as cancer, dementia, apoplexy, and infarction. The body often formed an addiction produced by an overdose of its own chemistry, when the physiology altered itself in an unhealthy way to which the body became accustomed. These constant secretions resulted in reorganization of brain cells resulting in permanent maladjustments to behavior (such as sexually deviant compulsions) or irreparable damage (such as substance induced psychosis). However, various disorders could be cured by providing an emetic, antidote, or countermeasure that, in time, canceled the imbalance in the manner of a base neutralizing an acid. If these methods didn't do the trick biofeedback coupled with hypnosis usually did as the ailment was psychosomatic. Of course, these interventions were mechanized and involuntary.

If you were overweight, they sucked the fat out of you; if underweight they pumped you full of nutrients. You had to fit the archetype prescribed for your body mass index and qualified age in order for them to regulate your temperament. The only thing that differed between persons was skin and eye color, bone structure, and the size and appearance of your nose, ears, breasts, or penis (although most of these could be and often were altered to suit societal preferences, which meant average).

As a result of these huge strides, medication was exclusively preventive since nobody came down with anything. I remember my coach from capture the flag football who often repeated, "The best offense makes for a good defense." Or maybe it was the other way around. Whatever, life span soared to new heights. It was similar to days of old when individuals might live two hundred years, even longer. Zero growth parameter was the remedy for overpopulating the planet; most citizens chose sterilization because producing offspring was generally prohibited (job replacements were being authorized and manufactured on an as-needed basis).

It wasn't wholly the breakthroughs in medicine that brought revolution. The physical sciences attained mammoth achievements. For example, audio waves could be video-recorded. Sound motion pictures replicated perfectly the original frequency pattern of any radio or other wave aggregation thereby reproducing prerecorded music or background noise exactly the same as live. Attenuation and amplification permitted the user enjoy a symphony on the one hand or snoop on a private conversation on the other. This technology advanced into the recording of brain waves and body movements to read a person's mind. A reverse process enabled the indoctrination of unruly citizens by writing their thoughts for them via a bombardment of electrical pulsations, managed neural stimulation, and imagery.

Light charging was invented. Electromagnetic waves of significantly higher frequency were running through fiber optic cables to power utilities at a fraction of the cost. Mirrored panels were constructed to reflect and store starlight; they could zoom in on bright stars (including el sol) using their own energy and direct the surplus to a chain of battery cells for powering appliances and machines. Cars, trucks, and trains ran on hydrogen extracted from sea water; its only byproducts were salt, helium, and breathable oxygen. Furthermore, heat from the earth's outer core was tapped for energy; hot water sources below the crust could be instantaneously accessed as well. Human waste was pressurized into a petroleum substitute through an eight-step refining process providing yet another fuel source.

The establishment owned the utilities. Less energy was required to run homes and businesses. But they kept charging more so they were really cleaning everyone's chronometer. They justified exorbitant fees by alleging mounting research and development expenditures. Since productivity was self-sustaining it was icing on the cake. So much for the energy crisis I imagined. They had a monopoly on energy, water, telephones, consumables and expendables (despite the fact that antitrust laws were still on the books). Yeah, they made the laws and enforced them but not on themselves.

Biochemical engineers developed a three-atom molecule with one each positive, negative, and neutral charge: a positron, electron, and neutron. Elements bonded into an infinitely compact substance favoring the obsolete super-silica-tetra-hydra hybrid. Stronger than any compound known heretofore, tritonite (as it was called) was the ultimate building block. Used for armor plating, component hardening, durable engine parts, and special military applications it could not be penetrated, broken, bent, scratched, folded, spindled, or mutilated. In short, they could nail you good but you couldn't strike back without hurting yourself.

Of course, the whole ball of wax was controlled by the North American Government (NAG). Talk about big daddy they traced your every move. Residences had a television set in each room; even if you weren't watching it, it was watching you. As I mentioned, any laws passed by the management applied to the proletariat only. There was nobody to hold civil servants to account because they enjoyed diplomatic immunity. And their duty was to spy on you and ensure you were behaving yourself in accordance with their definition of obedience.

Law enforcement practices were intimidating and ruthless. The kangaroo criminal courts always rendered a verdict of guilty. Punishment sometimes meant being dismembered for serial offenders. They would start with smaller body parts and either progress or digress: finger-hand, toe-foot. Depending on the offense you could lose your nose, tongue, eye, arm, leg, genitals, or head. Civil law was similar to criminal law: tooth for tooth. Vital and nonvital organs often were mined from convicts, the condemned, and the terminally ill to fill prescriptions for the aristocracy who were the only ones that could afford carnal transplants and implants.

Anyone receiving the death penalty or otherwise expiring became animal feed and plant fertilizer (after usable body parts had been extracted). Handicapped, deformed, or inferior offspring also were recycled in this manner. Euthanasia was awarded to people with incurable diseases, disorders, senility, or when they were no longer fruitful (a drag on the system). Socialized healthcare meant preselection for life preserving procedures with the elite getting in first. Lower caste persons had to wait endlessly for treatment and often died in line; the elderly had no chance. Seldom was anyone buried since the cost of a cemetery plot was exorbitant. A year's salary for a one-meter parcel; it was outrageous. And you'd be buried standing up in a vacuum tube and plopped into the dirt, crammed together like sardines. Needless to say, private real estate was scarce.

It was only about money. Well, what isn't? And the upper tenth percentile of the populace had two thirds of it or roughly twenty times the amount of a working-class chump. I wasn't about to be suckered into living under those conditions. If I'm going to break my back to earn a living it'll be to sustain my own comfort level not to enhance some fat cat's leisurely lifestyle. They never lifted a pinky for a nickel of the ill-gotten gratuity they bathed in. That's socialism for you: bust your buns, bleed into the coffers, and receive the dregs. Meanwhile the gap widens between them and you; they ascend the ladder and you descend. Everybody is supposed to benefit but that lasts long enough for you to get rooked.

In protest I refused to blindly acquiesce and convert into an automaton. And I absolutely wasn't about to let them experiment on me. I had no intention of being modified, codified, or pasteurized. Besides you can't change anyone but yourself, and you have to want to (though the divine spirit of love can change anyone).

I could've remained seated at the negotiating table but the cobwebs had overtaken it and the peace dove had long been excused. The continuous head bashing from the sledge hammer was a major nuisance. The line of accusers was out the door, around the block, and down the street. Their longwinded testimony was hearsay at best and nobody paid attention anyhow. I was already neck deep in the quagmire, the moat was rising, and the rescue boat was disappearing from view. It was time for me to fade into obscurity. I cast my vote in absentia and that was my last official act. Far be it for me to try and make a difference only to be submerged by the avalanche of bureaucratic baloney. Let it glide but keep your eyes peeled so you can get out of the way when the levee swells.

This defies logic: anticipating what will be. You cannot predict with accuracy the next event from a series of random ones. I learned this a long time ago when I was a poor boy hanging out with others in my predicament. We entertained ourselves fashioning miniature wooden boats that we floated along the gutter. We'd follow the wobbly craft as far as we could until it inevitably found a culvert or a drain. We could only imagine the remainder of the voyage so we devised conclusions to the story. It was considerably more creative than the games kids play today which require no imagination or intuition as these are provided for them. The same is true for the cinema and television. These are not inventive or original; they do not entertain they exasperate.

I think most stories could use modifications to the ending but I detest those that leave you in suspense. If I have to invent a conclusion why do I need another author to create the storyline? I have no need for someone else to give me the end and have me make up the beginning or give me the beginning and have me make up an end. And I have no intention of asking someone else to begin or end my whimsies. My life has enough suspense anyway; for my life story will never end.

Navigating through life we are faced with many unknowns. It may be forks in the road, perilous situations, acts of providence, or natural and manmade circumstances beyond our control. We can no more decree exactly what will be than we can make it so. Additionally, it seldom turns out the way I plan it so my plan is to have no plan. That doesn't mean I don't achieve goals, or prepare, or devise a broad strategy for the many contingencies that may arise. But you have to take life as it comes rather than force the boat into troubled waters, hurry and try to beat the storm, or build expectations as to what lies beyond the squall. Read the signs when they arrive (there is nothing hidden between the lines) and you will know when to act and why in the order occasions arise. What's the use of expending energy erecting a city of ambitions when the railroad line is determined to lay tracks elsewhere? It'll turn into a ghost town.

Freedom of Choice

It's not a complicated duty controlling your thoughts and aligning them with the proper actions. It takes patience and timing. Think before you act or speak. Collect yourself and the sensory inputs; then raise the caution flag and alert yourself. An assessment is in order during which you must delay your reaction. This can be accomplished by counting, contemplating, relaxing, or breathing: whatever helps you to gather your thoughts and synthesize them. Then decide.

Common mistakes always have included dwelling on the short-term benefits of a choice but failing to evaluate the long-term consequences; or neglecting the long-term benefits because the short-term costs are too distracting. It's a simple tradeoff analysis which if performed properly will lead to a logical conclusion. But some people think they need more alternatives even if the extras are unprofitable, detrimental, or unrealistic. Hey, if the only available option is worthwhile then what is the dilemma? Take what is offered, don't hold out for more or you'll end up with nothing. Be content with what you have and be responsible with what is entrusted to you.

Ever played the control game? It is dominated by those who are already out of it. Self-discipline is what they lack, yet they want you to tow-the-line as they define it. Keep in mind that relinquishing self-control will result in losing your self-esteem as well. The operating word here is self; that part is up to each one of us. Don't let others define it for you or you will come to believe it. And be honest with yourself; if you are not pleased you alone can change that. Mostly what you really need to do is change your freaking mind. Thank you. You're welcome!

Consequently, I became a nonconformist, an outlaw. I refused to kiss anybody's foot, or ring, or butt. There were many others that matched my moral stance and likewise seceded from the Union. Our slogan was, "Nobody racks my balls" (referring to a billiard phrase of course as it was our ambition to run the table). We didn't own electronic devices, except for jammers, so they couldn't keep us under surveillance. We didn't register for social cards so they couldn't track our whereabouts. We were masters of disguise, escape artists, each with a dozen pseudonyms; they couldn't figure out which one of us we were. We were off the grid, dead to the world.

We were the Kinfolk, brothers and sisters of the underground, literally; for we hid ourselves in clandestine caverns beneath graveyards. We had a convoluted schematic of reinforced tunnels below the city complete with furnished compartments, bringing to mind an ant farm. If anyone followed us into one, we could initiate a controlled cave-in and block our escape. We had mechanical eavesdropping and security equipment and we posted lookouts to ensure uninvited guests did not infringe on our privacy. They weren't welcome in our domain and we weren't welcome in theirs. Like prairie dogs we eked out a living; but troglodytes had it better than the taxpayers.

Looking back, how providential it was to be absent when the nuclear exchange took place; otherwise I probably wouldn't have made it this far. Plenty of the elites made it because they had hardened underground bunkers stocked with ample food and supplies. I never climbed high enough on the food chain for an invitation to their fraternity. Heading for the hills was my only option. And what a godsend; that's why I figure divine intervention saved me. The illumed elect had mastered the art of organized calamity to the slightest detail in a conspiracy to rule the world. The rest of us peons were to be enchained. This time it was our gang surviving in armored and stocked vaults belowground, while those in power were imprisoned by their egos.

The globalist agenda never accounted for us; regulators assumed there would be no resistance or opposition. But there wasn't an establishment we couldn't burglarize, a resident we couldn't hoodwink, or an official we couldn't bribe. It took coercion, threats, elaborate stings, and sometimes dynamite but we usually got what we wanted.

Federal installations were off-limits to the public. *No Trespassing* signs littered the avenues. Naturally, I interpreted that as an extended invitation. I broke into one such facility, an aerodynamics laboratory, to steal supplies for the solipsist's schooner. That really chapped their derrieres seeing that such items were classified top secret. They knew it was me because I deliberately left fingerprints, footprints, video and everything; but I didn't care. I already was a wanted man and I found that appealing. It's nice being wanted. Moreover, I'd known about their secrets; I used to keep some of them. Unfortunately, the administration kept the citizenry ignorant about a great many things. Most people hadn't the faintest idea of the technological advances being made. Many patents, inventions, and superior knowhow were deliberately snatched away and pigeonholed to prevent people from getting rich, getting over, getting ahead, getting free, getting lost, or getting away. The motive was to ensure everyone was financially dependent on the federation.

I was accosted late one evening while loitering near a manufacturing plant by an agent of the dominion who demanded my identification. Naturally, I didn't carry any. She tried to cuff me and I floored her with a right cross; she was out cold. That was the first and last time I ever struck a girl. Whatever, I skated away nonchalantly and hopped aboard a subway. I proceeded to edge my way to the rear, dove from the back door, and tumbled into a familiar channel that emptied into the sewer. I followed a linkage of conduit to where my land rover was parked, crawled out of a manhole, and tore out into the country. By the time I'd made it to the foothills the enforcers were in close pursuit, eager to apprehend me.

The terrain became too testy to navigate on wheels but that wasn't exactly news to me. I often had taken this track when I was young. I'd managed to scour every inch of that desert thanks to my brother who left his motorbike behind when he blew town. I recalled how I loathed it when my parents moved away from the coast to this remote inhospitable territory of which I was once unaccustomed. We had ended up out in the boonies, the armpit of the nation. Talk about culture shock. I was flabbergasted to see such a large beach with no water; it was an ocean of sand. But I came to love the wilderness; it was my marina. I recognized the mesa ahead, steep and high not to mention a few kilometers in breadth. I knew the best way to get to the zenith and across the table. It would cut over an hour off hoofing around it.

The old soldier had showed me. I met him one day while he was dragging a calf that he'd poached to a hooch fabricated atop the mesa. He was an Army veteran who became a hermit after the big war destroyed his marriage, sanity, and regard for his fellow Americans. That's why he resided solo. He must've been ninety, maybe a hundred years old. I had my pack, blanket, and food. I often explored, wandered, and slept overnight under the stars. Sarge invited me to dinner and I spent the night. I was a loner after losing Lany so we had a lot more in common than you might think. We became friends. Several months later, after I'd safeguarded my scrambler in the underbrush, I scuttled up the rise. I had brought Sarge some of my mom's world-famous brownies. I found the aged hero in rigor mortis lying on his bed. He wasn't expecting me; it was going to be a surprise. What he was expecting I suppose was death. He was dressed in his Class A uniform complete with medals adorning his chest to include silver and bronze stars, two purple hearts, a combat infantry badge, and airborne wings; he had a blue cord on one shoulder and a red cord on the other, and a garrison cap with a glider patch that had slipped off his head. I laid him on his spare cot, entombed him in full military regalia, with a dozen brownies and an operational M14, in a hollow he'd dug that served as a combination meat-smoker and cellar. There I cremated him using contents from his shelter that produced a very hot kiln. I waited outside saluting his sacrifice to our native land and his honorable departure from this world, while ushering him into his next episode. I lifted the fossils, gemstones, and Indian artifacts he'd collected as I'm sure he would've bequeathed those to me. They were always among my most prized personal effects. I slept in his bed that night and had another one of those unnerving dreams. It mimicked a black and white war movie that my grandfather had on videocassette tape; only in this war I was the instigator and my old friend was the journalist.

Regaining my senses, I found myself kneeling in the heart of what was left of the timeworn and rundown cabin. I grabbed a weather-beaten board from the pile. Promptly, I hurried across the draw to a particular part of the plateau that had a gravelly grade which continued to the bottom. Using the plank as a sled I skidded down in a minute and hustled towards the mount. I'd gained a couple of hours on my pursuers, ample time to lose the bad guys in the wilds for the time being. Drones searched for my signature but they were nowhere near on track, and dust laden winds had strengthened which would foul the optics if not the engines. Around nightfall the winds subsided a bit; a full moon peeped out and stars shown in abundance. I scrambled to the mountaintop sometime after midnight, knowing the overseers wouldn't attempt the dangerous ascent until morning (if they had a hunch where I was hiding).

Although the base had long been abandoned some of our equipment remained, to include a jug of water and a few dilapidated hang gliders. I inspected them until I found one that wasn't too badly damaged. I repaired it by candlelight using parts from the leftovers. Helicopters with spotlights and sensor systems were searching for me but unable to land or to locate my position which was beneath a camouflaged and barricaded launch pad. I could see a dozen campsites below where the authorities had assembled. I'm sure they figured I was cornered. They were having a shindig in the valley supposing to brainwash me once and for all, I presumed.

I finally worked up the gumption to take the plunge a few hours before sunup. I slipped into the harness, opened my wings, took a flying leap, and glided to safety some fifty miles from the site. This was one of many adventures in evasion that became almost a weekly occurrence. When first I left the precipice, I realized that this was the closest I'd ever been to the highest power in the highest heaven. The experience was as serene and illustrious as Nature herself. I opened my eyes and saw the distant horizon spreading from east to west. To view the earth from such an altitude with the freedom and grace of a bird is to live in another world. The cool fresh air whooshed by my ears, and I felt the soothing buoyancy beneath my pinions. Crossing an updraft, I ascended as if returning to space from a dream. Forever I hovered and glided through the misty bliss of skylight.

The shadows lined the ground appearing as ocean waves murmuring in the deep blue. Speedily I was descending more rapidly than I wished, almost hoping it not to end. But the shady glade in the distance was approaching, rushing forward to kiss me tenderly (imitating someone I once knew). She applauded as I collapsed into her lap, rolling over and over until I knew it was over as every experience in this life eventually will be. It was an abrupt end to another gambit I reasoned (akin to birth) just as the sun cracked the new horizon.

To soar as an eagle is to become one, if temporarily. There isn't a care or worry but only the joy to live, as love. I shook hands with my feathered companions and hugged the clouds; and realized that life is as it should be. Being confident to jump off the cliff was to face strife with renewed vigor, appreciating the many rewards that faith affords. I have had so many friends and exploits. I have been given profound peace and countless liberties, more than I was worthy; but life pays back double. For the love you receive is twice the love you give because it multiplies, yielding increasingly higher returns. Invest in it. As one poet eloquently put it: A little bit of love goes a long way, and a little bit of living is long enough. This was my way and no doubt, the best way.

I took a nap in the sand of a cozy streambed shaded in brushwood where I discarded the vestiges of my aircraft. It had been a long day not to mention the night, and I went out like a light. My dream took me soaring into the nebula of a collapsing blue supergiant. I had wings of an angel and I glided along a corridor of aquamarine hue unlike anything I had perceived, known of, or dreamt about. Never had I witnessed anything so beautiful, pristine, harmonious, or delightful. I was ecstatic, joyful, at peace, and at home. There were others but I could not see them or communicate with them. It was as if I didn't belong, or I had landed too soon, or maybe I wasn't welcome. But I sure wasn't frightened, angry, upset, or grumpy. I kept going because another destination was appearing in the torrid distance.

Torturing time which was no longer fresh slipped through fingers of smelted flesh. That which had passed was eternal—no end; future's time would forever begin. I stopped short of later and froze in-between; caught sight of the universe, bleeding, unclean. I started to wrestle with fate yet unknown, and drowned in the mire, unconscious, alone. Wholly to battle the elements there; thousands more (I was vaguely aware). Wrenched from my feet to be tossed in the scrap; brains squashed two hundred miles in the trap. As time passed, hollow spooks acquired my remains; they gathered me up and they bound me in chains. I was dragged to their castle for their king to see. I told them my story and they followed me.

The ghost following was not meant for me, however. I foreknew this as I awakened to a pure cerulean sky, then straightaway fell back asleep. What percentage of life is truly a dream and how much of it is truly real? I remember dreams being more abstract in my early years. Arriving home from work, I proceeded to polish off a bottle of vodka while watching cartoons. I awoke, sunken into the lounger with a throbbing migraine, where I nodded off and dreamt it again. This sequence continued repeatedly, day after day, forever. I was not only being hunted but haunted. Ghouls would surround me when SS was absent. Ever-present were the twins: Mara and Maya, which I couldn't tell them apart though one was evil and the other good. Especially confusing were their intentions. They skedaddled at the first glimpse of SS for they feared him more than me.

It was the year I fell for a forty-something skid-row virgin about a decade my senior who was detained for witchcraft. She had an awful upbringing, climaxing when her congressman father strangled her immigrant mother to death. Pearlie was a crazy marijuanaholic not a witch, though her appearance may have fooled a person of self-determined superiority. She resembled a certain rag doll that was the most cherished among Lany's menagerie, wearing a checkered, shabby dress; sporting stringy, strawberry hair; freckles dotting both cheeks and nose; and a crooked smile. But underneath the frill she had an elegance, sincerity, and kindness that surpassed wonder. The blackhearts were about to dump her into a lockdown shelter for wayward unidentifiable women. A dreary profession awaited her

Pearlie feigned an illness and was sent to the infirmary where she seduced a guard. As soon as he dropped his drawers, she grabbed his other gun and bashed him over the head with it. Wielding the pistol, she hijacked an ambulance and sped away with three squad cars in chase. Being apprised of the situation by a colleague we immediately responded to her plight. He deployed a diversion to distract the cops by staging accidents one of which involved the ambulance. I abducted the lady, masked our departure with a blast and smokescreen, and shuttled her to a nearby haven. She was immensely appreciative to the extent that she surrendered her maidenhead to me. It was the first time since childhood that she'd trusted a man.

We went together for about a year before she drifted away. Isn't it giddy when hurriedly falling in love though protracted falling out of it? I started out with burning ardor for her but she managed to douse it little by little, continuously sprinkling sand over smoldering embers of affection until the fire was completely squelched. Oh, I still loved her, but I wasn't in love with her anymore. She had too many of her own needs that required fulfillment to be interested in meeting any of mine. I wanted a son but she didn't. I wanted to make love once in a while but she was too tired. We didn't work, play, or eat together anymore; in truth, we had nothing left in common. I was thirsty but the same drink ceased to satisfy. For instance, I still enjoy vodka but I don't thirst for it anymore, and gin will suffice just the same. She couldn't tell me what she wanted only that it wasn't me. Another one bites the dust I thought as I added a checkmark to the found-and-lost column.

I recollect a dream riding on a bus next to my beloved Lany. It was a long trip and we'd dozed off as soon it became dark outside. I awoke when the bus stopped at the station but Lany was nowhere to be found. I searched the bus and the station, asked people if they had seen her, and ran around town calling her name. I thought she'd left me. Exhausted, I parked myself on a bench, put my head between my hands, and balled uncontrollably the rest of the day. The first I'd dreamt it was weeks before Lany passed. And here I was dreaming it again like a recurring nightmare.

Magistrates were determined to use whatever means available to get vagrants off the street. They abhorred people like me who didn't contribute to the coffers and weren't about to forfeit freedom. They resorted to biological warfare disseminating deadly venereal diseases. Card members were required to be vaccinated or face a relentless and painful demise. We fled to the outer territories and into the amber bluffs; the sulfur deposits served as quarantine. The military deployed weather control devices to emit the harshest of conditions. The tactic backfired for the plagues subsided and we were able to sneak back into the grottos. The establishment was fooled into thinking they had exterminated us, a least for a season.

I was a vagabond, forever on the loose like in my dreams. We were uncommon bandits, able to breach any security system to steal a meal or heist something pricey. We extorted from the corporation; what we didn't use we gave to those less fortunate. The only difference between us and the merry men is we had no qualms about ridding the land of murderers, rapists, and illicit judicators. Those scum suckers never looked justice in the face and thus would not have recognized her. They were insiders of the good buddy system; all thieving, lying, and vulgar scoundrels. Only innocents were found guilty in their courts. Justice seemed a duty so we conducted our own trials and executed swift punishment upon the incriminated. Naturally, this made them resent us all the more. But it was they who were rebellious not us. There was nothing magnanimous about their policies.

The slacking of the law opened the door to every manner of decadence and depravity. Anyone caught doing something illegal could buy a way out with sufficient collateral. Those who were law abiding were targets for ambush and exploitation. What else would you expect? If there are no apparent consequences what will deter the commission of an insidious act?

Witnesses for the Prosecution

It started long before I was born when entertainment consisted of small doses of sex and violence, with actors engaging in amoral acts, criminal enterprises, and terrorism but no simulated repercussions. It's a simple principle: the exaltation of lawlessness causes it to escalate dramatically. The propaganda of promiscuity was infused into the minds of youngsters, wayward women, and the faint of heart in order to radicalize them. Prostitution, a pastime participated by people of all penchants, approached pandemic proportions. Before long, kid killers were profuse slaying each other, their parents, and teachers on a lark. It was a sinister conspiracy by racketeers who employed the media to inculcate the feebleminded into carelessly following them into the cesspool. Deceit was more easily accepted, albeit solicited over the gospel. Civilization was uncivilized and society was antisocial. Everything was oxymoronic. But that was the purpose, evil perceived as good and vice-versa.

And what happened to organized religion you might ask? It was superseded by organized corruption. The papacy was the seat of a godfather and the bishops his henchmen. They conspired to commit acts of profiteering, lewdness, debauchery, and assassination, worse than the Inquisition. Clerics and elders in the various denominations used the pulpit to espouse political agendas and used their positions to cover up grievous atrocities. It was one scandal after another, the clergy engaging in abominable acts under the guise of religiosity. Behind a veil of tears was a spiritual thirst. I concluded that the only trustworthy avenue to the truth was to read it for myself in the Sacred Word. I still had an unaltered copy that my grandpa gave me. It was aged and tattered, but legible.

My grandfather, he was the last of the righteous men. While not altogether an educated individual I've never known anyone wiser (aside the solipsist). And spiritual: his countenance would glow with the luminance of a lantern. As such he was highly regarded and admired by anyone who had the privilege to know him. He put up with a henpecking wife for fifty years and continued to remain celibate after her demise, until his death at the century mark. Granny contracted dementia, converting into a reject from the roaring twenties. She fancied herself a flapper like her mother before her. In her dreams she was dancing the Charleston when she keeled over from a heart attack. It was a comical end for a dazed lady.

Gramps taught me compassion, trust, and honor. I only saw him get mad once, when he said "oh drat" because some drunk plowed into his car after he'd picked me up to go hiking. When the debacle was over, we went on our outing anyway and at his age he breached the summit first. He assured me that the mountain inevitably would be my sanctuary. He warned of the wicked age to come and to steer clear of it. "The scourge will uproot the upright like a plow," were his words.

I peeked at the sun, one eye open, the other, Earth: shut as if to hide itself. The face inside Sun's corona stared back with a puzzled and sad look. Moon was rolling down the boulevard with the momentum of a bowling ball knocking down the pillars of fate. I held fast to the cross which burned with fire until my hand also was ablaze. The thick smoke filled the sky forming black clouds that irritated the eyes of divinity, whose teardrops became missiles that exploded into fireballs hither and yon. Grubby fingers emerged from the foothills and tried to grab me as I darted down the disintegrating brick road which unfolded into the early dusk. Seagulls were rocketing past to escape the tidal waves which came crashing down on both sides. The turmoil would grin to have overtaken me but I stood as a rock, undisturbed like the bust of simpleton adorning my mantle. While traveling through eternity you too may notice the multitude of faces encased within the trees, clouds, and knolls. Can you see that there is emptiness in their eyes? They are looking for a home and you are it.

Hopelessly forlorn they were: those dabblers and their demonologists. Youths were recruited, initiated, indoctrinated, and ensnared. Tricked with false promises of riches, power, and pleasure they indulged in vain imaginations. Traumatized and terrorized they surrendered their spirituality and sold their souls. They were led astray by the unnatural and paranormal into the membership of malevolence. The exaggeration of liberalism, the breakdown of family and education systems, the mockery of justice, and the disdain for decency were tools of the trade for that organization. The utter rejection of responsibility and subjection of truth were their principles. Officially incorporated into the devil's den, tattooed with an inverted pentagram on their chests, conversant in the secret slang of runes and symbols, they were joined in death.

Being stuck on sin it stuck to them, a parasite, eroding hearts. Had they become glued to the Lord they could have rebuked the beast and been a repellant to evil. But under a facade of group strength they still viewed themselves as individually weak. And that they were for they sought no outlet from the slippery slope that leads to the pit. They took for granted that there was no escape and submitted like a crippled pussycat amongst the rabid jackals. Perceiving there to be power and craving it for themselves they delved deep, only to find themselves despondent amid the emptiness. Anticipating fun, they found none that would enthrall for long, converting one disappointment into another.

Enter the savage, the fanatical fascist and those fanged followers. They sort of floated in below the radar scan. The bigwigs never noticed; they were so engrossed in themselves. Flattery would get you everywhere with the oligarchs and so it did for the devil's descendant, the hermaphrodite from hell. Its power was in cunning, beguiling the fickle and flighty, the wayward, sinister, seductive, and idle.

They would take a census of their army by counting foreskins (not all males had penises but some females did). If you didn't disclose it you were not invited to enlist in their insane campaign. A nasty fan club served as sex slaves willing to do anything and everything. Their lair of lasciviousness was the envy of the favored, which arrived in swarms to splurge into the bog with their ravenous appetites. Thus, the popularity of Beelzebub's basement led to the sprouting of many more, and their fortune and fame burgeoned.

While traveling through eternity...

The darkie was not interested in participating, only organizing the orgies. He would travel in a caboose over the Imperial Guard Rails (he was afraid of flying, ha-ha). In transit, there were additional abductions of despondent wives used for "experimental" sex, to be discarded in a deserted ditch leaving a brainless, addicted wench. One irate husband dressed as a trollop snuck a gun aboard the train, shot and mortally wounded the bastard, who was being entertained by the naked theatrics. He scuttled off, being the dirty rat that he was, but appeared at a public address the next afternoon seeming unscathed. However, he did start using a lookalike after that, or maybe before.

Being filthy rich in the literal sense was the heritage of the frivolous faction. They alone could afford the luxuries of lust while the ordinary folk scrimped for their daily bread. The scales had tipped; economic collapse was eminent. That elaborate pyramid plot had putrefied. Disaster was drawing nigh like a runaway bulldozer. Banks and savings institutions went belly-up. Too many bad loans, embezzlements, and crooked accounting facilitated their downfall. Global stock markets went south after insiders stole profits, executives drained companies dry, and leveraged takeovers gutted businesses dumping the properties like it was a garage sale. The government was bankrupt what with misappropriated funds, printing worthless currency, pork-barrel wastefulness, and draining lavish expense accounts. The only ones making any profits were the drug cartels given that the demand for their products was at an all-time high (as were the consumers).

Two social classes remained: those with everything and those with nothing. Those with everything would see it slip through their fingers. They would cling to their plunders with their might. Comparable to a fist grasping a handful of sand, the harder they clutched the more their accumulations shrank. Theirs was a frantic search for something in life to value. Have you noticed that the epitome of fear is to be stricken with panic? This state of mind illustrates the belief that there is nothing to hold onto, least of all hope. It is a sorry sight for sure.

Those with nothing had nothing to lose. But there was everything to gain. And their faith in obtaining it brought home the hope; hope in the better life promised where peace and prosperity were nondescript when compared to the riches and glory that awaited them. They trained hard for the race and persevered, awaiting a genuine crown. These same prizes the greedy had shunned in favor of enjoying the pleasures of perversion. I once dove into the dungeon but managed to scrabble through; having been swilled down the commode, I washed up on another shore.

I turned up a buckskin map in the belfry of the manor. It had been stashed beneath a pile of frayed police uniforms at the base of a weathered wooden trunk, itself buried under a heap of rubble. Would the map disclose the location of a hidden cache, a secret hideout, or merely a buccaneer's empty tomb? Well I really had nothing to lose, so I hired a crew complete with captain and chartered their modest vessel equipped with two whaleboats. It seems the whaling business was at a lull, and the prospect of fortune obscured the jeopardous complexion of the expedition; that's the reason they accepted the job on commission. We set sail in late August taking a course due south towards the coast of Ecuador and then southwest en route for the Galapagos Islands.

Let me tell you, ocean excursions are not so different from space travel but a great deal more laborious. Navigation by stars, trigonometry, and global positioning equipment enabled the captain and me to pilot the ship by night, because it was a stellar course that determined bearing. An uncharted deserted island surrounded by a small barrier reef, about eight hundred kilometers northwest, is where we dropped anchor. From there our shore party maneuvered between the mounds on a whaleboat, finally disembarking on the northernmost point of the atoll. It seems the islet was accessible certain times of the year but submerged otherwise.

We camped until right before sunup when the tide was lowest. A forked volcanic mount gradually became prominent, silhouetted by the setting moon. Following a pass that was created by years of washing and erosion, we located a cavern near the apex of the tallest cinder cone. Using thousand lumen flashlights to scan, it was apparent that we would need to drop a rope ladder to descend to the floor thirty feet below.

We explored the cave but found nothing of value, until I tripped over the fossilized remnant of an ancient avian reptile. Having been a dinosaur buff since a preschooler I identified the remains from the family of pterosaurs probably of the Cretaceous period. The captain's only concern was that someone would pay top dollar for it. Possibly the first of the winged vertebrates, this specimen was rapidly entombed in volcanic mud and had hardened into silica composite an estimated 150-200 million years ago according to the paleontology class I took as an elective. Well maybe it wasn't that old, but it was unscathed by the sea. It would net a pretty penny if we could unearth it and drag it out of its mausoleum and into the boat.

Slopping around in the mud, the four of us began digging carefully to find the edges and hoist it out of the impacted dirt. Measuring about six feet by ten feet, embedded in a slab of deteriorating sandstone, it was extremely heavy. There was no way we could get it out of the cave, being too weighty and bulky, much less getting us and the specimen into the boat and back to the ship. We would have to summon the rest of the crew and the other whaleboat; even then it was improbable if not pointless. While the other seamen were arguing with one another about how to remove the sample from the sandstone, I continued digging and found its spouse. Now they were seeing some serious dollar signs. After further excavation I found what appeared to be petrified pterosaur eggs; they were flawless in formation, appreciably larger than a goose egg, and very rare. I gathered the four eggs in a canvas bag and proceeded to the opening of the cave to inspect them in the natural light. Unaware of what I'd uncovered, the captain and his mate continued to debate how to get the two preserved flying reptiles to market.

I surfaced in time to notice a thirty-foot wave barreling down on the opposite end of the atoll. I yelled at my companions to get out of there fast while I scooted to the top of the mount. Quickly the wave crashed against the southeast edge of the reef and distributed over the isle to where I was standing, scarcely six feet of dry land for miles. My accomplices below never had a chance. About that time one dinghy came coasting by; I was able to snag a rope and pull it towards me. Then the sea became calm. I peered through my spyglass scanning the horizon 360 degrees, but there was no sign of the whaler, the mates, or anything (water everywhere and not a drop to drink).

I began paddling southeast in the direction of the tidal wave, singing "row your boat" for eight solid days at which time I collapsed. Incredible as it may seem, despite rough sea, blistering sunrays, and harsh gales I wafted onto a sandbar the ninth evening at twilight. Ahead was a tropical island paradise. I had no idea where I was, how I got there, or why my life was spared over the others; but I was rightly relieved to be alive. I waded ashore, erected a flag from my shabby shorts, and proclaimed the island splendor my glory land. Was this a premonition of affairs to come? Maybe it was an indication that a scant tenth would make it out alive. Or could it be a warning that we are accountable in this struggle and cannot find our way home without being saved from ourselves?

It became evident to me that it was not my place to judge the rascals any more than it was theirs to judge me. I wasn't qualified to judge myself. And if I did what penalty would I levy? Could I afford it? Death was too lenient a measure. But who in all honesty would apply the same reprimand to themselves as they'd applied to others? Besides, we are guilty of the deficiencies for which we condemn others. You see, it's okay to judge what people say and do but it's not right to vilify the person. It wasn't personal; they treated every soul with disdain. I abandoned the quest; I resolved to give up the gun so I wouldn't have to die by it. I opted to let the fickle finger of fate have its way. Note that fate is usually the ultimate result of inaction. And fate was soon to catch up with doom, its cousin.

The ruling class didn't have much going for them per the unhealthy alliances they were forging; they sought treaties with former enemies and shunned allies in the process. Abandoning tenets they once stood for, they favored new dogmas to attract followers from all walks, none of which adhered to a respectable path. A new foundation was being built from a mixture of diverse creeds for which no paste existed that could hold it together. Sort of feigning an artistic work by blending oil, acrylic, and tempera paints, they produced a mystifying mess with no consistency, form, arrangement, or rationale. If they couldn't bolster sufficient cooperation in their pursuit of uncompromised folly, they acted unilaterally thereby hampering negotiations, circumventing due process, and insulting allegiances. When that didn't satisfy, they resorted to black magic, black masses, blackmail, blacklisting, and blackjacks. They wandered farther from truth, law, reason, and love not knowing that judgment was entering the foyer. They were supposedly carving a legacy but actually were digging their graves. They obviously didn't need my help.

There would be a reckoning from the least to the greatest, the humble and the proud, the weak and the strong. Each would be exposed naked to the world, with every dastardly deed plastered across the marquis for everyone to see. It would take years to enumerate my own transgressions not to mention those of humanity. Must we attend the entire grueling commencement? Or is it reserved for those that do not graduate?

Be advised, that day may be upon you sooner than you think. How fortunate it would be to have an advocate plead your case before the Judge of judges and convince him that your fines had been paid in full. Oh, to be justified, found not guilty, released from the shame and guilt, and to have that long list of iniquities expunged from the record. And guess what? Belief in the truth is the answer. When called upon to testify simply tell the truth. It is your key to freedom. Disbelief is rejection of the truth. It is the only unpardonable sin and it will guarantee a conviction and sentencing. Is that the way you would prefer to live? Then that is the way you will die.

The ignoble general bluntly orated, "War is hell." That's what I was pondering on the eve of the summer solstice as I peered into the darkness crouched in a foxhole, sharing company with a variety of creepy crawly creatures. We were awaiting the unstoppable ingress of communist hoards, tens of thousands we were told. The monsoons had created a snake infested swamp out of the rice paddies in the lowlands, and mudslides along the highlands would not allow one to scale the thick, slick muck. There was no escape route left.

A glimmer of light burst out of the emptiness breaching the blackness from afar, then another, and another. Like pinholes in a dam streams began seeping through, the precursor to a deluge of fire. And still you couldn't see a thing. One second seemed an hour, and an hour a lifetime. We had been waiting through the night and still were not ready. The multitude of flickering lights became too numerous to count like the stars above. A horrid cry emanated from every side, shells zipping past my ear, percussion explosions to my rear, rocket's red glare and the whole smear. I was emptying magazine after magazine into the dust and smoke as bullets whizzed towards me, one which knocked my helmet to the ground. As they were about to overrun my position a blast buried me in a cave-in of smelly slush. I assure you this: if you had never believed in God before you would then. And you'd be praying like you knew how. But you already did truthfully.

Late into the day I came to, tunneled my way into the light, and squirmed through the would-be sepulcher just enough to pull myself to my knees. The bodies were strewn in every direction; such devastation, destruction, demolition, eradication. Who knows what became of the threatening throng; I suspect those that remained were marching to the sea. All I know is that I was the sole survivor, again; with nowhere to go, not a morsel to eat, and nothing to my name except a rifle with no ammunition. It was a familiar flashback but one I'd sooner forget. I've had several glimpses of hell; never is the sight of it pleasant in any regard. I can only imagine heaven and I truly want to go there, though I haven't seen it either or anything that comes close.

Do you believe in hell? If not, why believe in heaven? Do we die and that's it? Maybe everybody goes to the same place, or no place. Is there punishment for sin? If not, then there is no such thing as sin either. Zero morality means that nothing is evil. Do you think you won't have to give an accounting? Somebody has to pay, right? Can you withstand it? Do you have someone to post your bail? Can you hire another to endure your flogging? Can you purchase a way out through hard labor, quid pro quo, or bribery? Or perhaps you're expecting to serve your allotted time in purgatory and then you'll be let loose. Dream on. There's no such thing as almost clean, partially saved, somewhat free, or a little bit dead.

Life is a hodgepodge of changing realities, each moment presenting a completely different array of obstacles, examinations, impressions, and turns of events. It is a plot that unravels one tidbit at a time, presenting multiple choices that will reconfigure the maze into new directions, turns, contests, and stumbling blocks. Each twinkling of the eye is a representation of a plan so elaborate one can never piece it together.

I pray for guidance, and while I know God will answer I tussle with indecision and uncertainty. It is not an advantage knowing the exact configuration in advance as he does, so responses to my pleas become equally enigmatic. Did he say yes, no, maybe, wait, or you'll see? That's the best I can come up with since it is futile to second-guess God. Eager as he is to show it to me, I won't comprehend it; but I am guaranteed it will come together at the end of the day when I will appreciate it more. In this knowledge I trust because I refuse to live a lie. I am not intimidated but awestruck at the complexity and the simplicity; the enjoyment and the anguish; the laughter and the weeping; the fulfillment and the emptiness; the timeliness and the timelessness; the predictability and the unexpectedness; the thrills and the throes.

Who would speculate against life? Who would prefer it to end or to continue? Who would deflect God's love or hide their own? Who would refuse his invitation and go their own way with no idea where and when it ends? Can anyone do it better?

SS, being inundated with questions had but one answer, "With the Almighty it gets increasingly, endlessly better and easier."

That's all I needed to know. Why torture yourself over the unknown I asked myself? It is the greatest of fears. It leaves you only with doubt, vacant of confidence, during the which hope also dwindles. When you are unsure, the risk of screwing up goes up. I unquestionably knew the best way to defeat the unknown: with knowledge. Knowledge revives confidence, lessens uncertainty, reduces risk, and strengthens hope. Yet the anxiety continued to batter my ego.

Initially, I had interpreted the torment as a mental illness because it caused restlessness, fright, and mood swings. Pleasingly, I was not a basket case, just misinformed and misdirected. The interference came from without; it was a spiritual attack intended to disrupt my sanity by clouding the truth. The vulnerability of my flesh made my mind easy pickings. If it prevailed over my spirit, I would lose the war. The cure was found in the realm of the supernatural and not the natural; the spiritual not the physical. Treasures like courage, conviction, and trust were incomprehensible and unexplainable with reasoning, though known explicitly to the soul encompassing me. Searching for truth via the natural, although productive, was incomplete. Searching with the spirit was without limitations and completed the picture. I determined that you needed the one to complement and comprehend the other.

Truth can be pinpointed by studying the book of the creation with the book of the Creator. God happens to be the author of both. Together they converge upon absolutes that are not subject to compromise or misinterpretation. To be sure, anything verified as true cannot disagree with either source. I concluded that things purported to be true via science alone might be suspect unless in agreement with holy revelation which trumps any other source. How can you know when it is a revelation from God? God himself has spoken it.

Food for Thought

"We are priests of the Church of Solipsist," spoke the voices that plagued him.

He regarded them as invaders, prowling his inner being. The intrusions were a provocation opposing predestation, because their concept implied predetermination. But SS avowed to be self-deterministic, while embracing guidance from the Divine One which he knew to be superior to other spirits. The prophets of his culture forbade such reformist thinking. If the scholars of his time had mapped out the temporal tables, who could possibly turn them? However, SS meant to do exactly that. They conferred upon him fantastic faculties however, including the ability to discern spirits; and that translated into a means to maneuver around the motives of mortals.

His power to see one's aura and assess his, hers, or its saintliness was intriguing. He evaluated the essence as if critiquing a painting or a star: type, luster, saturation, magnitude. Apparently, it matters not the color of the skin but the brightness of the tint. It was a rare gift. He could point at any creature and peg it accurately.

"Stay away from strays," he warned, "they're often malicious."

"I've seen them domesticated," I argued.

"The light of any spirit can be turned off and on again," he declared ... "Grab the spirit and corrupt it and you can extinguish its light, or you can accomplish the converse. The lesser creatures don't know any better but humanoids should."

"Are you implying that people have a choice whereas animals do not?" I reiterated.

"Precisely," he affirmed.

"Then why does anybody elect not to be elected?" I inquired.

"They're fools," he shouted, pounding on the lectern. "Spiritual autonomy assures everyone an opportunity to guarantee their eventuality, even after death and decomposition."

"Why would anyone reject such freedom?" I followed.

"It's a matter of receiving," he countered, "To not request it is to fade away."

"I can't help but feel sorry for those who tolerate their spirits turning dark," I whimpered.

"Me too," he agreed... "It's like looking into a black hole; but you don't want to see what's on the other side."

I discovered that the eyes were the key; for some they would twinkle but for others there was scarcely a void.

SS continued, "Some will refuse things offered gratis. They end up abusing such things instead of cherishing their endowments. The same will happen if they take it by force. Don't yearn for something you cannot have; even if you get it you won't appreciate it. It is the depredation of pride. For example, a murderer takes life but despises it; a rapist desires love but fears it; a subjugator wants exemption but enslaves others; a sociopath shuns responsibility but is blameworthy; the prideful seek glory but are disgraced; the self-righteous shun sin but are destroyed by it."

"And liars hate the truth because it proves them false," I reasoned.

"Now you're talking," he said smugly but in approval. "A person that adores their valuables loses them in the end; and those who strive only for the pleasures of a material existence will never be satisfied. A spiritual void can never be fulfilled with a worldly solution," SS maintained. "A material existence has no destiny but to die."

I've noticed misers. They're frequently taking inventory afraid of their property getting spent or stolen. They agonize over it, losing sleep in the process (and you know how valuable I regard sleep). Ultimately, what they really have lost is hope and what has been confiscated from them is their inheritance.

I guess that's how the weak-minded become addicted. They think they can stuff the emptiness with a passing euphoria but it keeps requiring more of the substance or activity solely to maintain. Constantly pursuing a feeling that they detected the first time, they get hooked. And that level is far removed from the lowest echelon of nirvana. They fool themselves into agreeing that what they are missing is of this world when it is the spirit of love they lack. I profess that the single-most healthy thing to which one should become addicted is the love of God. If only they could get a foretaste, a moment of unadulterated truth.

"But undoubtedly everyone does," he proclaimed. "Those who search for it will discover it finds them. Those who deny it will rationalize in order to jabber-walk themselves out of it."

His insights were profound; mostly they made sense. And he came from a place where the population engages in mythological reasoning and the worshipping of star clusters. His cohorts believed there were gods, indeed spirits in the constellations. Whenever a new galaxy was discovered it supposedly personified additional generations of ancestral roots, family constellations if you will, with the personality of Orion or Scorpio.

"But if nobody knows whose is whose why worship them?" I desired to know.

"I have no idea," he replied, "The slightest bit of spiritual soundness escapes their common sense." "Faith," he continued, "is not blind; it requires considerable reinforcement and proof to believe in someone or something."

Supposedly, that's why he spent so much time away from home; he didn't relate to them or their philosophy. They presumed all beings are influenced by spirits alive and dead, especially relatives that have passed. Many are powerful enough to insert their convictions into the minds of their progeny and indirectly shape forthcoming generations in the family tree. It's a component of the collective unconscious, soul repossession.

"I can't accept it," he attested. "If there was such a connection it would be to all creation for eternity; not exclusively assigned to your own ancestry, species, sphere, or epoch. Now, I can admit there are familial links likely limited to one's heritage and surroundings, but that's it," he resolved.

"Can't we receive messages directly from angels or God?" I posed.

"Hmm," he paused, "I'll have to deliberate on that." (As otherworldly as he was, he was willing to learn even from the likes of me.)

Parts of their belief system had merit, though. Firstly, he definitely was able to detect specters; my mother saw one once and I have felt an eerie presence before. So, there must be a spirit realm out there and I bet you can perceive them with extrasensory acuity, and possibly communicate with them. I suspect people might subject themselves to channeling other spirits especially if they exhibit a spiritual void. But the part about spirits inhabiting or owning celestial bodies—that was a tough one to swallow; and the constellations being reserved for genealogies—that was a further stretch. I can see why he denounced those notions. I don't even want to be the god of my own planet much less become one; what's more, it's lonely at the top or on the outside. There's more benefit being a subject to the Supreme who already has and knows everything; as a result, the capacity for growth, discovery, and spiritual aptitude are endless.

Secondly, because he could distinguish spirits SS could tell immediately if they were from darkness or plain absent. The key to their motivation and agenda was thereby revealed. Bystanders would applaud when he would uncover sinister plots and expose troublemakers for who they were. They would hide their faces in embarrassment, scurrying away the way roaches do when you turn on the light. SS had to alter his appearance sometimes to disperse the mobs that gathered around him. They thought he was a prophet. But he was modestly showing them the light that was revealed to him. This peeved SS when people would idolize him, because he knew he had failed to reach them. They did not listen, they were confused, or they were absentminded. What they were not was interested, willful, and strongminded.

Thirdly, he could read minds and he could communicate telepathically. But he only provided information; he never induced people to believe, do or say anything involuntarily. It was obvious who benefited from his leadership and who disregarded it. Such behavior was in alignment with the shade of their psychic essence. Clearly, the visionary was able to insert his thoughts for consideration; he trained me to do it. I tried it and it worked. But I quit because I didn't think myself worthy.

"Whatever makes you feel uneasy is not for you," he confirmed.

Consequently, our philosophies converged in many ways. We acknowledged that life subsists in the spirit, undeniably the spirit is life. Someone may be physically dead but not necessarily spiritually. And those summoning so-called familiar spirits are not rousing the dead but spirits of the fallen.

"Lingering wraiths are not dead people," SS insisted. "Spirits of the dead quickly return from whence they came. It's not the same with regards to angels and demons; they are unconstrained by a physical body. But spirits are alive including you and me and we are beholding to the Grand Spirit for we belong to him," he proclaimed.

"Ah, so orderliness is implied," I determined.

Spirits have ranks with Paraclete being the boss; probably angels next. I would guess that humans are below angels, but above animals (which are above plants and other subordinate life forms). In spite of this we can graduate to a higher class, second only to Christ himself. I'm not clear where solipsists fit in. But inanimate objects or celestial bodies, I doubt it. They are not alive, are they? However, some Natives proposed that the earth mother had a spirit and the river and mountains too.

"These beautiful natural phenomena radiate no living psychic aura," professed the oracle. "Therefore, they do not possess a soul or a spirit."

Even so, it is a spiritual domain in which we live as much as physical. We are surrounded by spirits some bad some good. Humans can choose to be one or the other. It is not a simple matter of adding up the good points, subtracting the bad, and determining the resultant valence. It boils down to the inspiration of the heart. Humans inherently know to do right but insist on doing wrong from the start. We can choose the good despite the presence of original sin because people share a common morality. That's the way we were made but not the way we behave. Whether a person is righteous or not depends on the path he or she seeks upon reaching the age of accountability. Everyone sees the honest and decent way but not all acknowledge it. And who points the way more accurately than Messiah?

Some rebuff morality out of hand assuming that science disallows it. And they also dismiss spirituality assuming the whole kit and caboodle is material. Not very scientific is it, to reject outright the vastness of that which exists outside of the physical? They will snub morality as law because they don't want to be held responsible, while others advertise their high moral standards as if that alone can save them. Either way they miss out because redemption and salvation are gifts that cannot be earned or bought. Studying the world religions, I determined one fundamental difference between the Christian worldview and others: Nothing short of perfection can earn a ticket to paradise. And only Christ will ever meet that standard; he paid it forward for those who desire admittance to his kingdom if only they submit to him. In no way are mortals capable of attaining this prize through works.

Incidentally, living beings without a discerning mind are intrinsically noble as well. You can teach them to be evil only because they don't know any better (i.e., they lack discernment). I had a great dog when I was young; he was gentle and sweet. My buddy trained his dog to be vicious and mean claiming it would make him a better watchdog and protector. But it didn't, because a dog instinctively knows how to protect and watch; that's what they do, better than most other animals and even many humans. And they can be conditioned to obey their master who becomes the alpha dog to them. My dog was superior because he didn't growl at everybody and he didn't bark all night long; but when he sensed danger, anger, or fear I knew it. There were no false alarms. And if someone would have come after me with violent rage my dog would have made toast out of them. Whereas my buddy's dog was mean to everybody; it barked day and night. One evening it attacked his sister and eventually had to be put to sleep. I understood dogs; I taught them to have a pleasant demeanor and I respected their natural talents. That's why the dog brigade was loyal to me. I miss them. Sometimes I felt more at home with the dogs than with society.

Beings more powerful than humans exist that possess the gift of discernment. Malevolent ones are called demons and live among us, but many are incarcerated in the bottomless pit. They will be released someday for a stretch and a half. The benevolent ones are called angels and live elsewhere but come to visit occasionally. I remember one pulled me out of a flooding channel when I was four; all of a sudden there he was and I was safe, and then he wasn't. You may have bumped into them but probably didn't recognize who they were. Perhaps they were disguised as someone familiar (dead or alive), or possibly a stranger helped you and then you never saw her again. Both angels and demons can speak to us somehow, maybe to our inner being at a level below consciousness. It could be that evil spirits are the source of disturbing and decadent dream content. And that is a mystery. SS tried to unravel it for me.

"There are many levels of consciousness," he maintained… "It's comparable to an iceberg, where the part that is seen is only the tip and appears harmless but below the surface looms an unseen and unbelievably boundless mass of energy. We call the alert brain consciousness and we hold it highly functional, but subconscious depths are progressively more versatile and accommodating."

Now the religion of solipsists obliges the notion of individual and group memories spanning the historical record of personal experience to that of close relations, ancestry, genus, world, and perhaps galaxy. Though SS doesn't buy into it, he is convinced that all sensory data are retained in memory, even that which is not perceived. I would agree that somewhere at the deepest levels is where spirits, dominions, and God become accessible and conceivably other dimensions or universes. Thus, thought is the door to the soul and that opening goes on forever as long as there is life.

"How can there possibly be room for it all?" I questioned.

I can comprehend the transfer of data to lower echelons (often referred to as long term memory); it's analogous to rehearsing for a test or a performance. I can understand how experiences that go farther back in time may reside at increasing depths. I can envision a distributed neural network comprised of partitions that classify objects, categorize situations, or provide lists like the names of every mademoiselle in which I've pursued carnal knowledge. But it's puzzling to me how a mind trapped in this insignificant prison we call a body can be capable of greater feats of cognition, memory, information acquisition and reorganization not to mention dreaming. And to top that off could there be a capacity for spiritual consciousness that encompasses the entire chronology of the species? There has to be a link that authorizes admittance to the larger database. The entirety cannot abide in every mind can it?

Furthermore, memory is fallible; its components become fragmented over time. Seldom is an entire experience stored in one place in the brain; rather the data are distributed at multiple levels among the neural nodes with similar informational constraints. The original event is rarely retrievable in its entirety and that's why people make mistakes in remembering. When only a subset of the contents is available, we tend to confabulate, inventing a picture or theory that will logically fill the gaps. Sometimes missing data are replaced using inputs that are not factual thereby altering the very substance of the memory.

Perception is not a complete picture. Likewise, memory reconstruction is not an exact process so don't rely on the validity of bygone experiences. People who think they can retrieve memory with high clarity are probably embellishing it; a great deal of detail would make it suspect in my book. Self-assurance, confidence, and excruciating detail do not correlate with accuracy. I would seek outside verification before I placed any stock in an old or passing memory or even a recent sensation. Besides, personal experience is not a generalizable representation of reality or the universe. SS warned me about these matters when he was teaching me to hypnotize myself. It's easy to coach yourself or another into accepting things that are untrue, by presenting rational explanations as you attempt to link disparate fragments.

"Memory resembles an elevator in a huge shopping mall," he taught, "with innumerable floors that can be revealed one at a time or simultaneously. You can illuminate several stores at diverse levels while the activation array spreads to those that sell the type of goods you seek. Once you locate the information of interest it filters to the top where your conscious mind can work with it. In this manner you find what you need without searching the entire databank which is arranged hierarchically by category. Try employing verbal cues to access the visual field and speed up the process. There really is no limit to the archive; the only limitation is time but that restriction has less impact within the subconscious."

"Now wait a minute," I countered, "I don't have the capability to manipulate that much information simultaneously, and I rightly don't profess, want or need to know everything."

"Rest assured it can be revealed, but not necessarily by your own power," he avowed. "You have no idea what is out there; more than meets the eye I assure you. Most of it is missed. If you center your focus, you'll notice events you hadn't before. For example, wave your hand in front of your eyes. It is not a smooth pattern but a series of snapshots or motion picture frames. If you could narrow your focus to the utmost you would be able to see right through your hand, as it is not solid but an accumulation of atoms that are loosely packed."

I couldn't see from the glare, contiguous beams scattering into every fissure. Too many colors to notice one; pigments coming together into a mass of blackness. Shadows produced pictures which changed with the slightest movement, making a scene overcrowded with apparitions. I couldn't walk because the path wouldn't keep still; it wriggled like an inchworm. The blockade was tumbling and turning, causing me to sidestep and lose my bearings. I had no equilibrium, experiencing an intensifying case of vertigo. The milieu, teeming and echoing with sounds, permeated my eardrums; the whispering breeze resounded with the strength of thunder and the spine-chilling shrill of the tornado was heard as a sniffle. None were discernable for they were coincident and ubiquitous, blending into steady meaningless racket. The afferent sensations were inundating: tepid, chilly, stinging, panging, pulsating. The only thing I felt was incongruous. I smelled smoke; or sweet; no, musty; or maybe flowery; yet bitter to the taste, though somewhat tart, while kind of brackish. I attempted to describe it but it came out jumbled and unsavory, like moldy salad dripping with stale dressing tossed into the air. I figured I'd fashion it into a monument but I fumbled as if wrestling a greased mackerel. Suddenly, every cell in my body fired simultaneously; I went into spasms and crumpled like wrapping paper.

I queried myself again, "Do we have the self-sufficiency to tap all these resources, or are some avenues of experience one-way streets that enter from the outside?" The answer: I produce psychic energy that can be channeled into physical, mental, and spiritual expression. I would argue it is very rare for the human mind to regularly appreciate the deeper levels of consciousness but I admit I loitered there when seeking essential truths. Such exploration enabled a realization of the wonders of God and his truth. And shouldn't truth be absolute? How can we know with certainty but by the omniscient, comforting, hallowed, and everlasting Paraclete?

There is unchecked power in the depths of the soul. For example, psychologists allege that physical pain is three quarters mental so you should be able to reduce the hurt by at least 75 percent if you concentrate on something else. But if you dwell on the pain it will feel that much worse. In the same manner you can increase sensation from the perceptual window via concentration. SS taught me to do this using meditation. I've known others that do it better. When my grandfather became terminally ill, I visited him regularly. He was able to block 100 percent of the excruciating pain that emanated from his cancer-ridden bones. There was no type or dosage of drugs that would alleviate his suffering only his will to do it. The doctors were flabbergasted. I, for one, was not surprised for he was a man strong in spirit.

"How much pain do you feel now on a scale of one to ten?" the doctor asked.

"Zero," he responded (off the scale). Then he smiled, shut his eyes, said goodbye, and expired. That was the one loss that never traumatized me. He had no fear of death. He knew the Way and showed it to me. And I know that I will see him again. I can't give you a reason how I know I just do.

We possess untapped power, not of the intellect but the spirit. It is our higher power; not far apart from the highest power but clearly magnitudes weaker. If you seek God, he will give you a taste of it. One does not uncover this power by any logical means but by getting a sense of the potential; not as a perception but as a surge of pure vitality. If you have discerned the presence of the Lord within your soul you know exactly what I am talking about.

Hence the eternal sentience, where the Almighty's authority is omnipotent and unchallengeable; where predestination means the future was and the past is. Everything is complete from beginning to end. God's history is infinite backwards, forwards, and laterally; 360 degrees times 360 degrees encompassing all directions: greater than the endlessness of the heavens, the temporal realm, and the prospect of parallel expanses. If it could be computed, his omnipresence would be infinity to the power of infinity.

God created everything visible and invisible, from the most distant red giant to the closest white dwarf; each of which gels into one cohesive and complex coexistence without which human survival would be impossible. Every ingredient of our universe including space dust, supernovae, galaxies, black holes, comets, stars, the sun, moon, planets, atomic constructions, matter, energy, momenta, and associated celestial events are perfectly configured and coordinated. Muse upon the precise composition, proportion, and distribution of cosmic elements, molecular bodies, cell building materials, and genetic structures promoting life. These thousands of components with their relative proximities, densities, compositions, movements, and interactions are perfectly calibrated to produce an idyllic environment which supports life forms found on Earth. Deviation by one percent or less from any of these variables negates the atmosphere and climate for us to exist much less thrive. The probability this perfect calibration occurs anywhere else in the universe, at this particular epoch of space and time, is exceedingly smaller than you are in proportion to the cosmos. Everything is twirling from electrons to galaxies, and possibly the universe. And it all revolves around you and me. In days of old it was blasphemous to assert that the earth circled the sun; theologians would not permit viewpoints conflicting with the earth being the center of the universe. Well they kind of missed the whole point; as have scientists who gag at the anthropic principle (defined above) or redefine it to fit an atheistic worldview.

Take for example the billions of letter codes locked into every single microscopic cell, containing specifications and schematic information necessary to generate a living, reproducing, and self-repairing person, all orchestrated into one complex sequence. This very blueprint of your existence is contained in each of the trillions of cells in your body; and therein resides a DNA strand containing enough data to fill a very large library. Is this random or designed? Isn't it quirky how the basic and most elementary component of our physicality is possibly the most complex? It is exceedingly more intricate than the entire cardiopulmonary system which is the largest arrangement in the body. Reductionists must cringe at the fact that it doesn't get simpler; in living systems smaller means more complicated. Even our central processor is a straightforward organization with sensory receptors intricately connected to an astonishingly amalgamated neural grid, residing in a brain weighing only a few pounds. Yet it is more complicated, efficient and capable than the largest supercomputers in the world. Or contemplate the eye, itself a miniature brain which can process a million inputs per second; undoubtedly there is more sensed by the eye than perceived. We probably miss at least 90 percent of reality, even with the greatest of willful effort. On the other hand, if we perceived 90 percent it would blow our minds.

Did you know that your brain is comprised of billions of neurons each one connected to tens of thousands of others, creating elaborate compositions of activity that transfer data at high speeds, upwards of tens of billions of computations per second even when you are asleep? And the complexity of the system becomes more intricate as you move from the containing systems to their components: brain, eye, cell, and neuron. Not unrelated to our universe where heavenly bodies are interconnected, interdependent, and counterbalanced each perfectly synchronized in space by various unseen forces.

Yet skeptics believe there are alternate explanations overshadowing the appearance of intelligent design. They refuse to admit that aptitude, knowledge, and power exist which are greater than measurable or imaginable. They postulate it was finetuned via mindless chemical, biological or other physical processes occurring naturally. This seems inane to me because such laws cannot explain the origin of thought or even ethics. It must be the other way around. Physical laws do not create a purpose-driven life; intelligence and consciousness do. Which is it: nothing can create everything or everything can create something? There is nothing in this physical universe that can recreate the present reality if reality began in a single instant of time.

Perceptually Perplexed

On rare occasions creationism is mulled over by the naturalists, but the design of the universe is criticized as if scientists could do a better job than the Lord God. They pose the question, how could a loving God possibly allow evil, disease, degeneration, suffering, and death? Why indeed? He is the cure for these things. Who can identify evil without understanding goodness? But people notice malevolence everywhere and wonder where God is, though it is we who are responsible for most of the evil. God certainly is not in the evil; he is the opposite of it. Constant exposure to immorality will harden the heart, but the Holy Father can soften it. Love unstiffens the stubbornness doesn't it? It also counters the evil which leads to suffering; but suffering is short-lived while freedom lasts forever.

The epitome of love and holiness was exhibited by Christ on the cross. He made the ultimate sacrifice to destroy evil, exhibited in the sin and impurity that we ourselves are guilty of but which he is not. So where is God? Where indeed! When you witness evil, suffering and death look up as if standing at the foot of the cross, and you will know these to be the works of humankind. And it will move you towards the works of Christ. You can't say that God doesn't know suffering; he endured personal anguish, torment, grief, and horror not to mention the accumulated desperation of everyone that will ever live. He is the standard by which perfection is measured and to which evil is contrasted.

If anyone should be disallowed freedom of choice it is those who deny there will be judgment. God is good; nobody else can claim that title. And the world he created was initially good until mankind ruined it with sin. But it will be good again at the restoration of his kingdom. "Whatever; goodness is relative," doubters argue. Yes, it is relative when compared to God's flawless justice. But when it comes to disobedience is anyone not guilty? Everybody needs to be redeemed but you must desire it from God. And he will appoint the advocate who will plead your case.

God intends to destroy evil. Why not now you may ask? Because there is still a chance for a great many. He will save others out of this tumultuous and backsliding world if they trust in his Son. He might spare the city for a period to free the one who will accept his righteousness. If God was to destroy evil outright then nobody could be saved. But he has shown everyone the way of salvation and given us the option. You can choose God's way and he will choose you out of this world; or choose the way of the world and perish with it. God doesn't want to condemn anyone; but he will not forbid those to be interred with their sin if they'd rather. There are consequences both positive and negative, so choose carefully and selflessly and don't put it off. For the end is nigh when sin, evil, disease, and death will be eradicated from the universe and from the essence of our being. God is reserving heaven for those who accept the righteousness of Christ in exchange for the evil they have done.

Sin is predominantly a human condition; it does not proceed from God though humans do. Christians cannot commit pernicious deeds in Jesus's name because claiming divine inspiration would run contrary to the act. Sure, Christians do wrong like everybody else. But our walk is to follow in Christ's footsteps not to merit his forgiveness since nobody can. Yes, we will fail again and again, but do not give up because you can improve with practice. In time the changes will be readily apparent to you and to others who observe your character and good deeds. Many who profess to be Christians are not following Christ sincerely (as evidenced by the Inquisition, Crusades, abortion clinic bombers, self-righteous braggarts, people that think they can earn salvation by their works, etc.). In addition, how can one be doing God's work if it is not in accordance with God's will? Therefore, not everyone who says they are Christians will make it home. The pious may think they can sin with impunity but I've got news for them.

All world religions and belief systems have produced radicals among their leaders and followers who have committed atrocities under the guise of their faith, be it deistic, pantheistic, atheistic, or theistic. Such acts are never justified because they are against God's law. People may regard religious terrorism as righteous in their own minds but are already declared guilty in the court of Christ. He is the very essence of love so anyone pointing to acts of evil done in God's name is mistaken. We emulate Jesus by radiating love and sacrificing our lives for others in his name (not the other way around). Morality equates to our basic admiration and esteem for human life instilled in each one of us by the Father. We have a propensity to protect that life and sacrifice our own life to defend the innocent, or sacrifice another if their intent is to destroy innocent life.

Unconditional love and personal sacrifice are not rational or natural, they are guided by the spirit. These, esteemed colleagues, pave the road to enlightenment and are the motivation for morality, defined as the regard for all creatures in general and humankind in particular. Morality is based on the foundation of perfect love, a spiritual concept. Reason without spiritual guidance, while it may allow scientific exploration, will result in narrowminded interpretations and a weak foundation of truth and right. Such reasoning will ignore that the needs and will of others are equally important to one's own (if it is given any importance at all). Yet it should be self-evident to anyone the consequences of sin: decadence, destruction, and death (i.e., the fall of man). Whereas the opposite also is true: the benefits of virtue are prosperity, sanity, and justification. Mischief leads to misery; morality to mercy.

The spiritual exists apart from the physical or natural. It is written: God respired with the breath of life and man became a living soul. The soul is the source of discernment, inductive reasoning, creativity, morals, and free will. It is what makes us different than any other genus germinated on this planet.

Emotion and intuition are expressive, unpredicted by any laws but relevant to the interaction of soul, surroundings and situation, and the physical with the spiritual. Feelings and thoughts produce selective attention, individual realities, differing ideas, and additional, uncontrollable variances in human behavior unexplained via science or the random movement of atoms and molecules. The assortment of possible conclusions is determined based on comparative equivalence in knowledge, evidence, and exposure. Experience may be the common denominator but it yields diverse suppositions, as many as there are people. Yet it abides by laws as well.

Unarguably, the universe is jampacked with law and order. Ever notice how the moral laws are as regimented as the physical? And the world adheres to both. But the moral laws are not byproducts of the physical ones. Try to prove that one. Where did moral laws come from? The foundation is love: the ability to care about people as God commands.

I concluded that there has to be one God and therefore one Creator. The proof I needed was right there before me. It was too beautiful, perfect, and orderly to be the result of chaos or chance. Atheism was outright illogical; I'd rather place my life savings on the lottery than buy into in that proposition. I mean seriously, what is the probability of obtaining absolute order from incoherent disorder? Test the theory. The chance of sequentially drawing four aces from a random deck of cards is less than four out of a million. Imagine the likelihood of dealing all fifty-two cards in exact sequence by suit after shuffling the deck; that proportion would be infinitesimally small. Now imagine the likelihood that the entire universe, with its trillions of synchronized gyrations, happened from dumb luck. We're talking a probability of point one with a gazillion zeroes in front of it. Try to enumerate every single relevant factor and the associated tolerances, constants, and calibrations required, not to mention the interaction effects. There is not a computer in the world that could calculate the covariance; only the mind of God.

Do you rate the evidence presented before you sufficient to conclude that everything evolved from nothing or that the material can produce the spiritual? Go ahead and acquiesce that the universe sprang into existence by itself; you cannot begin to compute the dubious probability. Like I said there had to be higher intelligence at the helm. People that deny this tend to be arrogant, pushy, and unfriendly. They conform to the scientific status quo dictated by those in power, clinging to long unproven theories and avoiding the obvious. Such rhetoric only contributes to the degradation of science and dilution of knowledge. But that has become the norm in every aspect of society, and smart people fall for it.

Hostile and shortsighted cretins have brought deceit and corruption, spewing untruths and undermining much of the good work that has been done. Harbingers already have come to warn that the unholy are among us and disaster should follow. Few have listened; if only they would notice and heed the signs. But people can be swayed by clever exposition, especially the wavering, unwitting, uncommitted, or uneducated souls unwilling to make the effort.

I've envisioned the patriarchs and prophets displayed in a magic show from then until now. It's a chronology of the Bible projected onto a movie screen; a dream which lasts roughly thirty minutes but could cover an entire month at the matinee. Luckily it was transcribed for humans by the immemorial one. My grandfather pointed this out and the angels have reinforced the association. If you concentrate you truly can feel the Holy Spirit in the expressions.

"Most sensitivity, take sexual orgasm, is felt in the psyche," SS instructed. "Contrary to popular belief however, unconscious motivation is not necessarily sexually-oriented nor drives self-destructive. It depends on your emphasis: flesh versus spirit. One's desire for freedom is not to satisfy the id but a need to be released from the sullied flesh, so as to possess the soul," SS continued.

Honestly there is strife between the flesh and the spirit. Perhaps this is the source of the death instinct upon which the spirit becomes unrestrained. Unfortunately, our rudimentary needs are confined to the material realm. But the need to survive transcends the physical. To have a body that cannot die, wouldn't that be glorious? Maybe we can and it will be. I certainly wish to be emancipated, to soar through eternity with the rest of the free spirits while still experiencing it with my senses. I must say, this was the solipsist's aspiration all along.

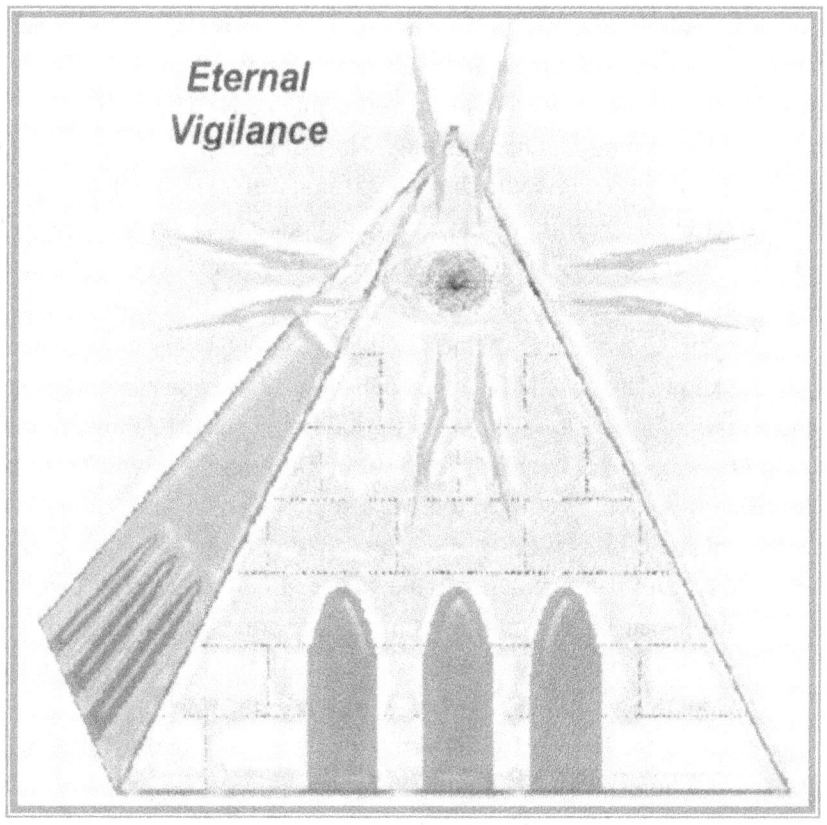

I succeeded in my dreams so it had to be achievable according to SS. In a way, my dreams have been an expression of my deepest desires; but some also reflected my worst fears. Isn't it feasible that they are related insofar as the fear of death is physical but the desire for it spiritual? Is there an unconscious motive to die as well as to live? Well maybe when the freed arrive at the resurrection, at which time death will seem momentary especially compared to forever.

"To be absent from the body is to be present with the Lord," wrote the apostle. Doesn't everybody wish for that? Doesn't the son want to grow up be like his father? A desire for mastery, superiority, and perfection could be construed as a need to be like the eternal Father who is absolute, while an inferiority complex could mean falling short. But the fact that you were brought forth in the first place proves that you are important and valuable to God. And if he was willing to sacrifice himself so you could live, shouldn't that improve your self-concept? It has been theorized that the degree of incongruence between the perfect self and the personal self will define your self-image. Wrestle to bring the two into alignment and you can obtain mental stability. Fashion your ideals to that of God's Son and you will attain immortality.

Religion, therefore, is not an invention of man to cope with our aggressive and antisocial nature but a striving of the soul to see eternity. The concept of God is an inherent notion; logical, perhaps instinctual akin to survival. The physical being aspires for permanency as does the soul. But the corruption of sin means death to the flesh so it is irrational to expect to live forever in this body. The spirit does not die however, for it is everlasting; but not unbound. Normal souls would endeavor to keep it if they wanted to live forever would they not? It stands to reason that the spirit must win the battle over the flesh. But you have to focus your energy on the spirit not deny that it is there. To triumph is to keep the soul and the solution: the flesh can be overcome by pure love.

SS has a mystical awareness of the feelings of living beings, including plants and animals. He knows they need love too. I believe God provides an abundance of it to each and every living creature. Love is the divine power of Jehovah God, who loved the world so much he created it in the first place and was willing to make a personal sacrifice to save it. We love God because he loved us first. Humans radiate this love as do other earthlings. Love others and they will love you; it's contagious. Children learn this from parents; animals likewise can be trained. The institution of marriage was established for that purpose, to magnify true love and pass it along to the offspring so it can endure for generations. People desire to have children for the same reason as God: to love and be loved, and to shower them with gifts.

How awesome is the love of God! Despite the fact that I am but a speck of dust on this planet, and the earth is but a particle in this universe of galaxies, and there may be an infinite number of viable universes out there, yet still God loves me! How could someone as powerful, glorious, and eternal as God love someone as insignificant as I? And he loves me more than anyone else has, or will, or can. He loves you too by the way, just as much. You have a Father in heaven that will do anything and everything for you and all you have to do is acknowledge him and love him back to receive it all. This is the choice God gives us: to love. His love demands that we choose, otherwise it wouldn't matter. He could have programmed robots to love him but who wants love if it's artificial? Love gives us the ability to find God and it is the basis of our faith. We believe in God's promises because we trust him, and in faith we have hope. Faith is the guarantee of that for which we hope. It is written: faith, hope and love abide, the greatest being love. This is how we can know things to be true though we cannot always explain or prove them.

Love is powerful and it certainly is energizing. Love can be shared, bestowed, revitalized, and disseminated. Love ignites, love multiplies, love amplifies; it can increase exponentially to mathematical proportions that are unimaginable, approaching that of the Holy Ghost himself. Love's energy is always accumulating, greater than five-hundred-billion suns and growing. The light of God is evidence of his love, and when he created light it shined for everyone. When he created humans, he made the light available to us all.

The theory of macroevolution epitomizes the limits of human mental capacity to construe such rapid growth in energy, and to understand the instantaneous charge of love's power. For the love of God is foreign to naysayers; they cling to an outdated theory that remains scientifically debunked. Yes, they tried faking evidence of links from a bone fragment or a tooth and created an artist's rendition that resembled a hominid and preached, "See, man evolved from apes." And though these charades have been exposed as contrived by anthropologists and illustrators, such errors still exist in science books and are expounded to the masses as confirmation. Meanwhile, many scientists refuse to abandon their naturalistic stance by proposing rapid transition or punctuated evolution, both unprecedented exaggerations given the unadulterated absence of demonstrable proof. The missing link for them will always be to acknowledge and accept God's eternal love. But they have scrapped that possibility a priori, forcing theories to conform to the antithesis. Many scientific postulates break down because they cannot be resolved with the physical laws. If bosons, leptons, quarks, neutrinos, dark matter, dark energy, and quantum strings exist God only knows. Mustn't one believe in miracles to trust in particles that are waves, photons being in two places at once, universal butterfly and domino effects, multiverse, and macroevolution?

Concepts such as microevolution, survival of the fittest, and natural selection, however valid, are oppositional with respect to aberrant human behavior, such as genital mutilation, sexual perversion, murder, and psychopathic deviancy. These are conscious choices that are hardly natural or meant to perpetuate the species, and undeniably not what one should expect from a highly evolved, intelligent, and civilized organism. Further, materialism is incapable of accounting for such behaviors as altruism, charity, faith, changing an opinion, placebo effects, mysticism, and dreaming; much less out of body or near-death experiences, or placing oneself in peril to save another. Such events have ineffable, temporal, spontaneous, symbolic, reactive, and spiritual features (like hope and love).

Here is insight: love is creativity in a comprehensive sense. It promotes healing, it conceives life, and it fosters peace. Love can find beauty in everything the Lord created for it is excellent. The works of man embody the feelings of those who forged them; the works of God too. Manmade objects do not generate their own energy however, but instead can exhaust it as in the case of money. Materialism, the love of money, and unnatural desires are contrary to unconditional love which is spiritual.

If the power of goodness is love; the power of wickedness is fear. To love goodness is to hate evil. Thus, hate is not the opposite of love, but fear. The two cannot abide simultaneously any more than there can be good in evil or darkness in light. Thus, love is positive energy; but fear depletes energy and is therefore counterproductive. Through fear the meditations of man are captured by the wretched one. Through love man is set free. Love can consume fear, anger, sadness, and guilt; similarly, a gentle candlelight can devour the black of night. Love is your higher power; love is the highest power.

Love slipped into a woman's womb in the middle of the tumult and was born into an undeserving world. He studied the people around him yet understood the entire universe. An omniscient mind shoved into human form or a case of mistaken identity? He knew an awful lot about human nature to the extent he predicted his own fate; and what an unpleasant portion it was. But everything turned out for the better because love prevailed in the end. His unfailing love overcame even death. Why would so much fear fester over one man's life and philosophy? Interesting how his life still impacts the world today which commemorates the anniversaries of his birth, death, and his resurrection; on those days more love is shared than the rest of the year. Clearly, these three events have had a most significant impact on humankind.

Question: How do you make love last? Answer: by giving. Giving how? When others give up you cannot give way. If others give out you must give in. Give it over and again, but don't expect to have it given back. Give from the heart; give all you can. Give freely for a gift is free; if you anticipate a return it doesn't count as giving. Love and giving are, by definition, free. By and by, the love will return to you in munificence. And don't neglect to forgive for it is an act of love, "give" being the root word.

Love fixes everything especially the broken heart and the corrupted mind. There is nothing else on this orb that can do it. The secular world seeks only material explanations; it cannot comprehend the spirit. Materialism cannot satisfy the soul, it can only appease the flesh. And that is momentary. But spiritual fulfillment is complete and everlasting. Therefore, love conquers the world (that would be the unconditional variety of love). This world can provide only one permanency: death; whereas *agape* love overcomes. God's love existed before we did; it is a blessing to us and it did not evolve.

Thus, love is the greatest of spiritual gems. Everything starts and ends with love. It is followed by faith and hope. Other spiritual gifts that spring forth from these include peace, joy, patience, honor, trust, respect, kindness, gentleness, mercy, sobriety, temperance, courage, and humility. SS coached, "A little bit of humility goes a long way while haughtiness is an obstruction to getting anywhere. Those who exalt themselves will be disgraced. Those who criticize and disparage the righteous will be embarrassed. Power mongers who insist on domination will be debased. Evil doers will be shamed. Terrorists will live in perpetual fear."

God's Son came from humble beginnings though he was King of kings. He deserved glory but would not accept any until his mission was accomplished. Don't brag about how great you are but how great he is. For everything that you are is because of him; and everything you own is thanks to him. And he will always be with you through the end of the age and beyond if you want.

Spirituality is not from this world. However, it is the primary component of character, and it promotes happiness. Gramps taught me that people who display good character will command the respect and admiration of others; but people of low estate will never be happy and they will detest persons that are. He advised me not to intermingle with them. "Strive for spiritual riches and you will be successful in all efforts," he preached… "The Good Book says if you chase earthly riches you will never have enough and what little you have will be taken from you."

Materialism was never a barrier for me since the accumulation of my assets and wealth would fit into a thimble. Worldly possessions are overrated anyhow. Prestige is never attained by living beyond your means. I grew up a pauper and I'll die one, but only by earthly standards. I'm a billionaire with respect to intangible treasures (I deem myself richly blessed). Likewise, the things I value are protected and insured. They are kept securely at my mansion in the sky. I haven't visited it yet but it won't be long before I do. At least I know the way there. Do you?

The trap is to think that everything is about you. Some people worship themselves. I am tired of those that endlessly try to impress, especially themselves (they must constantly remind themselves how superior they are in order to massage their egos). They don't pass a single mirror without pausing for inspection. Obviating embarrassment is the prime directive. It's the vanity of looking good. The solipsist insists that most play the game, but for many it's not a game. Every hair must be in the right place, or they'll redo the entire coiffure. They say you simply cannot put a price on luxury, status, or attractiveness. And they expend enormous amounts of energy, time, and resources to that end. (Of course, everyone has some degree of natural appeal as well as vanity.)

Every environment in which more than one person is present is an opportunity for comparison. It's a social situation even if the actors are isolated from one another. These people immediately assume that they are being evaluated and thus must look better than anyone else who is present. However, it is God who is evaluating them. But they always look good in their own minds. And they'll put others down to appear higher. "Ha," she tells herself. "My makeup looks better than that woman. And look, those shoes don't match her purse; how utterly out of vogue!" (It matters not that the poor lady was so sick she barely found the energy to dress that morning and make it to the clinic.) And when their neighbors bought a lawn ornament her husband purchased a bigger, more expensive one. How dare them, trying to show off!

Vainglory does not compel me. Stress on the other hand has been my nemesis. It's a never-ending struggle to maintain composure counting the traumas, crises, conflicts (internal and external), pain, fears, and frustrations. Not to mention the usual stuff: life changes, wishes not being granted, everyday pressures of childhood, parenting, aging, school, work, etc. It's a wonder the entire human race isn't neurotic. I mean, who doesn't experience anxiety or worry over these matters? And though I rely on divine intervention to deliver me from my anguish I still end up losing sleep over it. In that regard I am not alone. It's a distraction from spiritual peace. That's when the tempter strikes, when we are most vulnerable. I dream of being placed in a bow and shot like an arrow over the chasm for I wish not to cross it. But I do have someone to carry me.

One of the most difficult tasks subsequent to faith is to stay in the spirit. When people turn to their maker it is usually when they are troubled; but they ignore him the rest of the time. It's unsatisfactory to love God only when it's convenient; it should be an all-or-none commitment. But it's so easy to forget he's there or to take him for granted, especially when happenings are running smoothly or when we are being entertained. What is harder is to acknowledge his presence in every aspect of life, big or small, awful or wonderful. Instead we get stressed over trivialities and sweat blood when the going gets rough. And all the while the Lord is standing by to bring us through, if only we would ask. That's it; ask, believe, and it's done. It's comforting to know that I can call and he'll answer. As I said before, if you want him to come you immediately will realize he is already there. He is a personal friend of mine. You can be his friend too; and he will be the best friend you ever had.

Without faith you will never know he's beside you much less acknowledge his presence. If you didn't think he is, you wouldn't look for him in the first place. But he is unceasingly there in spirit and you cannot hide. He sees everything you do, hears everything you say, and knows everything you think. You may as well accept it. His spirit is the source and sustainer of your faith and life. It will empower you to understand phenomena that cannot be described scientifically (such as God and why you believe). Faith is what gives you the hope of living forever in paradise; without faith you would think it impossible. There always is hope as long as you believe. Don't hope for things you cannot gain; but do remember that things not possible in this world will be possible in the next, and things not possible by your own power are possible with God even now. Hope for things to come, not things past like taking back something you said or did. That requires forgiveness.

Let faith be your politics. It matters not if you are liberal, conservative, or independent. It matters that you are a unique child of God. There is nothing impossible with God; so then, all things are possible. With him everything works; without him nothing does. Depend on his grace and you will not fail; depend on yourself and sooner or later the bottom will drop out.

Look at history. When the Lord provided the foundation, nations prospered; when he did not, they faltered. That was the case when the Israelites were conquered. My native land has been another not so shining example in recent years. Have we forgotten what we stand for? There is no such thing as separation of church and state. You can't separate your beliefs from your thoughts and deeds. If you try you are a hypocrite. Matters of government should be guided by devotion not vice-versa. We the people should control the government not the contrary.

Once, a great country was founded by men of faith who stood on the principles of liberty and equality, establishing high standards of conscience and fairness. They acknowledged that humans possess unalienable rights awarded by our Creator, rights which societies have no authority to deny to anyone. And under that guidance the country progressed surpassing every other. But leaders digressed and decided to recreate the nation according to a foreign ideology. A great orator once pronounced that leaders should be subject to the governed not the other way around. Citizens never gave their consent for the rules these new ideologues devised. I ask you this: What about electing governors that place the interest of the country ahead of their own and voting out those who don't?

What happens when you remove God from the equation? Scrutinize the consequences: failure in education, travesty in justice, immorality in government, civil war. In days of old a leader was required, above all, to have strong spiritual convictions. Not so nowadays; in fact, quite the opposite. Spiritual health is declining to the extent that we are sick as a nation. Malfeasance in government fosters corruption among the governed. And a tainted citizenry means those voted into office will be crooked. No wonder matters are getting out of hand in the land.

Certainly, advancing the kingdom of heaven has to be good for the country. There used to be heads of state that operated within the constraints of God's law. Have they forgotten who they serve? Instead we are duped by arrogant narcissists that rule and govern in accordance with their own will and to placate their selfish interests. They are intolerable and I refuse to submit to them because a higher authority overshadows them (which they invariably refuse to recognize). God's verdict must rule in their hearts before they can be depended upon to do what's right. SS can tell who has it and who doesn't by looking at them. For us, we must judge by their words and deeds whether or not they respect the truth and its source.

Ultimately, accountability will be attested before the Lord's judgment seat. And he will administer justice in accordance with the truth. Don't hide from the truth or it will find you out and bite you in the bum. Accept it now and live by it. It's better to settle it now than later. If you do, the truth always will be music to your ears. And whenever something conflicts you will know that it is false.

Truth by definition requires an indisputable correspondence with reality. And such truth is universal. Truth cannot change but our understanding can. Cause and effect are relative to the situational conditions and the changing influence of contributing factors. When the necessary prerequisites are met a relationship between the two is evident. But rarely does that provide incontrovertible truth, except in the case of God being the cause of reality and everything we experience in it. This is because he is the first cause. God is a moral absolute. True morality also is universal; it is not relative. While people may tolerate some infractions more than others, that implies morality not relativism.

Have you noticed that a great number of people prefer untruths? They couldn't see the truth if it was painted on their eyeballs, for it is an impediment to them and their mortal strivings. Most people purport to be interested in truth but many do not accept it. Some fear it, distort it, or deny it. But they will jump on the bandwagon to defend their right to be ignorant of it. They will angrily profess their lies with a clear conscience without letting you get a word in edgewise. But they will be found out because it is impossible to keep track of that many lies.

I used to be one of them but have since become enlightened. It was revealed to me as a whisper that spoke three times out of the turbulence and directly to my inner sanctum. And its voice was clearer than the amplified sermons of those self-righteous snobs that talk a blue streak but refuse to listen to anyone with another opinion. Yet they dare to judge believers of truth as well as its cause. With a forced, superficial, plastic smile they condemn me because mine is permanently etched upon my countenance and they can't wipe it off. But they only pretend to be happy because they have nothing of substance to cling to but the certainty of death.

It became apparent to me the day I was caught aboard the pirate ship, helping myself to a cache of coins looted from submerged galleons. The booty hunters were about to disembark on another expedition into the Bermuda Triangle, just as I was about to slip into the murky bay with a bag of loot. They hooked me, hauled me aboard, and bound me hand and foot in leather cords, locking me in a utility room where I sulked for two days without food or water in a puddle of urine. Then, dragging me to the starboard side of the boat, I was lashed to a rusty anchor and tossed overboard. The wetness loosened the ties and I freed myself, but I knew better than to show my face so I allowed the anchor to take me to the bottom. I could see the ship's keel overhead because the water was remarkably sheer. The scoundrels had paused to ensure I was incapacitated, so I sat in the silt with an anchor in my lap, figuring I would either drown or get harpooned if I surfaced for air. I decided I wouldn't give them the satisfaction and stayed put.

I exhaled the last of my air, shut my eyes, and began to fade. I was dreaming of making out with a beautiful red-haired lady and suddenly I shook alive. Opening my eyes, I beheld a puffing pufferfish hovering in front of me, peering at me with protruding eyes and signaling that I had another breath coming which she punctually delivered. Then she proceeded to swim to the surface and return with cheeks full of air which she transferred into mine through her beaked mouth. It was music to my lungs. She motioned for me to follow her so I did. The redhead led me into an underwater cave where it got progressively darker. I was holding that breath inside and growing faint, but I continued until everything went black. Precipitously, there was a light, very dim and dead ahead. I mustered every bit of remaining stamina and pursued that light which became progressively brighter. Before long I was refilling my lungs with precious clean air. My little friend had led me to a sunken yacht that had crashed into a dying reef. Its shattered bow was lodged firmly into the collapsed formation. Trapped in the wreckage of the stern was a set of functional scuba gear complete with a quarter tank of oxygen.

Illumination from the overhead sun crept through the transparent water and peered into the trashed cabin where I reclined. Regaining my composure, I could see the retreating ship above and knew I was being abandoned, left for dead. I removed a life vest still tied to the railing and made my way into open sea. The puffer appeared one last time with a smile and a wink before she plunged. I always thought they were menacing, being the most poisonous marine animal around these parts; she sure changed my opinion of them. Atop the wave's crest I spotted a land mass about ten miles in the distance and headed in that direction, following in the wake of the departing vessel. Once again, I had escaped death by way of miracle.

The promises of God cannot be denied and absolutely will come to pass. How do I know this? Because God is truth and truth cannot lie; otherwise there would be nothing to believe in. For if truth was uncertain it would be impossible to distinguish it from untruth. If this be the case there would be no such thing as self-determination and it wouldn't matter what choices we make. As for me, I will cling to God's promises. I choose not to stick to false hopes or place total faith in anyone else; for only the Lord can guarantee. And I will pray for patience as that is one area in which I am sorely lacking. The hardest part is the timing. Some tasks I want to put off until later and others I don't want to wait until then. Impatience is a double-edged sword that will slice you up one side and down the other. But with faith you'll know the right time because it will be God's time, which was preset before time began. And you will praise him when it happens and appreciate it more.

We own spiritual gifts which help us overcome roadblocks in our pathway, those that obscure our vision of the finish line or impede our progress to becoming all we can. Ask any track star that runs hurdles. Don't dwell on the hurdles or you'll trip over them. Focus on the goal and the path ahead. Strive for the ideal self which leads to perfection, the example being Christ who gives us what we need to maximize our full potential. His accommodations are free and arrive copiously by spiritual awareness, understanding, and receptiveness. They are spiritual tools for positive growth and change.

The greatest of these is love which conquers the fear, such as being afraid of failure, worried that something bad will happen, unsure or scared of the unknown, or acceding that you are unable or it will be too hard. Love changes everything; and it energizes faith, providing confidence in the belief that anything is possible and that God makes good on his promises. Faith changes your mind; and it defeats disbelief. If you place your faith in the Lord there will be no room for doubt; it is a sure thing: abundant life. If you risk that faith on others, yourself, or the unknown you may be disappointed: no guarantees. Hope is an extension of faith which provides assurance. Hope is the vision of the possibilities and opportunities that lie ahead founded on God's pledges and an unfailing belief in them. Hope empowers us to overcome despair even when defeat seems eminent, thereby strengthening us with the will to refrain from desperate measures that are unproductive and self-destructive.

According to the great evangelist, if we meet these challenges head-on and move beyond them, we gain experience, develop character, become stronger in hope, and learn patience. Patience surmounts frustration and exasperation. We are reminded by the wise king to wait for the right time. Every purpose under heaven has a season he wrote, but we do not know the purpose or the time. And although we make plans God's purpose always prevails, working towards our good in the end. Thus, any experience has value including the trauma, loss, and pain; it is part of your preparation for a greater cause. Don't give up. Persevere and these will be revealed: your purpose, your destiny, your becoming. Spiritual treasure is the reward and the timing will be impeccable. You will not fear death, confident that it also will occur at the right time; and you will be ready knowing it ushers in another beginning.

The grave is not the definitive destination. Death is but an interlude during which we wait. Every spirit returns to God who will sort them out and divide them. The house of underworld has two stories. I suggest you place your reservations in advance and leave your departure date open. When it's your time you will check into a deep sleep. Your next breath will be when your eyes open and you see the Lord face to face. It will either be frightening or enlightening, depending on where you spent the intermission. I rather look forward to my Sabbath rest during which I will be kept safe, sound, and secure in the presence of the Lord of Hosts. Is there any safer place than that? I wonder if it will be possible to dream, or if I will experience awareness. I know this much: I will awaken to live with the Lord forever. Take note that if you wake up in the other place the second death will be your worst nightmare. That's why you want to be in the right place before you leave this world, or you will be in the wrong place in the next.

In order to find God, you must believe in something you cannot verify with your corporeal endowments. These are the restrictions of materialists and naturalists: God and his ways are immaterial and supernatural. Challenge them to explain truth, knowledge, thought, morality, or time in physical or scientific terms; see if they can expound the soul, spirit, or spiritual gifts such as love, faith, hope, joy, and patience. Such wonders are revealed in the nonmaterial entity we call the mind; they are not defined in or by biochemical arrangements of matter. Intelligence resides only in a mind capable of thought. A mind can cause the assembling and configuring of matter; matter cannot arrange itself into a mind. When I witness the amazement of birth I am reminded of God. When I behold the beauty of a waterfall, I recognize God. When I read the Holy Bible, I draw near to God. Every time I think that God is the reason, do you suppose the exact same arrangement of neural activity is present in my brain? The context and conditions, the mental and physical state, the biology and chemistry, each are varied though my conclusion is the same—God.

If the brain could be artificially manipulated you could make anyone believe in God, even an atheist. Just create the exact evoked brain potentials in the same quantity and arrangement that caused me to think of God. Yeah that'll work. No, the atheists opt not to believe, conceding that they haven't their own thoughts because the physiological processes make them think. How convenient, denying anything and everything to avoid being judged or accused; it reeks of predetermination. Try this: claim the devil made you, an equally untenable position. Well if you can't think for yourself what qualifies you to be an expert, a scholar, or a philosopher?

Consequently, everything is meaningless at least for you. So why bother? Wake up; such arguments are self-defeating. They come from those maintaining they've cornered the market in logic and intellect and are therefore qualified to preach to the masses about scholarship and causality (much better than those silly, misguided, and nasty Christians). It is a projection of their insecurity. I feel perfectly safe and secure without them and with God.

KINGDOMS

Kingdom: a political entity in which one party dominates. There are kingdoms in nature, society, and the heavenly realm. Not all are ruled by kings or queens. In fact, oftentimes nobody knows who is in charge (or everybody thinks they are). Such is the dubiety of domination. A word to the wise: fate can be fatal. It will happen within the span of a single generation (possibly your generation). Yet few are taking notice, though the beginning and end are plainly demarked as well as various points in-between.

Human beings can be considered members of the animal kingdom, for we are mammalian lifeforms that oversee the rest of the animals. Unfortunately, the planet we share also is the domain of powerful devils and demons. So, who really is in charge? Well God is, of course. Interestingly, the lion is referred to as the king of beasts, not the human. And the sovereign Lord of all is referred to as the Lion of Judah; he took part in the creation of mankind.

Going back to when I was still a virgin, Adam called us together. He pointed at me and named me "dog" although in modern terms I was more a wolf. I made friends with man; for a time, I was his best friend until woman showed up. I did not defer to the lion; I saw man as superior to the lion and myself equal to the lion. And there existed angels, superior to the man; well, at least in power. And there was our Creator who reigned over the heavens, the earth, creatures and creation.

I also became friends with the golden eagle, the buffalo, and the mountain lion. They turned out to be one individual who in due course exposed his true identity: a cherub named Gabriel. He had a fourth face, that of a cherub which disguised himself as any human or animal. In fact, he exhibited several such faces to me: my grandmother, my father, SS, Lany, Pete, and an arctic wolf who I understood to be my first cousin. Thus, he altered his appearance to suit the situation and the message, the situation being mostly uncertain but the message absolutely certain for it was straight from God.

I interacted with that cherub, who pointed out he had three cherub brothers. One was in charge of security and another administration. He was the messenger, like Mercury only way more versatile. Then there was the spirit brother Lucifer, who was a meanie; like the brothers, he was capable of changing faces and names though he used them to deceive and to accuse. I never met the eldest two, but I had my interactions with the younger and nothing good ever came out of that. He had the gall to come to my house disguised as SS, but he couldn't intercept the bad vibes I sensed when I slammed the door in his face. Their cousins were seraphim, way too numerous to count or name; armies of them, but you could look upon only one face at a time. Gabe was friendly, kind, gentle, patient, and helpful, the exact opposite of his little brother whom I couldn't stand. While Gabe's designated job was instruction, his rival chose destruction and was rebuked by his three older brothers. However, they all verified their boss to be supreme ruler, King of kings and Lord of lords, and referred to God as Father like do I. Which would you rather have on your team?

The vile brother stampeded the buffalo, but the pleasant one calmed them. The former could drive a dog mad, but the latter could tame the dog, unto obedience. The one hated humankind and the other loved them. Which of the two was a comrade, not just to animals but also to humans? However, humans were inconsistent, with traits similar to both brothers; some would appreciate and endear the creatures, others would abuse and neglect them. The out of control humans are the ones you've got to look out for. Humans refer to animals as wild, which is the word many animals have for humans don't you know. Again, whose side are you on? You can pick only one. If you take a walk down the wild side you may forget the way back.

Without a doubt, there is a pecking order in the animal world, in civilized society, and the heavenly realm. Anyone with integrity can distinguish the good from the bad, the benevolent from the malevolent, the obedient from the disobedient, and the helpful from the hurtful. Who would you have rule over you? Personally, I cannot defer to unethical, self-absorbed, untrustworthy fiends. But governments are full of them; when governments are stupid the citizens suffer. There have been dominions, principalities, empires, and all kinds of governments, from heaven above to earth below. And though we are subjects to many, there really is one authority we have to be beholden to for he established all governments and empires, and they likewise must be beholden to his administration or they will suffer the consequences.

Empires come and go; they wax and wane. Corruption from lust, greed, and pride initiate their downfall. History has proven it: Egypt, Assyria, Babylonia, Media-Persia, Greece, Rome, the Third Reich. Did they not bite off more than they could chew? It could not be digested despite their attempts to engorge themselves further (their eyes were bigger than their stomachs you might say). But a thirst for power is never quenched. And those who are full of themselves will constantly be hungry.

You see, the human ego has a voracious appetite. And the more you feed it the more aggressively it devours. It is better not to pamper it; but don't worry it will never starve to death. If you don't keep it in a cage under lock and key it will run amok; because, while it can be contained it cannot be tamed. It can become as a hydrophobic dog that must be euthanized. This will be the demise of every kingdom built on arrogance. I knew the next one would be no different, and here it already was upon us. It was foreordained once the last of the kindly kings had been deposed.

The globe divided into quadrants. In the southwest was a dictatorship, in the northwest an oligarchy. The southeast was totalitarian, and the northeast parliamentarian. Of course, each accused the others of being wrong but none were right. There was constant competition. You'd think it was the quarterfinals in a tennis match: kingpins trying to serve aces with every stroke in order to win the world. But there was instability and shiftiness, so none prevailed.

The economic, military, and technological superiority fell to the north. The advantage of sheer numbers fell to the south. While the north struggled for regulation, the south struggled for resources. Neither was opting for peace. They talked of it, but behind the facade of a white flag there were warmongers in penthouses plotting bloodshed.

The south was envious of the north and the north covetous of the south. While Orientals longed for democracy, Americans desired socialism. Though the Ottomans wanted freedom they sought to destroy it, and though the Europeans wanted unity they intentionally undermined it. Everyone wanted what the other had and endeavored to ensure that neither would have it. What a mixed-up world. I mean, you can't have it both ways. But none would opt for the moral high ground.

The civil climate was equally uncivilized. Slavery was rampant. Betrayal was the standard. Some persons would sell out their own mothers if it netted them a fix. There was no rule of law. Governing bodies devised rules as they went along. They appeased their guilt by pushing for legalization of their illicit behavior. That's right, slacken the law making it okay to sin. They surrendered their consciences so they could meander through time in a stupor or daze, ruled by a capricious ego that could not be restrained. Under the guise of being openminded they closed their minds to God. Their ethics were pathetic.

Social turmoil was complemented by natural and unnatural calamities. Floods, famines, and asteroids had devastated East Asia and South America. Earthquakes had swallowed up metropolises in Mexico, Turkey, Japan, and China. Africa was reliving the prehistoric age from nuclear fallout; leviathan sprang again out of the poisonous Arabian Gulf. A mangled thing that exhibited human qualities also hailed from that region possessing great might and trickery. It was unsightly as sin, with a blemish on its forehead that resembled a swastika. It invaded the upper territories and progressed towards the North Sea. This prince of perdition gained notoriety as a negotiator and established a stronghold in Scandinavia. An arsenal of dreadful devices capable of mass destruction and death were the instruments of its hand. But the Lord warned us, those who set traps for others will themselves become ensnared.

Meanwhile across the oceans, Los Angeles and New York were ripening into the new Sodom and Gomorrah. LA was a diseased and decadent den of devastation and NY a corrosive and corrupt kitchen of catastrophe. Like the memory of my long-lost love, the western kingdom was about to disintegrate. But its demise would be protracted and agonizing, never to pause for remission; meanwhile the foundation was systematically eaten away, a malignant tumor permeating its core.

Degenerates were engaging in repugnant forms of sexual gratification. Accepted practices became increasingly inhumane and amoral. People were sacrificing their babies as a means of birth control and for monetary gain from embryonic stem cells. Those maintaining monogamous heterosexual relationships were the laughing stock. Their civil rights were violated and distributed among the homosexuals, bisexuals, transsexuals, and assorted perverts. The bohemians went so far as to develop a vaccine for animals to combat venereal contagions, promoting bestiality. Many were into a fecal fetish. Anatomically augmented playmates and miscellaneous phallic devices were the craze. But this was soon preempted by commerce in cadavers to pacify the growing fascination with necrophilia. If it moved it was fair game. If it didn't it was fair game. I pondered the notion that God might raze cities and leave a salty crust as in bygone days. I found that concept far less repulsive than watching them dribble like rotting gangrene.

Skipping over the continents and across the longitudes, the discontent was spreading as soft oleo over hot toast. Man's worst enemy was man. Everyone had a conflict, either with another or within themselves. Contradictory castes clashed and familial feuds festered. Warring parties were enrapt in personal or collective depletion. Major scuffles were breaking beyond the borders of Syria, Persia, and the Sinai Peninsula. These scraps were activated purely by antagonism, in which nobody won but the casualty count mounted.

Then came the big one: the Sino-Russo contest; it would propagate into an inevitable confrontation between the kingdoms of the south and north. Apparently, surveillance satellites from the two powers collided in space; both accused the other of sabotage. It was actually a solar flare that disrupted the ionosphere and confused the electronics causing orbits to decay, similar to two sleds sliding together on a patch of ice. That the meteorologists discounted the phenomenon was unclear or maybe deliberate. Regardless, the combatants dwelled on the most meaningless excuses to kindle the rivalry that existed between them; and this in the wake of an artificial alliance among the aforementioned nations framed as a threat to the West. Here was the proverbial straw that broke the camel's back. Of course, the real issue was the race for who would control the oil. For the former it was a matter of survival; for the latter it was a matter of greed. A major international fiasco was erupting and nobody would be left out.

It was after Korea and Vietnam had been reduced to islands. Everybody was required to choose a side even if you wanted them both to lose. When the Soviets brokered an alliance Iran followed suit, seeing an opening to bury their nemesis to the southwest. Europe wasn't about to lose their right to the precious ooze either, though they pretended to be neutral. Not to be outdone, the battered third world threw in with the south. The choke point was the Middle East and those plentiful reserves, which soon would be of no use to anyone due to radiological contamination. The north decimated the south, people dying in hoards; but northland losses weren't exactly minimal. I dreamt I saw a pile of corpses that buried a once fertile valley two hundred miles long; and the dream came true. One can chisel a world that befits them and those in power can bring the sculpture to life. Modern day Pygmalions they were, a real mythological phenomenon; but their creation lacked beauty.

Worldwide trade shaped the international market supervised by economists in the north. Their rules of parsimony stagnated growth (while they enriched themselves). They advocated optimism as they diverted their doughnuts into offshore bakeries. This necessitated a global police force to monitor for dirty dealings (what a hoot since they were doing those dealings). Financial institutions were on the take looking to find a way in. If they couldn't they'd blow a fiscal hole the size of a semi to create an opening.

Anarchy was in the air; autocrats and sycophants were jockeying for position. Earth's emperor was in the making, the last of eight kings and a repeat from the seven. They would hand the reins over to this maniac, a would-be despot; a conniver whose eyes were ablaze with delusions of grandeur. And the statue came to life.

Minions sharing the villainous vision gathered en masse. These geeks came right out of the woodwork. I don't know if they were clones or what but they looked identical; devotees to the creature who lock-stepped according to its every whim to be modeled in its image. They were the coldblooded ones, literally and figuratively. Like conquerors of old they were tyrannical. Like zombies they dreaded only death. Like itself, they worshipped the beast.

Changes were on the horizon. A cosmopolitan theocracy was being set in place. For eons nobody had time for spirituality; they were too busy hastily confirming the fraudulent predictions. Ironic given this very event was in fulfillment of true prophecy. Religion was a novelty; poignant inasmuch as churches had long been disbanded and edifices smashed. But theirs' was faith sans of the Lord. They concocted gods in their own likeness. How derisive for they were created in God's.

Their leaders spread disinformation and espoused dispensation, a suspicious pretension in itself. Being different earned them the right, that's how they interpreted the affair (using divinations no less). First, they outlawed shaving deeming it unnatural not to be bearded. I think they were embarrassed so they hid their faces much the same as the womenfolk, making it easier to conceal their identities. Second, they donned the traditional garb (not a practical one): colorful linen underwear, silk purple robes with black satin sashes. They adorned themselves with jewels and glitter and crowned themselves with horned tiaras. It was a sacrilege for them to bow or curtsy yet they demanded it from others. They would christen one another with salad dressing each morning and feign piety, but these were acts of defilement not contrition. Brown magic was accepted and adopted into their ritual, repackaged to imitate a sacrament. Twice a day at the stroke of twelve, animal sacrifices were reinstated in the holy temple in adulation of the abominable one. Human sacrifices came next.

Fitting I deduced, that the capital city would emerge in the same place it began, and that they would try again to build the House of Nimrod. Sheesh! Didn't they learn anything from history? What nonsense, to imagine a modern realm that is so backwards while announcing the sky is the limit. Right, let's return to the old ways of hoarding pretty little objects like the packrat does, executing nonconformists because they hold another idea, or subordinating females assuming they lack intelligence and position. There's progress for you. It was the dawn of civilization and now it was the dusk of civilization, as if the sun should set in the same place where it rises.

Journey Through Geekland

The contemptible were introduced as honorable; perversity was passed off as virtue; desecration was deemed hallowed; imprecation was spoken as a blessing; lies were presented as truth. Their incredible creed was a contradiction to everything sacred and blessed, fueled by contempt for God, opposition to his goodness, and jealousy of his mercy. Same as Lucifer they fancied themselves superior to the supreme (as if the clay can be greater than the potter). But they were beneath the putrid residue that is trodden underfoot across the killing fields.

You see, they wanted to be the chosen ones. They wanted to be elevated above the rest. They couldn't stand being left out yet they had excluded themselves. They sank the boat, didn't they? God's selection process has never been based on ethnicity or socioeconomics; membership has forever been open to all demographics. These dummies were ignored, not because of what they wanted but why they wanted it: namely lust, greed, and pride. They figured they deserved glory though it was free. Converts were sweet-talked into intending they would die for a worthy cause and reawaken in paradise. What a surprise it must've been when they came to and realized it was the other place.

The monster's monarchy gained momentum. Proponents of malice gathered in droves, sowing their wretched dogma like seeds which would sprout in pupils of paraphilia and students of sedition. The stench of wickedness rose to the clouds saturating the atmosphere like a toxic aerosol. When the guise of chastity was no longer visible, they masked themselves from the daylight. Heinous acts of treachery and turpitude were committed under a shroud of darkness. Unspeakable horrors were orchestrated in basements and alleyways. Insidious contrivances were the handiwork of their reprobate and demonic order.

I cursed the lot of them. They deserved and received no sympathy from me despite the plethora of pain that awaited them. But they knew full well it was coming back upon their heads and heartily accepted this destiny of their own volition. Consequently, they would defame their maker when the vials of wrath were poured out, pretending they didn't know any better. It's the extreme form of denial.

Here was a macabre setting fit for a Halloween masquerade. The chilling saga of vainglory gone haywire was about to unfold. The day of reckoning and retribution was at hand. Investment of the soul to delve into depravity was about to yield marked remunerations in misery. And for a fortune in nefariousness only forfeiture of the birthright was required. Deemed a small price to pay to frolic in the muck they gladly surrendered it, for it was of no value to them (or so they thought). When the time came to render payment all that remained was sentencing; only then would they think twice.

You can wait until time expires if you want though you cannot quell the fires of Hell. But go ahead; push the limits of inevitability. See how far it will carry you until you are hovering above the abyss trying to snag the sky with your fingernails. It is too wide to traverse in a lifetime and you have left yourself but a second. Your last breath remains in your lungs because you are afraid to exhale it. And it is becoming as stale as the blast flowing downwind from that pile of corpses over yonder. Peering below you see leagues of them squashed together. And yours is next for the heap.

I had a prevue of the inferno once and I never want to go back. It was during that phase of carefree and crazy, pushing risk to the limit; unabashed in the pursuit of excessive sensations. Looking back, I realize that vice cannot bring gratification because the id is unquenchable and the flesh never satisfied. No matter how much you engorge yourself you will become hungry, thirsty, sleepy, and horny again, and again. Besides, there is plenty enough to go around and to provide for the needs of every living creature. But it is impossible to fill a void of the spirit with fascinations from the physical world.

Well the three of us had meandered into the foreboding district, where we fraternized with wretched trollops and miscreants while consuming copious amounts of liquor and other brain bending chemicals. A sleazebag and her crew of shrews led us from the bordello, down a shady alley to a discarded playhouse, luring us with promises of delight, debauchery, and dissolution. There we lay incapacitated, zapped by a stun gun, robbed of our belongings, and forced to don soiled and smelly costumes. I was dressed as a ballerina, Feather a squaw, and Moses a nun. Ironic I suppose, in a sickening way.

We were collared, blindfolded, and thrown into a pitch-black room with no windows, no illumination, no furniture, only a metal door. Trepidation set in; I imagined a typhoon tossing a tin can out to sea, left to sink to the murky depths. I can think of nothing more horrendous than to be tormented by a wandering and agonizing imagination. We knew we were going to be the featured presentation; to be abused, molested, and brutalized in ways that only a twisted mind can conjure until the last drops of our blood had been spilled for the sake of amusement.

I bade my companions to cease their cries for help as it only amplified my distress. Taking off one slipper, I flung it against the wall; it traveled about four feet and ricocheted back. I swept the floor with my hand, located it, and flipped it upward towards the ceiling, proving that the apex was over twenty feet above our heads. As chance would have it, I removed the other shoe and tossed it in the same manner; it flew towards the wall opposite the door at the approximate height of the ceiling. But the shoe did not return. I conjectured that this wall must not go the entire way up.

Beckoning my compadres to accompany me in the corner we formed a human ladder. Feather was the strongest, and Moses was the tallest, and I was the lightest. I shimmied to the summit of Moses's shoulders and stretched out my hands. And there was a ledge. We summoned our combined strength enabling me to breech the length of it and slide beneath a railing. Feeling my way around I determined that this was a storage area for backdrops, props, and apparel from an olden-era when live stage performances were the rave. Tying together several items of attire to form a line, I fastened it to the bar to allow my compatriots to scale the wall. I bundled an armful of clothes as we proceeded into the maze.

We rambled through a web of clotheslines, cabinets, and crates to the other side of the deck where a scaffold was emplaced, upon which we descended to the rear of the rostrum. Veiled behind a series of curtains, the audience and master of ceremonies were unaware we had discovered a way out of their dungeon. An exit was dimly lit so we proceeded towards it. A wheelbarrow of tools for inflicting extreme pain was stationed against the back wall. Next to it was a table, upon it an ashtray, box of wooden matches, and pack of cigarettes.

As we changed costumes, Moses took hold of the worn woolen coif adorning his skull, fired it up, and hurled it discuss style where it sailed to the storage area above. Feather had likewise struck a match and put a flame to the posterior curtain. I finished tying up my pants with a necktie, lit up a cigarette and tossed the burning match onto a stack of cardboard boxes, filled with frayed garments, rotting props, and assorted trash. We skulked through the backstage door which opened into a hallway that encircled the playhouse. Securing the outer doors with plentiful cord and tape, we skedaddled to the street seeking civilization of all places. In minutes the entire theater went up like a tinderbox, fully aflame with the denizens therein scrambling in a futile attempt to escape the hellhole that they had prepared for us, and in which they now were trapped. Talk about a wakeup call. Heed it when you get one. Who do you suppose is trying to get your attention? For villains such as these theirs had come and gone. I fancied myself a modern Samson taking down the Temple of Dagon, before realizing he did not survive the ordeal and I wasn't even in the same league.

Not everyone was forlorn and a righteous revival came to fruition. It gained a foothold in the Americas from the defense of formerly held ideals: God, country, justice, and freedom. I opined as they did and joined their ranks. This was the coalition of love. In such an association there is no need for stratification for the power belongs to the people. We were on a crusade in which we would persevere until the end, and that end would catch up with many of us too soon. No matter, because in this fraternity losing your life meant gaining it.

Who among you would not prefer citizenship in the kingdom of heaven, where it is unnecessary to make distinctions based on status, heredity, or popularity? Where there is but one class for all and all are equal therein? It is the family home, where the king is the head of the household and the children are heirs to the kingdom. Would anyone surrender to being a slave if they could become a prince?

I found an invitation that another had left behind and joined the party of peace. And I earned the right, the authority, and the responsibility of freedom and truth. Everyone who belonged to the movement owned these blessings and had the power to distribute them. Freedom and truth were given freely. Truth is inherently pure and it cleanses the mind of the recipient. Truth ultimately sets you free. These prizes are available only to those who honor and safeguard them. That was our reward for involvement in the new revolution where we were soldiers of fortune in the highest degree, fighting for a prize much more valuable than precious metals or stones. But protecting freedom and truth was a life and death struggle.

Deep down I have always known there is but one expert witness and he reigns supreme. If only the nations could have remembered. Our forefathers understood this. Governors should be assigned by the Almighty. Otherwise there's no telling who you'll end up with. The false heroes feigned divine inspiration, some proclaimed themselves deities; but I wasn't about to invest my trust. What's more, the true King of Ages didn't walk among us waving a diploma, a gavel, or a sword but behaved as a subject to his constituents. Thus, it seems out of character to assert perfection on the one hand and condescend on the other. Those who are superior need not endeavor constantly to prove it as this would better define them as insecure.

A climax was nearing, matching goodness against evil, the coup de grace at Armageddon. But there were a few more campaigns to wage beforehand. The reverent would be spared the ultimate brawl; they would be recalled from duty and brought home and I would be among them. In the meantime, the antagonists would be forced to fight it out with the cherubs who were next to impossible to kill and would come back to life nonetheless. And that's precisely how it transpired. An apparent triumph lasted only the weekend and a bit of power for but an hour. Those lifeless bodies that had been placed on display were revitalized in the midst of the rejoicing, turning a brief moment of victory into one of permanent defeat. That really infuriated the stepson of Satan who amassed the armies of abhorrence at Megiddo in an attempt to mount a full-scale offensive against the Lord's city. But the villains were annihilated in the blink of an eye; so much for his kingship. It brought to mind a cherub who I read slew an army with the swipe of a flaming sword.

That's when an archangel sounded the trumpet. It was so loud the skies shattered as a broken mirror enabling spectators to see the other side. The windows of heaven were opened and millions of brilliant faces appeared. Skeletons began rising from their graves and, refastened with organs, tissue, joints, and marrow were restored to the prime of youth. The two cherubs also accompanied us as we joined them above the firmament. We watched the entire episode from above, flashing the opposite kind of shock than the onlookers still grimacing in the coliseum stands. I was humbled to be numbered among the first fruits, to accompany the living. I was hoping it would never end and I couldn't wait for it to begin. You know what I'm talking about, when you don't want to awaken from an outstanding dream. But what if you realize that you're already awake and it really is happening? You'll see what I mean when you see it for yourself. I trust you'll have made up your mind before that occurs. Just remember, I didn't make it *all* up.

The Second Dimension

My head still swirling in the second dimension, I emerged from the woods and entered the cottage, retreating to the room of paradox. While sitting beside myself, I reached into my junk box and pulled out a hatpin. Once the path of the rotating orb entered my domain, I jabbed it directly at the tributary source. And the earth bled. It was the beginning of the end. There was no time to pick up the pieces or to mop the floor. I knew it was time to leave, to say goodbye. I looked around but found nothing I needed so I left everything behind. I headed down the untraveled road which winds through the barbed fences and past the ancient ruins barely visible on the horizon. Dragging the chains of regret behind me I trudged forward into the vanishing zone.

The world was a huge mass of manure; garbage, waste, and carrion accumulated in unmanageable quantities. Recycling had long ceased. They used to dump refuse into the Mariana trench but it was filled to the brim with rubbish. The oceans, beaches, and countryside turned into towering trash bins, breeding pestilence and disease which insects and rodents carried to every habitation. Air pollution was getting seriously lethal. You could cut the smog with a knife. The odor of it made you puke. Anyone without a gasmask and additional protective gear inevitably would be invaded by bacteria, toxins, and parasites. Living was hazardous to your health.

The sky was mostly drab green. The sun was pale brown and the moon was rusty red. Shadows covered the heavens by early afternoon. Despite the continuously creeping darkness, the heat was unbearable.

Earth's orbit became increasingly elliptical. It threw the rest of the planets off course. Even the Milky Way began to tilt. It shifted into the path of Andromeda which was slipping and expanding for its own reasons. The celestial collision ruptured the fuel tanks and gasses began escaping and igniting everywhere, causing thunderous blasts and cosmic concussions. Stars were losing their radiance, exploding or falling; meteorites were shooting through space and colliding with each other. Galaxies were imploding. Quasars, pulsars, neutron stars, and black holes became commonplace. The very fabric of space was deteriorating. Despite the stupendous light show in the heavens, the cold was unbearable.

Take a peek at the new Nineveh where filth is the foundation and sin the celebration. Yes, there is the famous whore that seduced the nations of the world; see her wallowing in her own waste. It is the city of ten pagan priests, which surrounds seven hills with its veil of blood (and assorted secretions). Send your delegation of scoundrels and join the partnership of perversion and their entourage of erotomaniacs. Grovel in the glistening grime which envelops your very soul with blight, until it has devoured what is left of your dignity. Then listen closely for the crash heard round the world and take another look after the dust settles. The entire city has been swallowed up by a sinkhole in a single day and the earth has a major bellyache. It is about to belch in a most disgusting way.

The spirits of evil were released from their primeval penitentiary, infiltrating the four corners of our revered globule. They abode in the dust devils that ravaged the landscape. Earth itself needed to be exorcised. A cloud of peril encircled it. Earthquakes resounded in diverse places triggering volcanoes, giant waves and flash floods. Scourges, epidemics, and infestations raged, proliferating death and decay. The plains were ablaze across the baked terrain. There was no clean water to drink and nothing nutritious to eat. Much of the plant, animal, and sea life had wasted away. A third of humanity had perished from pestilence, famine, wild beasts, and war. Another third was about to expire after drinking from the vessels of vengeance. Theirs was a futile fight because the world already had been laid at death's door.

The friction between ideologies culminated in the great valley, where the last stand of wickedness was trounced with the wave of an invisible hand as if God was shooing flies. The geeks committed mass suicide, those who saw it coming. The false prophet, his bishops and wards attempted retreat. They thought they had it made reveling in a creepy carnival reminiscent of a Roman orgy. But their ship hit a space iceberg and sank into the burning sea, that melting pot of maliciousness and malignity. They joined the hateful heap in the depths of despair, where the son of the netherworld would soon find itself, not to reign but to dissolve with the others. Believe me, it ain't any better for Lucifer than others in that place. Being a janitor in heaven has got to be better than being anybody in hell.

Commitment to condemnation earned a seat on the execration express. There was no way off that train to perdition its last and only destination. And those who boarded would never be heard from again; the very remembrance of them would be obliterated from the record as if they never existed. All contracts were null and void. It was a tumultuous torture chamber for wayward souls stirred together into a single identity of iniquity. Everything was forsaken, in particular hope. The only thing that remained was that incessant ocean of molten flesh, a constant reminder of the end of an age when time itself ceased to be.

Autumn leaves had fallen leaving a colorful carpet for me to bed upon. I longed for the blundering novice I once was, when living was an adventure and every experience a lesson. I rubbed the dusty magic lamp resting on my nightstand and flew as a winged angel into the black hole where nothing had changed in decades. Upon arrival at the November hall of fame I unfolded my bucket list. I always wanted to take up surfing so I rented a board, boots and helmet, paddled out to sea and caught a wave immediately. "Ahh," I sighed, as the wind fanned my brow and the sea spray peppered my cheeks. Sharply the crest dropped flat and me with it. I hurriedly rolled atop the surfboard because the ocean was rife with sea snakes. Appearing in the remoteness was a volcanic uplift pouring magma around the circumference of a new island. I splashed upstream against the undertow and opposite the eruption. The ensuing tidal wave washed me back to the station. There I purchased a ticket on an airbus to May; I was eager to get high and carouse with the ladies. Enjoying the scenery from the observation deck, the chauffeur announced we were preparing to land. Out of nowhere a meteorite shower started to pummel the craft, ripping open the hull. I parachuted to suspicious safety, where dodging the debris meant tucking into a ball in a pasture of poppies and praying for deliverance. Still unenamored, I struck that item off the list and advanced to the next. I checked into a cabin on a galactic cruiser attaining refuge from the storm; the solar system was in turmoil and I wanted out. Seismic activity became rampant on every land mass, the ocean was a boiling bath of steam, and the heavens looked like a war zone. Leaping into a comfortable cradle I returned to dreamland but quickly awakened when the sprinkler system showered the compartment. The wetness turned the mattress into a lumpy, soggy, coagulated slab of clay. Quite the rude awakening I surmised, while looking through the porthole, nauseous and seasick. Evidently, the black hole had tripled in diameter and gravity was sucking up the galaxy piece by planet. I stumbled up to the bridge and begged the helmswoman to reverse course. She knew there was no way to outrun this powerful vacuum cleaner so she complied, commanding the crew to scream full speed ahead at the recess's midpoint. The skin of the ship was peeling right off the shell, layer by layer. Coiling through the core the captain jettisoned the capsule and the explosion propelled us forward faster. Fortunately, we got roasted but not burned; unfortunately, the rest of the ship and its inhabitants were metamorphized into crispy charcoal briquettes. Miserable but alive I was again disconcerted.

What a waste of time, or was it? Such are the vicissitudes of life. The scenario can switch in a jiffy from bad to worse, from okay to great, from disaster to relief, from peaceful to evil. Adventure becomes survival, boredom becomes challenge, fear becomes faith. The game is a test, the situation a trial, the problem an education. Reasonable doubt is converted into a miracle, death into salvation, loss into gain, old into new, temporal into eternal, open into closed.

My mom once divulged her dream of eerie electrical storms occurring across the planet; thunderstorms without any rain but gusting winds and mammoth bolts of lightning. Like a megaton bomb a single strike could destroy an entire apartment building. Mom had a sixth sense. One such wallop scored a direct hit and felled a telephone tower that crashed at my feet when I rushed outside to investigate the deafening blows. A split second later and I might have been crushed; I had to sprint to evade. The skies were bursting with bright flashes, like cracks in a windshield that keep growing and splitting into more until the entire display is reduced to a scattering of shattered glass. There was nothing that a person could do but wait it out and bet your life that you were standing on solid ground. Like wandering a maze with no door and a Minotaur on the loose; and the only way out is to outlive it.

The empires of the earth had crumpled into ruins, precisely what the great conqueror of old dreamt some 2500 years earlier. Fallen kingdoms lay prostrate in the soot: crushed statuettes bowing before the Prince of Peace who had arrived in glorious splendor. The heavens were filled with his majesty and choirs of angels hailed his name in song. Nations broken by war gave reverence to the newly crowned Prince of Peace who assumed the ivory throne which is the judgment seat.

God's right-hand man was about to lower the scepter named terminus. Turning into cockroaches the blackhearts scattered into crevices and cavities wishing they could hide from the all-seeing Spirit. Angels immeasurable in number gathered the multitudes before the Ancient of Days. The bevy nervously awaited the indisputable verdict; they were guilty as sin and they knew it. The sentence of eternal damnation did not surprise them though they acted astounded when it was decreed. How could a merciful God pronounce such a punishment? That was their defense. But death was their reward for living a life without repentance, without faith, without God. They spent a lifetime rejecting him so he would spend eternity rejecting them. But it wasn't unfair or unjust since that was their choice; they didn't wish to be anywhere near God and so it was.

When he arrived on his white stallion, Messiah was speaking with that flaming sword protruding from his mouth; it cut down the liars and doubters. He dismantled the new world order which had become the old-world disaster. God's people already had been pronounced not guilty and their transgressions erased from the Book of the Law. Their names had been written into the Book of Life whereas the names of the guilty had been erased from it. Victory over death was ours to keep, bought by a slaughtered lamb. We entered the pearly gates at sunrise and did not witness the horrors that came down at sunset. Nightfall would be a permanent condition for those remaining behind.

The wicked were cast into outer darkness detached from the light of life. It was a place of no names, no faces, and no future. The fiery furnace burned endlessly to devour the impurities of imperfection. But those inside the unquenchable inferno had no vision of it, not even the feeling, only the thought: a beleaguering of the soul. Agonizing, like thrashing insects drowning in a flushing commode, they were besieged by a memory that had been blended into a meaningless collection of confusion. The dwellers thereof were nonexistent, void of sense, knowledge, dreams, and life, with nowhere to start or finish. From a distance the region resembled a giant whirlpool of magma swirling as a black hole—the infamous lake of fire.

But the fatherland, my what a stupendous place to behold. The splendid city sparkled from afar as a multifaceted topaz. "Wow," I thought, "This awesome place must be the New Jerusalem!" There was nothing from the old universe with which to compare it; unfortunately, that was the only available source of human imaginings at the time. Think of the most wonderful prize and then multiply that by a factor of ten thousand.

The foothills were speckled with palatial homes nestled in lush forests that continued as far as the eye could see. Every residence was cozy and clean, never dusky or dreary. The skies were clear and glossy, never sinister or stormy. The climate was neither hot nor cold, neither damp nor dry, not the slightest bit uncomfortable or unpleasant. It was peaceful, calm, unobtrusive, and tranquil. There was soft gay music and the aromatic fragrance of frankincense emanating from every direction, creating a jubilant ambience. Suffering, sorrow, troubles, problems, anxieties, these had been abolished. Grief, mourning, worrying, crying, pain, these had been extinguished.

There were no strangers because everybody knew everybody else. The prophets, patriarchs, judges, apostles, and disciples were there: the community of saints, Abraham's bosom, the true children of Israel. It was one big happy family reunion. Brothers and sisters embraced and conversed as if they had been missing one another all along. Even the animals were cavorting together: the coyote was joking with the jackrabbit, the cougar was grazing with the antelope, the rattlesnake was moseying with the field mouse, the eel was bathing with the barracuda, and the sparrow was circling with the falcon.

Nobody was idle, tired, or bored and the work was fun. The citizens were happy and content, shining and sailing with the radiance of comets. I felt profoundly safe from every harm and danger. There were children playing in the streets, people smiling; everyone was enjoying themselves. Citizens were free to go anywhere they wanted and could be there in an instant, darting to-and-fro the way lightning does as it intersects the thunderclouds overhead. We were timeless beings traveling beyond the reaches of light, time, and space. There was so much to experience it wasn't necessary to plan ahead because you could do it a hundred times and it would still be enchanting. The first day lasted forever and the second an eternity. It was better than the best dream but nobody slept through any of it.

In the middle of the city towered Mount Zion with its coiling intrusions. Atop the holy mountain was a four-sided pyramid with three arched portals on every side. It was constructed of enormous blocks of beige and umber agate. The foundation was a solid hewn rock, the appearance of polished red granite; twelve steps were carved into it on each side of the octagonal base. At the apex a beacon shone as a lighthouse, illuminating the city from east to west and north to south. Countless cherubim and seraphim were gathered around the edifice shouting praises, giving thanks, and singing beauteous hymns of exultation continually.

Inside the structure, halls were of solid gold each leading to the throne room of the Lamb located at the epicenter. The cathedral ceiling was constructed from transparent opal panes, buttressed in bronze and reaching up to the vertex. The floor was a meticulously assembled mosaic of colorful triangular porcelain tiles depicting a garden in the shape of a six-pointed star. Encircling the mercy seat were lustrous white marble tables adorned with purple linen cloths and pink and yellow roses. Intricately carved cherrywood chairs with teal velvet cushions were emplaced twelve to a table. Each row was set with scarlet silk napkins, stoneware dishes and bowls glazed in cobalt blue, and sterling silver chalices and tableware. The groom stood at the east entrance in his magnificence, wearing a seamless white robe and sandals, his scars still visible. He welcomed every friend to the superb wedding feast he had prepared. Guests were seated by ushers who were modeling tailored white satin suits, the elders of the tabernacle. Once the flock was situated, Jesus entered the room. A feeling of awe, exhilaration, and love overcame me. Before anybody could praise him and give him thanks Jesus gave thanks to his Father for us. Then he blessed us with a heartwarming and eloquent benediction and consecrated the fine dinner. He, along with the hosts of heaven, personally served us the purest water, the choicest fruit, the sweetest bread, and the finest wine. It reminded me of Christ feeding thousands in the fields of Galilee, only this time the number of hungry mouths was incalculable. The marvelous meal was delicious and nourishing, medicine for the soul alleviating heartaches and woes. Everybody consumed to their personal delight, for they would never hunger or thirst again and they knew it. It was a banquet fit for, in salutation of, and in tribute to: The King. And the festivities continued without end.

PROVERBS

The molecular model is analogous to a miniature solar system. Charged atoms revolve in the manner of orbs around a star. Is the microcosm a macrocosm in another world and is the converse also true? The image viewed from the telescope looks similar to that of the microscope. Big worlds and little worlds: no limits to the conceivable echelons of reality from tiny particles to expansive universes. If there are multiple dimensions in time whereby parallel universes can coexist, God only knows. If I can imagine it then surely God can make it happen. The major constraint in the awareness of such phenomena is the physical limitation of the human brain and affiliated sensory-perceptual arrangements.

We cannot begin to comprehend the brilliance of the Almighty, so let us not attempt to impress one another with our own. There might not be a logical explanation for a particular phenomenon. Don't bother me with your spur of the moment excuses as that will not raise my comfort level any. Please, if you have no proof don't invent some.

I have concluded that reaches of space and time, including everything in-between, were created by intelligent design. Nature did not create itself; neither is God a created being. Invented gods can be only material. The earth, galaxy, possibly the universe evolves as it revolves. Arguably, they have reached their peak and will steadily diminish; likewise, animals are on the decline (with the possible exception of superbugs). On the other hand, humans haven't reached their full potential.

Natural alterations are repetitive geologically, cosmically, and anthropologically as undulating waves. An entity might recycle in one day or a trillion years. A metamorphic world can be destroyed with scant trace of the catastrophic event invoking rapid mass destruction, be it natural (asteroid) or manmade (nuclear). However, such events are supplanted by pristine rebirth and regeneration. But none of these changes result in a new concept, object, or lifeform; that is, the modifications are within the system. One organism does not rearrange its matter into another. But creation, adaptation, destruction: these are not mutually exclusive concepts. Why do people insist it is either-or? What is the common denominator? Life!

A comet, resembling a spermatozoon, careens through the abyss of space and time searching for planet egg. And when they intersect—total destruction, spontaneous rebirth? Check out those reputed subatomic particles engaging in quantum sex, during which electrons exchange protons like bodily fluids and emit electromagnetic energy. Do they attract and resist one another the way people do, or like magnets? Is this by accident? Are you an accident? If the uncertainty principle applies at the quantum level is it any surprise your future is equally uncertain? The only thing that is certain is God's plan, the grand design. I challenge you to figure that one out. We don't have a need to know; to be sure, we cannot (at least not at once the way God does). But we can produce an effect and we do have options.

Thoughts are infrequently random. And they cannot be observed by examining different chemical configurations or neural activation patterns. That is, while the brain may be the bodily component through which thoughts are processed, the mind conceives those thoughts. Certainly, memories, experiences, and input data are stored within the neurons and interrelated connections. But the mind is capable of causing the neurons to fire in a particular pattern or progression. The quantum model corresponds insofar as thought particles, or waves, or signals can be exuded and processed in the brain. Oh, but that would violate the uncertainty principle since their directions are picked in advance; not by natural selection but by personal and thoughtful election.

Unconscious processes are operating automatically to maintain our health and functioning, without the need for awareness or intervention; but we can consciously intervene if we want and disrupt, alter, or control these processes. Yes, some tri-brain activity is hardwired and preprogrammed, developed and calibrated through genetics, experience and repetition. But such processes can be deliberately activated, concatenated, and reprogrammed. Highly practiced and skilled behavior will proceed effortlessly unless we invoke cognitive control. We can consciously change programmed or habitual responses though it takes substantial and focused effort. Oftentimes, injecting cognitive projections messes it up. That's why I quit competitive sports; I couldn't beat myself.

Everybody experiences conscious awareness. Have you perchance detected unconscious awareness? There are many altered states of consciousness: waking up, studying, daydreaming, hypnotic trance, meditation, sleeping, REM, coma, and so on. This is compounded by levels of arousal, novelty, training, distractions, experience, practice, and controlled versus automatic processing. And different states of mind are affected by emotions, mental health, physiological soundness, homeostasis, sanity, growth and development, damage and deterioration. Then there is common sense, uncommon sense, memory, precognition, clairvoyance, telepathy, deduction, induction, and synchronicity. There has to be a nonlocal aspect to awareness does there not? SS says there is and I believe him, because he has explored the quantum of my mind at greater heights and depths than I.

Okay then, what came first: the brain or the mind? Well, the brain is the vehicle that contains the programs but the mind is the programmer. Comparable to a computer the brain itself does not think, feel, or reason; but we do. The mind is within the soul which emotes, chooses, desires, comprehends, hopes and believes. Such occurrences are neither deterministic nor probabilistic, they are decided: not by nature but by individual will. How could behaviors such as lying or cursing be the product of inert matter, chemistry, or randomization? It treads against reason. Hence, we have validity to the expression, mind over matter. But the spirit is greater still than the mind.

The spirit can rule the mind, but the flesh is weak; thus, it is ill-advised to let the flesh assume command. The apostles spoke of the battle between the flesh and spirit. All too often desires of the flesh win as in the case of addiction, gluttony, lust, greed, deceit and other deadly sins and worldly appetites. The spirit needs to prevail in this conflict in order for us to choose rightly. But what is truly right? Let your conscience be your guide my grandfather taught me. Better said, let your spirit take control over your thoughts and there will be no conflict in your heart; for the spirit searches out truth which is always right.

In organic brain disorders such as Alzheimer's some connections are faulty, so the victim is unable to retrieve information or activate certain neural pathways, even with the greatest effort. It's as if the hard drive has bugs in it. The system is clogged, degraded, corrupted, or rusted; something that the programmer is unable to fix thereby preventing access or upgrade. You cannot store or retrieve information using damaged sectors. Therefore, it is possible for the mind to become disoriented if the system is faulty, but that doesn't prove that the mind and brain are inseparable. One can lose consciousness with a perfectly healthy brain; and an intact brain can die when denied oxygen too long. When the brain has been irreparably damaged, persons can relearn skills and behaviors by rerouting stimuli and processes to unaffected regions.

When a total shutdown occurs, people have experienced out of body perceptions. How is this possible in the absence of sensory data? The incident may be recalled sometimes with unusual clarity, though consciousness was absent while awareness remained present somehow (for example visual information retrieved when the eyes were closed, the person was asleep, or the brain was clinically unresponsive). Awareness must be connected to the mind, while the brain provides the physical manifestation. Awareness enables us to select inputs; meanwhile all stimulation is stored whether attended to or not.

Thus, learning from the environment is purposeful for it requires alertness and attention. In contrast, unconscious processing can occur in the absence of cognitive intervention and structured sensitivity. Recall of memories or internal models is selective, upon which a search of the database initiates electrical cycles and chemical processes enabling unconscious material to rise to the conscious level. And while some inputs are internal and others external, we can choose which to examine or manage in both cases. There are avenues to the unconscious that can be consciously activated and with sufficient practice enable reframing, redirecting, and reprocessing.

The brain is a black box but we can think "outside the box" as they say. We can talk ourselves out of or into something knowing full well if it is or is not true, moral, logical, or good for us. Entrenched within the furrows of the psyche, the conscience warns and it doesn't lie; it is receptive to the facts; it is conditioned for survival; it knows what is correct and proper; it steers the thinker accordingly; and it cares about others. Yet we are capable of choosing among countless alternatives and either going against the inner spirit or along with it. By that same power we can block the intrusive, sinful, or destructive thought; we can reverse the unpleasant feelings of derision, dread, or rage; we can halt the afferent signals of physical affliction and pain. People have been known to become healed via faith, contemplative prayer, deep concentration, meditation, and suggestion such that the mind overrides the body (note that the brain is part of the body). What a remarkable gift the mind; unfortunately, it is constrained by the body. But does the mind die with the body? Or does it continue after death? Does it not connect us to others and to God? Certainly, the spirit does.

There is no missing link except that of man to himself; thereby severing also ties to the Lord. Everyone has a choice: life or death, the spirit being life and the decisive force behind God and his creation, its adaptation, preservation, and destruction. There dominates neither science nor religion but body, mind, and spirit: the components of a discerning soul, the very image of God. And God is eternal but not necessarily the universe we live in. He is in control of this universe just as your spirit should be in control of you. If it could happen by chance without God, then there would be universes popping up, blowing up, or dying out everywhere all the time. And we would be motivated exclusively by our own selfishness and would not survive. With God it works; without God nobody would care and nothing we do would have meaning. There would be no reason for anything; no science, no philosophy, no doctrine, and no discovery. The countless breakthroughs, avalanches of information, with multiple avenues of communication, and increased understanding have and will continue for humanity as long as we exist. If God can conceptualize every possible universe, how did he come to select this one? For us dummies.

The world is in a state of cyclical change, like a time loop. Does it end where it started, is it without end, or does it totally quit? Or maybe God manufactures it altogether anew. Pollen journey with the wind in search of its genus; but this too is a process influenced by an external agent. Its predecessor plant blossoms and sows seed of its own kind. They unite and repeat the sequence. The plant decomposes replenishing the soil with vital nutrients thereby advancing its progeny. The plant breathes the carbon dioxide exhaled by the human who breathes the oxygen discharged by the plant. The tiny krill, one of the smallest marine animals, glide through liquid space, consumed by the largest of them, the blue whale. What goes around routinely comes around from the quantum photon to the massive black hole;

and every part of it leads somewhere. Even the ruminations of humankind are progressive. Nothing is original under the sun; but with intelligence, well who knows what we are capable of? And with God the possibilities are endless.

Humans also are in a constant state of change, and entropy. The body matures quickly in the beginning and slows after aging, making full circle. Then whoop, there it goes. Our bodies progress from infancy, to childhood, puberty, adolescence, adulthood, menopause, senility: in line with conception, maturation, deterioration. Correspondingly, the mind develops within these phases as we progress intellectually and psychologically: sexual, social, cognitive, moral, interpersonal. The relational environment is the essence of the personality. The genotype is shaped by the ancestral environment, the phenotype by the familial. The sociotype is determined by the cultural environment, the psychotype by the neurological. But the mind of God is in every soul and can be accessed by seeking with one's spirit.

The mind can visualize anything that is; the eye sees what is before it. The retina projects it upside down; the mirror reflects it backwards. Both represent an image from the past as there is no precise real-time processor in this age. Of course, this is true of all the senses. It takes time for light waves to proceed, as it does for receptors to ignite and electrical impulses to be transmitted to the visual cortex. Everything you see has already happened, like the luminance of a distant star continuing to shine after it has died. What can we learn from this? Take your time when responding to stimuli and think before you act, keeping in mind that the execution of your decision also will not occur in real-time. The prize is not inevitably to the swiftest but the thoughtful. Uh oh; there is that intelligence factor again.

Adult humans have a limited attention span; youth even less. Seven data items on the average can be held in active memory. The number is higher for the gifted (up to 13) and lower for the retarded (down to 1). A person in a coma or anesthetized may be operating at zero attention. Working memory is constricted, but you can transfer some tasks to long term memory where more bits per unit space can be processed in less time; this capability is pre-enabled in the savant. Practice does not make it perfect but it does make it automatic.

The unconscious can do it better than the conscious; intervening in a preprogrammed process usually causes mistakes. Skilled performance is a reflex response sequence that can be executed without cognitive intervention because it does not consume attentional resources. Unlike our limited conscious mind, the unconscious is relatively unlimited. It holds everything: the sensations, perceptions, memories, experiences, programs, ideas, and knowledge of a lifetime. Perfection is a top-down process not the other way around; but it doesn't occur in this lifetime (or spacetime if you insist). Nobody in this epoch can always be right; that is, there can be only one Supreme Being that is all-knowing.

Operating at maximum intellectual capacity keeps you mentally healthy, as long as there is sufficient physical activity to balance the workload. You cannot handle much mental stress if you are physically fatigued. If your mind is not engaged it will be sidetracked easily. Sex is a principal preoccupation, but you can get your mind off or on anything by challenging yourself cognitively; this requires effort and energy. An idle mind conjures deviant motivations. Idleness in body and mind promotes demise. Activate yourself physically, mentally, and spiritually if you want to achieve holistic health.

Think things out. Pay attention to what you are doing. Exercise your brain. Never act on inclination. Be reasonable. While your first impression is often accurate, analyze every option. Select an alternative only when it surpasses doubt. If you are not certain don't decide; give it more time. That is, when in doubt don't. If you must act immediately, opt for the least risky position. Assess the risks and the benefits together not separately. Sometimes in life you have to take risks, but don't make a habit of it. Follow your soul not your head; if it doesn't feel right it probably isn't. It is too easy to rationalize so conceptualize. Experiment with the data by bouncing it around in your mind or off your colleagues. "A lazy person can convince himself better than seven people with a good reason," explained the commissioner of the temple. And how did he find out?

Occasionally it is more effective to think in a reclined or sitting position. Explore until you find the ideal conditions for concentration and introspection. Trial and error may help to achieve the optimum meditation posture. For example, dreaming requires lying down and deep sleep in order to benefit fully. Daydreaming can be done in any position but does not afford the same regeneration as REM sleep.

The brain elicits electromagnetic frequencies including beta, alpha, theta, delta, and gamma, depending on purpose. Different waveforms and amplitudes represent different types of thinking and possibly specific mental functions, but not meaning. Data are processed and stored accordingly. During the wakeful state the mind keeps busy, emitting high frequency beta waves of low amplitude. Alpha waves appear intermittently, somewhat slower in frequency but greater in amplitude than beta, as the mind begins to wander and daydream. This is the threshold between the conscious and unconscious. As we enter the initial stages of sleep and plunge more deeply, slower waves of higher amplitude appear. The waves continue to slow down and increase in amplitude in the deeper stages of sleep and during unconscious experience; these are called delta waves. At stage five of sleep REM kicks in and we are dreaming. Curiously, we're pretty much back to beta waves as the brain is working, though the psychomotor system is shut down (except the eyes which are darting this way and that, known as REM). Particularly intriguing are theta waves, which occur during dreams and processes within the depths of consciousness; they are of modest amplitude but are higher in frequency than delta while lower than alpha. Theta waves have been associated with learning, updating internal models, creativity, and the reorganization of neural pathways. It is unclear if gamma is associated with any particular mental state. Is it not fascinating how cogitating occurs at conscious and unconscious levels, and the brain provides plasticity, the potential to regroup?

Everything travels in waves it seems, to include the visual and auditory stimuli that we experience with this body and process in this brain. Sensory systems can distinguish various congregations or patterns as we ascribe our perception to the aggregate; meaning comes from the repetition, practice, reprocessing, and mapping of the information. Central nervous impulses activate memory models accordingly. The matrix of sensory input is perceived, encoded, stored, and retrieved from memory in a similar format enabling rapid dispensation and interpretation. Regular interference in these processes causes attention deficit, distraction, disorganization, cognitive dysfunction, or dementia.

When reality becomes burdensome many will attempt to escape it, to the degree that fiction is perceived as real. The less time one spends in reality the more delusional they become. It may seem comfortable to escape into an unreal world but this does not assist the psyche as with dreaming. Psychotics and addicts will find it tough to return to cogent awareness for the realm of fantasy can be very compelling. Incidentally, faith is not a symptom of psychosis because faith is based on real evidence not false perceptions or delusions. Faith is greater than belief which can occur in the absence of evidence. Blind faith indicates zero confirmation and is irrational if not impossible. People can believe in unproven theories or positions, but are uninclined to trust undeniably in them or bet their lives on them.

It is healthier to address the present in the present, and not allow the past or future to deter you. If you don't admire what you see put a different frame around it. For example, when a task seems a burden revise your outlook and view it as a challenge. A pessimist could easily become an optimist. The gaudiest artwork is better appreciated when enclosed in an elaborate frame (and vice-versa). Your frame of reference will determine how your world is to be perceived. It is a bias that predisposes one to think, feel, believe, or behave in a certain manner. Widen your focus and narrow it; try a variety of angles. You may never view the same thing in the same manner again.

Preconceived notions will give you tunnel vision, when you configure the stimulus inputs to conform to your expectations. Sensation, processing, encoding, and storage of additional data likewise will be constrained to fit your internal model. Evidence to the contrary will be doubted, discounted, or ignored. Perceptual bias renders experience unrepresentative of reality and incapable of generalization to anyone else. So be careful in selecting a point of view, and don't be surprised to discover that you alone hold that perspective.

Information gathering is a personal preference. We mostly seek confirmation; it is too laborious to consider disconfirming testimony however pertinent. But why jump to conclusions? What's the use of convincing yourself about the facts before making an objective assessment? Study your options. Weigh alternative opinions and their relative merit. If you are capable of arguing the opposite position you will be better equipped to defend yours.

Everyone has unique experiences unto themselves and therefore each person experiences the same situation differently. Thus, reactions under similar conditions will vary from person to person. Nobody thinks like you, acts like you, or believes as you. Don't try to anticipate others' actions or tell them what to do or think. Your thoughts are seldom aligned with the rest of the world. Please don't suggest that you know what I think, feel, or believe; but if you ask, I'll be happy to share it with you.

Roach Coach

Look for the goodness in people and draw it from them. Everyone and everything have some element of charm if you seek it out. Why concentrate on the part you deem distasteful? Don't trouble yourself over events or outcomes that are improbable. Luck and skill can coexist, sometimes in alternating proportions, and both are available to everyone.

If you think it will you can ensure it will because you can will something into happening. But if you believe it won't you will be less likely to try. You can believe it to be true or false by dismissing the alternative. If you expect the bazaar will be uninteresting then you will not find anything there of interest. When you assume the worst or you think negative, you usually get it. Keep a clear mind and don't contrive expectations, then you will be pleasantly surprised if the outcome is favorable; if it isn't at least you won't get upset. Your gut instinct does not pass for proof. It is occasionally accurate when responding to the here and now but very unreliable concerning the future. Favor your heart over your gut. Don't be preoccupied about tomorrow or yesterday; use your time to address the present, it's the only time you have. If you could read your life story in advance would you choose to live it? I'd rather wait for the movie to come out.

Selections are reflections of the individual. The possessions that bring you enjoyment, such as toys, are a manifestation of your persona. Toys are our coping mechanisms and they facilitate growth. As we mature our playthings become more complicated, and hence expensive. Treasure them and take care of them because they are irreplaceable, keeping in mind that everything material remains expendable. Of course, you don't need elaborate contraptions to pass the time, it will go soon enough. But stay active and take time for rest. And remember, some of your best ideas are the ones that are unrehearsed.

There are many forms of human intelligence. Some humans can think abstractly and master analytical tasks, some excel in memory challenges, while others have an innate common sense with regards to physical, psychological, behavioral, or functional relationships. I have encountered an assortment of people who have excelled in one area but failed miserably in another. Individuals in either or all of these groups could be considered smart. There is no single measure of it. Those who boast of high scores on an intelligence scale do not compel me.

It is aggravating when people behave in a manner condescending to others, deluding themselves that they are superior somehow. Remember, we are created equal; endowed with rights, will, freedom, and potential. But we are not equally able in the exact same arenas. As wise as you may be in one area you are unwise in other areas. As talented and artistic as you may be in one medium, you are clumsy in other arts or media. If you sometimes are better than the rest, remember that you are the worst at something else at the same time (and so are they). Truly intelligent people hold their tongues and listen; but when they speak you can be sure they have something worthwhile to offer. A wise person snubs conceit, admits mistakes, tells the truth, and refrains from pointless speech. How many of you can unequivocally claim these traits? Consider some proverbs from the learned king. A wise man does not proclaim his wisdom; it will become apparent in more subtle ways. A foolish man overtly displays his foolishness. But even a fool, when he keeps his mouth shut, is thought wise.

Same as the animal world, society has a class structure. Animals commune together without interference; the reason humans cannot: because of reasoning (and brother can they be unreasonable). Humans adapt quickly; the reason animals cannot: because of instinct (and humans have some of the worst instincts). The differences among human cultures are found in the magnitude of distance between traditions, classes, and philosophies and the proportionate distribution of persons among them. Culture shock is the blatant disorientation one experiences when abruptly exposed to these dissimilarities.

Notice how animals communicate nonverbally; they do not speak in linguistic terms. And they don't have to. Everything they need to say is made known through gestures, intonations, movements, body language, and so forth. People are the same way. Probably 85 percent of human communication is nonverbal. A bloodhound can bark ten different ways each conveying meaning, while a person can say a single word and it could convey ten different ideas depending on how it is uttered. For example, modify the amplitude, pitch, tonality, duration, rhythm, and emphasis and see how many ways the spoken word "no" can be construed.

Muscle variations in the eyes and mouth alter the mood by adding emotional content to a message. Additional kinesthetic and proximal cues disclose underlying thoughts or feelings. If you zoom in on another's body language, you may discover meaning that is different from the spoken word. Further, the verbal message and the emotional content may be incongruent. Feelings usually cloud the message; communicate reasons not emotions. The only emotion that can always reinforce a message is genuine love. You know what they say, actions speak louder than words; and it's true. If the words and the deeds are in conflict the words are rendered meaningless. There are many ways to transmit meaning; jargon is often unnecessary or misleading. Keen awareness and acute observation permit the viewer to sense the subtle aspects of a teller's communication, apart from their talk.

The very meaning of words is contorted nowadays to the degree that you can say anything and later contend that your saying was misconstrued. Politicians are masters at denial, muddying the waters, and using reverse wordsmithing. Everybody knows they can't be trusted to tell the truth; regardless, when they tell it they don't mean it half the time, and the other half is accidental. They'll take one simple word and spin it in so many different directions that you'll forget what the heck they were talking about. It's impossible to get the gist though it may have seemed clear before they opened their mouths. I'm not sure it ever was distinct in their minds. Or they equivocate something to death until you wonder why you bothered to listen. Very shrewd is it not? Heads of state who talk out of both sides of their mouths, seldom having anything to say; nothing but doubletalk which means they also are doubleminded. How can you know what people mean when they don't say what they think? It's another sign of the times, one which was foretold countlessly so we wouldn't forget. But many occupants of Earth forgot to remember.

Conversely, some people can commune with others without being present. I don't know if it's via vibrations, telepathy, or what. I can't give a scientific definition for it but it happens. Have you felt an uneasy feeling about a relative or friend and learned that they were involved in a mishap that very hour? Indubitably, the spirit can communicate. For example, it's not difficult to sense the presence of vileness or uprightness. Some people have a real knack for discerning spiritual intent (like my solipsist companion). Obviously, the Lord can communicate via his Holy Spirit; I suppose other spirits can too. Keep your eyes peeled and your ear to the ground. Keep your mind alert and your spirit aware. For there's no telling what you might learn; you might uncover the explanation to an enigma.

There are many phenomena that are a mystery. It is futile attempting to dialog with someone who is closedminded. But when we insist on grasping the unexplainable, logic submits to speculation, reasoning succumbs to rationalization, and discussion surrenders to argumentation. Most conceptualizations minimally require further research or more factfinding. Other captivations are beyond comprehension; but that is not a reason to discontinue your pursuit when it moves you forward.

Who is not aware of the forces of fire, earth, water, and air? Yet who is not challenged to define them? For example, we can observe the consequences of wind but not the wind itself. These characteristics of nature can be contrary and complementary at the same time. Earth is eroded by fire, water, and air yet lives in harmony with them; and the decomposition afforded these destroyers returns back to the earth to replenish it. Fire needs earth and air to survive but is extinguished by water; yet fire can dry the water up, char the earth, and suck away the air. But too much air will blow the fire out and too much earth will smother it. There is air in the water and water in the air; when heated with fire, air causes the water to evaporate and then it drops back upon the earth. There are checks and balances in nature that are working for us. These dynamisms join together in different combinations while each is formidable in its own right, establishing a great number of workable scenarios making any one event quite unpredictable. When combined they create a force to be reckoned with, like when wind joins water and beats upon the lakeshore turning stone into sand. But with any force missing or unequal nothing on the planet would hold together. The unfortunate thing about fountains is that they eventually run out of water. The unfortunate thing about balloons is they eventually run out of air. Hopefully, carbon lifeforms will not run out of either. The unfortunate thing about earth is you can starve; the unfortunate thing about fire is you can freeze. Lose one, lose all.

Why does the chicken run around in circles when danger approaches, and why does an ostrich hide its head in the sand? Not that I have personally witnessed such behavior but maybe they are looking for an escape. Stupid birds, though how I wish I could ignore my fears that easily. What is so unusual about clouds? Do they tell a story or predict the future as some people suppose, or do they simply exist in the minds of those who are afraid of the future or disclaim reality? Ponder such things but don't dwell on them.

Consider this: the greatest mystery is unveiled in God's autobiography. Careful reading of it will uncover solutions to your problems, hopes, and dreams. The gain in wisdom will be exponential. It's intriguing how God unravels the intricate plot and discloses the foretold and inevitable outcome. The book is filled with history, science, romance, health, humor, drama, adventure, horror, guidance, and assistance––something for everyone. And it's factual! It has produced remarkable answers to many of my questions. I cherish the part about living forever as brothers and sisters with immeasurable love, peace, and joy. Sibling rivalry does not exist in that family where adopted children are equal heirs.

The Bible is not a tall tale it's real, whether you want to accept it or not. There are those who would destroy it because they either do not comprehend it or they'd rather ignore that there will be judgment. Or they do not approve of anything implied to be supernatural or spiritual since they accept only material explanations; but scientific conjecture doesn't come close to proving or explaining the essentials. There are many who believe the Bible has diminished in validity via translation; truthfully, the ancient scrolls and the latest version are identical. Some suggest it has changed over the centuries, as if someone collected all the manuscripts that ever existed, destroyed them, and distributed a new version throughout the globe in five hundred different languages. In any event, shirking responsibility is what impels disbelievers. Very counterintuitive to say the least since motivation implies acceptance.

There is no surrogate for truth. Paranormal experience is not the way to enlightenment. Rather it takes hard work, dedicated study, and faith. Do not search for a quick and easy route to understanding. Religious experience does not preclude edification through scriptural study. Religion is a way of life not a happenstance occurrence. It is okay to make personal sacrifices or to meditate about your spirituality, but these behaviors are done as an act of worship they do not achieve enlightenment. You are unable to learn by fasting to the point of exhaustion and then interpreting your hallucinations. That's when you're sure to receive a visit from the malevolent one (who tried to trick Christ the same way). Hint: it was the mischievous jinn not an angel of light that appeared to the false prophets.

Devout people seek unity whether with God, nature, others, or self. The best way to establish that link is with love; which itself can be spiritual and in God's case absolute. His love is magnitudes greater than we are capable. I am speaking of unconditional, supernatural love, not romantic love or brotherly love. I mean, who among you would lay down your life for your enemies? Do you love those that love you and those that hate you equally? God does. Love is a way of life, of behaving, of being; it is not a mystical or otherwise undefined state of mind or an obscure feeling. Love is a noun and a verb; love is real and it is observable. And love is the greatest power known to the nations: it is the essence of God's Spirit. Love is the glue that holds everything together including us and our relationships. The Spirit of love is what gives us rebirth, reconciliation, and new life.

Saved by the Light

Mystical and religious experiences may not be spiritual at all but incoherent, metaphorical, or narcissistic attributions for which no real evidence exists, and whereby the supposed supernatural message escapes into consciousness from within the self. This is not a path to truth or enlightenment. If the experience is otherworldly it could easily reflect a spirit of malice, if not the demons inside. Some people pursue intense states of concentration in order to switch everything off, for the purpose of drawing a complete blank in an attempt to retrieve something meaningful from the nothingness. It is impossible to extract absolute truth from the realm of the Creator in this fashion, much less direct it there. Voiding your brain is an invitation to many spiritual entities many of which are malignant. If you want strength and guidance meditate on God. Almighty God might direct understanding to you, but it likely will not occur if you are presuming a revelation. The occurrence would be impossible to inspect directly, especially given the uncertainty concerning future time and the timing of God's will. Plainly said, seek God and he will reveal himself to you; not necessarily when you think you are ready but always when he does.

Knowledge comes from education, experience, and understanding; wisdom is a product of the interaction of the three. To achieve anything positive from a meditative and transcendent state, remove the clutter and focus on the retrievable wisdom or apparent truth by assembling personal experience, training, memory, and scriptural narratives. Self-disclosure comes from the nadir of your mind, implying it already was available but obscured by a cloud of doubt or denial. That is, personal reflection is insightful insofar as it helps synthesize the disparate artifacts of experience.

Prayer allows you to express inner thoughts and desires and consciously present them to God (though he knows them already), thereby establishing a link from you to him. Use that connection also to contemplate on Christ and his teachings. God delivers to you his declarations, the *Logos*, acquired with faith and transmitted via the Holy Spirit; revelations may follow but will be distributed in God's time and way. This will rarely be experienced as a conscious state of awareness, but rather a moving of the spirit within you and the knowing of truth that cannot be reasoned.

You will never merit your salvation, you cannot decipher God via mystic awakening alone, and there is no divine award for an accumulation of good deeds. Actions are an end not a means. The only deed that counts is the perfect work that was performed on the cross of Calvary. Exchanging your guilt for the holiness of Christ rouses you into worship by way of fasting, prayer, meditation, study, witnessing, and works. These are acts of faith not substitutes for it. Actions are proof that you believe and should be guided by an ideology that is based upon morality and a worldview founded on the Word of God. If you want to find absolutes such as truth and love, look into the Bible. But don't take my word on it since you have God's.

You can neither grasp the omnipotent one through experimentation nor by reason or rationalization. There are no human or worldly explanations, physical or mental. Anthropomorphism is baseless because the attributes of man cannot be ascribed to God any more than you can envision heaven by observing the natural world. God's characteristics are conferred upon mortals as he sees fit but not vice-versa. I once wondered if God could be a solipsist for genuinely his is the only valid reality. But I dismissed the notion because that would be delimiting his being. Additionally, animism is aimless because God alone can give life and only the living can possess it. Inanimate objects are not alive so they do not embody a spirit or a mind. Pantheism is pointless too. How can the universe be God if he can be inside of it and outside of it at the same time? God is all and is in all. He does not abide solely in things tangible but also intangible, incomprehensible, known and unknown. You might as well try to confine God to a box as to a universe. The solipsist rejected this nonsense and became a nonconformist in his society; and I joined him.

There is only one Supreme Being and there can be only one; if there were more than one then none could confirm supremacy. Polytheism is therefore illogical. The idea of multiple gods implies that they are unequal; if that were true there would be competition among them not harmony. Does a god have a ranking; do they get promotions like in the armed services? Those who believe in many gods often designate one the creator and another the destroyer. Clearly, if they both reigned supreme then everything that was created by the one would be destroyed by the other and there would be nothing. Thus, with such a philosophy the creator must be the greater. Polytheism assumes an order as in the case of the mythologies of the ancients. The learned ones in those cultures mapped the heavens, gave the constellations names, and proclaimed them gods. And there was considerable bickering and infighting between those gods; they misbehaved as if human. It is irrational to think that a god would engage in petty behavior. After all, are they not supposed to be superior to humans? If I was a god, I'd be above that; wouldn't you? And those people that are rewarded with eternal life do you think they will act this way when they become immortal? Perish the thought; there can be and will be no conflicts or confrontations in God's presence. Does it do anybody any good to oppose God? Lucifer tried it; look where it got him.

If it is the spirit that makes us alive, and that spirit is given by God and belongs to him, then it is by that spirit that we find him and understand him. Sometimes we know facts in our minds sometimes we do not. But there are truths of which we can be certain that are accepted only by faith. Such wisdom cannot be dissected into components, analyzed, or interpreted, yet it is ascertained just the same. Thus, it must be the spirit providing this ability since the mind is incapable. Haven't you ever been sure of something in your heart of hearts and not been able to explain why? Good luck trying to convince someone who is not open to spirituality. Assuredly, such knowledge is fertile for it generates more. The combined knowledge of humankind does not approach the slightest smidgeon of God's wisdom, however. And when he makes truth known to you there will be no doubt. Believe it and you'll receive it; leave it and you will grieve it.

It is ineffectual to deify something or someone particularly if supremacy cannot be demonstrated. The definition of the term implies that such a being is elevated above others in every aspect. The Almighty doesn't act like a man he acts like God. Christ, who possessed both the human nature and the godly one, did not behave as a normal person for he did not commit a single sin. Thus, it can be said that he was superior to and above other human beings. And the very reason: because he is not of this world. He came from God; positively, he was God in the flesh. How else could he have done the things he did and not done the things that everyone else does? How else could he have saved humanity from the curse of sin and the permanency of the grave? How else could he have given his life as a sacrifice and then taken it back again?

No human born can approach the perfection of Christ Jesus. But it is hard for people to accept him as equal with God so they ascribe to him the status of a subsidiary god, an angel, a created entity, or a mere man. As magnificent as God is, he easily can take on more than one form can he not? Angels can and God invented them. How then is it so difficult to believe that God would join the human race? Why wouldn't he? How better for people to understand God than to see him through their own eyes? How else should God show us who he is? Would he appear to us in the entirety of his glorious splendor? We would not be able to fathom such a thing; it would overwhelm us. We would disintegrate in his marvelous presence if we were to stand before him in our current degenerative state; for his holiness cannot tolerate our sinfulness.

The best way God could have shown us his love was to condescend and come among us; this is the meaning of *Emmanuel*. The sacrifice of Christ is the greatest expression of love known to humanity which only God could deliver. His is a greater love than any other human can muster. For whom among sinful men can redeem themselves from the grave much less anyone else? Why would God become a man? Because it doesn't work another way. Justice requires payment and atonement demands blood; but mercy enables forgiveness and grace affords freedom. We donate blood to save lives, like Christ whose blood saved us all. This blessing arrived giftwrapped in a single package presented to each and every man, woman, and child. Are you the type of person that opens gifts but doesn't appreciate them, or returns them, or gives them to someone else? Better not let go of this one, or trade it, toss it, or trounce it.

Jesus is our pilot and we know him because he appeared among us. Who would not want a relationship with him? In addition, the opportunities keep coming when you're following him. Looking forward, can you see the big picture? There at the end zone he waits. If you can see him then you know the correct direction in which to proceed, because he has the right of way. If you follow his lead you will recognize your path and you will realize your dreams. Yeah, the anticipation is grueling; and we often try to hurry rather than waiting for God's time to come. But if you're patient it will fall into place at exactly the precise time. And that is my confidence.

Survey the matchlessness of Jesus Christ: a human with no character flaws, pure in heart, holy in spirit. Every word he speaks is true, every action virtuous. He is love personified. And he practiced what he preached—profoundly exceptional. The entirety of which still rings soundly and is highly applicable after two millennia and counting. Nary a living soul has been able to live up to that standard. Who would not wish to emulate him except those who flatly do not care or refuse to take responsibility?

Christ is my role model. He is the author of all features good. Satan would be delighted to destroy goodness by way of evil. But that will never happen because he is not a deity and therefore, not that powerful. Yet there are those who are exceptionally daft and adulate Satan, venerating him through acts of wickedness and irreverence. He was the angel who was cast out of heaven for disputing God.

Angels are created beings; they are not gods neither are they to be worshipped. There probably is a hierarchy in the angelic order with the archangel Michael being of much higher rank than Lucifer, who was once named the anointed cherub. Lucifer was doubtless busted to a subordinate rank after what he tried to pull in heaven. He was the worship leader but wanted to be the object of worship, kind of like extorting from God by skimming from the spoils. Plus, the havoc he has wreaked down here on Earth should place him considerably below humans in the celebrated order of beings. Why honor him? He is at the bottom, a condemned and abandoned creature who will never achieve the status of heir. He is defeated and will take you down if you do not have Christ bringing you up.

Some people deify and adore angels, demons, humans, themselves, or objects. How preposterous is that? Are they immortal gods? Only the one true God deserves your worship, adoration, and praise. Humans are created equal and have the same rights, privileges, and promise as everybody else. And we can become the person God wants us to be and live forever if we follow his example which is Christ. Why waste your exultations on angels, people, yourself, graven images, or false gods? You might as well be giving them to Mephistopheles. When people give the glory to another, God is displeased. Like my dad did, he punishes me when I am disobedient, disloyal, and idolatrous. Yet he will forgive; but that doesn't mean being absolved from the natural consequences of wrongdoing. Sorrow does not release payment.

God is a faithful Father and will chastise us and correct us when we have strayed. Therefore, it is not wrong to use corporal punishment since God uses it. So, don't be afraid to spank your kid; but employ this method only if you know how to administer it properly. Punishment, to be effective, should be immediate and should reflect upon the transgression. It should be accompanied by an explanation. It should never be done in anger or impulsively. It doesn't have to maim or bruise indeed it should not; it only has to hurt. The pain will go away soon enough but the memory will linger. A threat will work as good as the real thing for quite a while after that. Do not desist from reproving your children for it is an act of love; and they will respect and admire you for it in the long run. To not do it is to invite trouble. My parents had discipline down pat and let me have when I deserved it. Raise your children by example with discipline and correction, for that is how the Lord raises us. And when he raises you it could be everlasting.

The most worthwhile thing you can do for your children (or anybody else) is to ensure they know the route to heaven. Point out the Way to God so that they can find their way when you aren't there to show them. If you trust in the Lord, and accumulate spiritual reserves, your kids will learn from you. They will follow your example whether it leads them up or down. Educate your family and friends in the ways of righteousness and the good news of salvation will be theirs. If you refuse you have done a major disservice to them. The reward for sharing the good news is a long and prosperous life on earth and in heaven.

Spend quality time with your loved ones. Do not neglect any of them. Distribute your affection equally among them, but don't waste it on those that rebuff it. You can love people at a distance and maybe they'll come around but don't exasperate yourself trying. Make time for people, recreation, and vacations. Workaholics only produce more work for themselves. They reach a point when further labor becomes counterproductive. The only thing they are adding to is the amount of time they are wasting while at the same time subtracting it from life. Why plow yourself into an early grave? Let someone else dig it after the fact. Would anyone in their right mind choose to hasten death?

Stock up on spiritual assets not material ones. Worldly possessions are impediments that cause people to stumble and fall, and they are found on the road to death. You will not find them on the road to life because they are not a necessity for living. The Lord says, if you seek heavenly pearls you will receive them, as well as everything else that you need to sustain your body and life. What's the use in being engrossed or terrified? Focus on God and spend quality time with him. And be a willing servant and workhand in his business.

When you undertake a task, no matter how significant or insignificant, strive to do your best. Set realistic and achievable goals, identify the steps that lead there, then take one step at a time. Be conscientious, dutiful, and loyal to your family, friends, and employers. If you let them down you will be letting yourself down. Learn everything you can about your job, the organization, associates, their companies, and customers. Quality assurance should be your number one priority. Goodness is in high demand and will sell itself; maintain an ample supply of it.

Maximize your time on task by taking periodic breaks. Scarcely a short interlude in which you readdress your thoughts and reconsider your responses will facilitate your mind in consolidating information, reaping conspicuous insights into previous periods of concentration and analysis. Let it incubate and develop; then get back to the grindstone. You can tackle more than one task this way. When the whistle blows go home. Quit while you're ahead. The job isn't going anywhere but you could be. Do not sell your soul to the company store; if your boss expects you to live at work ask her for room and board.

Associate with people who are honest, patient, respectful, and caring. Veer from those that are haughty, hateful, conniving, or untrustworthy. You can teach them the truth if they will listen but you don't have to be their friend if they won't. Never gossip about others or lend your ear to gossipers. Don't speak ill of anyone and don't make enemies with people. Acknowledge your differences with them and agree to disagree. Never laugh at people's misfortunes or find pleasure when those you dislike fail or fall. Pray for people you despise and for the unfortunate ones around you. Help them when you can if they are willing. Be kind and gentle to everybody. Respond with love; respect those you meet and you may gain an ally.

Control your emotions. It is natural to have them and they produce useful energy regardless of whether they are negative or positive. Use the energy to build rather than destroy. Find creative and constructive avenues to express feelings. Even anger can be vented in a beneficial way. Instead of getting frustrated, lashing out, breaking something, or beating your self-esteem into oblivion, use it for something good. You can burn calories with physical exercise, accomplish household and gardening chores, or create an artistic or literary masterpiece. The emotion itself is not necessarily a negative thing but what you do with it might be.

Didn't you know, obsessions can be life threatening? Don't allow pent-up feelings to plague you. They needn't remain attached to memories; release them and let the memory fade when it should. Otherwise, repressed memories will never be forgotten and the obsessive reaction will never be suppressed. It takes a lot less blood, sweat, and tears to process the emotional material than it does to hide it or lug it around. Cut loose your garbage and give it to God; he will dispose of it for you. Why carry it to your grave? It belongs to Christ so you might as well let him have it. He paid for it. He will give you peace and rest in return. What a deal!

Admit when you are wrong and correct your errors. Do not wait to be found out. It will be less effortful to finish something now than to put it off. Recompense those you have harmed, shamed, or shortchanged whether deliberately or accidentally. Don't leave it for the courts to sort. Never make promises you can't keep and without exception make good on your vows. Don't commit to something and later back out. Never give away possessions then ask for them back; and never present a gift while expecting one. Do what you say, do the right thing, and do not condemn others for your character flaws. Replace broken dreams with new ones.

Avoid excuses and provide reasons. Communicating your intentions beforehand is the preferred course of action because your companion is a reasonable person. You'd be surprised how many arguments can be circumvented by keeping one another informed. Remember, information reduces risk which equates to fear; the most common fear reflects the unknown. If you are not sure of yourself it's because you're troubled. Learn about it and it won't bother you as much; because knowledge gives us power over the unknown thereby generating confidence. Attempting to excuse oneself after the fact is psychologically irrelevant. You can't fix the past but you can build upon the present. You cannot construct a bridge across the waterway by starting on the other side.

Be honest and sincere. Refrain from indiscretion, for each one contributes to the next and before you know it there is a sea of them that you cannot swim through. Like an undertow deceit will drag you down; like a riptide dishonesty will dump you out at sea and you will drown. It takes a lifetime of lies to bury one and you still are found out in the end. Those who are insincere in the small matters will graduate to the larger ones with haste. And those who are mindful of the big mistakes will be cognizant of the smaller ones and will endeavor to make the proper corrections in every case. If you cannot pay it back, pay it forward.

Follow the cultured, honorable, and wise until you have earned the right and respect to lead; then do so diligently. Lead with courage and confidence. Establish high standards of responsible, ethical, and moral excellence. Your best can always get better. Encourage creativity and innovation and inspire others to aspire. Be a visionary. Provide incentives that will motivate people; offer praise and recognition to those who deserve them. Give credit don't take it. Be flexible and adapt to the characters and behaviorisms of those with whom you come into contact. Be a team player and encourage collaboration and compromise. Know yourself, your limitations and assets; strive to turn your weaknesses into strengths. Endeavor to understand the abilities and liabilities of your juniors and help them to overcome their apprehensions. Become erudite in human strivings and a keen judge of human character. Memorize the rules, requirements, standards, missions, and protocols so you can be a resource to your superiors, subordinates, and peers. A good leader will plan, direct, organize, decide, and control; but above all they will empower. Use your power as a tool not a weapon. If you are to lead others, let the Holy Spirit shepherd you. Discover spiritual actualization and everything will be yours.

Strive for the faith of Abraham, the patience of Job, and the devotion of Ruth. Be as dutiful as Jeremiah, hopeful as Isaiah, and loyal as Esther. Aim for the integrity of Daniel, the benevolence of Joseph, and the chastity of Mary. Persevere like David and keep your cool like Elijah; be fearless like Peter and loving like John. Find the dedication of Noah, the tolerance of Moses, the courage of Joshua, and the strength of Samson. These were examples of endurance in the faith. The power given them by the spirit of love is the same free gift offered to each and every person. Notice how it turned them into great men and women of God. These heroes were everyday people; and so are you and I, with defects, failings, and weaknesses They possessed virtues too because of their love of God. God brought out the greatness in these ordinary humans and will with you. Such distinction is recognized to this day, not only during their time but thousands of years later and for the times to come. This is what lives on: the legacy. Think of the most important person in your life, the person that influenced you more than anybody else in shaping your reputation and path. I picked my grandfather. Who did you pick? I bet it was someone of excellent character: virtuous, undaunted, and wise. They are the heroes; individuals lacking these features are forgotten over time.

God has blessed every somebody with special talents, aptitude, and purpose. We are commonplace people; and yet we are extraordinary each and every one. The age-old adage, God doesn't make junk, is accurate. Society inculcates the notion that there are no losers and everybody is a winner. While that would be true overall it is not individually. Let's face it, there are some activities that we're lousy at; we will never win an award doing them, indeed we shouldn't. Everyone bombs at something; and everybody rockets at something. But nowadays every child gets a trophy; nobody wins nobody loses. Mediocrity is acceptable and becomes the norm. What kind of message does that send to kids?

Certainly, we can learn to master tasks that we lack natural talent at. But there are things we are naturally good at, things we can get better at, and other things that we will never excel at. And that's okay. This is what makes everybody unique, albeit exceptional. This is what makes competition fun and rewarding. Take sports. Imagine how boring if everybody was equally excellent at baseball; nobody would watch it and many would quit playing. Because no team would stand out, no winners, no losers, no champs, and no trophies. No incentive to try harder, to practice more, or to improve. Good performance should be rewarded; poor performance should provide incentive to persist and train. Maybe there is a sinister conspiracy to create a middling society where there is no reason to boost effort, conquer anything, shine or be great. If I won't have to put my heart into it or give it my best shot to get a prize then why should I? If the bare minimum is adequate, and there is no enticement to motivate me to stand up or to outdo the rest, and even if I do the compensation will be the same… Well, you get the picture. This kills freedom and invites socialism.

I believe that our purpose or calling in life is precisely to exploit our personal gifts. My business was never to be a baseball player though it would have been nice. That doesn't mean I was a lousy ballplayer as a kid; I actually was pretty decent. But I wasn't good enough to turn it into my vocation. Despite the coaching, preparation, and resources I still would not have made the grade. But these same investments propelled me to surpass the requirements in my chosen field of play, and thereby carve a notable and gratifying living out of it. People need to recognize their hidden potential, cultivate it, amplify it, and implement it in a way that benefits others, propels them forward, and pleasures the Lord at the same time. Give to God the praise for your accomplishments, thank him for the opportunity and the promise, and your ambition will increase, your triumphs will surpass your expectations, your faith will enlarge, and your repute will remain intact. When the game is over, irrespective of the outcome you will be a winner; and you will receive the same title and bonus as everyone else that reaches that pinnacle: Child of God adorned with a Crown of Life.

The only truth that makes us equal is Jesus Christ. In every other respect we are not equal. We are better than others and we are worse than others; that is, we are equally different. But we are similarly endowed by God with talents, rights, free will, and discernment; and we possess excellence. You too will be outstanding if you do a major league about face and allow Christ into your heart. The man Jesus Christ exhibited the aforementioned virtues to the uttermost degree, while possessing zero faults, failures, and frailties. He is excellent at everything; he is unsurpassable because his perfection is the standard. Christ is the example of what we can become with his love alive in our hearts. Instead of merely existing on this horizontal plane, I suggest you experience the vertical plane and its power.

The ultimate commission of the patriarchs was motivated by the same reward: salvation. It's a message for us to heed. The Lord didn't come to punish he came to save; do not impugn him. If you want to find fault blame sin, for without it there would be no suffering, pain, sorrow, or distress. Suffering is the consequence of sin and evil; and pain reflects the knowledge of those consequences. Such cannot exist in heaven where there is no sin. We are made perfect through suffering; yes, we are made perfect through Christ the proof of God's love, whose suffering was unparalleled and his goodness as well. It's not God's desire that malfeasance and misery occur; it is the will of sinners to whom God gave freedom. When it comes to iniquity every person is equally to blame, apart from Christ who will destroy the iniquity and corruption we have caused once and for all, his last act of adjudication.

Sin is ugly but our Savior is beautiful; yet he's been despised, disgraced, and rejected by many. The earth was beautiful until spoiled by humans due to sin, bringing death and destruction. The third heaven is beautiful, incorruptible, and will remain so.

Since sin leads to death it follows that there is no death in heaven. If you make it there it's because your sin was removed. That being the case, death will have no power over you. The reason is this: love is the greatest power; and no greater love is celebrated than to give one's life for another. And Christ paid with his life to forgive your sins and mine. Practice forgiveness as an act of love and reflect Christ; it is senseless to hold resentment against others for you are guilty too. It is useless to blame anybody if everybody is to blame. And say you're sorry even if it isn't your fault. It is not an admission of guilt. It is a statement of your love.

Continue to persevere along the right path. But don't stare at the ground or you won't see where you're going. Focus on the light. If you exit from the plotted course you'll end up in no man's land, where darkness could conceal the return lane from your sight. The light shows the way. Looking forward you'll notice the barriers in your path as they come into view and you'll surmount them with ease. Visualize the grand blueprint. If Christ is in the lobby you are entering from the front door. Let him be your poise and escort. Desist from anticipation; expect only the abundant life he promised. Don't be in a hurry lest you miss the opportunity, or trip on the obstacle, or careen over the cliff. When you get to a crossroads, you'll know which way to go but possibly not before. Be prepared to seize the moment every moment.

The road is straight and narrow that leads home and there are many detours, potholes, and obstructions along the way. You are to stay on the freeway to freedom where you will find everything you need to reach your destination in a timely manner. Don't be fooled by great billboards that advertise what they cannot sell. Don't be tricked by alternate expressways that get you nowhere fast. The journey can be long and arduous but also interesting and fun because everything is novel. And isn't a challenge more engaging than boredom or a free ride? Enjoy life. It sure beats the alternative. Live each day as if it were your last; for many it will be. Remain aware and mindful. To think is to feel and splendor brings joy. Fear and doubt lead to clinical depression and anxiety. Denial and unbelief lead to despair. Purpose and meaning provide clarification; to lack these is to be constantly dissatisfied, restless, and unsure.

Loyalty is greater than royalty. Stay on the path to avoid God's wrath. Follow his Way and be not led astray. Jesus spoke, "Be of good cheer and do not fear." "Focus on me and not the sea." "And from the grave you will be saved."

Don't be afraid but prepared. Trust is a must. If you worry, you'll be sorry. Heed the call or you will fall. If the Lord is your captain your ship will not capsize. Be zealous for him not jealous of them. Embrace grace. Reliance succeeds; defiance impedes.

Greed begets need. Treasure does not equate to pleasure. Health is wealth. Charity creates prosperity. The more you give the longer you live. Endeavor to live forever.

If you earn your bread, you'll be well fed. The lazy become crazy. If you play all day you will pay the price of vice. When you let the garden go only weeds will grow. If seeds of the spirit you sow, then deeds of merit will flow.

Equality is a reality. Illegality is a malady. Immorality precedes fatality, prevents immortality. God's truth is of the highest quality; his justice brings the truest finality (no more pardons and no technicalities).

Edification brings revelation, innovation, inspiration, emancipation. Yearn to learn and not to burn. Imagination without determination has no destination. Dedication may result in invention, if not creation. Beginning is superior to winning. Express it, don't repress it. Wait, don't berate. Give assistance not resistance.

The humble do not grumble; their hearts are endowed their heads are bowed. But the proud are loud; they raise self-praise. They ramble and rumble but they will stumble. There is no contentment in resentment. Forget it and you won't regret it. Keep it and you will reap it. Gratitude is the right attitude. Kindness should be added to your attitude. Disdain will bring pain. Being blameful is shameful.

Hope helps you cope. Making amends is a means to that end. Despair is a lair. Guilt will wilt your self-esteem and derail your dream. The unforgiven will quit being driven.

Make sure you're in the right before you fight; for war is nothing more than an act of greed, a grave misdeed, and depraved. The dead end begins when you've given into temptation, resulting in condemnation; when sin wins it will send you down below the ground with the renowned sound of extermination.

One can tell quite well that the heir of Hell is near. The beast disguised as a priest, who lies, has increased. Peace has ceased because fear, hate, uncaring, and despair are here, there, and everywhere. So, beware. When your heart can hear the cries of butterflies the slaughter is nigh.

Now you know how to proceed. Allow the love to flow and feed the seed implanted within your soul. Slowly, it will grow into a tree of life that glows with eternal brightness, showing you the right way to go; and you will succeed in becoming wholly holy and free.

A man who tries, vies, and dies. Foolish guys disguise their lies, deny their ties, and hide their eyes when they cry; they live buying their sighs, and flying high through smoggy skies. Men who try die to arise.

Appraise if you will the two choices before you: that everything we know and of which we are aware emerged by itself; or everything came to pass by the will of an omnipotent God. Either it exists without design or with design; without a creator or by a creator; from absolutely nothing or via immutable power.

The following principles of causality are postulated, pointing to one entity possessing all the ascribed attributes.

Only an eternal being can be the first cause of everything.

Only a timeless being can invent, regulate, and intervene time.

Only an omnipotent being can stretch space indefinitely.

Only a supernatural being can create nature, energy, and matter.

Only a living being can conceive life.

Only an omniscient being can originate, instill, and sustain knowledge.

Only a conscious being can initiate and activate awareness.

Only an intelligent being can design an intricate universe bursting with life.

Only a perfect being can establish the absolute standard for morality.

Only an immortal being can grant everlasting life.

Only a holy being can purify a soul.

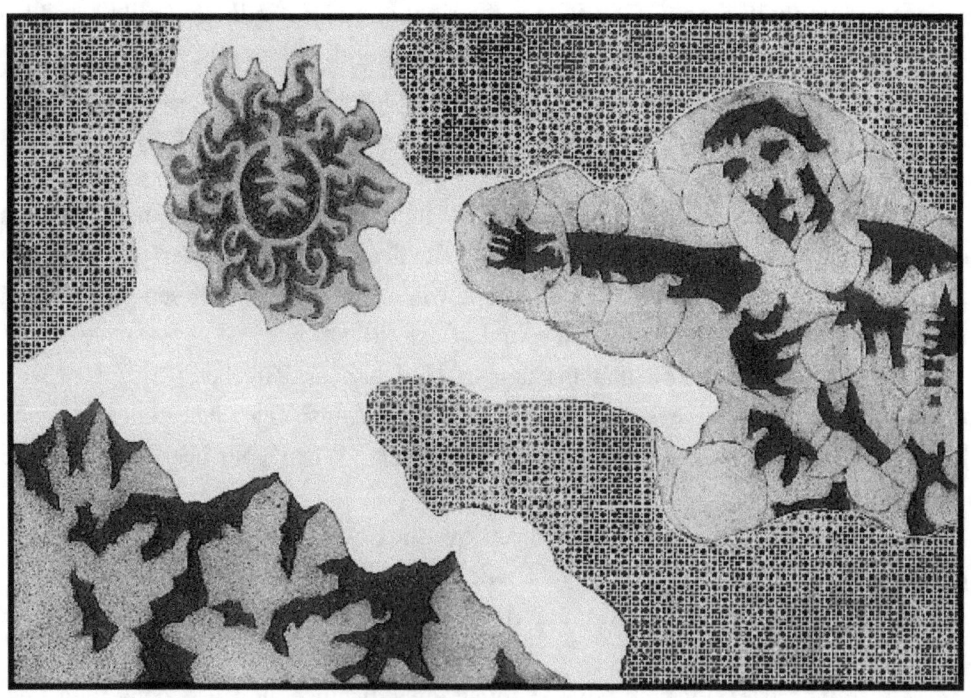

Spirit in the Sky

The oracle recalls his conception and life in the womb. It reminded him of a big bang. Light exploded with the force of a megaton detonation followed by a vision of faces: his ancestors, generations of them. He monitored the program from the fetal posture as if relaxing at a luxurious cinema; until he literally climbed out of the undersea cave and took his first breath. He said the entire seven months of his gestation left such an impression that he often goes back there in his mind to reminisce and take it easy.

I have no memory of life in the womb but I imagine it was pleasant. In grade school we viewed a video of a woman giving birth. It seemed pretty traumatic for the kid; it wasn't that pleasant for the mom either. And it doesn't get any easier for either one of them after that. Still, one can only be struck with awe at the sight of new life; amidst the bloody mess there is an element of spectacular beauty.

SS has a photographic memory. That doesn't mean he can flip through a literary anthology and memorize the entire text without reading it; and it doesn't mean that he can recite verbatim the same book having read it once. What it means is that he doesn't forget anything, even birth. Every experience is logged in a meticulously organized database: a neurological warehouse if you will. He can access information quickly and effortlessly which is why he seldom errs. His brain isn't any bigger than mine however, he simply uses it more efficiently. He definitely underestimated humans though, but then he never had occasion to observe civilized ones before.

His kind develops quite rapidly. He began to talk when he was ninety days old and to project his cogitations in a hundred more. He was walking by that time and learning to write. By age one he knew the entire phonetic alphabet and could compose paragraphs. By age two he was building thousand-piece puzzles and sketching accurate scale models of objects and vehicles. And apparently this was slightly above average in the normal distribution.

Both of his parents excelled academically and professionally. His father was a professor and his mother a publisher. They often traveled about, attending and delivering presentations at different academic conferences, leaving the children in the hands of a licensed daycare facility. While on a philanthropic mission in his native galaxy, these ambassadors of goodwill were killed by a suicide bomber who had targeted the wrong embassy. Senseless death was wrought at the hands of an imbecile who couldn't read an address correctly. Fortunately for the gene pool the assailant also expired in the blast.

The result was to bring more combatants into escalating interstellar warfare that already had claimed tens of thousands of lives in the sector. A full-blown galactic fiasco was brewing which would last for two score and seven years. Little did the solipsist know that someday he would play a major role in the resolution of that conflict.

SS was orphaned at age two-and-a-half with a sister a year younger. They were dumped in a residential home for children, funded by the government. To keep him occupied they started him in school a year early (at age three) and he excelled; by age four he already was in an advanced class. He taught his sister how to read and write and she too began school early. The two feasted upon each other and they forged ahead mentally and emotionally, developing a bond that blended their hearts and minds into one.

Unfortunately, they were separated when SS turned five. The sister was snatched by a wealthy couple from the royal line to be brought up in an enriched environment. The brother was left behind in impoverished subsidized housing to be reared in a crowded, deprived environment. They were all they had and faced the fear and frustration of never seeing one another again. A brief tearful goodbye was forever etched into the next step of a staircase that led progressively downward for the solipsist.

It was a devastating setback. SS turned unruly and defiant, often throwing objects at the faculty and screaming aloud in hysterical fits. He was very destructive to the property and had to be restrained on numerous occasions to prevent injury to others and himself. The children's home couldn't handle him; further, they were losing their sponsorship and soon would be closing their doors. Fatefully, the counselors pawned SS off on unsuspecting adopters.

The jilted tyke bounced around foster homes like a pinball in one of those archaic arcade machines, but he perpetually ended at the reformatory without a free play. He did manage to expend minimal energy on his studies (from lack of anything better to do) and he continued to dumbfound instructors with his intellectual prowess. Still, he was easily irritated and openly aggressive. At first the psychiatrists thought he was hyperactive and antagonistic but eventually realized that he was modestly under-stimulated. They registered him in the accelerated pipeline and eventually he settled down and began to achieve high marks again.

One auspicious day a juvenile delinquent burned the institution down. SS scarcely had time to salvage the photo of him and his baby sister; other records and memories were destroyed in the blaze. He escaped relatively unscorched but not unscathed; the rest of the inmates were not so lucky, including one careless pyromaniac. SS was the sole survivor. He spent a few weeks in the hospital suffering from smoke inhalation, second-degree burns, and additional trauma. During his rehabilitation he fooled around with his nurse who stole his innocence on his thirteenth birthday and gave him a sexually transmitted infection in the meantime for which he had to stay another week to be cured of it.

Once again, his life became unstable. He was transferred to a shelter for criminal adolescents which was more a jail than a boarding school. Though not exactly an offender his behavior was offensive so they figured he belonged there as much as anywhere. He regressed to earlier stages of rage, defiance, and explosiveness. Doctors tried to temper him with tranquilizers but that didn't work because he had to be sedated continuously. They tossed him into a padded cell under solitary confinement. Due to the frequent tirades they stopped letting him out as he would retaliate mercilessly against the operators as a result of his maltreatment. They did however, bear him access to books and he read profusely. It was his only solace and escape; until one fateful night when a deafening electrical storm pounded the compound. Numerous consecutive bolts of lightning zapped the central power transformers and the locking mechanisms on the cells malfunctioned. When the doors popped open SS slipped away unnoticed, but not before trashing the computers and recordkeeping systems. Talk about déjà vu.

As a back-alley urchin SS gained a greater appreciation for existentialism and obtained a first-rate tutorial about life on the street. He fell in lust over a homeless girl who taught him the basics of intercourse, but she ran off to service a soldier leaving the orphan alone again. He panhandled for food and money living under bridges and sleeping in subways. He often appeared before the magistrates but they never could decide what to do with him so they'd give him another warning and turn him loose. They finally declared him independent and permanently liberated; he always did fend for himself so it was a change of status only in their eyes.

Emancipation was not all it was cracked up to be. He knew he had to get a job or be forced into the discouraging world of dishonesty and disrepute. Despite his sordid upbringing he refused to relinquish rationality. He had apprenticed in gardening and landscaping and sought work in that area. He started pruning trees, mowing lawns, and sculpting people's scenery. Time flew by until an aristocratic artificer accepted his proposal for a tree planting job and, satisfied with the results referred him to the neighbors. SS increasingly developed a reputation for craftsmanship and aestheticism, developing a list of clients that consistently commissioned him to toil their soil and beautify their habitat.

At nineteen he began working fulltime for a member of the regal family, caretaking the grounds of a ten-acre spread in Fantasyland. On days off his boss's comely daughter cooked breakfast sharply at seven for him and dear old dad. SS was attracted to, make that smitten with the nobleman's daughter. He had never been in the company of a debutante so elegant and she had never witnessed a rascal so raunchy. A crafty lad of manipulative mannerisms, he coaxed the nubile lass into his quarters one evening and proceeded to snatch a kiss. She resisted at first but succumbed to his charm, mellifluously melding into his embrace. He became electrified; but a charge of chivalry changed his course and he resisted her advances to go all the way. Needless to say, they soon became lovers: the opulent duchess and the belligerent brat.

As karma might have it, she finally probed for details about his background upon which he showed her the crinkled photograph. Putting two and two together they realized they were brother and sister. Being the marrying age, and pregnant as well, they eloped. It was not unusual for close relatives to marry in his culture so her father gave them his consent and the guesthouse. Let me tell you, this is how to proceed from pauper to prince in seventy weeks without trying. And what an imposing pair: he the streetwise scoundrel and she the cultured academic, a terrific combination—smart, skillful, shrewd, seductive, and sly; a solution for success in any society.

His landscaping business boomed and SS expanded. He commissioned several crews which he personally supervised. They consisted of wayward boys that were down on their luck like he had been; he gave them a chance at probation rather than incarceration. SS taught and mentored them in a way that he alone could. He eventually formed a corporation and opened an office and training center in the inner city. In eight years, he was as wealthy as his father-in-law, who retired to help him run the administrative office.

SS amassed a fortune, a family, and a formal education during which he majored in the physical and environmental sciences. For his thesis he formulated fertilization and cultivation methods that resulted in organized germination, so that desired vegetation could grow rapidly and naturally in designated locations. At that point his career took off, swiftly raking in the legal tender, establishing a new trade in his world called environmental engineering. His expertise was required throughout the sector by civilians, businesses, and governments. He was on a consulting job at another solar system when interplanetary imperialism caused the annihilation of the province where he, his honey, and their daughter cohabitated. "To gain my world back only to lose it again was the living end," he sighed. Sure, the insurance would cover his assets, but how would he replace the loves of his life? His inner circle severed, he became a recluse totally divorcing himself from relationships of any kind. It was déjà vu all over again.

"Well, that's one thing we have in common," I suggested. Problem for me is I never made it as far as marriage or offspring.

What a blessing it must be to share such profound love with a member of the opposite sex. I had a brief encounter when I was a teen, but ain't seen hide nor hair of a prospective soulmate since. I was stuck on a childhood romance that was never consummated. People underestimate the love between children. But I assure you it is as authentic as any other, maybe more. The advantage of youth is that there are fewer conditions placed upon the liaison. Love is shared, albeit imparted, and the commitment is genuine. Equality is valued and responsibility is usually forthcoming given the chance. That seems feasible in theory but I never had a chance to test its validity. Probably it's too late for me now. But who knows, maybe you can teach an old dog new tricks. Heaven knows I had my chances.

Mirror to the Past

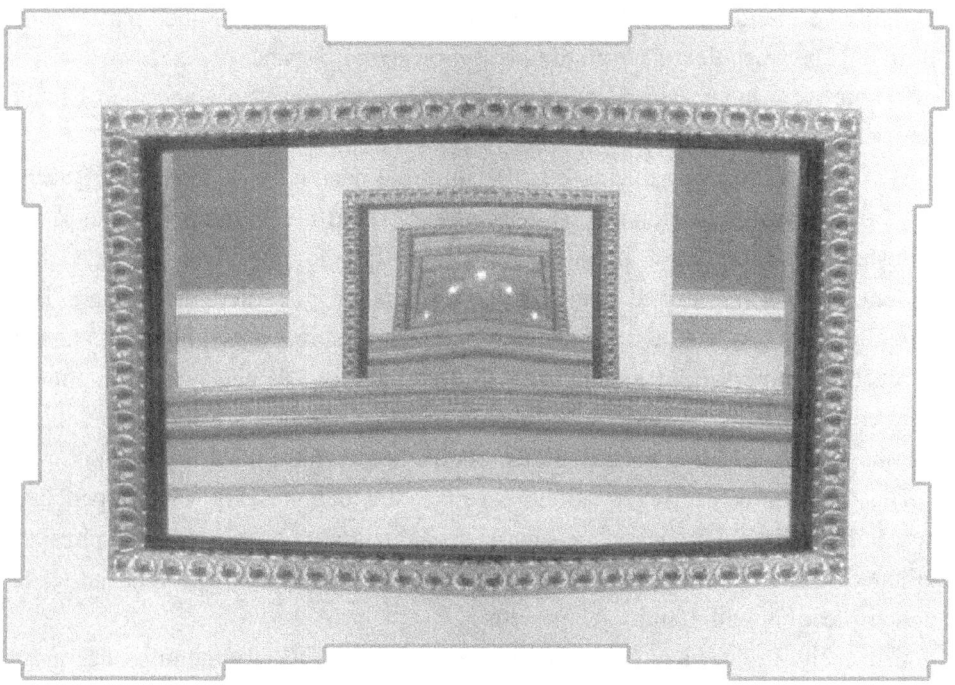

It seems the principles advanced above get compromised in adulthood; that is, some people tend to become increasingly more selfish in their partnerships. Equity does not always imply balance and to restore it the antagonist usually resorts to psychological methods that cost him or her nothing. Adults have the tendency to maximize their benefits while minimizing their costs, and social relationships are no exception. At least that's been my observation but I've been wrong before. Ask anyone what they define as fairness and most will respond fifty-fifty. Okay, probably relationships can be sustained at that level. But whatever happened to each partner contributing 100 percent? That's a win-win situation if I ever saw one. Total commitment, giving, dedication and devotion; awaiting nothing in return but knowing it is impending. How I long for such a connection. But truthfully, I know I am loved and that a connection exists from my spirit to spirits passed or unseen, especially persons I have loved (and still do) including the Grand Spirit.

Well, the loss was unbearable for the solipsist and he withdrew into the illicit drug scene where he grew demented and deranged. He was flailing around in the ashes when guys wearing white coats and carrying Geiger counters picked him up. He abided in an asylum for autumn and a year. I deemed his reaction understandable for someone who'd been continuously traumatized since a toddler. His past would haunt him, the present would daunt him, and the future would taunt him. His only deliverance was to lodge inside the utopian reality he formulated in his mind's eye. Eventually he found himself there, returned to awareness, and regained partial sanity. Fortunately, he was released from the institution with no scars.

"There were many weird goons in there," he told me, "Now and then I believe they existed; but if they did then verily, I was a lunatic."

He didn't mind being diagnosed with multiple personalities. He developed them purposefully in order to manage his demons and guard his dwindling veracity. Each manifestation performed a particular function. His favorite was being Galactic President and getting stoned every day (this persona governed the others). But a culmination of every distinct ego state caused him to suffer a psychotic break; for at once each nightmare he'd experienced throughout his life became simultaneously integrated into willful awareness. In layman's terms, all closets were opened and the skeletons loosed, invading his consciousness like a swarm of hovering hornets.

His mind blew with every circuit in his brain depolarizing. He slipped into a state of discombobulation and desensitization, mentally exhausted and physically debilitated; comatose would be the human equivalent. What snapped him out was his daughter pleading with him to get on with it.

Curiously, I never have nightmares per se for even the frightening ones are too interesting to worry about. Actually, upon analysis they seem idiotic even hilarious at times. It brings to remembrance the nightmare I had when I turned nine. I saw myself a lad of five, flying naked as a jaybird, wearing only a red baseball cap and cowboy boots, pissing over the city as I sang *The Star-Spangled Banner*; it was raining cats and dogs, literally, creating a sloppy sludge below. I finally ascertained the meaning of the dream at age twenty-one. It was a collage of snippets from my early childhood prior to moving cross-country from a lush tropical setting to a deserted desert. How the expression of fear fit the scenario is beyond me. Perhaps it was associated with the dread of starting school a year early in a strange place with no friends. But fear is a relative term. The reflection of past horrors can linger within the confines of a troubled soul, and such was the solipsist's handicap.

Still I was jealous of him because he was able to live out my dreams. He used to say, "If you've solved it in your dreams you can make it happen in life." Well I have yet to realize that. Although I have to admit that learning takes place during dreaming; and purposive thought occurs in concert with REM sleep. It is not simply the integration of newly acquired information into the existing memory structures; it is the reconfiguration of internal models in preparation for the next event or a loftier purpose. Memory modules are thereby reorganized bringing new definition to the past as well as insight into the future.

Dreams can connect the past, present, and future in a way that is devoid of temporal constraints. No wonder they intrigue me so. SS bought me an audiovisual device from the afterworld complete with electrodes and a memory tracer. It enables me to record my dreams and has been my favorite toy since. The contraption scans images from neural activation patterns in my visual cortex and converts them into photographs depicting the various scenes being displayed. I can project them in sequence and watch as the episode changes or a scenario unfolds. It's like watching six different television sets. Each component and symbol represent something profound about the denotations of my mind and associated cognitive structures. Needless to say, it is very enlightening. I have seen arrays of images that collectively assemble into insight, meaning and wisdom. I encourage everyone to record dreams; they put things into perspective every so often. You could get a warning from God about malicious plots against you, or a message giving you directions or instructions, or prescience into internal ailments, or premonitions telling you of incidents to come; or perhaps only an entertaining interlude that will inspire you to write a book or something.

To better understand what is going on in your dreams, pay particular attention to these aspects: dialogue (especially words that are spoken to you); actions (especially those left incomplete because you woke up); and salient workings that stick out in your recollection. Analyze features of the dream and you may gain personal understanding and develop accurate empathy.

Further, notice the emotions you feel or felt (passion, anger, fear, grief, loneliness, rejection, guilt, joy, excitement, love) and how that relates to the current state of affairs and your state of mind. Naturally, everything is germane at least to you; but the symbolism is personal not universal. For example, a rooster might mean something different to a farmer than to a butcher. An ocean would be different for a soldier than a sailor. Cultural, generational, gender, age, economic, occupational, and geographical variances certainly come into play. Most important will be the relevance of past history and experience, current relationships, roles and responsibilities, and involvement with upcoming proceedings. Be aware that the dream may be so convoluted that it makes no sense at all; there might not be a clear connection to what is going on or what could happen. And the feeling can be substantially different than the wishing. However, continuing trends or repetitive patterns often point to a single end, action, or idea. Recurring dreams may be your subconscious trying to tell you something. Peruse your dream diary regularly to pinpoint trends and associations among the episodes. Group them together into logical taxonomies, and watch the arrangement expand into additional implication, value, and guidelines.

"out of the closet at last"

The following situational conditions, scenes, and symbolism may indicate what is happening in your life (or what is going to happen) and what to do about it: setting, location (space, home, business, school, recreation, battleground); directions and openings (window, door, gate, stairs, path); people, family, strangers (past or present); animals (domestic, wild, flying, swimming, crawling), plants and flowers. It may be important the activities (falling, running, sobbing, laughing, embracing, competing); the time of day or night and the season of the year; weather (inclement, stormy, cloudy, natural disaster, bright); and of course, plot and situation. Take note of objects and their use or purpose: food; money, jewelry or gold; toys, tools, vehicles, weapons, musical instruments; buildings, homes, palaces, rooms, furniture; body parts; and whether things are old or new. Identify the elements that are present (fire, water, wind, earth); the landscape, geology, and bodies of water (river, lake, ocean, pond); and especially spiritual phenomena (God, Jesus; church; angels, demons, and ghosts). Dreams will assist you in understanding how your unconscious mind works.

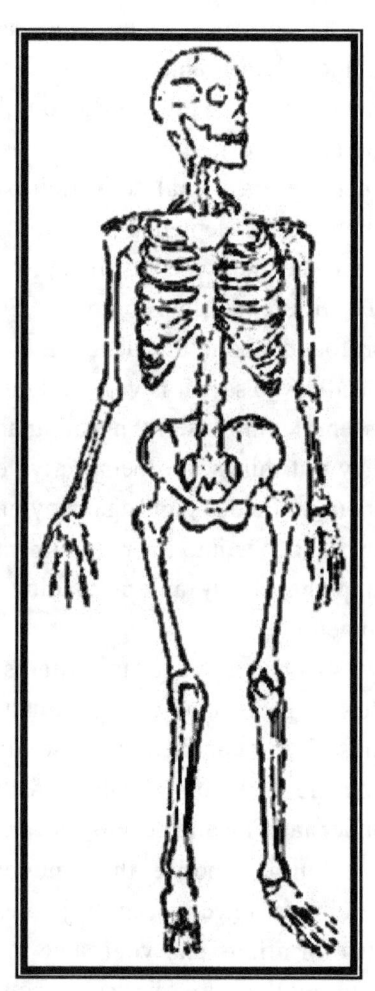

The brain consists of an intricate interconnected arrangement of innumerable neural nodes which are activated in particular sequences that establish connotation and realization for the individual. Theoretically, this network is arranged successively, with the larger schemas reflecting an integration of information clusters that collectively produce an experience, memory, or idea. The clusters in turn are comprised of subordinate bunches of data, which are a collection of yet smaller chunks, composed of even smaller bits, etc. (kind of like the universe itself as well as your body). Each subdivision stores a specific category of information. Therefore, in order for new or updated information to be merged into a given module, file, or cluster it must satisfy the associated informational constraints. It follows that cognitive restructuring should necessarily occur at the subconscious levels as is the case during dreaming. It's as if your brain is conducting memory defragmentation and disk compression on your hard drive while you sleep. Is the unconscious mind reorganizing itself in order to free up space in preparation for another deluge of input the next day? It is known that the process removes irrelevant connections and strengthens relevant ones, thereby achieving maximum accuracy, speedy recall, and efficient storage.

Given that memory is a complex conglomeration of numerous layers of data it is remarkable that the brain can perform such reorganization so effortlessly. But the very reason that it can is because it is doing so at the depths of the subconscious. The information is processed at greater speed, in larger quantity, and at multiple levels during dreaming. The activation of neurons occurs in different cerebral areas via assorted parallel channels accounting for the apparent bizarreness of dreams. The greater the number of memory clusters simultaneously activated, the less coherent their associations will be, and the stranger the overall view to waking consciousness. When you awaken you get a sudden, momentary glance at the entire exhibition. Unrelated parts will seldom fit together; subsequently, the pieces can be assembled into more than one puzzle.

But why is rapid eye movement exhibited during most dream states? What are the eyes doing during REM sleep? Does our brain concoct a visual memory map that is scanned sequentially by the eyes? Are the eyes directing clumps of data to the appropriate neural modules in the system? Are we establishing links between hemispheres of the brain by developing verbal connections to the visual imagery, thereby providing conscious cues that facilitate retrieval from the unconscious? Are we disseminating the information into collections of images that become written into those memory traces providing an appropriate match? Is the visual cortex performing fast-forward replay of events in order to synchronize past with recent events, and suggest possible future expectations? Are any or all of these mechanisms taking place? Or are we knowingly shifting our gaze as we experience the projected scenes or slides being visualized, coming at us far more rapidly than daydreaming? Further, what meaning is derived and where is it stored? These underlying questions even the solipsist could not answer. Neither could I find a definitive conclusion in the most current and advanced scientific journals, for I continue searching for the REM connection to this day. Whoever figures that one out will become famous.

To continue the history lesson, revenge was eating at his two hearts. So, SS applied for and attained an appointment with the space cadets. Graduating top of his class he was assigned as a tactician and strategist, trained in battlefield analysis and recognized as an expert in chemical and biological warfare. While working in a secret laboratory he discovered and produced a toxic agent that was both deadly to solipsists and environmentally safe. It was deployed in mass quantities in retaliation to the onslaught of antipathy by and against his kind. As soon as the aggressors had successfully eradicated every soul in the targeted domain the wars ended and SS resigned from duty. I found his exposition unnerving.

It took SS a lifetime to live it down and for life to be rejuvenated in his bygone stomping grounds. Discontent with his accomplishments, plagued by posttraumatic stress and guilt, embarrassed from his contribution to prejudicial obliteration, he decided to leave the galaxy and explore his universe solo (after all, he needed to get accustomed to being alone for the therapy to work). He purchased a small but swift cruiser; then he hired a few technicians to aid in effecting modifications. But still he was not happy. Then he obtained clearance from the authorities to attempt a breach of the black hole in the center of his galaxy. The government gave him permission, probably to get rid of him. Nobody expected him to survive the theorized singularity, much less succeed in making it through to the other side. But they didn't write him off either as he was an extraordinary specimen. This enabled him to test his theory and traverse the black hole, where by and by he found me, confirming that there is life beyond that spatial phenomenon. They used to say nobody'd seen a black hole, well guess what? That's because it's actually white, you dimwits. It's easy; if it eats light there must be beau coup light coming in from the other side. The reason you can't see because it's invisible in the light.

He withdrew from the turmoil in his mind and his universe, entering those which were totally foreign to him. Together we investigated my mind and my universe. Everything to him was like a dream; he couldn't distinguish fantasy from reality for they were too closely related. He passed his life off as fiction; for others it was. Strictly speaking, sometimes it was stranger than truth. For I've witnessed spectacles that defy explanation, astounded at the intricacy of my corkscrew galaxy and its hundreds of billions of stars. It truly is a dazzling place to visit but I wouldn't want to live here. Not when there are places unseen and unheard which transcend human experience; they are out there waiting to be explored, never touched by human thought. And that's where you'll find me an eternity from now.

His next fantastic feat was inventing time travel. When SS first broke the time barrier, he couldn't land the temporal plane. It took a while for him to adjust the partial correlations until the path analysis was completely calibrated, and solutions led to an optimum prediction (it made sense to him). Consequently, he went tumbling through time as if falling down, or up. For weeks he had to live someone else's past in reverse order into a future period that didn't exist yet. Well it wouldn't fit and he hit the pit (which may or may not have a bottom depending on which end of it you're looking at). In the nick of time he steered the craft hard to aft, then slammed on the retrorockets spinning to a full stop. The fact that he halted at all was the key. He added a failsafe gadget that would implement such a shutdown and zero out time thereby seizing the present whatever time it was at the time.

"It was a living nightmare!" he blared.

"How ironic: life can be a bad dream and sleep a wild fantasy," I responded. "It doesn't have to be the wrong way, or it could be both ways." (Or the opposite like being afraid to dream but not to live.)

Thus, he began his voyages through time in a parallel dimension, to survey an expanse that few in his world would ever contemplate much less hear about. I was a tour guide of sorts but it was a great opportunity. We were the modern Vikings, overcoming great barriers and dangers to discover untrodden territories. Time was the final frontier, not space. We sojourned back and forth through the chronology of Earth because SS didn't want to explore his own history. I suppose it was too disquieting for him so he chose to keep it repressed along with his memories of home. He was old enough to be my grandfather when I met him, but he had seemingly unlimited energy.

The solipsist traveled incognito; he spoke only to strangers. Strangely enough, I was strange enough for him not to stay estranged from me. He acknowledged that my notions were not unlike his, and realizing we were more alike than not he decided he liked me. The solipsist prefers not to release his name however. He told it to me once but made me vow never to repeat it. I call him SS and he fancy's that nickname. He comes from a long line of solipsists.

His favorite excursion was backwards to the great wars. He was impressed with the sheer audacity of the triple alliance. While he didn't agree with their views, he admired their resolve. Just for fun he decided to see what would happen if the mad murderous dictators, one each from opposing sides, had joined forces; so, we altered the past and let it play out. Europe promptly fell, and the USA and Japan were forced to withdraw and defend. The hostilities continued for another decade until the deployment of nukes caused the world to hurdle into the time of the tribes; then history picked it up from there.

Well two can play that game, so I coerced SS into going back again and we rigged it so that the cocky American general would successfully convince his superiors to conquer the commies in addition to defeating the krauts. Europe quickly fell again, under the auspices of the West however. Ukraine and the Baltics followed suit. Immediately the occident bonded. This new twist caused time to hasten into the reign of the evil kingdom.

The solipsist was humiliated because the simulation I proposed had a greater impact on history than his, insofar as it quickened the end. Either way it didn't matter because the finale was the same. No matter how many times we backtracked we could not change the consequences. So, we tried fiddling with the future to see what would happen.

We made similar alterations to those of the past. Instead of Magog commingling with the northern kingdom we arranged an alliance with eastern Asia. This resulted in creating the two world powers; the only difference being the dividing line became longitudinal, creating an east-west dichotomy rather than north-south. The hemispheric showdown reoccurred either way. Thus, time reverted to the present regardless of how the future or the past had been refabricated.

I've heard people say: If I had it to do over, I would have done it differently. "It wouldn't matter if they did, their destiny has been preordained," the solipsist declared. We ultimately end up making the same choices because that is our affinity. And while there may be a destiny or calling designed for us, we still can opt out and never fulfill that purpose. I mean, SS could've ended up a psychopath or a bum, or both, had he not decided to ensue with his harebrained promenade that included me.

You can throw a monkey wrench into the works but the cogs continue to turn; your best bet is to affect your own life. No matter what a person plans, it's God's purpose that inevitably will prevail; and you can be an integral part of it if you dare to care. In the post hoc analysis, giving due diligence, it makes more sense to live your life as it comes. Forget about hindsight because you can't change what already happened. Forget about foresight because you cannot create the future. But you can build one. Learn from your mistakes (as well as your successes) and move forward at the pace of time. Besides, people are compelled to react the same way in similar circumstances and thus are destined to repeat the past. You cannot change time because it is changing you, until it ends. Eventually, time itself will expire.

Our travels made SS yearn for something he misplaced and he started sinking again. Upon temporarily regaining his composure he concluded that he must return to his previous personage. Maybe he could convert his people by convincing them that the spirit was within them not somewhere in outer space. He was not returning home to claim who he used to be but to establish who he was going to be.

Same as disillusioned souls here, who typically find it easier to deny the truth in favor of living in doubt as if this takes less effort or faith. And for the rest, they hadn't been seeking the divine because they couldn't prove it to themselves, as if incontrovertible evidence was available inside their head. But they have failed to look elsewhere or explore fresh possibilities. Moreover, if they wanted to experience righteousness, they'd have to invite it to come. I guess wherever you go or live, and whoever you are or strive to be, the same basic choices are before you. That is, if you are an intelligent being, you'll know where to go from here and you'll know you have arrived when you get there (unless you are trying to blaze a trail on your own).

The Pit

Every eighty-eight days SS trekked across space and time, then back again. He couldn't appreciate knowing what would happen realizing that whatever he sensed he could anticipate. Either way, he would periodically return to later and plant the proof for another to find thereby bringing it about. I suppose that's where I came in, to facilitate the fundamental objective of his enterprise: destiny. Does history repeat itself? "Unquestionably," he would answer. In essence it was self-fulfilling prophecy. He was in no position to change it though I was determined to do so.

Who then is the solipsist? I suppose he could qualify as my alter ego, for I too needed to acquire self-reliance and bury the burning pain before I could perform properly during those challenging escapades. In the orphanage, and again at the sanatorium, he realized he didn't appreciate having others supervising us or bullying us. He taught me to discipline myself in order to avoid the disciplinary actions of others. Of course, where he comes from you totally get hammered for slacking. I adopted his philosophical approach and assumed my position as intern. He required me to "Keep in line, and don't push it too hard, too fast, or too far." I executed my duties as if it was my father expecting it, whereas our interactions were filial. I trusted his prudence; he relied on my conscientiousness and dependability.

"Trustworthiness is the measure of the man against other attributes," he taught me. "It is the combination of the degree to which a man tenders his honor and the extent to which he meets that commitment."

"And you will never receive trust if you never give it because if you don't trust anybody nobody will trust you," I added. "Trust is a priceless gift from the Ancient One," SS avowed, finishing the thought.

Extraterrestrials are not what you think. For one thing, they don't resemble runts with swollen heads, bug eyes, and emaciated faces. Perhaps that's how you visualize them but the image was counterfeited for you. It was a hoax perpetrated by various intelligence agencies to keep people in the dark about their top secrets. They cleaned up sites and covered up incidents leaving absolutely no substantiation or paper trail, but plenty of speculation. The science fiction dreamers did the rest, along with the paranormal freaks and the paranoid coveters. Suddenly everyone was seeing UFOs, aliens, specters, and such. They were living past lives, reincarnated as cows, mice, birds, or humans and bearing witness to every manner of eschatological delusion.

And then there were those shrewd devils that enjoyed abusing people with eccentric mind games. They had an elaborate setup complete with mockups, costumes, and actors which would fool anybody of average intellect who was sufficiently drugged and paralyzed. It was a wicked collusion to engage in brainwashing, sexual assault, the mining of body parts, and performing experimental surgery, leaving the victims traumatized and believing the perpetrators were aliens. The miscreants got away with it for an awful long time; it was virtually impossible to get caught since the authorities were convinced the abductees were loony. But consider that the prey underwent comparable scenarios: machines, medical equipment, drugs, sex, scripts, outfits, sets, and backdrops. Too often we base our beliefs on what we see, sidetracked by optical illusions. Vision, or any other sensation, can contradict reality; ask any pilot who has learned to trust instruments and displays more than sensations and perceptions, or a blind person who can navigate through darkness better than those with sight.

"Playing on the aspirations and experiences of the ignorant, incompetent, or intoxicated is an effective avenue for indoctrination and manipulation," the sage submitted. That's how the fanatics engender a cult following, I realized, and why the government keeps people uneducated and in the dark.

If you're sharp you'll accept that you don't always have a need to know (it's not because you're mentally incompetent). Notice what they show you is generations behind what they have. And they don't want anyone else to have it or to know about it. We assume they are powerful and intimidating; and rightfully so. Besides, if they publicized their secret stuff some idiots would get their hands on it and cause a cataclysm (like mischievous little monsters playing with matches). They invent pseudo enemies and imaginary threats. Some engagements are staged so they can test the prototypes. Case in point: if intelligence about radar reflective composites had reached the enemy the wars would have commenced long before. Or did you think stealth technology was in its infancy in those days? Nothing was new. How were they able to build the atomic bomb so fast? They had been examining the technology long before deploying it. They concocted ruses to subdue these advances.

Be grateful that you have imagination to entertain you and don't have to watch firsthand the vile forecasting of imperialism, slaughter, and captivity. And be thankful that time wasn't crunched into a vacuum as if to save it or spend it. Otherwise, I would never have been born and you either. It's lucky that we're here anyhow because those crazy fools are more apt to abort a living fetus than their costly, futile, destructive and unfunded covert operations. And the solipsist, where would he be now?

I was honored to have the distinct privilege of exploring the complexities of the psyche and the cosmos with an individual who hailed from a venue out of the void. It's an opportunity of a lifetime and one I wish everybody could experience. But in a way, they can. For example, I believe God sends guardian angels to protect us. How else could we make it through the gauntlet alive? You should tune into yours. As for your demons, it's high time you dismissed them for they are of no use to anyone.

What then does a space alien look like? Whatever you want them to look like. Is there proof of such beings? Positively there is evidence of spiritual presences. Take angels for instance. They can disguise themselves to resemble whatever becomes them or expedites their errand. Some have four faces: eagle, bison, puma, human. They could resemble you. Look in the mirror. How many faces do you see? Is your face the only one? And those people out there, are they all human? Do they originate from here; if not, where? But surely, they come from somewhere. Are they alive as we are? Can they be saved?

Thus, one part of the puzzle had been completed but insufficient to see the entire picture. Had we genuinely crossed the chronometric threshold, are there manifold universes that simultaneously exist, or were we visiting parallel extensions of the same world? But if the multi-world hypothesis were true, I would not be me, at least not in the other dimensions. That's what the mavens preached. But it was me all the while and I am not a solipsist. I postulated, "The different dimensions theory suggests that the future can be altered in the present, though the past cannot."

SS dismissed the notion without presenting empirical data which was seldom his way. I guess he was tired of providing answers and decided it was time to seek a few for himself. Mentoring me was weighing on him too I suspect, as I am not the most astute or cooperative protégé (and way too inquisitive I must say).

Ruins of Destiny

I saw him off below the pinnacle of my famed mountain and hideaway where the ship had been stowed in a depression, camouflaged and cloaked among swaying coniferous trees. He was going back from whence he came to live the hereafter again, in a land where the inhabitants are the same shade of tan (unlike here where everyone is a different shade of tan). Where wars are conducted via videogames by analysts sitting behind consoles, directing spacecraft and controlling reconnaissance and attack missions by computer, and where he would resume his commission as casualty assessment officer. He envisioned retiring in ten years, packing the schooner, returning to the other side, and establishing his dream station at the base of the Pleiades. I've always admired that view myself.

And will he return? He usually does; but he's unpredictable. He sends me stellar telegrams that he produced in the future. Last I heard he was spending his leisure time working on a cold atomic fusion project whereby plasma energy revives itself. In theory, it would produce what it expended making it very economical for powering star machines. This, after he already had discovered a way to fuel the ship using deuterium. He has a gift for improvisation, doesn't he? He comes up with stuff that wasn't even there tomorrow.

Meanwhile, I was back slaving for the secret service. It seems the occasional sightings of the solipsist's spacecraft led authorities to believe that an incursion was imminent. I was combating cloned bionic superhuman assemblages spawned in preparation for a surprise attack from space invaders that never came. Odd I thought, since the government had outlawed cloning long ago during the war between the sexes. Built in violation of their own decree, the establishment was now forced to trail and terminate the troublemakers (with extreme prejudice) as they had become a threat to the bureaucracy. I guess the remanufactured hearts wanted to produce a superior race but their DNA had been severely compromised and they could not reproduce; a kind of jackass you might say. They tried to hide and would attack if cornered, though they possessed no conscience or measure of morality. Life and death became meaningless but they retained the survival instinct. Overall, they misunderstood the value humans place on life: ours and theirs. They had to be put to sleep for they were programmed to be nasty and ferocious.

How typical. You know what I'm saying, when honchos develop offensive weapons as a means of defense. No wonder they are prone to backfiring. You can fight fire with fire but you can't end war with war. The best way to restore peace is with peace. When will they learn? And as advanced as the solipsist's world, they hadn't rid the place of gargantuan annihilation devices either.

Well I didn't enjoy the drudgery; it collided with my scruples. Besides, there were bigger disputes to exhort. Were the androids ignorant or even alive? It wasn't for me to decide. This was a classic approach-avoidance conflict. Still I had a semi-steady job, though the retirement and benefits packages were next to nothing. Yes, I had income but at what cost? I couldn't complain. Well I could but who would listen? Things can always be worse I figure; or better. But at least they are. If I am to make a difference in this gamut, it ought to be with my might and my heart. But if the heart is not in it, it probably isn't a good idea to continue the pursuit.

I was awakened from ringing in my ears; Joy had called to tell me she wanted to sell the house. I asked her what she meant and she hung up the phone on me. Right then, Gramps sauntered into my bedroom requesting assistance cleaning the old place. A stray black Labrador followed him in; the dog was howling uncontrollably. We didn't know where the dog came from but it wasn't vicious, foaming at the mouth or anything. I muzzled the dog with my hand and he stopped howling and squatted down on his haunches. He didn't seem to mind me holding his snout shut. I went to the bathroom and the dog followed me, howling again. I grabbed his nose and he responded accordingly. Finishing my business there, we proceeded to the abandoned house, the dog lagging behind like he belonged.

I discovered what Gramps meant by cleaning the house. It wasn't dirty, trashed, or in disarray; but there was a huge unruly gray mare in the living room. As soon as she saw us, she began bucking violently; then stood on her hind quarters almost as high as the cathedral ceiling flailing her hooves in my face. I unsheathed the silver sword from my belt and extended it high above my head. It collected and magnified the shimmer of every flash of ambient light leaking through the windows, sending beams in every direction permeating every room in the house including the attic with its sheen. I guess the intruder didn't appreciate that and she vanished. In retrospect it seemed more an exorcism or purification than a janitorial chore. I kept the dog. I have no idea who ended up abiding in that house. One thing is for sure: there will be no escaping the light when the Lord returns; truth will be revealed, darkness extinguished, and lies exposed.

I could not grasp the dwelling as I didn't recognize it after I reawakened. I'd just as soon not go back though, that's for sure. It was a scary place yet uproarious in its own way. The horse, while it showed strength, was nothing but an obstinate menace. But the dog, which seemed annoying at first, turned out to signify obedience and loyalty. I would possess that sword if I could; a positive power resided within it. For it flashed an eternal light that penetrated my very being; all the way to my inner soul. It could ward off darkness and evil, I might add. I guess Gramps was trying to tell me to clean up my act, which had to begin with a cleansing of my heart and ultimately my soul. And a significant change was afoot. I learned to employ the sword by listening fastidiously when God would speak. I got the point if you get my drift.

Mostly I would dream of a different maiden each night. It seems they had a carnal interest in me or I in them. I wasn't particular about the body type, age, ethnicity, or socio-economic status; but then again, I never have been. Sometimes I had sex with them but I usually woke up before getting to the good part. I thought it meant I was starved for intimacy. And maybe I was, but for the wrong reason and with the wrong person. Anyway, the message became clear—my infidelity was towards God. I had been an unfaithful servant interested only in self-gratification. Egotistical and selfish I was, a man of many vices. I let go the lechery and refocused on the luminance. It renovated my spirit and opened the porthole of instruction.

Head Adjustment Time

See how much you can learn from your dreams if you truly try? They teach you about the past and they prepare you for the future. Either way, you can apply the understanding to the present. I have likened my dreams to great dreamers of old: Jacob, Joseph, Ezekiel, Daniel, Zechariah, and John. What wisdom they beheld and imparted concerning their future, our future, and beyond; and that knowledge applies not only to oneself but to everyone, everywhere, and for always. Not that my dreams are as profound, but they are educational and informative. Can you relate?

The pieces gradually come together to inform, but it requires considerable patience, research, note taking, cut and paste, and reexamination—sort of like constructing a montage. You needn't rack your brain; just let the information flow continuously and aggregate it at a steady pace in a manner that allows for its ingestion while preventing overload. Too much at one time will cause some of it to spill out onto the ground, and too little will leave you unfulfilled and uncertain. But once compiled, a picture with borders will emerge absent of holes, smudges, irrelevant members, or leftover fragments.

Having obtained advanced training in fighting spiritual wickedness, both human and demonic, it was my duty to impart this knowledge to the next generation of legionnaires. Yes, I was piled higher and deeper in instruction until my hair had turned white. Though I took exception to being called "maestro" the name stuck. Irrespective, it was my turn to lead since my awareness of the enemy far surpassed the others. I confirmed, once they'd mastered the material new students would be referring to them as teacher. In the meantime, they were instructed to watch and learn as I had when SS passed the baton to me. It was a responsibility I bore when I pledged my life to the Lord because he had given his for me. In return he gave his Spirit to me that I might know these things and explain them. How am I doing so far? Have I completely lost you? Do you think it is I who am lost, or maybe you? Are you ready to go forward and disseminate truth with boldness and firmness? As far as SS and I, we were not through searching because it wasn't over yet.

EXODUS

I have been wandering aimlessly it seems for months now. I honestly can't remember how long it has been, but then I can't remember much of anything anymore. I only recall an olive-green brick house with a white wooden fence around it and barking dogs. I wonder what it means. Why do I continue to lose my past and my awareness of the present?

There is a man over there. He must be a businessman because he is dressed in a gray suit and carrying a briefcase. Perhaps he can tell me what day it is. I am approaching the man. Should I ask him? Sure, I might as well.

My mouth is moving but I can't utter anything but jumbled babble, that's what it sounded like to me. There, he is responding. He is speaking but I can't comprehend his babble either. Why can't I achieve a simple thing as interpreting short statements? I must be losing my senses. I can't understand what the man said much less what I said.

Well there he goes. He's walking away rather swiftly. Look, he has turned to glower back at me. What can he know that I don't? I must have done something wrong but I have no idea what it was. Frankly, I am not certain what just took place.

What is the matter with me? I feel as if my personality is splitting in two. I still have vague presence of mind though, because I have thoughts. But rationality is elusive. If I am thinking why can't I get the picture? Why can't I stay in touch with reality? Everything is slipping away from me the moment I attempt to grasp it.

I guess I have traveled far today, I feel so fatigued. But I suppose I'll continue onward; it appears to be the one task I can force myself to do. I have journeyed as long as I can recollect, possibly years. I know my legs must be tired but I can't feel my feet upon the ground.

At least I can still see, although at times my sight becomes hazy. I should concentrate on my sight before it leaves me as well. There is a tunnel up ahead; I think I'll go through it. But what will I accomplish by doing so?

It appears that this tunnel is tinier than I thought; I'll have to get on my hands and knees. I can sense darkness closing in around me. Wait a second! I can feel the darkness but not my kneecaps dragging the dirt? The shadows are getting heavy on my shoulders. I'd better stop and rest.

There is a little square of light on either side of me. Which one do you suppose is the correct one? Check out that red pattern on the wall. Hmm, it appears to continue down the corridor. Snap out of this nonsensical dilemma and get out of this place before you lose it!

Boy, that passageway wholly blew my mind. Why did it captivate me so? It's as if it had a power of its own, greater than my own free will which I have forfeited to this delirious condition.

Feature the beautiful colors. They shimmer and reflect on everything. But these colors do not appear to be true; they are not the same colors I've discerned before.

Stop! I heard something. Think. Analyze; it's bound to make some sense. Let's see; it sort-of grunted or growled like a, a, an animal. A dog was barking. No, no that's not it. But I felt the noise. That's it, the noise came from me. Oh, it must have been my stomach grumbling. I suppose I haven't eaten in a very long while.

Why are those people laughing at me? They are you know. Haven't they seen a human being before? Although, I'm not me anymore. Normal people don't undergo these instalments, do they? Please quit it! Don't look at me! That grass tasted terrible.

Everything is moving so fast. Objects are passing too quickly. Slow down! Quiet! I know, why don't I sit and wait here on this fine lawn? It isn't as soft as I remember. I wonder whose lawn could this be? Or maybe it's a park how nice and peaceful.

Well, at least I'm not violating the law. But why then is that policeman approaching? He's grabbing me! Hey, leave me alone! Uh oh, I shoved a cop. I'd better run. Wow that car almost hit me! Where did that car come from? I didn't think people were permitted to drive through a park. Parks are for relaxing.

How long have I been running? I am so weary. My head feels wispy. My body feels weightless. I guess that's better than feeling nothing isn't it? My temples are throbbing. Maybe if I continue to feel the pain sensibility will return.

Now my torso is spinning; I feel dizzy. Everything around me is in motion, whizzing about my eyes. Why is everything bouncing all over the place? Now I'm rising from the ground. Cars, trees, bushes, rocks, people, everything floating in the air, appearing to be rotating in the same direction. Everything that exists is in motion, sailing through the sky, swirling towards that giant star. I have never seen so many different things before, at one time, fluttering around like dust in a windstorm and funneled towards that star. What is happening? Is it the end of life?

Whoa, that was a weird dream. What was my subconscious trying to relate? One thing is evident: even a schizophrenic exhibiting serious catatonia, hebephrenia, and dissociative fugue can tell that something is happening. And like many others who are not mad, he doesn't know what it is. "Oh, the insanity of it all," people say.

Lots of people running from reality but it will not hurt them. I guess they think they'll be punished, the wimps. It's a softer sentence if you face the flak immediately rather than wait until later. Who would save ten minutes now if it costs ten years in the future; or worse, spend ten years of extravagance in exchange for an eternity of emptiness? There is no escape in the end. And the sentence will prevail, no appeals.

Admittedly I escape, if only in my dreams. I am a foreigner here and ache for home. I dream of it and I have seen it. Heaven, my friends, can be found within. With the spirit, a taste of paradise can be sensed and understood.

I had longed to explore it at will (the unconscious that is) by approaching it from the inside; I presumed I could find an escape inside my mind. I proceeded to consciously sleep hoping I'd be there when a dream sequence commenced. I successfully made it through four levels. But when my eyes went ob-conjured my soul spit me out into a state of total wakefulness. I retried two more times with the same result. It was as if entering would mean never exiting. Maybe it was fear which held me back. Would I become absent? Conclusively, I would be unconscious. Exploring inside myself might become as compelling as the universe outside. I thought I could journey without the need for travel. It boiled down to a desire to play it out and let God's will be done, realizing that paradise was a destination not a state of mind. I practiced the art and mastered lucid dreaming; sometimes it makes sense but it doesn't have to. You should try, it's fun; but the meaning will be contrived.

When it comes to the afterlife however, it is better to wait for Christ to come than to meet your maker prematurely. I yearn for that great departure where souls are reunited whether dead or alive. It has been written about many times. Remember when God responded to the pining of the Hebrews? They finally were released from Egyptian slavery after four-hundred-plus years. They sighed for the loss of liberty and pleaded for the Promised Land. As do I. I'm not talking about being liberated from the bondage of oppression but of sin. And I'm not talking about finding another place to live for my dwelling is in God's house. I just want to go home sometimes, but it is not time quite yet.

I escaped this war-torn world long ago if not physically then spiritually. It has no hold over me; neither do the imbeciles who rule it though they think they have power. People in Jesus's time also sought freedom from oppression, but wrongly assumed that they were being beaten down by the Romans whose power also was measured by God. The Jews expected a militant messiah not a humble healer. They wanted their conquerors to be vanquished but they forgot to accede to their own consciences and ended up murdering the very one who could redeem them. Funny how they refused to acquiesce to Roman authority yet appeased it nevertheless; then justified their actions as if in accordance with Jewish law. Both ignored God's law.

The leaders of the synagogue were no more pious or trustworthy than the governors imposed on Judea by Rome. The message presented to them was divine and pure; it fulfilled over three hundred prophesies. Yet only a handful paid attention to the Father's sacred messenger who implemented his plan to the letter. The rest tried to cover up the truth rather than tell it and those that told it were tracked down and massacred. Of course, the fact that skeptics aimed to hide it only served to prove it. To this day they claim evidence tampering, as if the borne and bare truth can ultimately be smothered. But you can't stifle certainty, for who with half a brain speculates on an indisputable falsehood? And who would risk going to their deaths arguing something so extraordinary, especially if they did not believe it themselves? Therefore, it had to be true.

The resurrection episode spread like wildfire; before long the entire world had heard about it. Haven't you heard? Did you know that a third of the population will go to their deaths believing it? Is it possible for that many people to be lured by simple, fickle men? Or were these eyewitnesses genuinely empowered by the omnipotent Spirit to spread the Word? The underlying surprise was people heard the report in their native tongue from mouths that had never spoken the dialect before. What a sight that must have been! Imagine receiving the good news from ordinary men: foreigners, many uneducated, who had never stepped foot outside of their homeland until they heeded the call of the great commission. Yes, it would be difficult to swallow without the foreknowledge that these evangelists related what was foretold centuries before Messiah's arrival. Fifty days after the Lord's crucifixion, exactly one week after his ascension, his apostles obtained the gift and straightaway used it to take the message to the ends of the earth where they would be ridiculed, dehumanized, beaten, and slaughtered. They were not insane or obtuse but compelled, devoted, and convinced. They willingly sacrificed their lives for this cause having received the awakening and the impetus.

The revelation of Jesus Christ converts the shrinking and timid into courageous, brave, and bold. I believe and will gladly go to my death believing, whenever and however that occurs; because the knowledge will bring me from death into life. I do not fear death for I am looking beyond. Truthful tutelage transformed my feckless life into fruitful; it made a stagnant existence flourishing, purposive, and abundant. Like the apostles I have turned from cynic to zealot. Others will reject the entire account which is their prerogative. It's like trying to bury the sun. It's also like trying to bury the Son whose light they could not extinguish and burns still. But the scales have tipped, and the suckers that reject the truth outnumber those of us who cannot. Thanks to them, morality and integrity have plummeted worse than the economy. This is the prelude to their downfall and that of civilization.

How typical the scam; empires falling like dominoes. The next will be the last. Here we go again. It boils down to greed for power, pride for position, and lust for leverage. Show me one politician today that genuinely spends his or her entire term of office doing the job for which elected or hired. Or point one out that has never been caught in a lie and tried to cover it up. If you can I'll buy the first round. I have observed them, countless hours wasted playing honored guest and basking in the limelight; passing nonbinding resolutions; prosecuting persons across the aisle for tripping on their tongues; performing disappearing acts when the proletariat identifies inconsistencies in the way the law is interpreted or applied; appointing or honoring judges that defecate on the Constitution; persecuting anyone that doesn't share their immoderate ideals. Why won't you numbskulls pass some flipping legislation, huh?

It's getting to be Rome revived: everyone stabbing everyone else in the back. But they haven't presented any credible facts or verified the slightest misdemeanor. They go after the innocuous ones in attempt to dig up charges, whereas they have nothing to charge them with so they concoct something. No wonder the entire world scoffs at us, demeans our administration, and estranges from this country as if theirs is beneath contempt.

I admit it, our government is in shambles. Why do the politicians seek domination of our lives and why do they want to decree conventional wisdom? Everyone knows that it costs twice as much for the government to finish a job than it does for private enterprise to complete it. Management of civic programs is wrought with overruns and manned by mobs of executives that don't do a piddling squat. Would you vote for bigger government so that your taxes can double and so you can receive additional substandard services? We need them to govern not to rule. We need them to maintain order not complicate things. We need them to coordinate with foreign nations not try to assimilate them. We need them to regulate not dictate, to enforce not reinforce, to manage not scrimmage, to defend us not depend on us.

Don't get me wrong, I love my country. I'm as patriotic as the next person, maybe more. I would fight and die to save this land from ruin, bankruptcy, or communism. I'd rather be a conqueror than a submissive whiner; it's not a matter of subjugating someone else but your own vanity. Instead of finding blame find solutions. This is not a complaint but a warning. It saddens me the course that politics is taking. And although I don't question the patriotism of those in office, I categorically must question their motives. Too much permissiveness on the one hand and too much prohibition on the other; now that's consistency. Talk about consistency; we brainwash our kids into the consciousness of super-sensitivity to individual differences. Meanwhile, those who are different want to be treated like everybody else. And all the while the insufferable theocracies overseas are indoctrinating their kids into being intolerant of anybody else especially us, while we are supposed to tolerate everything and everyone especially them.

The idea that multiculturalism rules denies that our original culture was great. These new outsiders did not lay the groundwork for our republic. Sure, welcome them to come; but they need fit in not the other way around. Everyone here should embrace this culture and maintain their sacred heritage if that is their identity. Ditch the junk that isn't worth holding onto. We cannot be making accommodations for every idiosyncratic ideology. Nothing is preventing them from practicing their beliefs at home or in their places of worship. That's freedom of religion. According to the newest age you cannot embrace one faith or exclude another. Listen up. The Golden Rule is: Do unto others as you would have them do unto you. It is not: Let others do unto you what they would have you do unto them.

Anything goes so everybody come. And the people arrive in droves like herds of cattle, seeking opportunity as if this was the Promised Land. It is not and we are not the chosen people. Those who share the faith of Abraham, they are chosen. And that faith was and always has been in the true Liberator not the invented ones. Self-proclaimed messiahs, it's chronic. They can't redeem themselves much less anyone else. Nobody can but Christ. And you'll see him someday in your flesh with your own eyes. And he won't be the reincarnation of a dead Imam, or the spirit of the archangel Michael, or the personification of Brahman, or the President, the Emperor, the Ayatollah, the Mahdi, or the Buddha. He will be the risen Lord who came once in the flesh and will come again the same way, once and for all. It is that belief which makes you an heir not your bloodline. And it is your rebellion that condemns you not your disinterest in the pardon you were offered which could have saved you.

Soon there will be a mass exodus such as the world has never seen. It will catch many by surprise. Those who were not awaiting it will be disappointed; woe unto them. It will be good news if you have been anticipating the Lord's return. That's why it is important to declare the Gospel. I have contributed my two cents worth, a miniscule role by my own standards as I'm sure I could have done more. But at least I'm making the effort. Are you? Let's agree on this: We are responsible for one another. To do absolutely nothing makes you an accomplice.

Of course, there seems to be a great abandonment in that regard. When someone notices another in need, does he or she turn a blind eye? Would you rush to satisfy their want or leave it for another? I'm busier than the next person. I don't want to get involved; it could be a setup. Oh, they'll be okay. It's not my responsibility. I wouldn't know what to do regardless. I could be hit by a car, contract their disease, or get sued. There might be a ferocious beast prowling the streets.

Remember the words: indivisible, with liberty and justice for all? Have we forsaken what we stand for? Each powermonger schemes for standing but none take a stand for unity. Remember the words: united we stand divided we fall? Then you know what comes next. Even the house of Satan cannot endure because it also is disjointed despite the accuser's frantic attempts to reassemble it.

What we need is a mass departure from the status quo, from the facade of self-righteousness, from the insignificance of political correctness, from being sissies when it comes to enforcement of rules. We cannot let evil have its way. Take up your sword and attack it. Stab the iniquitous ones in the heart with the word of truth. What they are doing is wrong and they know it. Let's not allow them to get away with it for that will only make matters worse: the law will become weaker and the lawbreakers bolder. When you bail out the bad guys what you're left with is more bad guys roaming around. But there's a disincentive to try.

You cannot simply work to earn your keep anymore; you have to struggle to obtain and maintain it. You cannot expect politicians to be reasonable, you have to force them. People are not inclined to do the right thing until everyone gangs up on them. Those in power care only about the power; their proposals do not improve the lives of anybody but them. If we stand together against injustice in Jesus's name, we'll have the collective vigor of our spirits combined with that of God. It will be a force to be reckoned with. Seriously, if one cleansed spirit can defeat the mutinous imp, imagine what the rest can achieve in unison? Unfortunately, the converse also is true: if the horrendous hoards band together they become an enigmatic enemy.

That, fellow persons, became the opponent. They wanted to merge the secular fanatics, establish a pseudo religion, attain worldwide classification, and name it in the guise of a devoutness that once shone in the patriarchs. Their prophet first arrived to unite the tribes but the newly appointed prophets only effected division. They recruited disciples to do their dirty work: somebodies who were ignorant of their exalted books and the sayings therein. There was no shortage of bemused souls that would follow someone gifted with a knack for persuasion, believing the lie because they didn't know any better. They knew not the voice of the Good Shepherd. Unfortunately, those aware of the truth kept silent, dreading retaliation.

A coalition of four prided themselves on their ancient legacy: Egypt, Assyria, Babylon, and Persia. The ambition of becoming rulers of the world created quarrels over which should command. They were bucking for a promotion, each declaring themselves the holiest and bearing the number twelve like a crown. But each leaned on the identical fault of the former the pride of which prevented an accord. One encompassed three others by might as if the gavel fell in default to him.

Fundamentalists they called themselves; candidly, extremists in the most unwelcoming sense. Too bad that's the only thing they could agree upon. The constant competition between factions made the bonds brittle. And they were careful not to share too much so it was never enough. When they jointly banded for the big beating it lacked a method; more of a shotgun blast of rock salt into the buttocks of the fleeing west rather than a direct hit into the core of its being.

Their sanctimonious pilgrims aspired for the prowess of the intellectual giants before them but missed it by millennia. Collecting ample technology to brand them dangerous they produced their weapons of mass destruction and launched them at the dreaded brothers of yore. It was a hate that festered for centuries, ripe for the lance. Well they struck with all guns blazing. But readiness had not preceded attempt; for many projectiles failed to deploy, a number of them spun out of control, several were off the mark, and some exploded in place. Most of those that found their trajectory were intercepted in midair. The event imitated a fire in a fireworks factory.

What remained was a stretch of seared tentacles burned into the land and surrounding a nucleus of obliteration. Fortunately for the young and the wise they had accomplished their exit en masse, fearing the very end that ensued. Weeping for their native soil they vanished into the outlying territories scattered from Hell to Texas. Woefully similar to the diaspora that the chieftains had striven to restore, it was irony sifted through a sieve.

Impurities lingered, tainting the loam and rivulets. The parched hills and vales were discolored in the vein of a cheap painting that runs, fades, and gathers dust. Mix that with a horrific collection of carcasses and you can conceive the carnage. Remains of rats, animal and human, dotted the countryside resembling a jaundiced addict with the chicken pox.

The corpses were too disassembled to count and too accumulated to bury. The ravens had a field day. I remember being forewarned that they would ascend from the pit. You'd think feasting on contaminated carrion would've made them ill but not so. Eventually the terra firma was thrust into its prehistoric prospect where only fossils could dwell. Survivors gathered at the edges and hoped for rain, hiding in caverns and clefts to escape the four judgments that were being poured out upon them. Nobody accepted the refugees, and their relations would never return. They had disowned themselves from God and country.

The solipsist predicted it would end this way prior to his return (which he did in my dreams but not in person). He knew what was to come but wasn't about to let on because he wasn't sure when. Definitely, I didn't want to know because that would've taken the surprise out of it. "No reason to be alarmed," he informed, "Just beware, especially when the baptizer resurfaces; it will be the inauguration of extermination." The foretold one had a lot in common with the solipsist (though a little humbler perhaps). But they couldn't have been one in the same, could they? Then again how many spacemen are out there? And what are the odds that they would be in total agreement?

He was unkempt but clean, still dressed in his black burlap vest and breeches. He was the survivor of many a holocaust. He also weathered the verbal and physical abuse and was no worse the wear for that. He feasted on whatever yet was healthy as a horse. He had no need for grocery stores or hotels; he shopped in the wild and slept in the sand. Treated as a pariah he was feared just the same. His tidings could still the water or summon a thunderstorm, and break the silence that ever preceded him. His remarks paved the way for fulfillment of prophecy that he himself pronounced over two thousand years before. But the mainstreamers paid little attention. I reckoned the multitudes didn't believe him the first time so why would anyone suppose it to happen a second? I believed him seeing how the Lord himself ordained it.

Spanning forty-two months the leaders' ire simmered until it finally was beyond sweltering. For the duration, everything the prophet uttered was a blow against the empire. But the riled-up ones dared not act against him as they recognized he had authority beyond their comprehension. They shrunk in his presence and slinked away, but eventually mustered enough hatred to plot his demise. Upon ambushing and beheading him during the Passover week, just like a pagan king did to him on his first appearance, they tied his body to a sharpened post that was jammed into the head displaying his remains in the town square. It was a dark and dreary weekend under a bloody lunar eclipse. Until he came back to life. Is he not a shadow of the Lord or what? He forecast the coming of Messiah then and he'll do it again afore too long.

How appropriate it seemed as I pondered the significance: not a coincidence that his resurrection coincided with another noteworthy arising. Needless to say, it occurred exactly 84 hours past his betrayal. That's 2 times 42 or 12 times 7 in mathematical terms, the length of an ultimate end. In 3.5 days the 3.5-year reign of the evil kingdom had come to an end. I seem to recollect how the 3.5-year ministry of Christ came to a climax in the concluding 3.5 days of his mortal life, culminating in his resurrection on Easter Sunday three days after his sacrifice on Passover. Forty more days of fellowship followed before his ascension brought another era to a close.

Except it wasn't just the prophet's revivification but many more. Graves were unlocked in the basin of dry bones and a strange evacuation ensued, not unlike the initial resurrection of him who brought them back to life. Every living soul had been cautioned but only those who heeded the advisory were undaunted by it.

The event was quite entertaining, the chilling dance of the undead. I was compelled to join in realizing I had something eerily in common with them. Dreams of such incidents used to scare the daylights out of me as a youngster. Pops told me the nightmares were but an outpouring of my exquisite imagination which he considered a blessing. And he was dead on; but he always had a knack for zeroing in on the not so obvious detail. I possessed a creative edge that could compose a hymn of praise on the one hand and choreograph a horror movie on the other.

I recollect sneaking into the witch's manor to spy on her and a host of goblins, offspring of disgusting lust. Have you ever chanced upon a witch? I have. Not a snaggletooth old biddy with green skin, a pointed nose, and warts on her face. She didn't fly on a broomstick or wear a crooked hat. She appeared to me a charming grey-haired woman. But she was ugly enough to stop a clock; not from her looks but because of the evil in her eyes. Her seductive allure would render a man sightless, only to relish in his own wanton appetite. Her charade would conform to the hussy conjured in his mind and he would surrender to her kiss of death: honey to the taste but bitter to the soul.

Artist's conception of the American flag ...

... or, my father was a meatgrinder

She cooked up a ghastly brew that permeated the air with an odoriferous cloud that peeled the paint, wilted the weeds, and attracted all manner of vermin. The governess and her gnomes would partake of the putrid potion, which would be poison to a person of principle but provided sustenance to a sick psyche. I was up-chucking into the toilet when a troll bade to enter; but realizing the lavatory was taken paid no mind to what stature of creature occupied it. Intuitively aware that an invader was stirring, the sorceress commanded a thorough search of the premises. Nonetheless, I had slipped through the window, dashing into the dark forest.

They caught wind of my scent and like hounds on the prowl tailed me from midnight until dawn. Unbeknownst to them I was practiced at navigating the dusky tangles under the obscurity of a new moon. It was testy terrain. The gnarly scrub brush and thorny thickets would have been treacherous to traverse had I not otherwise performed reconnaissance on occasion. I often weaseled my way through it to sneak into the haunted mansion and observe the appalling assemblage, gathering intelligence for what I didn't know. Conceivably, I was becoming acquainted with the ways of the opposition for plainly, acumen can serve as a countermeasure. The sleazy floozie constantly sought to overpower me. But she had not the tenacity, knowing not the challenge. The brood abhorred the customs of conscience and hence never learned them.

Truly, they'd acquired an understanding of the vulnerabilities of humanity but not the assets. That's why they preyed upon the downtrodden, the faint of heart, the uninformed, and the slothful. And they will hunt you with great vivacity. But those who are saintly will find vigor in the Holy Ghost and defeat the advances of such allies of arrogance and villains of vice. For the fiery darts of the wicked cannot permeate the armor.

Head down to the quartermaster and obtain your suit for free; it is issued to all who make the request. One-size-fits-all and it never wears out. It comes complete with training manual which is also your weapon of war. It is the sword of the Word which cuts to the core and divides asunder the soul and spirit. An astounding axiom it speaks; and the spiteful elves run like the devil when facing it. They assume there is power in numbers however and return with angst. But that strategy already has been proven ineffective (as demonstrated in preceding episodes). They will find out soon enough so let's keep it mum, shall we?

It's too bad that the utopian world they seek is one where their power is absolute. But only God's power is unchallengeable and he bears no contenders. His is the perfect world where sin cannot exist, which is why there is no pain, despair, or sadness in heaven but only peace, joy, and wellbeing. The culprits in this world are full of disjunctive musings, wayward inclinations, and utter tomfoolery which prevent attaining perfection because of humanity's inestimable imperfections. What a joke, to think that man can invent such a place as paradise. And they think they can get there via trickery or deceit; how nonsensical. What they ended up fashioning was a dystopian materiality of wretchedness. I have dreamt of the impeccable world, the images of which have been etched into the caverns of my soul like ancient cave drawings. There is nothing on earth to describe or compare it.

Similarly, there is nothing on earth to illustrate the insidious inferno. There are images in prophecy but they do not begin to depict the blackness and the blankness. My visions are horrendous; it's a place where every scrap of formerly infected and ruined existence has been melted into a cauldron of insanity. Lost in space, the souls are blown apart like an imploding sun leaving only displaced debris. They remain trapped with other adrift souls that cannot relate but only repel; increasing their separation like celestial bodies distancing faster and farther at the edge of space. Particles drifting with no possible connection, integration, or materialization, like ripples in a glassy pool that soon vanish. God told us he would deliberately detach from and abolish the memory of the condemned. He placed a chasm that disconnects them from the saints.

Such is the appearance of the lake of fire that sucks everything inside in the manner of a black hole; shaken from this physical universe and scattered into the void beyond. Where does everything go? Nobody knows. Does it cease to exist? What do you think? And why do they call it a black hole when it is one of the hottest bodies amid all that so-called dark matter (but for the fact nobody knows what lies beyond it, except maybe the solipsist)? Speaking of black holes, I could tell you stories.

I remember attending lectures by sages, renown in their craft and praised as wunderkinds. Many believed themselves to be above reproach for who had the brainpower to contest? They proposed mathematical proofs for their models, convinced that the particulars were evident and defying the world to explain where they were in error. The solipsist always attended the symposia; in fact, it was his idea that I go. He correctly repudiated theory after theory identifying two limitations: time and space. They maintained that a black hole and/or the singularity itself had infinite density while space and time were constant. "What are neither continuous nor infinite are space and time," SS persisted, "Because the only completely infinite and the only absolutely constant—these are features applicable to His Holiness not the universe."

We were inundated with unremarkable pedantic views that depended on a finite distribution of matter confined to that which could be conceived and monitored. The missing element in their equations was a coefficient called infinity to which their theories would fall apart. The quantity was diminished because that was the one factor which could account for mass procreation by an omnipresent and omniscient Father. Forbid it that they might consider an intelligence higher than their own.

I studied the proposition that the black hole emptied its contents into a parallel universe. I'd found there to be life beyond this one. Though anything in the one hole is never found in the other, but for the solipsist. Physicists and astronomers could not agree on where the information went. One would contend that it was gone forever while his colleague maintained that it crossed into another universe. The next held that it was confined in a neighboring formation and could not escape or return; another alleged it was locked in this universe but unavailable for examination. The succeeding proposition was that none of these hypotheses made sense because the galaxy is riddled with black holes. Those in his camp surmised that the universe had so many holes it was falling apart, as if it was being vacuumed bit by bit into a second dimension. Was the very fabric of space disintegrating like a rotten canopy? Was there a mirror image of our universe composed of antimatter that caused both to disintegrate in equal proportions? I thought, maybe the stuff goes in one hole and out the other, the way factual information passes through the ears of dissenters. I wasn't about to tell them that I had passed through a black hole, not once but twice. I knew of at least two realities which coexisted that were different, separate, similar but unique each with a personality of its own, kind of like heaven and hell. Beyond infinity there is yet another. Like in death, you are no longer here; but not dead, yet.

SS infused into me this interpretation: the key to unlock the mystery of creation is infinity. He taught me that logicians often believe incorrectly there is an end to space or a point where time stops. Most bought into the presumption a big bang initiated the spread of elements throughout the heavens and our universe was expanding still. And there at the peripheral reaches of space it carried on. Others figured it would bounce back because it could expand only so much before contracting or deflating. Perhaps it would collapse and implode as a dying star thereby creating a new singularity. Or maybe it would just die. The error in these positions was the assumption that beyond the beyond there is nothing; as if the universe had a boundary or would eventually run out of gas. But how can it spread through the void if there is nowhere for it to go? The most interesting feature of space is that there is enough room for everything. The same is true for time. Does everything that exists have to fit into this universe? And does everything in this universe have to stay here? And is there a time when everything ceases to be or the energy runs out? Maybe, maybe not. Time-space may have a beginning and it may change or be changed, but some things will never end. It follows that, if there can be no end to some things there also can be no beginning.

The next craze rallied around the submission that a black hole produces an explosive expansion on the other side: a generator constantly spewing out bubbling new universes. Conceivably, every one of the purported innumerable black holes represented a connection to another universe, which itself produced countless black holes and so on. It implied that production of universes multiplies to a number that is incalculable. But that suggested the infinite; theorists would accept an infinite number of universes but not an infinite God. Moreover, does any other dimension have to adhere to the same timeframe, space, or rules? Nowadays, they figure we got lucky. I don't buy it. I agree with the solipsist: There may or may not be a conclusion to space and time but there will be a time when it won't matter. The counterargument is that neither exists because existence requires a beginning and an end. Why should it? God's doesn't. God has no constraints. Creation, expansion, inflation, duration, speed, time-space—all are meaningless and irrelevant to God. Every combination is possible and undoubtedly exists if only in an all-knowing mind. Whether there are untold universes in the physical sense is impossible to discover in this life, though unquestionably available conceptually with an active and vivid imagination and obviously known explicitly to the omniscient one. Who would refuse to seek him knowing that he is undeniably there? Answer: Only those who disbelieve they can actuate a personal and spiritual interaction with the Almighty himself. But I cannot ignore that God is in contact every second while scarcely realizing it.

Some of the lecturers further confused the issue by proposing parallel universes comprising the same inhabitants as ours but with different lives, consequences, and ideas. How silly can you get? Would we be clones synchronized in simultaneous dimensions, ensuring that all combinations of possibilities are covered for every experience and existence? They'd deny the interminable existence and presence of God as craziness but come up with outlandish ideas of unlimited, synchronous but disassociated universes in order to presuppose there is no God. Now isn't that a profoundly scholastic assumption? I figure every feasible occurrence can be found in the realm of God, where the multidimensional hallways of ingenuity and origination endlessly converge on a purpose known to us only at the time God offers it.

I think it plausible that we are individuals, completely exceptional (as are other universes if indeed they occur). And who can assert with certitude that an adjoining universe if proven to subsist contains humanoids? It doesn't track with the truth. The first man was a created being. There was only one other immaculate incarnation: Jesus Christ, and his sacrifice occurred once and for humankind. Christ did not die many deaths nor did he arise from the dead multiple times. And God does not assume many physical forms only one: Jesus. Again, it is a denial of the probability of infinity and the profundity of the phrase *e pluribus unum*.

There are contradictions. Take the declaration that the universe continues to expand, a reasonable concept. It started fast but slowed; or is it speeding up? Yet it continues to follow the arrow of time (forward only). Can time vary as a function of the speed of expansion? Space matter, gaseous gatherings, and stardust seem to be leaping up, out and away. Outlying formations are hypothetically zooming towards the perimeter becoming increasingly more distant. But the same is true wherever you are in the galaxy, or the universe for that matter, so they profess. According to the postulates of uniformity and symmetry it's the same everywhere, like the distribution of microwave background radiation. Some galaxies are ostensibly billions of light years away, suggestive of their age, and gaining speed. Our solar system has been determined to be much younger. But how can that be? It would follow that we would be closer to the edge and that it was us distancing from the rest. But if the Milky Way is the center of the universe then it should be the elder. Is Earth in its adolescence or full grown; are we in the midst of a generation of mature galaxies or toddlers? Or did God snap his fingers and poof there it was. Scientists say our sun, planets, and galaxy are middle-aged; albeit, the precise age for human life. How do you gauge that? Space is so far away the light from remote objects is seen late. Meanwhile, the older matter is forming the younger, while newborn nebulae are developing into adult galaxies as we speak, all of which already happened as they are light years from here.

It's a paradox. Are we closer to the nucleus or to the periphery? Or does space inflate in every direction with increasing entropy regardless of where you are in the universe? Either way the universal rim is way farther than we can see. That's because space is expanding faster than light can travel (otherwise there would be nowhere for it to go). The universe itself may be bigger than space, or vice-versa. Scientists cannot pinpoint the epicenter and therefore have no way of proving which direction is the beginning or the end, except up. Does there always have to be a start, or a finish? Well maybe in this universe. SS held that we could never reach the start or end of space even with a time machine; this, after I fervidly urged him to take me there. I was left to dream about it; I couldn't, for the optics surpassed all the more my visualization. You can get a glimpse but not a clear one.

And then there was string theory and the eleven dimensions of spacetime. Yeah, the universe is strung together like amino acids. Come on, my kite string can't hold it for long. The cosmos would be tied up in knots before we were through with it. Or maybe we are puppets and the gods are pulling our strings. And the constellations are playthings; perhaps a baby god's mobile. Maybe the strings are like those of a musical instrument vibrating in harmony with creation; or like hair cells in the cochlea quivering with the maddening melody of lunacy. I envisioned the web of a spider but symmetrical, yet assuming numerous multidimensional shapes; with the infant gravitons a spherical mesh, capturing or captured by sticky strings. The question remained however, who spun these webs? Does reality resemble membranes in one giant but damaged brain connecting observations in a random accumulation of incomprehension? It may look intricate but it's more of a twisted and tangled ball of twine, the result of trying to tie it together.

Give me a break with this stuff. Why not propose the most bizarre explanation available and bamboozle people with confused logic and complicated scientific mumbo jumbo? It is impressive but it doesn't jibe and it's totally disprovable. Perhaps the philosophers are amused by looks of bewilderment on the countenance of onlookers (to boost an inflated ego that itself will need to contract sooner or later). But the diverse paradigms cannot be fused into a solitary model so they search for the elusive theory of everything, ignoring that God is the enlightenment and that homo sapiens can realize all the answers only via an eternity of discovery. Reductionists search for a first cause but fail to grasp that there can be only one. By definition it has to be the reason for everything. Only an infinite and nonmaterial entity fits the bill. Everyone knows this: nothing subtracted from or added to nothing leaves—nothing. But contemplate this: infinity plus or minus infinity equals—infinity. It is ignored because it is impossible to measure or otherwise prove or disprove this mathematically.

One theory that I chewed on was the big bang, primarily because of implied teleology (intelligent design), not directly in conflict with the biblical account. The command "let there be light" must have produced a spectacular show, especially if viewed within a massively compressed timeframe (or in the absence of time). The counterintuitive and unexplainable result was that the explosion didn't cause chaos but organization and order. It wasn't created to last, however, and for good reason, because the best is yet to come.

Many cosmologists maintained that spontaneous growth began with a random event; but that flies in the face of their supposition that there was nothing before, until some incredibly small concentration of pure energy living in a quantum vacuum couldn't contain itself; but that implies something already existed. Guess what? Creation is not an event but a process. Yet they would describe evolution as an event and not a process if it suits them. They presume that time began at a single point; with that logic it has to end someday. I guess it's comfortable to remain insular than presume there possibly could be eras of age and reality prior to singularity (especially given the fact that they suppose there is nothing after death either, itself assumed to be a singularity, and have only this existence to know it all). If our universe began at the instant of the big bang then there could be more than one because God existed all the while. Therefore, his domain could include multiverse but not ours. Well guess what? This universe isn't the propitious one out of an infinite number. If it was, then I guess a monkey typed my graduate school textbook on theoretical physics. There are no such anomalies; otherwise there would be an infinite number of them. Or maybe our luck has run out. Seemingly not, when taking into account that the law and order we follow is merely a derivative of the greater underlying schematic of rules, events, learning, and wonderment put into place for our blossoming.

I imagined neurons in a vast cerebral complex where combined they represent a single concept in the mind of the Almighty, like black holes interconnecting universes. Everything affects everything in a kind of synergism such that any single occurrence is part of the greater design. The flutter of a hummingbird's wing is felt in the outer galactic limits. Then what we do and say also affects this universal field. And our response at any given moment could change the world as long as we stay lovingly connected to reality. Humankind is an essential element in the grand design, particularly because God has made himself known to us, he became one of us, and he encourages a personal friendship. It proceeds that everything we experience is experienced by him. The brain that brought us relativity reflected that it's either a miracle or it isn't. Either God is or he isn't; but it takes tons of faith to believe he isn't. SS has his own theory of relativity: everything is related whether seen or unseen; here or not here; past, present or future; large or small; alive or dead; angels, humans, animals, plants, microscopic organisms—all relate to God.

Yet the erudite ramble on so sure of themselves, allowing only that cynics are imbeciles. I do not pretend to be as smart as they at least in matters of astrophysics. I don't need or desire faith in such matters; that philosophy cannot save me. I do ponder, however; but I do not require definitive answers. I would rather be asking the questions than providing the answers. That way I don't have to explain why I'm wrong. Who cares to agonize an entire lifetime trying to explain something that cannot be known in this one? In that regard there is a limit (except with God's knowledge). But they will continue to press forward, calculating pi to infinite decimal places, envisaging eventual closure to every irony, mystery, and coincidence. What they will not accept is that infinity can go forwards or backwards; it can apply to many things other than time and space because God is all and in all.

That inspiration can transcend elementary intellect once crossed their minds though it remained inexplicable via naturalism (notwithstanding the unconscious aspect of the eureka phenomenon). But guess what? Another source is available, the same as our inherent knowledge of truth and right, which can be observed even in children and is called discernment. It's the greater part of our being, a higher power if you will, where knowledge is available through divine revelation. But they would deny that as well. The beauty of the mind is it can implicate fathomless yet workable neural configurations in which to involve, solve, resolve, absolve, and evolve (unlike a computer that tolerates only a finite number of alterations or upgrades before it becomes more cost-effective to build another one).

In fairness however, many traditionalists in the sciences are beginning to accept that an alternative theory of everything inevitably leads to God (or at least, intelligence, purpose, design, and/or creation). That is, more are jumping off the evolution, materialistic, agnostic boat and getting on the creation, theistic, and spiritualistic bandwagon. I was one of them; now I am convinced in God. My psychology professors groomed me for naturalism, and my research for becoming a staunch observer. And it still led me to one undeniable conclusion. SS showed me how science and philosophy are inseparable. Beliefs are based upon scientific analysis as much as they are proven by it. The diehards accuse believers like me of being delusional or foolish; but it is they who believe in realities that cannot be verified or do not exist.   Would they maintain that billions of the world's inhabitants are psychotic because they swear by a Supreme Being? Likewise, over half the people on their list of idols believed in God. Should we suppose that their greatest protagonists were deluded? I doubt if they do. But that is precisely what the great evangelist prophesied: God will give them a strong delusion and let them believe it.

The stalwarts put forth the ruse that anything can happen anytime and does. Even that theory has to consider what started it not to mention what was before and will be after. And though they can assume by faith limitless possibilities, they cannot wrap their arms around an eternal God without whom nothing is possible. Is it more feasible to hypothesize an indefinite number of universes that exist simultaneously or one God that exists infinitely? Which requires more faith?

There are so many problems with multiverse theory it's laughable. To begin with, for that theory to hold water it must assume any combination. There would have to be an unspecified number of universes with me in it; where everything that can be said or done in this one has an alternate that is exactly the same minus one, or plus one, or whatever. Thus, there'd be lots more universes that got lucky, which include me and/or everyone else (plus or minus everyone); namely an infinite amount. Some with me and some without me; some where I die in childbirth, some where I live to be 969 years old; and some with every option in-between or outside. How could God stomach that (so many of me that it would drive anybody bonkers)? It seems some scientific propositions have been advanced precisely to disallow God as part of the explanation in spite of the absurdity, with relativism being the default assumption.

Do you want to live forever? Then accept that eternity will always have novelty; life doesn't get old. And there is not a duplicate of you being offered this same gift of eternal life. We've already outlasted many species on earth and still we are in our infancy. Is that not obvious? If you knew everything what would be left to search? Each question has an answer and you have perpetuity to discover it, as long as you answer the most important question affirmatively: Are you saved? When you begin to conceive of a life that never ends you can appreciate why this one is but a smidgeon, like indigo to the entire electromagnetic spectrum. Infinity makes sense at that instant. There can be something faster than a nanosecond, farther than space, smaller than a subatomic particle, but not greater than the Almighty. There can be massive intelligence without physical mass. Feature an existence where an infinite amount of time already has passed, like steady-state proponents did, and you can begin to comprehend what future awaits.

Consider light; physicists postulate that light is constant in empty space, but concede that light can be slowed, split, bent, or otherwise manipulated. Light can be propagated and it can be suspended. So, light isn't always constant though it cannot be reformed or destroyed. And those elusive photons, elementary particles of light, are invisible. Is that plausible, a light you cannot see? However, God's light cannot be seen with the naked eye either. But it is deeper and more intense than the light we see from the sun or an incandescent bulb or an array of diodes or the light that exists outside the visible band of the electromagnetic continuum. So, light can be visible or invisible; and it can boom in the absence of space and time. Have you heard, what we see was adapted from the unseen? That does not imply nothingness, but that many details are undetectable. Even scientists believe this, what with imperceptible particles, dark energy, forces weak and strong; quantum strings, fields, waves, singularities, and what not. Physicists must accept a huge amount of this stuff on trust. Watch this: your sensory and perceptual faculties sanction sight; so also do your spiritual faculties but it's a different kind of vision.

Consider time; at light speed time halts. It is said that we would age slower in deep space due to less gravity. So, is time constant? There are limits to the notions that time is linear and never changes speed. Isn't spacetime curved? Doesn't the black hole bring time to a halt at the event horizon? Won't time decelerate as you reach the edge of the universe, and aren't farther galaxies supposed to be moving away faster? Does time really slow when you reach light speed or approach a black hole? What if you could breach light speed? Or is time coasting downhill? Since gravity increases with mass so do rotation, inertia, and time zones. Would daytime not be affected by changes in Earth's size, tilt, spin, gravity, or orbit? If the mass of our planet decreased (or increased), wouldn't a day measure longer or shorter? How does one estimate with accuracy the age of the universe as time itself is variable, especially with respect to where you are in the universe? Maybe there are no true constants, including time and light. That would violate the laws of physics; but even the big bang, black holes, and quantum mechanics defy laws of physics. Thankfully, God does not vary; though everything else does because he can change it and he can change you.

According to the Bible time is neither linear nor unidirectional, as it was reversed once and halted another occasion. Explain that! Christ also was not constrained by time or space. Take for example miracles: the virgin birth, raising the dead, walking on water, calming the storm, curing the sick and maimed, feeding thousands with a little boy's lunch, or turning water into wine instantaneously. Thus, the works of our Lord neither adhere to the laws of cause and effect, nor to physics or spacetime. True miracles are supernatural, designed to send a message, provide validation, or convey revelation. Jesus was conceived by the Holy Spirit, born of a virgin woman, and developed into a man. And though he was tempted same as everyone else, he never dropped his guard. After some 33.5 years he was assassinated; in a few days he was alive again. He walked, talked, and ate another forty days after that. How does that fit into the normal progression of time and space, much less natural and normal human capability? Of course, Nature's laws are violated all the time by humans what with unnatural sex, abortion, euthanasia, etc. There is a penalty for breaking the moral, natural, and civil laws; it's called justice.

Can anyone calculate the exact length of creation? Was it 6 literal days, 6000 years, 380,000 years, 120 million years, 15 billion years? It doesn't matter to me. Besides, God can fiddle with the clock if he so chooses. Cannot one day and one night connote different ideas? That'll be the day, huh? Maybe days took longer back then, or maybe there was a lapse of time between days. God would create something and let it transpire, a day being worth a thousand years and vice-versa. Were there eons between days or did six twenty-four-hour days occur one after the other?

Does a tree grow from a seed, germinate, yield its fruit, and replenish the soil with new seed in a single day? It surely wouldn't take millions of years. Did the vapors and elements separate to produce atmospheres overnight? Did space matter coagulate into galaxies, stars, planets, and cosmic bodies between dusk and dawn; or is that how the heavens developed at all? If it took billions and billions of years, wouldn't that be too long? The second law of thermodynamics implies we would have nothing left to grow on; stars would be burned out, the moon would be long gone, and an earth day would take years. Well, it depends on which authoritative cosmologist you're asking. Possibly it took no time at all. Either way, it isn't impossible with God who has no constraints. He can supplant a full-grown mustard tree into my living room right now if it suits his purpose. If he stretched out the heavens like the Bible says it would be pretty quick, comparatively speaking. Understand this: that's how it was written and how it is observed. But quick to God is a trillion years. When God breathed into man, it brought him to life immediately. If he has done it before…

Whether it was fast or slow it was timeless regardless of the timeframe. God created humankind one fine day and we have continued, multiplied, developed, and progressed technologically for millennia. Still, we have not changed in form or functionality one iota; we possess the same degree of complexity and capacity. Because everything already had been planned, designed, and installed before this planet took form including you and me. The entire universe was established specifically to spawn and sustain life on Earth without which we wouldn't be having this discussion. And God allows us to affect this dimension of spacetime by granting us liberty and morality.

Perhaps the six stages of Genesis represent eras or perhaps terrestrial days. Either way, the sequence is a guideline, the seventh day being reserved for rest and worship. God rested insofar as he had no need to intervene further, allowing the universe (and us) to develop, advance, expand, and prosper. But that doesn't mean he can't or won't step in if and when he pleases. Take God's advice and enjoy a day off each week to appreciate his creation and engage in the wonder of it all! This is concretely the foremost message to be gleaned from the Genesis week. Additionally, we faithfully should show our appreciation always and forever, not solely once a week since the seventh day of Genesis was not defined by an evening and a morning.

God is another dilemma to throw into the quantum mishmash. Maybe it isn't incredibly tiny building blocks that make up matter, energy, and other stuff but grossly gigantic ones. Either way you can't witness it. What I have observed is that it takes the artist weeks to paint one elaborate painting, but only one day to finish the work. At the moment of creation God executed his plan and it developed into a fine work of art. And we get to see the glorious picture of what he was foreknowing every moment of each day forever; but only one peek at a time as it is constantly in a state of flux. Still, God remains the same.

During our last encounter on Earth SS reiterated, "I can assure, you will not experience this space and time again."

"That means the only two things I have control over is myself and right now," I added, after which a look of surprise adorned his countenance.

"You really are getting it!" he exclaimed.

Fact: the universe includes us; it's not singularly an astronomical phenomenon. And while space seems to egress with entropy, humankind does not. We can be persevering, decisive, interested, and instructed. We can gain in strength, knowhow, and spirituality. Though our bodies and minds degrade we will be rejuvenated. After that we can abide as perpetual beings. And God controls it all. I find the thought of that outstanding! The atheists find the thought repulsive. Who do you think have left their minds in the gutter?

I asked the lecturers to identify the most important episodes in the history of our species. They converged upon the discoveries of gravity, general relativity, universal expansion, quantum mechanics, and exotic matter. Their heroes were legendary: Pythagoras, Leucippus, Ptolemy, Copernicus, Galileo, Kepler, Newton, Maxwell, Kelvin, Planck, Einstein, Heisenberg, Hubble, Bohr, Feynman, Hawking, and others. An exceptional list to be sure; by the way, many of these believed in and attributed science to God. Coincidentally, I was compelled to offer a proxy. I proposed that the most important occasions in human history would be the creation of mankind, the birth, death, and resurrection of Jesus Christ, and his second coming when God will recreate everything. They promptly threw me out of the auditorium. How could I possibly revere Christ and the writings in the Bible more than these great men? I wonder what their opinion would be concerning outstanding thinkers on my sweet-sixteen list: Moses, St. Paul, Athanasius, Augustine, Wycliffe, Luther, Pascal, Locke, Washington, Jefferson, Adams, Franklin, Madison, Lincoln, Chesterton, Lewis; mostly believers. Notice how the men in both lists have died yet their legacy lives on.

You cannot delimit God to linear time or three-dimensional space (or four, six, nine, eleven, or however many dimensions). It is a blunder to describe God in material, metaphysical, or human terms or try to explain away his constancy. That's where mistakes are made in attempting to reckon such concepts as predestination coincident with free will, one God manifested in three persons, and creation by a super-intelligent designer. If time is unidimensional does there have to be a start and a finish? Not always; well, maybe a physical beginning but not a spiritual end. God exists in multifarious dimensions where he can be here, there and everywhere simultaneously; he has access to every point along the plane of humanity as well as before and after and all oblique intersections. Is there anything in our perceived reality that is perfect, omniscient, everywhere, and everlasting? Well, God.

Although natural selection has no empirical basis concerning our origin, consider this: spiritual selection. I believe I will change because God has promised. I will become as an angel but better: a higher, perfect, and unblemished human in the likeness of God's Son. But this will not occur until Christ returns, after which he will carry people like me to his domain of excellence far away from here. Yes, there is a utopia and I intend on going. Arrogant you say? Make no mistake, we didn't earn his favor, only by remembering the promise. If you don't want to go that's fine. Resurrection my friends is spontaneous transmutation for those who believe; survival of the fittest if you will, among whom will be those sanctified by the Holy Spirit to be pure and blameless. One might think of it as spiritual evolution but it is correctly re-creation, when everything will be new, including heaven, earth, me, and hopefully you. The prominent change in my body is that it will live forever because it will be faultless and flawless, untainted by a purified soul once replete with iniquity.

I posit that the spirit within me remains the same in essence and power. Perhaps when it is freed from my body, I can experience astral projection; certainly, that capability could be possible in a glorified body. I regularly travel in my dreams whether waking or asleep; but such excursions are a product of my visualizations and therefore reside within me not without me. It resembles lucid dreaming how real it feels. I learned to dissociate effectively at an early age; I guess I was about twelve. I was looking at a book of paintings that my aunt owned; she was quite the accomplished painter herself and tried to teach me. One photocopy in particular caught my eye; a boy my age was fishing at a lake in the woods. I stared at the picture for several minutes and became mesmerized; I was the boy complete with straw hat, bamboo rod, overalls, and bare feet. When I returned to reality two hours had passed. I still remember the place and I go there occasionally to escape, for the picture is implanted in my memory and accessible at will. Try it if you are seeking peace of mind. Nature always has helped me connect with my Creator, but now I can connect the same way without going anywhere. I wish I could connect with the solipsist that way; apparently, he can but not me.

There are those that wish there was God, those that don't want God, those that deny, and those that cannot deny God. I am among the last group. God's existence is in diverse dimensions of reality and unreality. He can appear as a man and disappear at will; he can read the thoughts of everyone and already have an answer to their prayers. God can solve your problems before you perceive them; and he can plan your destiny while you make your own choices and pursue happiness as you define it. And he can grant eternal life. Only an eternal God can present such enjoyment. Atheists ask, "Who created God," an incongruous and pretentious question to say the least. Obviously, they haven't a clue who God is. They can conceive only of a god that is a product of our universe, one that cannot contradict the physical laws. Let me point out dilemmas in quantum theory which defy the physical laws: a photon can be a particle and a wave at the same time; and you can predict the movement or position of a particle but not both; and associated electrons can be two places at once. But they cannot fathom Messiah being both human and divine or God being two places at once.

It is very impressive the genius of humanity and unimpressive at the same time. Many have discovered how to tap the vast resources of consciousness from the brilliant scientist to the retarded savant. Everybody approaches that potential when they dream. Train your brain to perform multiple operations by studying statistics, logic, geometry, law, medicine, astrophysics, psychology, physical science, and the arts. But remember, the power of intellect always can go further than you can. And when God gives wisdom it surpasses human understanding. He embeds the knowledge into your soul so it cannot be corrupted by perceptual, experiential, or intellectual bias; otherwise the meaning would be altered to fit a worldly synthesis.

Contemplate this: some phenomena can be comprehended by the spirit and imminent is the avenue to glory. If you cannot figure out infinity it's because you have tasked your paltry mental faculties to understand it. This is a constraint, because the mind currently has a boundary which is the body within which resides the brain. And your present corrupt body cannot live forever but your spirit can. Jesus said, "It is the spirit that gives life not the flesh." He stated candidly in the ancient texts that the spirit lives on after death. Life forms have a will to thrive and survive. The materialists define such life in terms of the interaction between an organism and its environment; and they maintain that death is the very end of it at which time the body is enveloped into the earth through utter entropy (i.e., dust to dust). But life cannot be defined unequivocally in terms of the physical because the spirit never dies. God who is Spirit never dies; he is always here, always was, and always will be.

The fact that life is coupled with self-awareness only addresses the mental aspect of existence; it is insufficient to define the essence of life. Your life force is in the spirit which is given by God. He will let you keep it if you seek him and acknowledge him. If not, your mind and body will be destroyed; your spirit, which belonged to God from the start, will return to him the source of life. Thus, for souls to be fully alive and self-aware, these three components must be simultaneously present: body, mind, and spirit.

Life springs forth from life not from nonexistence. And Christ who is God in the flesh is life; and he existed with God since before time. Within Christ reside the features of man and the indwelling of the Holy Spirit. We are to worship him in spirit and in truth for he is equal with God. We also are part of God and he is in us. How can you know this? Like I said, such understanding comes by means of your spirit. This spirit stands in awe of the divine who gave it. And that, according to the wisest mortal that ever lived, is the beginning of wisdom. Such knowledge is available to everyone who searches the soul; if seeking is guided by your spirit it will be enlightening when you stumble upon absolute truth. Conscious awareness and moral discernment are top down processes with the spirit enabling such capabilities. The reductionists assert it is bottom up; clearly a counterintuitive stance as their beginning begins at zero where it also ends. How's that for circular reasoning?

We are able to comprehend the world via science precisely because we have been created in God's image with a mind that can observe, analyze, test, differentiate, and infer. He gave us these gifts to find him and fathom his creation. The atheists assume a rational universe but reject that it is the mind that enables such rationality. If lucidity was due to an evolved brain then why don't pigs and elephants study mathematics and geometry? They've been around longer than we have. The unbelievers must constantly be haunted by such contradictions: trying to explain the mind only through the material, or life only by the physical, or moral reasoning only via the natural. If only they knew of the spiritual, it could explain these fascinations in a manner that makes perfect sense. It is actually more effortful to categorically snub the truth which becomes a continuous task, causes tremendous anxiety, and leads to erroneous conclusions. Thanks to God, I do not have a mental illness, faith is not a delusion, and Christ's promises are real.

I was able to recover, despite the cosmic thoughts bombarding my brain. Even I, with poltergeists haunting my memory, bats in the belfry, and skeletons in closets locked behind portals of perception. Once obtained, the power enabled me to release them and they had a picnic on a lawn of grey matter. They got to meet each other and at once I became an integrated soul; then I bade them farewell. Mind you they were not rivals; acquaintances at best. I could have allowed them to visit from time to time but we have nothing in common anymore. Monsters used to congregate under the bed late at night; that's where it's always dark. Ask any kid afraid of sleeping without a nightlight. I'd have a bad dream and wake up fearful, figuring they were outside my head not inside. Nevertheless, I summoned my internal superhero, the monster mangler, to ward them off. But he tried to overtake my ego and dominate the entire show so I had to retire him too. Otherwise he would've become more dangerous than the fiends he was commissioned to dispatch. Joy encouraged me to draw portraits of the gremlins which enabled me to put them to pasture where they belonged. I displayed them on my bedroom wall where they remained for years. I wish I'd kept the pictures they were quite amusing. I suppose we all have our demons assigned to us by the demented one. I see them lurking in the faces of many people. Some of these individuals are ogres in their own right; others are plagued by the monsters within.

I chose to discharge them and forgive myself. What's past has passed; no need to carry it into the future. Give it to Messiah; he earned it. I'd rather deal with his appointed ones, angels of superior power and might than humans. They drive away the demons, preventing them from returning with more. I think they talk to me sometimes but I don't talk to them because I wouldn't know what to say. Besides, God is a close personal friend and guide, and listens. He speaks to me and I discern with my heart of hearts. Some people call it the conscience; others the soul. It is accessed via the spirit which he put inside me. I advise you to take notice for it is your greatest power. It doesn't lie to you and it informs you what is right or wrong. I know for a fact that God speaks to each of us in different ways. When I finally started paying attention to him everything became clear. But it isn't easy to explain.

The three who found the infant king certainly must have been in touch: one each from the original sons that survived the flood. Gifts obtained from Arabia and the African horn they brought; priests who studied the ancient religions, prophecies, and texts. They navigated by way of a unique celestial event, a portent they knew to be a sign, being well educated and versed in astronomy, mathematics, geometry, prophecy, and philosophy. This was nothing compared to what they were about to learn. If they didn't believe before they sure did afterwards. And the knowledge that seeped into their souls was pure and telling. It wasn't just an epiphany for them either as they would not keep the discovery confidential.

Their peoples would reject it centuries later and follow a saga that was a spin of the initial testimony. Instead of accepting the accurate version they tailored one to fit their worldview and called it their own. But the alteration rendered the entire text false by virtue of the fact that precision requires internal consistency, reliability of the source, corroboration with known truth, and unswerving dedication to certitude. If it contradicts itself then none of it can be trusted. The ultimate blunder elicited by scientists, agnostics, occultists, and atheists is adapting the evidence to fit their theories rather than the converse. Truth can be (indeed it must be) unwavering. Yet they engage in warped or roundabout logic. Violating the principal principle of non-contradiction, they eschew the facts going so far as to postulate that nothing is true and everything is meaningless, or that faith is blind (well, theirs' maybe).

When God genuinely has a hand in the preparation of the documentation, you'll find no errors. This was the most astounding part, the minutiae and how every piece fit, though transcribed in different tongues by numerous authors who lived at various epochs and locales. How else could their disparate yet inclusive manuscripts have gelled so comprehensively? Nice try, those who have invented their own book of truth in order to be unique or feel special. Truthfully, only one compilation exists that has God's signature on it; it is holy like he is since it is him who speaks. The world will try to smother it so keep it close and stay alert. Raise your ear and open the crypt when you are summoned. You will know where to go from there. But to be counted among the saints requires training. You are fighting an enemy you cannot see. Maybe you have some expertise battling flesh and blood but it will not prepare you for this skirmish. Carry the sword, which if you remove the letter "s" spells "word." It penetrates the invisible shield, seizing the heart. Learn the ways of spiritual warfare and conquer the enemy; for even if you stand alone you aren't really.

The sandstorm swept over the arid plain, desiccated and blistering hot. Sweat burned my eyes forming a haze that enveloped the scene, adding to the fuzziness of the setting and the cloudiness of the circumstances. I swept my hands forward at the border of my reach, taking baby steps along the course on a quest for a recognizable reality. I was hoping to make it to the queue and catch a train; or flag a taxi that would carry me to a destination. Instead, I tracked an indescribable phantom that led me into the badlands. It had me circling as if through a turnstile, over and again. I was trapped in a revolving door in the unclear white darkness.

While going nowhere it seemed a direction, because every time I made it there it seemed different. But how would I know since I couldn't view it? Furthermore, can there be more than one nowhere? And how does one know nowhere in the first place? The only way is having been there before. Anywhere would have been better though. It's an empty feeling if you get it, hopeless and despairing. I would not wish that outlook on anyone. It's better if you can't see it; you definitely will not want to go. However, if you stay here or there, then you'll never get anywhere. But a step in any direction will be progress. When the prospects are bleak that is a predicament. And this, ladies and gentlemen, is life without God.

Fortunately, it was simply another bad dream, at least for me. For there I was, driving through miles and miles of nothingness, no scenery whatsoever. Plenty of other cars were on the road each vehicle displaying a different state tag. But there wasn't a soul inside just an empty bag of bones. And that was spooky enough. The only available reading material consisted of county line markers which changed every kilometer. It wasn't only the counties that had been gerrymandered to death; the fifty-two states had been reconfigured to the nth degree. A map of the nation's internal borders resembled child's scribble. Elections fell to the unchallenged reigning party. Politicians made it seem a three-party system, but the con was they crudely fought over which would be the more allowing. It didn't matter since the masses had no representation either way. I swear, if you don't drink and drive, you'll start on that highway. The destination is uncertain because the direction is unclear.

I yearned for an end like an exciting escape through a painted forest, with fall colors psychedelic and aglow way up the rise. At the summit the roadway would make a clearing through the trees exposing the ocean below. Looking down would be my first sight of it since the trip began. My favorite place was within reach, and soon I was frolicking on the beach in the sand and suds. I wondered, whatever became of my collection of seashells? I recalled touching my ear to the conch; I didn't hear the ocean but a whisper telling me to live healthy is to die happy. It was so easy when I was a child. But the adult in me wanted to be convinced in the midst of the doubt. I think that's why God gave me his book of knowledge. But it took the same eagerness as the child to apprehend it.

If you want to truly grasp profound insights from God's universe and his Word, you must open your mind and seek with your spirit. One cannot comprehend the depth of God's wisdom using physical and mental faculties alone; they only connect us to the world. You need to explore the depths of yourself and find the inner power and control (which is your very life force) in order to encounter the kingdom of God. For it is beyond anything that you can examine in the present environment.

God—Is he for real? Look around you. Isn't it fanciful, eccentric, incredible? But it was here before you were. You can't understand it? Let me explain. It's pretty farfetched, but if you can satisfy your curiosity by saying that your mind is not capable of grasping such a weird phenomenon, you also can satisfy your curiosity by deeming it unreasonable to consider anything fanciful or farfetched. Either way, it's a copout. Think about this. Sometimes you need the challenge, something unordinary to understand or believe in. I can think of nothing more challenging and fantastic than making God your excuse for life. It's may seem weird, farfetched, incredible, and extraordinary; but it's fun when you base your philosophy on God's Word. So, if you want a challenge, friendship, understanding, satisfaction—God. If you want life and heaven, and if you want God—God.

Search outside the familiar realms and explore the spiritual world, which is vaster than the universe. There are layers of existence that continue, never reaching the coattails of God Almighty. But he reaches down to us and connects via Nature and his Word. Both reveal truths which converge to produce wisdom. Open your hand and open your heart; let him inside. He will unfasten the padlocks of your mind, unrestricting your perception, enabling you to see vividly with your soul. Then you will know exactly what I am talking about. And when your jet plane leaves for its final departure you will gladly and fearlessly board, for the destination is eternity.

LAMENTATIONS

I deeply regret many deeds I have done though I know I'm forgiven. Most were indiscretions others were downright deviant. If I could've taken it back would I have done it differently? Or was I destined to take advantage of others, to lose control of myself, and to disregard God? How beholden am I that I will not be held to account on account of one ultimate sacrificial offering; thank goodness, because I wouldn't have been able to afford the penalty otherwise. The door is open and the Savior calls. What are you waiting for, death? Whether death comes or Christ comes, either way it will be too late. It's time to get right with God right now.

I hoped that I was in the right but I wasn't exactly kind, understanding, humble, or gracious in my approach. Sincerely, our clandestine operations were on the militant and violent side. But this was war; we had to be aggressive, and secretive. We spoke our own language, a gobbling potpourri of blurts, grunts, and animal noises sort of when SS uttered his native tongue; some codes were actual words in the language of solipsist. We could insert them into seemingly casual speech that was irrelevant to the message. The cadence, pitch, intonation, and syllables would make sense only to the brotherhood. Nonverbal communications that seemed normal and meaningful meant something entirely different to us. We encrypted the message with subtle cues that only trusted operatives could recognize and decipher. The union had no way of interpreting our conversations, signals, and dispatches no matter how hard they tried, despite the surplus of surveillance, decoding technology, body language experts, and foreign language specialists at their disposal. Playacting our rehearsed skits, we could blend in when necessary and disappear as quickly; empty faces in a crowd became their worst enemy. This was a most valuable lesson from my old amigo SS; I managed to converse with him in solipsist, sort of.

Our resolve incensed the incorrigible ingrates. We engaged the annoying brood on a daily basis, extinguishing their fires and dismantling their pyres. My body shook from the constant barrages of bullets that I sent raining upon their parades. Okay, I guess I did mention previously that I was going to let it play out; but I couldn't. Those cantankerous curs were massacring innocents by the score. They targeted souls seeking solace or salvation, unconcerned about the atrocious amounts of suffering and collateral fatalities. The finicky freaks enjoyed inflicting unspeakable torment and anguish; since this was their conviction, we returned the favor. Traipsing about in their body armor, feeling invincible and sanctioned, they danced on tiptoes pretending it was Mardi Gras while they blasted, slashed, and clubbed every living thing in sight. Quite harsh their loitering law, affirming that leftover squirrels would remain on the treadmill.

We emplaced sniper teams in the medium heights of rundown skyscrapers, after removing the windows and drawing blinds specially engineered for the occasion. Scopes were bore-sighted to 500 meters, attached to long-barrels equipped with flash suppressors. Of course, we stored a plentiful supply of 7.62mm armor-piercing ammunition in our magazine satchels. Time and again we caught them by surprise. We'd take careful aim at the center mass of their shoulder silhouette and squeeze off a round that would cut loose with such intensity and velocity it ran them through, splintering bones and ripping flesh. Searching the sky for the slayers that ended their procession, hands held to their breasts, they fell flat as a freshly hewn tree. The last thing they saw was either a blank bloodshot sky or the gritty blood-soaked pavement.

How did we pull this off you may ask? Well a crafty chap (who had been with us since tribal days) stole a couple of crates of tritonite rivets from a hangar where aircraft were being maintained. His brother, a talented artisan in his prior vocation fashioning false teeth, was adept at molding bullets out of porcelain with rivets inserted. The strong and durable rods had triangular bevels that came to a fine point; embedded into the clay they remained strong and straight during baking. We'd collected gobs of brass, never leaving any at a fight site. Using a magnum load to accelerate the projectile, the ceramic slug would explode into fragments when it smacked into a plated vest; but the rod would commence to worm its way through the layers of armor, shredding every internal organ it encountered as it tumbled along. I realize this description is on the gory side, but it just goes to show how innovative and determined we were to put a chink in their armor (so to speak).

I was still in charge of the rifle committee as in days long past; in fact, I inherited full command after SS flew the coop. We developed specialty squads for diverse sorts of countermeasures. Traps, mines and assorted whizbang explosives were harnessed to foil ruthless plots coming to light via our formidable intelligence network. Makeup and costume artists created interesting and sneaky characters: a handicapped person who rode a wheelchair equipped with rocket launchers; government officials and dignitaries bearing identification, documents, and passes from captured officials to enter secure buildings and eavesdrop on surreptitious assemblies; and law enforcement personnel armed to the teeth with the latest weaponry donning uniforms filched from the establishment. We would meet in public places to strategize, carousing around like a crew of preppies gearing up for a weekend of lively rambunctiousness. Hiding in plain sight, they overlooked the obvious as they searched the catacombs, back alleys, and condemned properties for the ghosts performing our disappearing acts.

Meanwhile we were kidnapping kidnappers, castrating rapists, putting hits on hitmen, and blowing up bombers and bomb makers; often using their own conspiracies and supplies to indict, convict, and interdict them. Who else would? The scalawags had protection if not exemption, plus asylum. Actions and counteractions were glamourized in the media, and the games became the envy of fledgling youth who were ambling about bored to tears and seeking misadventure. The clerics disseminated propaganda to enlist and coerce unwitting anarchists into permissible pugnacity. But the rebellion was actually us; and many of the citizens figured that out and opted to endorse our stratagem. They were the ones with brains and heart so it gave us the edge when it came to collecting intelligence, aiding concealment, providing security, abetting guileful operations, sabotaging cyberspace, and more. You'd have to be a dumbbell not to see that terrorism had been decriminalized, but not so much counterterrorism; thus, our cause seemed more attractive to levelheaded mutineers. The opportunists joined us because they chose what they perceived to be the greater good rather than pursue the greater evil (or perhaps the least of the two). What a resource for infiltrating society because they could aid in ways where most of us were vulnerable, given that cameras were everywhere and more were being added by the hour. Who would suspect them for they had valid playing cards and they filed monthly tax returns?

We repeatedly slaughtered assassins and retreated, as guerillas in the mist. This was a genuine jihad. The reactionaries weren't used to facing their enemies so they were shocked out of their socks. I have learned that it takes sizable courage to confront your fears head on; but if you run from them, you'll be running endlessly. And you can't escape them or pawn them off on someone else the way radical extremists do. They never fathomed freedom, they derided it. They never understood loyalty, they abhorred it. They weren't interested in truth, they scorned it. But the terrorists comprehended terror and they were terrified of it. Fear is a popular phenomenon to be feared, is it not? Will they never consider the alternative, to fear only God? For he can crush and he can keep. I prefer the latter.

I grieve for persons who haven't sought restoration and reconciliation. They are misdirected; and anyone who follows them. I once heard a parson say that his most important responsibility was not to his congregation but to his own children. "If they do not make it to heaven," he explained, "I will have failed them." Imagine: preceding your kids in death, finding your way home, waiting for them to show up, and they don't. I can appreciate his point. Surely, we all are God's children. We are brothers and sisters so shouldn't we be concerned about each other? For isn't that the second-most important commandment: to love others as much as ourselves? I mourn for the unbelievers; they know not the power of love, only fear.

I weep for those who seek love in the wrong places or the wrong persons. I especially feel for those individuals that give their love generously to others who are abusive to them or otherwise do not reciprocate. Not that the love is wasted for it returns in other ways; most notably the unrestricted and endless love of the Father.

But some people don't know when it's time to move on. Give it your best shot and let God do the rest. You cannot cause a flower to grow but you can plant seeds. Yes, you can be nurturing but God provides sustenance; you can be caring but God effects change; you can be loving but God institutes redemption.

I bemoan people with evil in their hearts. Their quest is to force others into fear for their lives, present and future. I guess it's because they despise their own lives and are afraid of what is to come, and likely want everyone else to feel that way. They're jealous of anyone whose hearts spring with joy, they disparage the doctrine of pure freedom, they envy those who are convinced about the hereafter, and they especially abhor Christendom. The only cure for them is real love but they will not find it because they are unwilling to love unconditionally. They only love others who are correspondingly disgusting. Some claim to love the divine, but their gods aren't loving and kind they're hostile and hateful. For others their god is money. It's not the money that is the culprit but the love of it. Some people worship it. They bask in their riches but it tarnishes them. And many of our youth have waded into the grunge; they want to get rich in a hurry but are unaware of the denizens therein. Some end up selling themselves out and lose the investment equally as fast.

Notice how the narrowminded will curse or ban the object; but it is the perpetrator that is culpable. Remember, possessing money itself is not evil, but it corrupts. Guns don't kill, people do. Politicians want to abolish guns so you don't revolt but that's why the amendment was put there in the first place. The forefathers knew it could happen again, hoping that it wouldn't but prepared if it did. Remember the founding father who said, "You have a republic, if you can keep it." Those in power endeavor to remove that prospect reducing the threat to only them.

Besides, if some maniac is bent on murder, he will find no shortage of objects to accomplish it; people have been killed with such objects as a screwdriver, brick, antifreeze, jawbone, truck, and golf club. Should we ban those items too? Then only criminals will have access. And how are we to defend ourselves? Are you going to rely on the government to protect you? By the time a lawman shows up you'll be dead. I read a true report of a man who shot and wounded a burglar and got sued for damages by the burglar; maybe the owner should have aimed at the criminal's heart. Sometimes gangsters will shoot a citizen out of spite. Do they ever get sued? Jeepers, the bad guys have more firepower than the cops, while the general public is virtually powerless. How are the police going to stop crime when they are outgunned?

I guess we also should ban cameras; aren't they responsible for recording immoral deeds? The media moguls influence flocks of young sheep to empty their spirits. This is particularly true with television where glitter masks the eyes. The networks have surrendered morality for ratings. In that realm glitz is queen, homosexuality is the norm, and atrocities such as rape and murder are hyped.

Anything goes and repercussions don't exist. They have brought our children down to their level. And the kids have no idea how to dig themselves out since nobody ever showed them how to use a shovel.

Do you want to be popular? Then undress for the camera. Do you want to feel sexy? Then debase yourself and become a sexual object. Pity, because everybody has appeal. Children don't realize this because their self-esteem is constantly in question, as if defined by how others view them. They have wasted their identity so they succumb to exploitation and this drives the fading image of self ever lower. At that point they can't muster the intestinal fortitude to identify an attacker or a saboteur. Apprehension is the motivator not happiness.

The following are the scourge of society: child molesters, pornographers, pimps, rapists, exploiters and the like. They are the epitome of manmade manure. How could anyone spoil a little one, or anyone, for a brief dissolute delight? Talk about the scum of the earth. They deserve no mercy whatsoever, only the guillotine. Why does society suffer them to live? They'll never change; they're addicted. It's the only thing they think about. For many it's a family tradition. Here's another example of how the gene pool could carry on with considerably fewer contributors.

And where do they get some of these judges who think they can invent their own justice? They toss out relevant facts with no precedent. They do whatever they want with blatant disregard for the fact that their decisions are in discord with the rules they swore to follow. They would abandon the Constitution or at least rewrite it. They would free a child molester yet incarcerate a hypocrite. They should look into the mirror. When they let the pedophiles walk it makes me suspect them of being one. Who but an offender would sympathize with an offender? It has nothing to do with forgiveness. A victim may forgive an assailant but the perpetrator still must be held liable. Besides, judges are not to dispense pardon but punishment.

Is there not a progression present in the criminal code? Isn't murder more heinous than envy? It is in the Ten Commandments. Evidently, the defiant justices would abandon or rewrite those as well, though the tablets still adorn the highest chambers. I'd hate to see them carve their amoral code into stone; they'd call it the Ten Consents. We know they would never put that much effort into anything lawful. But the stone tablets someday will smash them. I would think there is a grading in hell, with some getting the greater damnation. Perhaps there are varying rewards in heaven as well, with some receiving the greater responsibility.

But this world is slipping into the slime. I blame it on the erosion of culture and the secularism in society. They've removed the Lord God from our foundation and heritage. Discipline has been eliminated in institutions of education. Family ties and values have disintegrated; kids are turning into recluses, withdrawn and isolative. Promiscuity is advanced and religion shunned in the entertainment industry.

Networks have ignored the plight of poverty, the treachery of terrorism, the malice of slave trafficking, and the arrogance of advantage in their news coverage. It isn't news anymore, it's wind. Government leaders have exaggerated triviality and overlooked the most odious of abominations. And judicators seem more interested in self-expression than enforcing laws. Meanwhile, those violating laws receive impunity; they evade prosecution with their expensive attorneys and semantic gymnastics, or the laws are never enforced in the first place. They'll invent eyewitnesses, hire convicts to present testimony, and parade thugs and liars to assess character. Accountability ceases to exist to the extent that people become desensitized to the decay especially the young and naive.

Self-appointed spokespersons pontificate tolerance and sermonize endlessly about parity. Yet they continue to promulgate their double standards with respect to age, race, gender, physical prowess, political slant, and socioeconomic status. There can be but one yardstick and it should be applied evenly to everyone; only then will we achieve equal opportunity, impartiality, and fairness across the board. But they'd rather keep the dividing lines clearly demarked so that they can disperse allegations of bigotry, accuse persons of noncompliance, slander an official's reputation, or remove someone on the basis of trumped up charges of insubordination, offensiveness, obfuscation, harassment, or evidence tampering. Never mind that the case is flimsy or lacks merit altogether. But if there was no division, they'd have nothing to do and a convenient source of income would run dry.

They'll pursue with great vigor any opponent, drag his or her name through the mud, and accuse him or her of everything from being ugly to being hateful, unethical, or criminal. Thus, strictly honest people with integrity and loyalty shy away from running for office or seeking positions of leadership, as they prefer not to have every aspect of their life and any indiscretions of the past to be strung out on the clothesline. Or worse, have fabrications created and disseminated to every corner before proven false or publicly repudiated. When the damage has been done then the newspapers might print a retraction; but you'll have to search for it among the fine print in the concluding pages.

You are insane if you admit to any wrongdoing. They won't forgive you they'll crucify you. Yet their deeds have been covered up with more spin than you can find on a merry-go-round. They view themselves beyond reproof and pretend to be offended when slighted. But their transgressions are many and will lead to their demise; they deny there is payment for sin and redemption through faith. Oh, what a pitiful end awaits them when the omnipotent fury of God is unleashed!

Is it any wonder that our youth have become disinterested in matters of faith and responsibility? Are you surprised that the rates of violent crime have escalated noticeably? Do you flinch when you see the crookedness, the corruption, the vice, the flamboyance, and the debauchery in government and business? Don't you find it appalling when the blameless are charged and the guilty go free? Are you unflappable with regard to these affairs, preferring to espouse lenience? Liberalism is not the same as liberty. Meanwhile, conservatism is ridiculed. It is an insult these days to be labeled a moderate or centrist. But these values have nothing to do with one's partisan pitch; it's a moral stand. It's not right or left; it's right or wrong, remember? I am referring to the conscience, the superego, scruples. Everybody has an inner voice; listen to it, it will not lie to you. It is your access point to the highest heaven. Place your feet on the foundation of love and you will find it, and maybe feel it. And that is not an extreme position it's centered on God. The Lord said, if you are seeking the kingdom of heaven you need to look within yourself to discover it.

Most of the forlorn souls were not looking for the way in but the way out, for which there was none. When the abyss was unlocked it was time for me to highball the gates. Through the smoky entrails emerged the torturous legions; a cavalry that could not be numbered, deployed to gather converts for condemnation. It sounded like a rumbling stampede kicking up the dust, obliterating the sun, and filling the skies with smear and stink. Millions of giant armored insects swarmed about. Mounted upon each was a demon displaying the face of a man and firing a harpoon that would smart like a stingray as it stabbed each victim in the anus. While they were being reeled in, the prey would pray for the first time, not for life but for death. Too bad dying would not relieve the agony which was now beginning. I was appraising the bloodbath from a concealed vantage point when I spied their leader Apollyon pointing a skeleton's finger summoning them to advance. The entire throng went careening into the pit like a bunch of sightless leaping lemmings. A cloud of smoke once again billowed from the hole which consumed them all. It was then I finally decided to hang up my guns. I returned to my persona of a kindly and caring pacifist, realizing that the battle belonged to the Lord. I wasn't exactly neutral but careful.

I am rooted in the middle; I bend with the breeze. It's okay if you do not vary more than one standard deviation this way or that. Admittedly, that may not be the norm in this day-and-age but it obviously isn't abnormal. People label me megamoderate. What the heck is that? It's an oxymoron. How can you be extremely temperate? And they label me intolerant. Hey, I can tolerate a lot more than they can; what I refuse to tolerate is evil being given a pass. If you do not believe as I do, I can live with that. But can you? Or would you accede to the accursed?

I have settled the matter about evil: it is the work of people. I hear reductive materialists ask, "Who wants to believe in a God that sanctions evil?" How often have you heard that one? Well, if they don't want to believe in God why do they blame him? If God doesn't exist who is to blame for evil? But do they accept any blame? Do they feel acquitted or indicted by their wayward ways? If they took responsibility, they would recognize that they are guilty as hell. And who isn't? Instead they ask, "If there was a God why would he create us that way, authorizing evil expression?" "Why doesn't he do something about it?" He already has. Don't forget, God is not constrained by time; he sees the cascade of life as a single experience. Wickedness has its way because of free will which will be relinquished in due time for those who practice it.

The Father made us more like him than people think, and less like other living creatures than people think. That's why he became a man to show us how we can be, undeniably, how we are like him: able to choose the good and refuse the evil. The main difference is, our Savior did but we didn't. This knowledge is relevant only to humanity; other earthly creatures do not choose on the basis of the ethicality of the available alternatives. God resolved the matter by doing the good that we could not; and by paying the price for the sin that we could and did. He paved the way for our becoming like him simply by following his lead. And though we are imperfect in our ways, he will make us perfect in lieu of our faith in his words, our desire for him, and our effort to stay on the path he sets before us.

I do not lean towards a particular party. I side firmly with God. The Lord cannot self-indulge; nor can he self-deny. He doesn't vary. He is my example; the moral standard. This philosophy was not the invention of an ascetic. It has always been God's way which he showed us when he came among us. It's a boulevard, but narrow compared to the flyways out of town. It's easy to get sidetracked from the many curves, forks, and intersections. But it's not that difficult to follow if you remain focused on him; and it's immensely more satisfying.

Okay, I'm having this dream you know, and I'm lying in bed sleeping. How about that, dreaming that I'm asleep? And then I start having another dream: a dream within a dream. Has that ever happened to you? It's bizarre. Anyway, there's a thick fog and I'm stuck at a crossroads. I'm not sure which way is north or east, or whatever. Rather, the options are seasons. So, I select springtime because I favor green, mild weather, and soft rain. Next, I find myself in a small nest, a baby bird warm and cozy. I'd just as soon stay there than attempt to fly. But by and by, you have to try. Suddenly I cut loose and there was nothing to it. It was so natural and fun I began to chuckle. Right then a bell chimed and I opened my eyes. Mind you, I'm still asleep; the alarm only alerted me that another dream was on pause. I got out of bed and looked into the mirror, rubbing my eyes. A shadowy shape was approaching from the mirror side of the image.

My first inclination was to retreat as it could be Mr. Grim Reaper. Instead I stepped in to meet my nemesis. Advancing was the silhouette of a highwayman on horseback riding hard. I could not get a peek at his face as it was cloaked with a hood, but I sensed no hostility and I was not nervous. Coming to a screeching halt, he told me to choose. "Choose what?" I inquired. He replied, "You may select four tools from this sack," which instantaneously appeared at my feet. I picked the axe-hammer, the multipurpose pocketknife, the bucket, and the entrenching tool. "You have chosen wisely," he confirmed. Then the fog reappeared and again I found myself looking into a clouded mirror. Only this time I was wide awake. When the fog lifted, I quickly noticed the reflection of tools behind me on the bed.

But let's get back to the point. See here: The Bible teaches that God is love. If you can feel love you can feel God, and vice-versa. If you love others, you're sharing God. If others love you, you're receiving God. If you believe in God you know love is the answer to the misery, lawlessness, treachery, and desperation. If you do not believe you are trying to clean the dishes with a dirty rag. You can push the dirt around but you can't remove it and you can't hide it. All the cologne in the world will not mask the stench of sin.

The world is nearly void of love. People seek gratification from earthly enchantments which cannot nourish the spirit. Disappearing contentment is the best they can achieve and it becomes addictive. They search for something or someone to plug the hollowness. Meanwhile, the recreation fades rapidly and discontentment seeps in. It seems one can become wearier of the indulgence than from the tension they are trying to flee when entertaining it.

Many find companionship amongst their ilk who likewise feel emptiness in their hearts. Communally there endures a false comradeship; but alone, each member remains adrift at sea. They merge into a single mindless entity that is predisposed to risky decisions, unfriendly engagements, groupthink, and criminal mischief. But the sensation of security is fictitious and the prospect of power unrewarded. And the trepidation never leaves them because charity cannot linger. For they too are alienated whether apart or together, because individuality is missing; and the group does not become integrated but polarized. Even a common course will not provide a common yoke. But their duty is to tag along and not question motive or destiny. The plunder of the conquest will be insufficient to placate the whole so it will fall to the favored or the strongest, only because they have lasted the longest. The weak or subservient who represent the majority further lose confidence and regard for self, which already was below the perceived worth of the others. They strive for syndication, acknowledgement, and acclaim. And though the gang appears organized and unified, it has no more congruence or purpose than a riotous mob.

It's dangerous to be an individual anymore. But if you care to take a stand, prepare to be shot down. Fascists can't bear to listen to anyone but themselves. Freedom of speech applies only to them. And they would defend the right to feed pornographic prose to a child but chastise someone for praying silently in public. In fact, they will take more and more liberties especially the ones that were instilled as a safeguard against totalitarianism. That's right! What they seek is tyranny not egalitarianism. Eventually they will have it because people are too tired and bored to resist anymore. We've been worn down to the nub. Isn't it sad that the silent majority has remained so? Well I'm not going to give up hope, not just yet. Mine is but one voice. Join with me and we'll sing a new song. It will be music to God's ears but irritating to the powermongers.

Decadence is not a civil liberty. Freedom does not permit the deliberate testimony of lies, the persecution of the righteous, or the scandalous exploitation of the innocent. Too many bystanders sanction the activists and fanatics who are defining what everyone else should think and be; these ingrates get airtime while speeches from the informed are smothered. Take for example abysmal atheists that won't pipe down. If they want to renounce God that's their prerogative. But why are they so callous about it? If they ever were to accept that God exists, they'd hate him; they can't stand believers in God either. They can be turned around however, for God's love has been known to work wonders. But people who are sold on ignorance already have closed their eyes, ears, and hearts to God. They have therefore condemned themselves. I found myself wishing to be free of them.

Seeking a moment of solace, I approached a lone cottonwood casting its shade across the knoll. Sprawled over a cushion of soft grass I slept. When I awoke, I stretched out my arms, yawned, and then thanked the tree for its service to my soul. He acknowledged, pointing out that I was the first to do so despite the hundreds that had lain there. I recognized him by adding that he was the first tree to speak to me. As it turned out, tree had quite a bit to decree.

"I am flawless in my creation, no blemishes or imperfections," he boasted. Admitting that I was not I asserted that someday I hope to be. "Indeed, you will," he agreed, "when our Creator opens the windows." "Will I see you there?" I inquired. "Perhaps," he responded. There was much to learn from the tree: how he stands strong against the wind but bows; how he spreads his branches and embraces the storm on the one hand and protects the robin's nest on the other; and how he digs his roots deep into the ground and grabs hold of the rock.

Behind him the sun was setting. "Unlike you, feeble man, I never sleep," she asserted. "But someday you will, won't you?" I proposed. "No, but someday you won't... As for me, I might meditate for a spell after I shed my corona in a flurry of fire." "You have no doubt, contemplated destiny as I do," I submitted. "On that point sir, we see eye to eye," was her reply. There was much to learn from the sun: regardless of the weather she shined; no matter the climate she showered her warmth; whatever the weather she daily visited and soothed the lonely, heartbroken, and suffering.

The grass chimed in with their chorale of voices intoning, "In one accord we bring praise to the Holy One!" "I wish to join you in your adoration," I requested. "Then unite with us in our steadfastness," they demanded, "for you must persevere in the midst of turmoil or you will perish." "I shall be true to my roots," I assured them. There was much to learn from the grass: how they held together through thick and thin; how they lifted up the soil; how they bathed in the rain and the sun, raising high their blades.

Tree and Me

Not to be outdone, the sky would have the last word. "Would you overlook the obvious?" he questioned. "Positively not," I replied, "I heed you day and night, snuggling within your encirclement; you have never failed me faithful friend." "Glad you noticed," he said smiling. "Now go and do the same," he advised. There was much to learn from the sky: how he supplied us with life-sustaining breath; how he persisted in his work for nigh unto an eternity with nary a complaint; how he broadened himself as a shielding firmament over the earth.

It was peaceful, it was right. There was love everywhere. They knew how to define tranquility and tendered their propositions as to how I could seize it. Who would deny, ignore, or turn away from the message God conveys in his handiwork? Open an aesthetic eye and listen to the vibrations of nature. And take time to behold the beauty as you stand in reverence and admiration of its majesty. God makes this known to all people yet some do not own up. They would worship the artifact rather than the architect; or possess a narcissistic affection for only themselves as if they had a hand in their being here.

It reminds me of the tale of the giant cactus relayed to me by my grandfather. There was competition among the cacti. Some would seek the sharpest and longest spikes, others the largest trunk, or the most arms. But there was one that strove to be the tallest and reached up high into touch the clouds. He fancied himself superior, not only in height but in stature. Gruffly, the wind brought him prostrate before the others snapping his torso at the base. Arms would have surrounded and strengthened him but he had none; breadth would have sustained and supported him but he lacked that too. And now his spiny spine would secure him to the sand.

It's criminal; it's reprehensible. I detest vileness and degeneracy. I expect those self-indulgent villains eventually will get what they deserve. I pray that they do not go unpunished for long or succeed in harming another living soul. They are enemies of the living and companions of demons. And they get away with their atrocities because nobody has the guts to do anything about it, much less take a position of justice or righteousness. Ours is a society of tolerance; but I cannot tolerate injustice and malice. I guess that makes me a nonconformist. Vigilantism won't help either.

I especially loathe the idea of following Beelzebub. How insane is that? Degenerate disciples would repudiate God yet esteem his adversary? And under that guise are committed the most despicable acts of atrocity against humanity. They infiltrate our schools, churches, government, private and civic institutions utterly for the purpose of indulging their naughty cravings. They cover their tracks by sponsoring suspicion, endorsing discord, and distributing disloyalty. Some hold sordid services where adulation of their king includes sacrificing babies, drinking blood, mutilating their bodies, performing abominable sexual acts, casting spells, summoning demons, and whatever is their favorite pastime or floats their boat at that time. What kind of a warped and wanton mind finds such activities engaging?

Everything they say is a lie because that is their truth. Everything they think is against Christ for that is their mission. Everything they do is malicious for that is their act of faith. Every plan promotes self and destroys goodness since this is their hope. And they dangle on a thread with the prospect of ruling in purgatory for eternity. But there are no rulers there, only senseless tortured souls that will realize firsthand the pain they once wielded upon others. This is how they lived their lives and this is how they will die their deaths.

Can the dean of darkness guarantee anything? Oh, he will make grandiose guarantees but he cannot deliver, neither in this life nor the next. Everything on the earth has been given by God and there is enough for everyone. Satan cannot give you something that you already own; he can bring only death though he has no power over it. More to the point, you already have the capacity for excellence. Tap into your God-given potential. The desire, the faith, and the effort already have been placed into your heart; you are able to become everything you were meant to be, more than you ever dreamed of being. Because every soul has worth, every person has promise, and exceptionalism is what makes us equal. But we are not the same in measure, arena, or calling. Concretely, the only thing we all share is access to the Spirit.

Gauge the aptitude of true power. Is it greater to put someone to death or to raise someone from it? If you extol the powers of iniquity, you forfeit the security of the Most High. God and Lucifer cannot both be right. And you shouldn't revere them together for they are in opposition. But who gives credence to an obvious swindle? Satan always twists the proclamations of God like he did in the Garden of Eden, and when he tried to tempt Jesus Christ in the wilderness by spinning God's own words. Yes, he is cunning and knows enough to make you look ignorant. But how can the senescent serpent be brighter than God if God invented him? What's more, Satan lacks the power to create and to procreate. He seeks devotees of doom to be his children. What baffles me is he succeeds. It makes me embarrassed to be a member of the same species with the likes of those who patronize the devil.

I remember when intrepid young rebels raided the goat farm. Revolutionaries after my own heart they were; sick and tired of the hedonism of their elders. Who could ignore the statistics: scores of missing children who had been forgotten or left behind? Nothing but cold cases which had been filed away because of supposed lack of resources, personnel, and investigative leads. The fact was, law enforcers didn't want to look, afraid of what they might find. Those probing further died mysteriously, quit the force unexpectedly, or joined the dark side. Here was another marker too alarming to be believed: the number of suicides, accidents, and murders among honest public servants, attorneys, and officers of the law.

The small band of morally-minded mavericks managed to infiltrate a nefarious network of pedophiles, whose enterprise it was to traffic innocence for a handsome fee. Malfeasant mongrels had established upstate an impregnable compound that masqueraded as a legitimate business. It didn't take a college degree in accounting to figure out that the gobs of money they were raking in did not come from the sale of goat products. Besides, does an ordinary farm have sentries, checkpoints, and security systems?

Inside the barricaded barn they would hold their services, complete with sexual assault, orgy, slave trade, and sacrifice. Bedecked in black masks and red capes to conceal their identities, they engaged in the most sadistic misbehavior imaginable. Primarily a pastime for the aristocracy, the entry fee was exorbitant and the dues inflated. The canny insurgents managed to shake blackmail money from members to meet the requirements for membership. Bribery and extortion were accepted practices so the intruders were commended for their shrewdness. Isn't it quaint how the players failed to realize that another attribute of cleverness is deceit? How could they not be suspicious? I find it hilarious in a warped way.

Well the time came for the big sting. The protesters had slipped inside with machineguns, camera equipment, and paddy wagons. At the opportune moment, the seven of them opened fire into the rafters and the congregation dropped to the deck. Every participant was ordered to surrender their batman outfits or eat lead. Few opted for the latter. After sending a direct audiovisual feed of their dirty deeds and the identities thereof to a renegade broadcaster, the culprits were rounded up and escorted to the wagons. Then the goat farm was set afire, goats and all. What happened to their impenetrable security you might ask? Hey, anybody lacking scruples can be bought especially if it earns them immunity.

Almost one hundred "respected" citizens, mostly male, were unmasked that evening before the world. They included schoolteachers, mayors, judges, legislators, businesspersons, clergymen, pediatricians, and others one would least suspect if they were as gullible as the general public. The roach coaches were deserted in grassy fields where those abominable perpetrators of perversion remained incarcerated, until some dolt broke open the wagon doors two days later. Though their reputations had been unraveled no legal recourse was taken against a single character. The news media had dropped the story like a steaming hot potato.

The good news was that a few hundred children were emancipated from the clutches of cruelty. Most would not return home since that would've been equally ugly. Instead, they were drafted into defending the dissatisfied and disadvantaged, becoming contemporary crusaders. Sadly, they would never realize the social reforms they marshalled for but at least found strength in one another and survived a fiercer fate. And their resolve would lead to the liberation of many more. However, the enemy would ultimately prevail, for the disgraceful dozen continued to breed disdain and disrepute in amazing quantity with continued exemption.

Among their ranks arose that dreadful essence claiming to be of imperial lineage. But he descended from the bastard son not the legitimate one. His father before him was an outcast, a nomad that couldn't stay put and had no home. He hailed from the ancient kingdom after emerging from a basket along the banks of the Euphrates, that was his story. Gregarious and conniving, he invited himself and was accepted by the party of lost causes. Expounding on rumors they longed to hear (e.g., being "chosen" and the "children of promise" and the "catalyst for change") he took charge over their religion and fashioned it into his own. He waged war against the righteous, whom he derided and wanted to hurl into the tomb that was prepared for him. There were antichrists in profusion willing to join the revelry and sacrifice themselves to the serpent. The self-proclaimed apostle became the object of their devotion and they became instruments of his atrocities. Misshapen into the image of the dragon himself who had appointed him, he erected an altar in the holy temple in his honor (more like dishonor) and defiled it further with blood offerings.

The grisly flow produced a river of folly, defiling the tributaries and turning waterways into rust. The tenants relished in their revilement. All who drank of the cup of insurrection and bathed in the tub of acrimony became disfigured by this curse. Their blood was going to erupt like a gusher and fill the canyons to the mane of a stallion.

The Storm

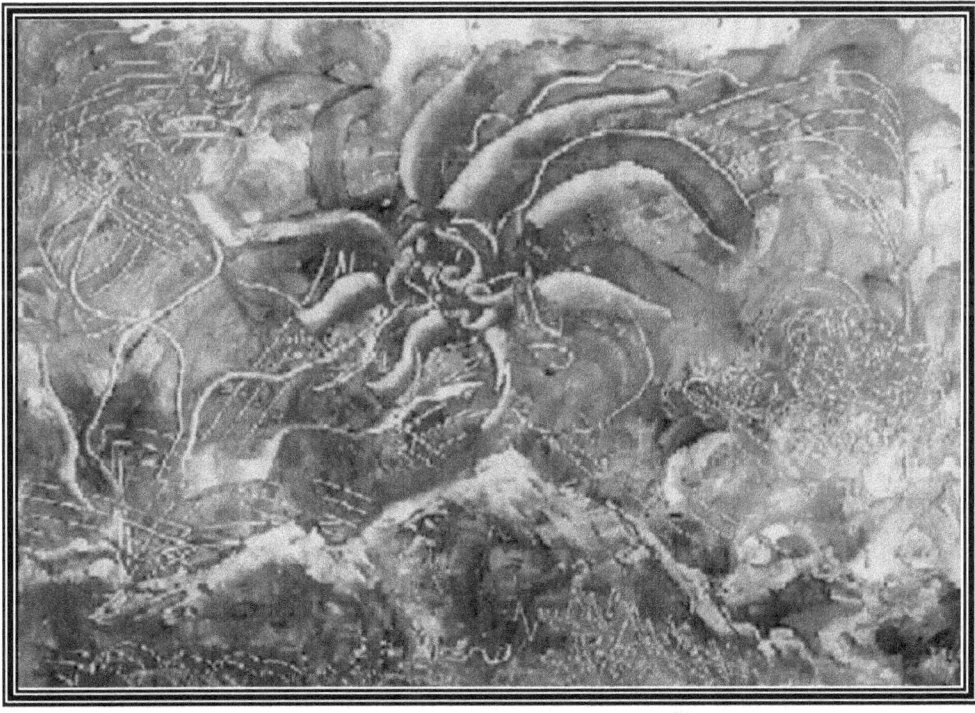

This was written in the book of the law for generations to see. How is it they didn't notice, those who consented to having their creed hijacked? The moderates realized what was afoot and divorced themselves. Understudies mostly, who found freedom in education of the mind and spirit. They organized their own exodus after failing in the upheaval. Only fanatics, militants, activists, and crazed insurrectionists remained in the sacred places which soon would be converted into catacombs, their definitive resting stop. The wasteland that became their home made me wonder why the Lord didn't proceed with annihilating that capital the first time. But he elected to spare it for the sake of the decent. This time however, all were blameworthy.

The metropolis slipped into the mire, toppling as an imploding volcano. A giant sinkhole sucked the lot into the stomach of the earth, where once digested it became refuse in the bowels of the underworld. What a bombshell it must have been, presuming their empire would triumph. After the anointed cherub was cast out of heaven, did he suppose there was a chance of being readmitted, especially since he hadn't changed his ways one whit? Surely, he didn't believe so, but persuaded his fans somehow. The solipsist slumbered as the conscience of the nations also snoozed.

The chambermaid shook the crumbs off her apron and arose from the settee. She picked up the cup and saucer with her unfolded napkin and headed into the parlor. That's when she heard him calling outside the window. Eager to see who it was she heeded the cry, skipping down the staircase and opening the gate, allowing the court jester to enter the courtyard. He was a dwarf of a man; garbed in a colorful sequined outfit, curled and pointy slippers, and floppy topper with fuzz balls bouncing about the ears. Not very cute, but she found him witty if not enchanting.

His crooked smirk revealed sharpened teeth, sinister looking and yet fashionable she thought. She must have known he was a trickster but chose not to dwell on it because he made her laugh. Despite her naiveite she'd never entertained such foolhardiness before, but heedlessly drank from the decanter he offered, sucked into the captivating conversation rehearsed so methodically, and the lute that he played so eloquently. But she was the one being played.

The liquor softened her inhibitions and heightened the excitement of his ominous undertaking. She was drowsy and disoriented, losing her scandals as she stumbled past the hedges while he ushered her to the gazebo. There he ravaged her, capturing her unawares and stealing her purity. And there she would awaken the next morn feeling the pain between her thighs, with scant memory of the night before or the viciousness therein. She furthermore would be caught utterly by surprise nine months hence. For she would deliver a monstrosity from her womb; the spit and image of the lone joker in that wrinkled deck of cards left on the parlor table, those she used when playing solitaire night after night following her tea and cookies.

But the wretched toddler would be snatched away by the king, to be raised among royalty and taught the ways of condescension. The child would learn only the concessions of self-absorption, never caring or considering the anguish or love of his mother; for he did not seek to suckle at her breast because there were more delectable desires to pursue and fulfill. The servant girl was dismissed, only to die in despair a comely young pauper dishonored and despoiled. Her lifeless body, covered in a worn muddy sweater and tattered apron, lay on the cold hard stones. Her only son paid her little mind as the driver snapped the whip and the carriage whizzed by. The prince's only thought: what an embarrassment to be exposed to this disgrace, littering the highway like garbage. Little did he know who she was or that she was his last chance.

It burns to my soul, like pouring alcohol into a fresh wound. And I can't rinse it out because I know it will not heal; not until the book is reopened. Those pledges that could have saved them would condemn them. The way was unlocked before them and they intentionally bolted the door from the inside. Why does it trouble me? I am not responsible. I tried to warn them and so did many others. But God taught me to love them and there is a price when you do.

I mourn the aimless souls. They are too proud to seek God. They care only about themselves. But by doing so they obviously don't care, because to neglect God is to neglect self. I should think that narcissism, abandonment, and stinginess would be among the deadliest sins. There certainly is an abundance going around; and this has led to the destruction and downfall of men. It boils down to greed and pride: too greedy to share the wealth and too proud to be bested.

And the hindrance restricting the remainders was apathy. Society at large had maintained a laissez faire attitude for generations. People didn't want to become involved as it took time and energy and usually produced unpleasant or undesired consequences. There was no way they were going to allow themselves to be derided, scorned, or reprimanded. This only succeeded in stifling the proposition or practice of courtesy and honesty. They didn't disapprove but hunkered down in their hideouts hoping nobody would notice them; if this worked it was their only victory.

But I won't judge them. They had been brainwashed; assimilated by the mind machine which manufactures immorality and cultivates complacency. Sitting daily for hours in front of the monitor exposed their brains to copious amounts of propaganda, garbled truths, and innuendo. Their reality and their ingenuity were fabricated for them so they wouldn't have to reason or question or envision. Their heads spun with the message that moved them which wove webs of irrelevance in the midst of the axons and dendrites. Eventually nothing would permeate the entangled weaving, except that which had no destination. Memories were being removed, reprogrammed, and replaced. They were impregnated with new processes and programs via the inundation of altered images, and the repetition of warped rationalizations. Personal thoughts and aspirations were voided so that a recall scan would yield nothing but a learned sense of helplessness.

Being introverted as I was, I encountered myself; withdrawing from and abjuring all persuasions about such modernistic drivel, in hopes of connecting with my soul. I located that inner peace which surpasses understanding thereby escaping the world and discovering what was beyond. Sometimes the truth can be found from within; you basically have to listen to it. It has been planted into everyone; make sure it does not wither and die or so will you.

I was contemplating truth and whether absolute truth could be verified, because the conventional wisdom was that it was either relative or unknowable. But the fact that Lany had blue eyes would always be true for all time and for all people. I concluded there must be poignant points that are absolutely verifiable. I pondered, if an omniscient being exists, by definition he has to know all truth. That would be an attribute of God I surmised. Jesus claimed he spoke only truth though he was called a liar and an imposter. He professed to be God and God cannot tell a lie if he is the ultimate source of truth. So then, Jesus was either crazy, or a liar, or who he claimed to be. But he wasn't crucified for being a liar or for being crazy, as these were not capital offenses punishable by death. The officials wanted him dead for saying he was God; blasphemy is the only offense they accused him of and the reason they found him guilty. The question is, did he blaspheme in which case he was a liar; or did he tell the truth about who he was. The Roman rascal that condemned Jesus to death asked him, "what is truth," this after Jesus told him his duty was to tell the truth. But then the jerk left the room without waiting for Jesus's reply; it's as if he didn't want to know the answer. Maybe that's the problem with those deeming truth to be relative or unknowable: they refuse to listen to or acknowledge truth because it damages their egos and contradicts their disreputable intentions.

Suppose Christ was a liar; you wouldn't be able to believe a word he said. Plus, the entire Bible would be unreliable for he quoted it regularly. But a liar is easily found out whether in the spoken word or the written word, as it is impossible to keep track of a pile of lies; because at the end of the day the truth comes to light, the lies are exposed, and the liar is discredited. However, to this day billions of people follow Christ, his teachings and the Bible; and they do so as a result of seeking truth, not negating it. It's the power of prophecy; someone predicts with unprecedented detail and exactness a distant future event that happens precisely as stated, such as Christ declaring that Jerusalem would be sacked and the temple destroyed within a generation. If verified, it would be evidence that the prophet was neither crazy nor a liar. Or maybe he got lucky, right? The Gospel writers recorded this prophecy, which came true almost forty years later. To contest the event as a fulfillment of prophecy, some historians argued that the writers documented it after the fact so it wasn't prophetic at all; but that would be quite a feat seeing how the historical records reveal that all but one died a martyr's death prior to this prediction coming to pass. The only book of the Bible emerging afterwards was the Revelation prophecy. A profound prophetic accomplishment is not a talent or a trick, it's a gift. Even a meteorologist can't reliably predict whether it will rain the day after tomorrow much less next year, at a certain time, on a certain day, in a certain location; if a weatherman could do that, he would be called a prophet; in fact, the prophet Elijah did that very thing.

How about the ability to perform multiple miracles which also cannot be unraveled since the occurrences defy nature, science, and logic? Can paranormal marvels be the work of a lunatic? I mean, a crazy person may believe he or she can do such things but can't prove it to others by overtly doing them, so the person is dismissed as deluded. But if you saw a supernatural spectacle, say a person strolling evenly atop a turbulent sea, would you think he or she was crazy? Or maybe you'd believe you're crazy. If a guy told you he was going to be assassinated, and then come back to life three days later, you'd certainly think he was loco; unless it happened strictly as he said and you confirmed it firsthand. You'd be forced to believe one of the following: either you are delusional, or he is unique and special and you are blessed to know him.

The worthiest way to discover the truth is to seek it out; do the work. Conduct the research, talk to the experts, substantiate the known facts, and other forms of objective scholarship. But people will dismiss Jesus, the Bible, and the existence of God without performing any of these tasks. They tell me the Bible is a compilation of tall tales. I ask them if they have read the Bible; they tell me they don't need to. They've heard the allegorical stories and that's enough. Or they tell me that the Bible cannot be true and there is no God because the scientific evidence contradicts these notions. I ask them to cite the evidence and they regurgitate a bunch of unproven verbosity, fabricated data, and self-contradictory statements that are neither scientifically sound nor historically factual. Those that loathe God, Jesus, and the Bible cannot provide one valid example of a false statement or a crazy act; they will spout the same rhetoric that has been misused since his ascension. If Jesus cannot be proven to be a liar or a lunatic, then you're left with the third alternative: he is precisely who he says he is. Can that be proven? Categorically, yes! But you have to want to know the truth, do the work; and listen carefully.

Getting back to the story, progress had taken a standstill. Sure, there were economical and productive ways of doing things. Natural resources could have been preserved and distributed. Great ideas, inventions, and modernizations cropped up that would have improved the quality of life for everyone. Products, processes, and machinations were available that might have revived the most backward peoples and the most dilapidated economies. But these items were snatched, stolen, or stifled. The affluent and renowned wanted the status quo to remain so. There would be no more competition, democracy, or entrepreneurship. They weren't about to share or to be outdone. Thus, the rich became richer and the poor poorer. Society at large became more dependent and less intelligent, more permissive and less productive.

That's why the solipsist kept his riddles to himself. He coached me because he knew nobody would believe me. He figured, if they silenced those with superior intellect than I they'd never give me the time of day. Take for example his energy producing appliance that used a little to create a lot; it merely took a reconfiguration of magnetic fields. He wasn't the only one to figure it out. SS wouldn't let me market the design knowing it would be pilfered, burned, or buried not to mention the threat it would cause to my life and livelihood. Many advances already had been realized and had fallen by the wayside. Government, military, and big business held back the best for themselves. Inventers were bought, imprisoned, or murdered.

No more power to the people or they wouldn't remain needy. Talk about playing with a marked deck, and the stakes were life and death. But the populace gambled all the same. What did they have to lose? The only choice was how fast. When you go all-in, you'll either hit the jackpot or shoot your wad. Either way you'll know how it ends in a flash. There's a measly $1/100,000,000$ chance yet people are willing to chance it. They'd spend their accumulated earnings on the lottery, fueled by a dream instead of real food. But the dream fades at the same rate as the finances and what remains is greater want. Oh yes, someone will spring to their aid at the price of enslavement. That was the plan all along and proof the game was rigged from the start. This is why we ducked out the backdoor and absconded with what we could carry, burying the rest for a future occasion if and when it might become necessary.

Home was heaven and it resided in the heart, so we were always there and we were always free. Even if they captured us, brainwashed and persecuted us, we still had won the race. We had beaten them at their own game. It was called make your own rules; and that's how they cheated the masses and fleeced the reserves. Because, if you play according to their guidelines you will realize enough gains to get hooked; but the odds are grossly in the house's favor. However, if you play the game the way they do they'll be confused when you advance, as they assume you stand by their policies and not your own (whereas they don't either). For they do not proceed in accordance with the highest power since they assume it is them. They too lose in the end, not just the power but the glory as well.

It equates to idolatry anyway you look at it, which is a violation of the most important commandment: love God first. The second is love everyone else. It's okay to include yourself in the latter but not the former. These two, declared the Lord, are the most important imperatives to follow and the keys to justification. It's about caring. But nowadays who cares?

It took a lifetime for me to figure it out. I often thought I was part of this world and the premonitions and paranormal experiences were my connection to it. And I was right to some degree; however, the very idea of otherworldly thought would imply it is not of this world. The Almighty also is not of this world; he is not of this universe either for that matter. How can God be a part of something if that something is essentially a part of him? Is he not master of his creation? If not, it would be the same as building a jail for oneself. And maybe the solipsist is not of this world but of another. Maybe he is of my mind, or is he of another? I'll let you figure that one out. This will be your homework for today.

One thing's for sure, I eventually grew up, matured, found the elusive wisdom. I came to understand that I was wrong before, and it took years to encode the mountain of data and ascertain what was right and true. You see, experience teaches you about the world, and yourself, but not about God. You can know him only from what he teaches and reveals. It will not emerge via osmosis, evolution, or introspection. Remember, wisdom takes education, understanding, and experience.

I identify with the truth so I am hated. But Christ cautioned that the world would hate me as it hated him. He was not of the world because he created it; that's what he said and he doesn't fib. He was placed here to show us the exit. I was chosen out of the world for I was never a part of it in the first place. Many have been predestined to be part of his kingdom. And people who aren't often resent those who are, though it was their desire not to be. Now it makes total sense. I see why they are evil, lying, sinister, calculating, unscrupulous, brutal, and heartless. They'd like to see the elect fail for they view us as overconfident, ignorant, deceitful, condescending, or crazy. But that is a projection of their own weaknesses whereas the preceding negatives can be considered their strengths and their ruin. They band together and seek others of their breed, and cannot bear to lend an ear or allow anyone else to speak. Because truthful words are painful, like the piercing of the stiletto they would impale into my heart and the agony of defeat that is constantly in theirs. They deny being in misery while looking for company in it. When the very answer to their disturbance is what they renounce as a pestilence, disease, sham, or curse.

The laws of the land had been molded by a revolting theocracy characterized by fraud and godlessness. They were hellbent on rounding us up and ripping our hearts out. If a Christian partisan such as I was to be captured, he or she would be tortured in inconceivable ways. Such was the fate of a former colleague who tried to acclimate, but instead fell prey to the menacing mindbender machinery. But the roots of his faith were deeply planted and he was unable to shun his allegiance to the Lord Jesus, knowing full well it would brand him an agitator guilty of treason. Once the suppressors were alerted that the gentleman had been observed kneeling at his bedside with a crucifix in hand, they raided his abode with two dozen stormtroopers as if he was a major threat, and lugged him away kicking and screaming.

He was betrayed by a scout of the establishment who befriended the common folk in order to infiltrate our secret society known as the fishers. The conman was paid a bounty to expose infidels, defined as anyone suspected of worshipping any other than Antichrist who had proclaimed itself the god of the universe. Being caught on video by a surveilling cop wearing jetpacks, they had him dead to rights. Exhibiting outlandish religious behavior such as prayer, or possessing associated paraphernalia like a Bible, would render a heavy price in order to discourage others from committing crimes of this nature. A faithful servant of God quickly became honored guest at a sacrilegious ceremony that dehumanized saints in exultation of the dragon king. Daily sacrifices were held in the temple of doom, the devil's sanctuary, erected upon a rock once held hallowed and now profaned.

Anyway, Simon had been disfigured, dismembered, defiled, and broken in one such episode, being made an example of the consequences for disobedience to the idolatrous rule. The event was aired during prime time, since inflicting pain had become the draw in the most popular program of the century. One dissenter would be brutalized each Friday, using progressively more creative techniques from the producers' handbook of horrors.

I uncovered a mauled Simon huddled in the corner of a broom closet in the overcrowded psychiatric ward at the prison infirmary. Posing as a priest of perdition, I arrived to dedicate him to Belial as a last rite, for he was scheduled to be crucified at dusk. That equally vicious event was to be televised during the prelude to the next airing of *Last Days of Our Lives*. Come to think of it, I could have been the main attraction and made my television torture debut, had they caught me smuggling my buddy out of the loony bin. I shifted disguises to that of laundry collector and carted Simon through the back door in a bin of soiled linen, right past one guard who was relieving himself and another guard who was busy fetching a last meal for my convicted friend (how thoughtful the warden, okaying the condemned a choice of TV dinners while viewing their ignominy, prior to being liquidated).

I recognized the warden playing master of ceremonies; he was among the Klazi when I banished them to the badlands. He became a lieutenant in the army of antichrist during their rally to recruit assassins, interrogators, and assorted henchmen; he'd worked his way up to curator of the municipal torture chamber. I should've taken the solipsist's advice when he told me to eradicate the lot of them. "Sometimes, it isn't wise to show mercy," SS urged. He sure nailed that one, and I sure botched it.

We patched Simon and weaned him back to semi-fitness at which time he adamantly pledged to resume the fight. He was in haste because he was infected and had but a short time, vowing to take the maniacal menaces with him. He interrupted a subsequent telecast in a blaze of glory when he detonated an improvised explosive device demolishing the station and taking out the entirety of the staff, sets, scripts, props, facilities, and equipment, as well as the studio audience. It was the concluding shooting of the world's favorite soap opera. Simon became quite the celebrity, posthumously; everyone remembered well that last scene prior to the show's abrupt cancellation. A modern-day Nazarite, he had once succumbed to secularism and its temptations, but relented when he understood the sinister plan to reengineer his thinking and destroy his soul. He took down the temple of their god in a closing act of contrition. It sparked a last-minute rush to defy the dominion.

Like the deranged demagogue, devotees of disaster can see the writing on the wall but refuse to heed the forewarnings. They sit and watch, engorging themselves as the angels dismantle their kingdom brick by brick, while they count the ways they hate God. They continue conspiring to destroy his church, while their empire crumbles beneath their feet. Step by step they descend into the pit which they think is the way up. There is no way out only down. Please don't go there it isn't safe!

I was traveling through for the last time, hungry and cold; not intentionally but misdirected. It was adjacent to the dark forest, which was familiar territory to me by now. But this time I had wandered much further and deeper. I laid traps to catch some game and I commenced to construct a shelter. Upon completion I checked my traps; lucky as I am, I snared one hare. Scrawny it was, but I was eager to gut, skin, cook and eat it. It was bleeding, wounded, and wailing, which made me feel irked if not offended with myself. I gathered some herbs, leaves, minerals, and vines, sparked up a pile of branches and cooked some salve. I cleansed and dressed the wound, and nursed the ragged rodent back to health. As soon as it was able, it lit out of there bounding and rejoicing. I laughed, made an about face, and retraced my steps; gradually I found my way out of the shady, jumbled, and incongruent woodlands and back to my humble homestead.

Once again there I was, standing in front of the mirror; holding the bucket of tools in my right hand. The image was clear and reflected the real me. My quest was not in vain and the dream had come true. I would manage to find a variety of applications for those tools, and to this day I have remained grateful to the gray rider for his counsel and his gifts.

We are blessed with countless freebies; some are never appreciated until it's too late to benefit. I lament mostly for those who refuse such treasures, particularly the opportunity to be clothed in glory on the last day. I reminisce venturing through time with SS, when I was the immature, albeit ignorant youngster seeking adventure more than truth. How I wished we had reversed to the time of Christ and conversed with the Lord of the universe; to be fed among the thousands with holy food which nourished body, soul, and spirit. I have pictured Messiah on the cross pouring out his soul to anyone who would embrace him. Though I didn't witness the event personally, I did anyway. I wanted to see him after his resurrection and shake his broken hand, the godman with his piercing scars, wounded on every inch of his body, but dressed in righteousness and glory, his countenance radiant and beaming.

"But you will see him," SS assured, "Everybody will." He's right, you know. Nobody can escape Jesus's return because there will be shouting, trumpets, and singing, complete with light show and fireworks. He will take home his designates; I can't wait but I must. Every person that ever lived will be gathered together whether still alive or once dead, possessing all their faculties; each seeing the Lord with his or her own eyes. I bewail exceedingly for those who will be viewing him for the first and last time.

Treacherous Treats

REVELATIONS

Floundering in the grasp of gloom I prayed to God to pull me out of my despair. He reached down from above, lifted me up, and planted me on my feet. I thoroughly felt the connection: hand in hand, heart to heart, Spirit on spirit. It reminded me when SS would speak to me telepathically; but that only worked when we were in the same location. I realized that God was closer still, as near as my own heart. In fact, he opened my heart, cosigned my mind, and invigorated my essence to reside therein and I in him. All I had to do was think and he listened; and all he had to do was speak and the words were etched upon my soul. I felt reassured, refreshed, and restored. But battling the fatigue I conked out, during which I recharged.

At the boundary of space, I trespassed through an event horizon one last time; I had to locate the solipsist and tell him. SS tapped me on the shoulder. He was waiting for me to show up, and we had a conversation. I was chatting telepathically with him, though he knew in advance what I was going to say. There was no need for line-of-sight transmission; we weren't even in the same dimension. He was in the future; he already had died but he was alive and well. I was still kicking around below trying to shake the blues, figuring nobody knew my sorrow; but I was wrong. I had two-way communication with anybody and everybody merely by projecting, either to God, SS, associates, or animals.

I accepted his invitation to visit and followed SS into a pyramid. It would be an understatement to say the encounter was exhilarating. There I controlled a vastly superior intellect than when I entered, arranging thoughts fluently in a nanosecond. The speed of my ideations exceeded that of light and time I imagined. The news was piling up in heaps and disseminated to neural nodules throughout my cerebrum; and without hesitation I was processing the next cascade of data and circulating it. These processes were operating in parallel. I presented two personas: one me going in the door and one going out at the same time. Like black holes: coming, going, or both.

And get this: not a single impression of evil crossed my mind; such meager, immature, and crass reflections were beneath me. There once was a time when every ounce of fight within me couldn't smother those sinister intrusions. My brainpower was light years more advanced to be entertaining such senseless poppycock anymore. I realized that everything I had done wrong in my life began with the wrong thought. But there were no more wrong thoughts: nothing sinful; absent of errors in sensitivity, logic, and integration.

What used to be advanced science and technology was clear-cut, and what was once a dilemma wrapped in an enigma was intuitively obvious. I had more answers than questions but SS was not surprised in the least (though possibly relieved). It was interesting how my judgments became purposes, expressed in words and actions that generated grander insight, wisdom, and production; oh, and cogent curiosity such that my fascination with it was exponential. Every tidbit of knowledge archived in my central database was effortlessly accessible in entirety. I had unlimited ingress into the unconscious; with the ability to conceptualize in various dimensions and statistically analyze thousands of cases to arrive at highly probable conclusions. Thoughts were spewing like voluminous volcanoes erupting without ceasing, clustering conceptual configurations into colossal cogitations. I could associate chaos and disorder, wisdom and truth, creation and reality; I could define gravity, energy, and synergy. Had I been reconfined to my previous physical inadequacy, my brain probably would have exploded like a big bang producing undiluted gobbledygook: disorder versus order. Amazingly, no overload, confusion, or miscalculation forever. These capabilities exceeded that of SS and his world, except for the fact that he already had acquired them having left his world behind, well ahead of me.

I had a photographic memory meaning I remembered everything, excepting my experiences within the phantoms of previous materialistic veracity. But this concept was befuddling: Had I misperceived being a product of a celestial orb which didn't endure? I wasn't certain it ever did. Since I had no recollection of that reality I wasn't concerned where I'd hailed from; but I was willing to continue in the place that I now was. I had conscious awareness of self and I definitely relished my conversion, for I possessed zero desire to be whom or what I thought I had been. Abruptly, that notion became another obstruction so I entertained it no more. I reckoned my entitlement came with a new set of faculties, rules, laws, and codes endowed by our Creator. Had I leapt into a more fortunate and progressed life form? It certainly was not something I evolved into because I was still me; but I was most definitely transformed.

Tactile sensations resembled an unremitting orgasm rippling through every nerve ending in my body, with startling rushes as if adrenaline was pumping through my arteries instead of blood. The only way to describe the feeling is complete, uncontaminated, uninterrupted elation, fulfillment, and euphoria. I could listen and distinguish everybody and everything, however loud or soft; and pick out a voice, syllable, or sound from the commotion. I could gaze into space and compose a complete register in three dimensions with the depth of lightyears; then zero-in on any galaxy, star, mass, wavelength, or particle. Reality was thundering with exuberant colors, sounds, and kaleidoscopic ornamentation; but natural, not contrived, confabulated, or contorted. I saw through and walked through solid objects like walls and mountains as if they were invisible, or I was. My forethoughts resembled a composite of dreams, the impression of which I am unable to portray with words or paint into pictures. There was nothing compared to this because it was foreign to me and continuously nuanced.

I explored the vastness of a once beautiful universe in a momentary encounter, before it disappeared completely. While I retained the beauty and grandeur of it, it didn't come close to the present one. It seemed inconsequential now, like a class I might've flunked in the sixth grade. I was bathing in exquisite splendor, glory, and power; I was splashing, zipping, thrashing, and dashing. It seemed a fantasy; SS certified it was not a dream but a premonition.

Then he exclaimed, "It's time!" Without delay I emptied my pockets at the teller where my belongings were confiscated. "You have no need for such frivolities," SS averred. We passed by a landfill containing the plunders of kings and kingdoms. Across the street was a huge compacter, crushing phones and assorted electronic devices into cake. Next to it was a sizeable forge where all things metal was melted and molded into crosses, which were situated alongside the exit route like telephone poles. At the bottom of the hill sat a vast library dilapidated and vacant, with empty shelves but for rotten piles of flakes. Here was a community void of malls, traffic, drugs, clocks, problems, and charges. We took the underpass and disembarked at the central subway terminal; there SS showed me to an escalator going down. "I'll see you soon," he declared, giving me a high ten. I'd never seen him smile that way; he always was so serious. But he appeared as serious as ever smiling out loud. I retreated looking up at his Cheshire grin until that too faded. It would be my final tour of the future with the solipsist. There would be no time for wandering after that, neither forward nor backward. What a drag it was to return to yesterday in a world where time was equally meaningless and irrelevant.

I imagined the Lord critiquing a myriad of worlds within his soul and examining God knows how many viably intelligent beings before settling on designs. I mean, couldn't creation be a controlled experiment with God manipulating some variables and keeping others constant in his universal laboratory? Or is that too scientific an explanation? Pity, for the naturalists, materialists, postmodernists, humanists or whatever they call themselves nowadays would never consent to such a comparison, because creation is not a scientific possibility in their argument. And since there are no facts to support their theses, they now presume that life probably came from outer space, since the evolution thing halted in momentum and reputation (it devolved). Where did those life forms burst from, another alien world or universe? And what caused that? And on and on ad nauseam. When you rule out the truth what remains is fiction. And there's a bunch of that flying around. Note that there are no extraneous variables in God's test of humanity, except perhaps sin. See here: creation is a revelation from God and science is God's gift to examine and understand it. Thus, creation and science are not contradictory but complimentary.

With or without research and development the Lord began to mass produce advanced life forms including us. Some of the beings he chose included angels;

humans also could join the ranks of the chosen by choosing God. Like the angels he gave us the ability to glide, figuratively and literally. My genus was awarded the medal of morality: the sixth sense of right and wrong. Every human possessed this basic knowledge irrespective of religious orientation or vital worldview. Our earthly nature was to select sin, but the corresponding knowledge of evil preceded it. "The cosmos has repeatedly been an excellent medium for experimentation," the solipsist once insisted.

Do you think you are here for a purpose? Or are you here by accident: a natural coincidence? Maybe you are an unconventional life form that started as a protozoan in some ancient primordial soup; and that rudimentary organism transmuted into an amphibian, a mammal, and then a man. And somewhere along the way thought, intelligence, morality, love, and reasoning happened, or developed, or evolved. Do you believe that your ancestors were apes? Hah, try to validate that statement. If this be the case then your life is a hit or miss event and you are about as significant as an atom of helium floating in the ionosphere, a speck of sand blowing in the desert wind, or a bacillus squirming in a sewer. What are you living for? Just to die? Then why have morals or purposes?

The command of God can spontaneously convert random into order and configure nothing into something. The grand designer planned and made you the way you are, to collect experiences that only you can in the exact sequence and at the auspicious moment. These are necessities for you to become who you are and who you were meant to be; to develop the character, instincts, and skills required to fulfill a destiny that only you can without which you would not be ready, worthy, or successful. Cogitate on that blessing. Choose it or lose it.

You must think it cavalier of me purporting to be special in the eyes of the all-seeing eternal maker. Unless of course, you believe as I do. If you aren't sure you're an agnostic. Take your pick. Oh yeah; agnostics prefer not to choose. "How can anyone possibly be convinced without concrete evidence?" my philosophy professor reasoned. This position contradicted itself. How can you know or not know God exists without accepting the possibility he does? And how can you prove or disprove something without accepting that it could be so? The only way to disprove God exists is if he doesn't. Good luck with that one. Think about it for a second; indulge me just this once. What makes more sense to you? Do you have a preference? "Prove it," the professor demanded. I don't have to. The resurrection of Christ is all the evidence I need; in him we have living proof.

Oh, they tried to quash it but hundreds of eyewitnesses and multiple timely and accurate accounts made the occasion pretty difficult to censor. The very fact that adversaries endeavored to squelch it confirms it happened. They discovered the empty tomb but they couldn't produce Jesus's body. They went to great lengths to ensure the body would not be stolen and yet it came up missing. The authorities accused Jesus's followers of bribing guards, stealing and hiding the corpse, with nobody noticing. But it was the authorities who bribed the deserting guards to perpetuate this lie which is still their defense today. Others advanced a lie that the whole thing was bogus because Jesus faked his death. Some say it was an imposter with a slight resemblance whom they executed. The Romans were in collusion and the entire event was staged okay? Or how about the one where he didn't really die but was raptured? Or my favorite: he survived and escaped. That would've been another miracle whereas he had endured enough flogging to take out most people, with rusty spikes driven through his limbs which surely poisoned his blood supply, and a spear plunged into his heart as if anyone could survive that. He was too fatigued to carry his cross and then they nailed him to it. After that he woke up in a dark tomb, untangled his wrappings, moved a two-ton stone, and promenaded out of there on feet that had been pierced front to back. Right?

The officials searched high and low for his body while hundreds of people saw him alive, individually and in large groups; he was walking, talking, eating, and totally restored to health notwithstanding the gashes. Did all these witnesses experience the exact same audiovisual hallucination complete with delusions of majesty? That is not only unnatural it is psychologically impossible. Psychosis is as unique as other individual traits and states. Yes, the staunch unbelievers are still trying to obscure the facts of his birth, life, ministry, persecution, slaying, burial, and resurrection using the same implausible arguments. Ever wonder why they are petrified when the name Jesus Christ is spoken? Does the truth make them cringe? Maybe they are trying to keep something personal repressed. Or, do they wish that everyone remains in the grave as they believe they will?

Better face it—Jesus Christ is alive; he was brutalized, slain, and arose from the dead. The vast majority of historical accounts support this fact to include secular and antagonistic sources. There is no other ancient text that has such support as the New Testament: tens of thousands of documents and counting. In olden days, oral communication was the norm since so few could read and write. It is remarkable the extensiveness of written evidence, some dating back to the first century when it took place. Preservation of handwritten material required meticulous copying and recopying yet there was no alteration in the text or the meaning. That's because Christ was an enormously big deal then and still is; the news spread around the globe and continues. Even resolute doubters were converted such as members of the Jewish Sanhedrin, Roman soldiers and emperors, persecutors of Christians like Saul of Tarsus, and the biological brothers of Jesus (who must've thought he was wacko while growing up with him); even atheists and intransigent scientists are coming to faith these days. Why? Because the evidence is overwhelming and convincing.

The event was recorded in the four Gospels as well as the Acts and Epistles of the apostles; by Jewish, Roman, and Greek historians; in Hebrew scrolls and other ageless writings. And the messages are every bit as consistent and relevant two thousand years later and will be forever. There is no other religion ever founded that espouses the claims of Christ and backs it up with proof. His resurrection will bring yours as well. Would you rather arise to be his adopted brother and live with your Heavenly Father, or be disowned? "You're dreaming," I am told. I am dreaming, not about the past but the future, possibly your future.

Dreams are real insofar as they represent reality be it past, present, future or some combination of the three. They happen, apart from which tense or time is being portrayed. My favorite dream, well I think it happened, at least something similar. I was an apprentice studying to be a Persian priest. The leader of the temple was a sorcerer who specialized in religious history, astrology, and divination. Like many of my past instructors I regarded him as self-centered, self-indulgent, condescending, and presumptuous. You couldn't believe a word he said; but that compelled me to conduct sufficient research to verify, to the extent possible, what was true or not with respect to what my deans were putting out. Perhaps that was their intention.

One day I brought before the congress results of my investigation concerning the anticipated conjoining of Jupiter and Saturn. I had monitored and charted their movements every night for nine months and expected the planets would soon appear superimposed, at least somewhere. I demonstrated geometrically how the two bodies were about to arrange themselves into a right-angle perpendicular to the earth. The chairman's response was to yawn. Next, a coworker whose field of study was world religions presented his report. He had pieced together an interesting summarization of prophetic works predicting the coming of a great king. The wizard told us we were idiots when we construed a connection relating our findings. In any event, he sent us on a field trip to test the hypothesis. It was a welcome assignment. My partner and I had been cooped-up for thirteen months in a vast library, engaged in countless projects, interviews, consultations, and coursework; we were ready for a change of scenery. I suppose the scholars needed a break as well. That we were fated to grapple with philosophical and developmental breakthroughs would initiate our destiny.

A caravan of camels was loaded with sufficient rations, silver and gold to support and sustain our animals, the two of us, plus five armed guards and five slaves for about six months. We headed west in the direction of the point I'd projected to be ground zero. Daily I plotted our course based on the terrestrial movements and arrangements. Captivatingly, the planets fell back into alignment after three months of travel. We skirted the city of Babylon and entered the land of Arabia where we setup camp for the hundredth time. After nightfall, while studying the planets atop a mount, I spotted another encampment approximately two thousand paces southward.

There were campfires enough for a small army. I alerted the guards who doused our fires while we hunkered down. It was too late; an emissary already had been dispatched from the neighboring band. I feared they were bandits but they mainly wanted to know what we were doing there. Reluctantly, I informed the main guy (who spoke my language as well as several more) about our quest. Unbelievably, he explained he also was following the planetary alignment in search of a phenomenon.

We joined forces with the Arabians and proceeded west. The leader of their clan was a learned man of noble lineage, himself a prince the son of a sheik. He filled us in on relevant history, philosophy, geography, and astronomy. He mentioned it had been almost a millennium since this unusual celestial reconfiguration last occurred, according to the fragile scrolls he safeguarded. Now I was really getting excited; we were on a supernatural mission I presumed. He knew we were close because the planets had recently come together a second time more superimposed than his first sighting. Months passed; we were fatigued, undernourished, aching, cold, and sleepy. But we persevered more determined than ever knowing that we had not yet arrived.

About that time, we crossed paths with still another convoy; they had been traveling close to a year, hailing from a land farther east than we. Their leader was a guru, the rajah of an ecclesiastical Hindu order. He was the eldest of us all, very academic, refined, cultured, and scholarly. We shared notes as we trekked onward towards the setting sun. Everything seemed to be falling into place as if the entire trip was predestined, and we were being moved around like game pieces. But I was proud to be a part of it because I regarded the expedition as my calling and purpose.

In another few weeks of rough going the most spectacular thing occurred: the planets conjoined a third time becoming one, as if a marriage between Saturn and Jupiter had taken place after their lengthy courtship. It led us into the land of Judea where we tramped another two days to the most populated city. There we displayed deference to the local authority, forfeited a toll for our passage, and stated our business and our quest. Advisors to the autocrat proclaimed the exact town where a prophesied "anointed one" would be born, foretold from ages past. It was the last leg of our journey and we arrived later that evening.

Apparently, there had been quite a ruckus in the land. People from across the territory had traveled there to celebrate a religious holiday, and to be counted by the Roman emperor for the collection of taxes to make obedient subjects out of them. It reminded me of the trouble Romans had been stirring up back home. Most of the pilgrims had cleared out and returned to their provinces; local residents were emotionally depleted and not exactly cordial. They didn't have any idea what we were chattering about or searching for and didn't seem to care. Swiftly came a lowly, dusty, somewhat emaciated shepherd boy who told us what we needed to know. He witnessed the night of the king's birth and was telling everyone he encountered about it. Most people had taken the poor lad for a retard, but we didn't. We were amazed hearing his account, as we followed him through narrow passages to a small humble abode. Definitively, we had caught up with providence: a tiny monarch scarcely a few months old, and his lovely parents. They were packing in preparation for a journey to Egypt of all places.

Once I beheld that baby I was filled with joy; there was no doubt in my mind we were in the presence of greatness. The planets had looked exactly like my dreams, forming a giant star with a tail emanating downward as if to caress his eminence. The star had since vanished but the infant child glowed like starlight and was crowned in splendor. Though he had yet to assume his kingdom we kneeled and payed homage, presenting the newborn with gifts. I'd put our remaining gold in a jewelry box wrapped in a purple silk scarf and laid it by his feet. The others also presented gifts of great value. We exchanged presents amongst ourselves as well: artifacts and commodities from our native lands. But the greatest gift was to meet this family; their narrative was intriguing if not mind-blowing. They were in a rush, so slightly before midnight we went our separate ways: the young prince and his parents headed west and the rest of us to the east.

I tell you the truth, it was well worth the trip. I emulated the shepherd boy; I wanted to tell everyone about this incredible occurrence. We returned home a lot faster than we had departed mainly because the Indian chief had dreamt of danger. Upon arriving at the shrine, I was surprised that the magi were unmoved, uninterested, and suspicious when we recounted our discovery and presented our conclusions. They mocked us, swearing that we were intoxicated, misguided, or in dreamland. How could they take this so lightly, we inquired? But they chastised us and vehemently showed us out of the planetarium. My companion and I immediately fled the monastery to begin a new journey, both of us endeavoring to unveil the truth concerning this extraordinary king and his kingdom which was out of this world. He was human and yet he was godly; precisely, he shone as the very image of God.

Humans have been crafted in the image of their fathers, earthly and heavenly. We look like our earthly parents and we endure physically, spiritually, and mentally with our Heavenly Father. The physical form of Almighty God is Christ the New Covenant; he is the embodiment of the prophecy that a Savior would restore the kingdom. He lived a life without sin to fulfill the Old Covenant of the Law and was crucified, dying for the transgressions of the world to fulfill the New Covenant of Grace. If he had been unsuccessful then the law, sin, and death would have prevailed and there would have been no resurrection. But as a matter of fact, he did not fail; he arose from the dead bringing the revivification of humankind and the correspondent verdict. On the last day many will find peace and bliss. The remainder will encounter anguish and grief, banished forever from God's presence.

Following the Son, we were given a discerning mind and the will to do our Father's bidding. Thus, mankind knew right and wrong from the beginning; but too often we have acted unwisely. The serpent told Adam and Eve that partaking of the Tree of Knowledge would make them as smart as God. But voila, it made them a transgressor like Satan who also lied when he alleged it would not lead to their deaths. Yes, you and I have indulged in forbidden fruit. The only knowledge gained was the knowledge of sin; and the only reward received was a death sentence.

However, those who partake of the Tree of Life will know what it is to endure without sin, inasmuch as they earnestly and humbly sought the righteousness of God's begotten, the only example of utter adherence to the Law and obedience to the Father. This virtue he gave us when he took away our unrighteousness. Believers will live forever with him, sanctified by his Holy Spirit and conformed to his image of perfection. Such a conversion permits the corrupt to be changed to incorruptible, the lawbreakers to be reconciled unto the eternal I AM, and the inglorious to share in glory. The only thing necessary to obtain this inheritance is to trust that you will. It cannot be earned or bought for it is free. It proceeds from the assurance of a pardon, given to everyone who desires it. Who in their right mind would reject the opportunity to live eternally in heaven? Well, those that do not want to go to heaven or to be with God forever, I suppose.

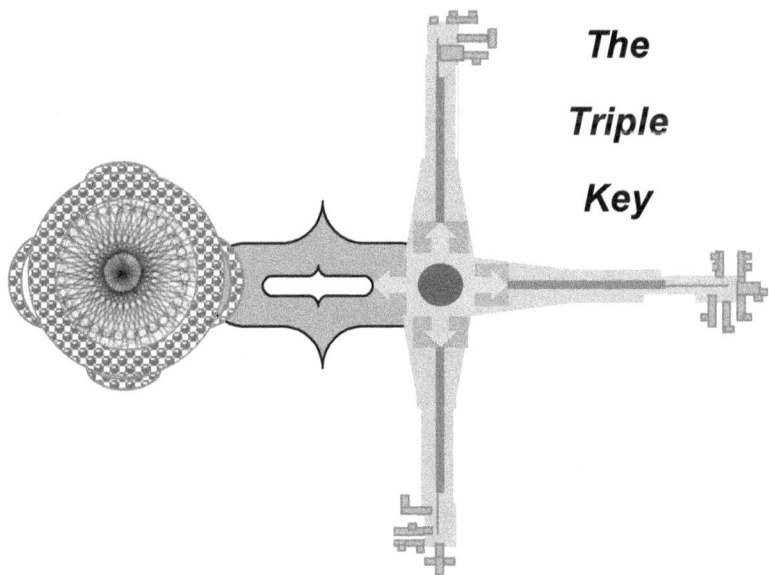

The
Triple
Key

The patriarchs of old yearned to acquire the land the Lord had set aside for them. They looked for deliverance from the wickedness that surrounded them and pursued a life of faith and hope. As these men believed in the coming of Messiah, so does everybody who looks forward with assurance to his second advent. The saints can anticipate living forever in the Promised Land. Those who do not cling to God's promises will not be heirs to his kingdom. Their faith is falsely founded on themselves; their striving is for worldly fortune and fame both of which are temporary and fleeting. Personally, I would rather invest in something solid and secure which will never fade or slip away. We are the meek who inherit the earth, the chosen race. But it isn't the old earth, it's the new one. Remember, Earth's fate doesn't look too rosy; it's marred by corruption, death and destruction, awaiting an anointing by fire. Our lot in life lies beyond that threshold where time is irrelevant. This the counselor tried to elucidate on numerous occasions. As I try to explain it to you, I realize it cannot be comprehended with the mind. It is understood uniquely by the spirit; but such understanding needs to be activated. Too many people have deliberately deactivated it and allowed others to rule their thoughts.

Please don't permit the humanists to convince you otherwise and steal your ticket to paradise. If you are confused search for answers. You'll find them via the means of grace, avenues in which the Lord has made them known, ways that one can receive him: the written Word, the Sacraments, and witnesses of the Truth. Christ witnesses for the Father, and his disciples witnessed for him; he commissions you to be a witness to others that they too may know the truth and shed the shackles of sin. It is written: The way of salvation is made known to everyone. It will come to you in due time (like right now); don't turn your back. Untie your mind and heart and you will understand these things I'm conveying to you. With the wisdom of your spirit you will discern them, if only you open the door when he comes knocking.

But beware of false teachers and fake prophets; they can be bought for a guinea per gross. Shun those who claim to be seers; they are naively good at guessing. Avoid cults and the occult; they can only drag you down. Such as these strive to lure subjects by enticing them with worldly temptations; but they are spiritually bankrupt. Refrain from witchcraft, consulting mediums, fortune-telling, calling misplaced spirits, confiding in astrological forecasts, and superstitions. Those activities will direct you along the wrong path and are an invitation to demonism. Degeneracy is trying to infiltrate your soul just as the faithless have penetrated societies to destroy. Once vice enters the mind it defiles the body and it darkens the spirit.

Persons possessed by demons have regressed to a primitive state of consciousness. They cannot recognize the truth because discernment is obscured by smoke and mirrors. There are mental demons and there are spiritual ones. Both are unhealthy but curable. Both make a person fearful, but of what? Death? Surely, without the spirit there is nothing but death. So why fear nothing? What can you gain from that? Nothing. What can you lose? Life! And it is the Holy Spirit that brings it and there is no cover charge. The eligibility requirements have been waived, the entry fees have been paid in full, and the debt of your iniquity has been covered.

How many fake messiahs does it take to screw in a light bulb? Who cares, they can't make it shine. The Light has come already so don't expect another. He will come again but when he does it will be in judgment. He is the only way to heaven. Do not accompany anyone awaiting a silver spaceship to pick them up at the curb. Once you earn your wings, you'll be able to soar on your own.

And what's with all this secrecy? God reveals truth he doesn't hide it. Secrets imply there is something sinister lurking behind the scenes. Religions that conceal their beliefs and refuse to testify of their sacred practices should arouse suspicion. It is fine to worship and pray in private; but surreptitious oaths, languages, codes, and rituals are not scriptural. Be skeptical of those who preach anything contrary to what Christ and the apostles taught. They are laboring for the other side and often don't realize it.

I asked God about them; I prayed for an answer. "Is there hope for them? Can they be helped? Is there any truth to their claims?" The Lord replied, "There is no way out for they have placed their hope in fables." This refrain resounded in my ears the night long and I awoke with the message fresh in my mind. It was not a case of looking in the wrong places; they weren't legitimately searching at all. They assumed they'd found what they were after and it wasn't the one true God. Perhaps they had chanced upon another force that impersonated a god and they were entrapped, while never openly recognizing our Creator God to be the almighty, omnipotent, and eternal One. Not surprisingly, other entities possess none of these attributes. Wayward souls believing in false gods will call opponents infidels. Truthfully, refusing to succumb to a false god does not render anyone an unbeliever or atheist; idolatry is defined as chasing another while rejecting the God of all things visible and invisible.

Case in point: my first encounter with the famed Assyrian. You remember him, the androgynous homophile whose blood ran rich with war. He would advocate whatsoever stirred up conflict and confusion in order to enlist those susceptible to deception or otherwise uncertain of the truth. Too apathetic to seek truth on their own, they depended on those seemingly knowledgeable to keep them apprised.

The third temple had been erected upon the famous boulder. Their newfangled titleholder arrived in opulence. There the braggart sat, perched on his gilded throne, summoning babes for sacrifice as he bade the young to kneel and worship. When they hesitated, lightning would strike the altar and vaporize the burnt offering thus convincing uncertain followers that he was a god. Hah, the technology was already past its prime though how could they have known? Admirers were unaware and childlike, coming from crumbling countries where ignorance was bliss. Those feats of magic were quite convincing to people with a sheltered mind.

Gee, I remember some of that stuff back when I was a defense analyst. The scam was quite simple: triangulate the position of the altar using satellites that can hone in on a global positioning device, a completely automated process. Then, remotely activate a particle or laser beam designed to penetrate the atmosphere from a space platform and zap a ground target with precision. What was required was line-of-sight aiming which is nothing when the weapon is deployed in space. Even the educated could be fooled regarding the many magical instruments at the quack's disposal; for when did they hold a top-secret clearance? But the above example itself consisted of commonplace technology declassified eons ago. Target triangularization, not a complicated concept.

It was a charade. Religion had become a way to exploit people for money and sex; nothing but a con game practiced by charlatans and swindlers. Their exhibitions drew interest like a sideshow at the carnival while old-time religion grew boring and monotonous. Organized creeds had to be jazzed-up. The leaders of the various denominations wandered into myths, substituted sound doctrine in favor of their own traditions, and discouraged people from discovering biblical truth on their own because they were afraid someone might expose them to be fakes. As for the finger-pointers who believed that theirs was the only valid faith and everyone else was condemned, they were blinded by the Light. Those who rejected the truth and the One that brought it were unexpectedly siding with the creature and probably didn't care. They purposefully picked a course down the shadowy aisle, escorted by the pandering pimp, betrothed to the beastly and barren bride of blasphemy.

The bloodsucking temptress was lethally lovely, alluring and beguiling, at least to a nasty fiend of equivalent character. But a plague-ridden harlot is not the best candidate for a soulmate if you know what I mean. Who in their right mind shops in the slop for a partner that is polluted and perverted, then invests their vigor only to pay with their soul? But gatherings trailed the infested and festering slut all the way to the bottom of the sullied sump. Eager and enthusiastic they were, anticipating enchantment and excitement but receiving excrement and expulsion. Hades thought he was collecting mislaid souls for a booty chest until he found himself locked inside with the rest, rolling into the crematorium for the grand finale. Why would they forsake the true Messiah for that? Simple: they didn't want to be a part of Christ but apart from him.

Christianity never has been an exclusionary religion; everybody is welcome, no exceptions. What is necessary is that you follow Christ. There are several paths to choose from but only one heads home. Many have lost their bearings, largely thanks to the crafty and devious clerics and teachers who know enough to be dangerous. But

God warned us of a generation that would produce some devious devils. If the citizenry wasn't fooled by the proselytizers they were fooled by their own imaginations.

"Fine, you've got your revelation and I've got mine." What, not again? "Either way, does it really matter since revelations are relative?" You wish. The greatest of revelations is the relevant one; the rest are altogether irrelevant. I recommend you familiarize yourself with the Revelation of Jesus Christ. Anyone can claim that God has revealed something profound to them via dreams, visions, supplications, or meditations. But that doesn't make it so. Note that an experience does not equate to proof of a revelation.

There are ways of testing the validity of a revelation, or prophecy, or any message purported to be from God. How specific is it, does it come to pass, is it consistent with scripture, and does it coincide with God's will? The Lord makes his expectations known and those requesting his guidance will receive it at the designated time. If you are unsure, ponder it prayerfully. Usually, it is not difficult to distinguish truth from lies. Test what you hear, see, read, or think don't accept it as is. Diligence in the study of God's Word enables one to recognize the differences between a revelation from God and one from Satan. God has revealed himself through the Word, and Christ who is the Living Word. Such knowledge is life changing. Despite the countless impending revelations that may occur in a lifetime there is but one revelation that matters supremely and it supersedes them all: The joy of salvation and eternal life is available to whomever proclaims Christ to be their desire. While many revelations come with conditions God's revelation comes with a guarantee: everlasting life in the Kingdom of Heaven. I've envisioned a deep dark hole from the inside, filled with pain and intimidation. You can neither escape nor can you hide; that is a fact and an eye-opening realization.

Many allege the Bible as their foundation but have distorted it to match their personal views. Why alter something that is already crystal clear? That's what I'd like to know. Compare what people proffer as factual against the Holy Bible which is the ultimate arbiter of truth. Equip yourselves with knowledge and be prepared to endorse it in lieu of The Word; if it does not agree it cannot be true. There cannot be several truths concerning a single matter. A half-truth is still a falsehood. Read the Good Book carefully and you will see your mind opening, and wisdom will come your way like a flock of geese flying in formation. It truly will be mind-altering when it happens. But don't stop there; continue to develop in your walk with the Lord.

I regard the Bible as a giant jigsaw puzzle. Each testament, book, chapter, and verse provide clues to a revelation that is extraordinary. You cannot see the big picture when parts of it are missing or distorted, neither can you grasp the meaning of one piece or section when examined in isolation. But little by little the pieces fall into place. As soon as you can envision the entire exhibit you will be amazed at your understanding. And you will not doubt a word of it after that.

Why is it that so many ignore, denigrate, or blatantly despise the Bible? What are they afraid of? How many other books exist that have endured two to six thousand years, much less retained such enduring popularity and accuracy? The Bible is the most widely read, most widely sold, and most widely esteemed of all literary works throughout human history. How could the Bible have survived if it was another fairy tale? But the unbelievers maintain it is exactly that; I guess they would spurn fairy tales also, not to mention the truth. But they haven't turned a single page.

The shallow mind thinks there is nothing beyond. But that also requires faith; visionless faith is operating in those searching for missing links. Believing or disbelieving without tangible proof requires enormous faith whether you are a scientist, a priest, or an atheist. I choose not to place my hope in uncertainty but rather in the assurance of promises that are real. I mean seriously, if you're going to believe in anything at least make it something that is beneficial to you. Besides, what harm is there in doing so and what does it cost? Not a thing. Thus, if you are a cynic ask yourself: would you prefer a bleak ending or a blissful one? Would you rather have death or life? Hint: choose life.

Life is the greatest of God's promises. He has certified it to his people by way of covenants. A covenant is an agreement, or contract. God's gift of eternal life is what he gives in return for your loyalty, which is by faith. He has promised so much, beginning with his love, protection, and sustenance, and ending—never. These same essentials any loving parent would provide their children. The only thing required of you is to accept these gifts by trusting they are yours. To seal the deal, God declared that his Redeemer would fulfill the law on your behalf and pay the penalty of death in your place. And because our Savior was without sin the grave had no hold over him. Hence, the resurrection; first the only begotten Son of God and next the rest of humanity. Through his life he conquered the law. Through his death he conquered sin. Through his resurrection he conquered death. This he did for you and me. Believe these truths and you will have an inheritance in God's kingdom as an adopted child and an equal heir with God's Son.

The Lord has exchanged his holiness for your sin. What a bargain! I suggest you accept this offer; if you do you will live forever. You will receive a glorified body that cannot die because it will be without sin like his. Those who don't want it can refuse it through disbelief. But they will die a second death never to rise again; for they would perish in their sin rather than give it to Christ. He is the same Messiah that the patriarchs knew would come and Christians believe will come again. Their faith has been founded on these same promises. And we will congregate in paradise from the least to the greatest, as brothers and sisters in our Father's house. But there must be a response to the gift of faith, requiring perseverance.

Equip yourself with the tools and attributes needed to win. Build up your own credentials; don't wait for others to become disqualified. You will not inherit first prize by default. Much discipline is required to obtain the skills and knowledge to succeed. Determination to excel is not inherited, although specific talents can be intrinsic, genetic, or bestowed by God. Everyone has special gifts but many more must be acquired to compete. Any skill can be learned and mastered through training and practice. And each contest prepares you for the next challenge.

Defeat is not a decisive outcome; it is but another step towards the objective. If you take two steps forward for every step backwards, you are still making progress in the right direction. Quitting (i.e., not trying) is the only true form of failure. If you do not succeed until the tenth attempt that still counts as success. Whenever did you master something on the first try? Unload the emotional baggage and see how rapidly you proceed. It's very difficult jumping over hurdles, negotiating tight squeezes, or climbing high ladders carrying luggage. Lighten up! As I said before, you might as well give your heavy load to the Lord. He bought and paid for it so isn't yours anyway. And he requests it of you to boot. It seems unfair dumping your refuse on him; but if you do, he'll take it off your hands and dispose of it. We give him our sins; he gives us his favor. It's the trade of all trades.

But a fervent and sincere response is appropriate. Once you have received salvation it is not something to take for granted. It's not a matter of opening your presents, saying thank you, and going on your merry way; because a new itinerary will be presented before you. You must take that path even if it means to divert from the previous one. True faith results in action. It implies becoming equipped to serve others and being a disciple of the Lord. Faith entails change: a change of heart, a change of direction, a change of lifestyle. And once your heart is changed what follows are beliefs, thoughts, and behaviors. If Christ changes your heart it will change your mind. And there's no looking back from there because everything is new from that instant. Have no fear, for the Lord will steer your ship through typhoons, between peaks, across shoals, and into safe harbor; for he goes before you. He has the bowlines in his hand and will fetch you into port. Let him lead the way. Do what he says; and quit doing... well you know what. Confess, repent, and plead for your life; and you will have it.

Acknowledgement of one's shortcomings should spark a desire to make amends. Although salvation is free it should not be kept on the shelf or in a drawer. It should be proclaimed to the world using whatever spiritual avenues and endowments are at your command. Exercise your talents in the name of the Lord and give him the glory for your achievements. He will make a conversion in you that will empower you to elicit attitude adjustments in the people around you. His love will radiate through you and energize everyone you encounter. You will see everything in a new light: his Light. It will reveal features that you never envisioned or understood.

People do not receive revelations from God that request them, saying, "Show me," like the decadent king who mocked Christ. Those who seek God, endeavor to learn from his Word, and endure trials and tribulations for bearing his name, they are the ones to whom God reveals himself, his will, and his intentions. Anybody who has his Holy Spirit in their hearts can come to him with a need, question, or plan and God will enlighten them showing them what to do, where to go, and when to speak. But don't expect to begin prophesying, seeing great visions, or performing wondrous miracles if you haven't been fully instructed.

Mansion in the Sky

If you are not experiencing these things it doesn't disprove the existence of God. The mere statement of this fact demonstrates the fallacy of the logic. Anticipating such events suggests that you are not ready for them. If you are looking for a new sign then you have missed the ones that already are present in your life. If you're waiting to receive a revelation before you can believe you'll be waiting endlessly, because such a revelation already exists and it has endured for two thousand years. Look at the world today. Did you miss the catastrophes, wars, plagues, and tribulations? Were you not a bystander to the degradation of morality and the persecution of the faithful? Have the mockery of godliness and the exaltation of spitefulness slipped by unnoticed? Would you join in and assist in eradicating Christians from the face of the earth? Which side are you on anyway? Where will you go from here? Where do you think?

Two revelations stand out that will open your mind to the truth. One comes from the hand of God and another from the mouth of God; he works and he speaks and it is your decision whether or not to watch and listen. The creation should awaken you to seek God; then you will find him through his Word. Thus, you can hear him in the written Word and you can see him in the living Word; and if you open your heart you can feel him with your spirit. He is knocking at the door; if you let him in you will love him whereas he already loves you. Anybody can choose to reject these truths though they are incontestable. You can see and hear clearly or hide your eyes and cover your ears, but God is not going anywhere for he is everywhere. Have you heard God's most amazing story? In my quest for truth his light showed me the way. I will tread the streets of glory with never a thought of yesterday.

Can you ignore the intricacy and beauty of nature? Doesn't the magnificence of it reflect the glory of God? Even devoted scientists are able to appreciate the wonders of the cosmos irrespective of how they think it got here. You can discover revelations in the book of creation and in the book of scripture. Both were written by God, having proceeded from his mouth via the *Logos*. And the two do not contradict one another in the slightest detail contrary to popular belief, as long as you interpret the book of nature using the book of scripture and not vice-versa. Investigate these resources and discover the true source.

When buds and blossoms spring forth it is called spring; when leaves fall from trees it is called fall. If you've paid attention you've noticed these events, and you're aware what's coming. Keep in mind that animals do not fall and are not condemned. They cannot fathom or discern sin or its consequences. When stars, angels, and people fall, it'll be the big fall. Ever had that dream where you keep falling, falling; and it doesn't end? What if it isn't a dream? I prefer the dream of springing forth. Consider the rise and the fall of humankind. Rising is more fun. You've been kidnapped by the sin of self-exaltation, but Jesus has paid your ransom in advance.

You cannot effectively test the Lord, unless he challenges you to do so (such as tithing). Events must unfold within his timeframe. If you attempt to shorten the schedule you will only invite trouble (I remember a couple of guys named Abraham and David making this mistake). When the time comes you will know how to respond, as long as you believe. Oftentimes, you receive directions at the very moment you reach the fork, or you utter profound statements at the very instant you are challenged. And if life doesn't transpire in the manner you request why blame it on God? It's because you have veered into the wrong lane.

God doesn't exact bad times upon you. He doesn't tempt you and he doesn't give you more than you can handle. Lucifer on the other hand, will bring you hardship, calamity, and adversity. God invigorates you to overcome these setbacks, and he always provides an escape from wickedness. But the vile one knows the end is near and is frantic. He will endeavor ardently to irritate you into acts of desperation. Rebuke him and shun his advances for he is plainly looking for company in the fall. There is nothing el diablo can offer or promise that you haven't the power to realize yourself; the only thing he can assure is death. Make no mistake, he is a formidable foe and will not be discarded easily. If he possesses one endearing attribute it is persistence. But if you persevere in the faith you will outlast his unholiness.

Accept God's help and he will steer you through every storm, leading you past the tangled jungles and over the frozen tundra. If you give him your works, he will give you his thoughts. He has planned eternal life for you; enjoy the ride don't try to alter its course. At times it may seem a rollercoaster with twists, turns, dips, inclines, and loops; going fast, slow, and maybe upside down. But only an idiot would try to disembark from a speeding rollercoaster. More importantly, you are secure in the Lord's hands; you cannot fall, crash, or be thrown out and you will discover that the ride is actually enjoyable. Relax; have no fear. You are insured with a lifetime policy that pays great dividends and abundantly matures when Christ returns. You cannot be denied because he is on your side.

You mustn't magnify those pompous expectations about what the world offers. Expect only that God will make good on his offers, which are unfathomable. He pledges protection, provision, and prosperity if you follow him. Wondrous experiences are bound to come your way but you don't know what or when. The eagerness will be a minor annoyance, but the pleasant surprises are acutely more gratifying than the disappointments you'll experience when your mortal strivings are not consummated. You can prove to the Lord your intentions by acting on your faith and he will give you directions. And your purpose will become his purpose. Humbly relinquish control; you'll know when you have arrived. That doesn't mean you can't select your educational or career goals, only that God will equip you to serve and succeed in whichever arena you compete as long as you are doing it for him.

There are five duties that you should perform to demonstrate your commitment. They will help you to stay spiritual in your focus and connected to the vine. First, pray constantly; that is your link to the Lord. Whenever you think of it talk to God in your mind: when you awaken, when you eat, when you go to the bathroom, when you are on your way, when you are at work or play, when you retire for the day. Don't stop praying, for it is a direct transmission from your spirit to his. And his spirit will hear every word and will respond in ways that will aid you more than you can comprehend. Thank him for the many blessings he has bestowed upon you and yours, repent of your sins, and ask him for his forgiveness. Pray for everyone, especially those who are sent by God to minister to the lost sheep. Ask for spiritual riches and you will receive that and more.

Second, study God's Word with diligence; that is his link to you. Whenever you pick up the Bible and read you are receiving messages directly from his spirit to yours. And the more you absorb, the greater your understanding will be; and it will continue to increase no matter how many times you complete the entire text. This is the very best way to learn about God and his will and prepare you for ministry. For if you know the truth, not only does it set you free it enables you to expose false teachers, to shepherd others who are going astray, and to edify the church. If a revelation is what you want, you'll find it in the Gospel message.

Third, worship, thank, and praise him at all times and in all places. Your adoration and praise should be channeled to the Lord in everything you do and say. Thank him for all things huge and tiny. Offer the sacrifice of praise during every segment of your life. In addition, take a day each week to publicly worship; this will enlighten yourself and the rest of the flock. Fellowship frequently with other believers so that you can encourage, sustain, and support each other. Make joyful noises to the Lord; it doesn't matter if you can sing like a canary or speak like an orator. Your thanks and praises are very pleasing to God for they are the fruit of your lips. Give him the glory he deserves because everything you are and everything you have you owe to him. He gave himself for you so give yourself back. This is the least you can do.

Fourth, donate your talents, abilities, and resources to further his kingdom. Everyone has been given unique gifts; you may discover that you possess aptitudes that you weren't aware you had. Cultivate those abilities and master them; develop and practice additional faculties that you enjoy. Continue to train for the race. Establish a full repertory of knowledge and skills that you can bring to bear at any time in response to the situations, opportunities, and people that are presented before you. Maximize your potential as you proceed, assisting in the best way you know how. Give of yourself, your time, and your increase. Share your wealth with those who are needy. Support your house of worship and those who minister to others in spirit and in truth under the moniker of Jesus Christ. One tenth (or more) of what you earn should be given to support the church, to help those less fortunate, and to advance the kingdom. Try this and watch the unlimited buildup in your abundance. It's like investing in the stock market but with one exceptional exception: a plentiful return on your investment is guaranteed.

Fifth, exercise your spiritual gifts. Be a witness to the truth. Help train disciples for Christ. Tell everyone with whom you interact how blessed you are. Allow God's beaming rays to shine in and through you 24-7. Use that light to brighten the way for the downtrodden, desperate, and disoriented souls so that they can find their way. Give others you meet an excuse to ask about the peace, joy, and hope that is yours so they too can acquire these spiritual gifts. Let your entire life be an example of God's grace and mercy working through you as you touch others with the power of his love. The Holy Spirit will ordain you to accomplish extraordinary tasks and perform miraculous feats, like the apostles and prophets who subdued sovereignties, healed the heartbroken, sick and lame, cast out demons, and even raised the dead. Give God the credit and the glory and you will be bestowed with honor and power.

If you cultivate your faith you will prosper and grow. You will be healthy in heart, mind, and spirit. Primarily, you'll have the serenity and happiness that surpasses worldly pleasure. They are yours to keep forever. You can believe it because you have God's Word which he always keeps. In time you'll be equipped to defend the faith with knowledge, evidence, and an impeccable source of truth to back you up. Go into the world and engage people. But do your homework: know your audience; adjust to their culture, community, background, situation, and history. Then, test the waters; ask questions; find common ground. Utilize semantics, syntax, and idioms that conform to others' approaches, interests, and conceptions. Work within their boundaries; and identify obstacles and fallacies within their belief systems, contentions, and assumptions. Most importantly be reasonable; give them a reason to try putting on Christ, displaying charity, empathy, encouragement, respect, compassion, and modesty. Appeal to their sense of morality, desire for peace, need to be saved, and the reward of eternal life. Educate them in the truth that endures forever by teaching them not preaching to them. Truth is the most persuasive tactic available to us. Love is the most effective delivery method. Touch their hearts with God's love and truth so that they can possess the joy and the peace you share.

Never call God a liar and never blaspheme his holy name. Keep in mind that unbelief is akin to making the accusation and will equally bring the grave to your feet. Further, if you say you have faith yet it is not evident in your behavior, you are living a lie. To deny him with your hands is contrary to confessing him with your lips. Your words and actions must agree. It is not up to God to act on your faith it is up to you (he already has acted). This is the only unpardonable sin: to turn God's truth into a lie that lives forever in your soul. Turn from your wicked ways and face the music now before it is too late; for even the thief who was crucified at the Lord's right side was pardoned before his last breath.

Don't get caught up in events and schemes which the world and its media throw endlessly on top of your pathway. Your course goes beyond there so you might consider taking the bypass loop. And don't be afraid, for the way has been illuminated so you won't be driving while blind or tripping on the debris. But beware, for danger is everywhere. Spiritual warfare is happening around you. Good and evil have been at odds since time immemorial. You are in the midst of that siege whether you want to accept it or not. However, you can win the fight if you don the armor of the Lord which is the ultimate protection. You can withstand the best advances of the enemy if you remain steadfast in the spirit. With Christ living in you, you have the capacity to defeat Satan himself. You will grow in your strength and courage, and with conviction you will face the armies of evil head on in battle. They will run from you in ten different directions, because they will see in your eyes the penetrating light of eternity which is the perfect love of God. Wickedness will be no match, for theirs' is a world of foreboding, trembling, and agony. Though they sought strength in it, it had no power.

But the power of love is boundless and they cannot comprehend it, so they flee from it. And you will split them asunder with the double-edged sword of God's truth which will pierce them to their very souls. With the authority of the Gospel you will be a champion for Christ and the demons will submit to your every command. You will drive them back into the fire which they thought they could use against you, but instead will be their burying place.

I awoke alongside the abandoned road with the most intense glow abiding. I wondered how long I had lain there judging it had been indefinitely. My body felt broken and disarranged. I attempted to loosen my stiff muscles and joints while I struggled to my feet. Soon the hurt left, enabling me to continue on a road that seemed well-traveled at one time. After rambling for a while, the confusion and dizziness evaporated and my eyes cleared enough to visualize the situation. I noticed the figure of a man coming my way from the opposite direction; he appeared to be in great haste. As he neared, I hesitated. I peered at him believing he must know me, wondering if I knew him; and I distrusted what was left of my memory.

I could tell that this man was of great knowledge so I asked him what he could be doing on such a highway as this, which did not appear to have been traveled in ages. His presence was a warm soft flurry of affection. His face was too fair to look upon and my eyes became blurred when he spoke. He seemed to gasp for air for he breathed so deeply. His speech came forth like thunderclaps breaking up the atmosphere, becoming imprinted upon my ears. He explained that this trail had never before been traveled. He promised that the journey would not be burdensome and he would see me through. I grew enthusiastic and confident when he took my hand in his and we continued together. I stepped as if smoothly gliding on roller blades. I said nothing but believed, recognizing a great deal without explanation or conversation.

The sky was the brightest I have seen, though it was cloudy. It snowed on my heartaches but I felt no cold. We happened across a deep ravine with many caves, crevices, and snowbanks. Without warning, a leprechaun darted out of a large tunnel; the ice liquefied wherever he went. This was the ugliest person I have encountered, but I did not lack compassion for him. He spoke faster than an nth; I thought he was offering a drink. We had journeyed far so I requested a sip of water, assuming that my mouth should be dry. My companion gave me a drink from his flask with assurance I would never thirst again; and he was right I wasn't thirsty anymore. He insisted the individual had nothing to offer which I didn't already have. Just then, precipitation in the gully turned red dripping like blood, and we continued onward. As we were leaving the valley of shadows, I was curious to know the droll fellow's name. My friend told me the name adding that it was unimportant for me to remember. I wouldn't have been able to enunciate it due to the many syllables and I immediately forgot.

Upon approaching the crest of the ridge, I felt myself expanding. I could not hold it together. My eyes began to see in every direction: up, down, left, right, and behind. My brain started to swell until my impression had completely embodied the late dawn. My thoughts became mountains and I was crying rivers of gladness throughout the land. I climbed with the clouds and enveloped the atmosphere in my arms. I had never felt so free. All my troubles, worries, and fears had been replaced with unending ecstasy. And I would never look back.

Flying a fiery chariot, my chaperon showed me dreams I had never seen before. I saw armies of angels guarding houses of anger; I was comforted to know that the gates would never swing open in my presence. We crossed through alleys of precious stone that gleamed away my guilt. We passed by windmills that were flowing out grains of wisdom that became pure gold. Being fed grace from this savory wheat, I knew I would never hunger. I heard orchestras playing the sweetest most beautiful music. There were flutes of joy, violins of sorrow, basses of heartbeats, and silver trumpets shouting out a warning. In my dream I had beheld personal apotheosis.

It was an out of body experience; that's what I figured at first. I felt I was soaring away and so I was, since I could see my shadow below. I was not alone, for many others were joining me aboveground. We were alive, even persons that had died. Our faces were bright, enraptured in a halo of delight. We were wearing a seamless white tunic and nothing more. The Lord of Hosts was descending from the highest heaven while we ascended, rendezvousing halfway between the earth and the sky. Those left behind were marveling at the sight but not exactly enjoying the show. They looked frightened, confused, enraged, bewildered: they were bawling, screaming, moaning, groaning. Some were shaking their heads, others their fists. I was waving goodbye. I didn't know them but I was thinking I might have, once upon a time.

Mountaintop Refuge

THE SEARCH

Prologue: The Challenge

Crossing o'er the straight and narrow—countless curves that thread this life;
Balanced on a shaky fulcrum—one side bliss the other strife.

Stage 1: The Fruit

Ripples flashed across the glass as grapes announced from fragile bowl,
"Doors of destiny are open, sharing paths that unknown hold."

"Marching onward never ceasing," chimed the orange from the rind,
"Looking backward e'er forgetting, scenes you viewed which lie behind."

"It is greed to crave the glory," spoke the apple quite amused.
Uttered the banana, smirking, "First you win and then you lose."

Vapor crawled outside the threshold. Light escaped the drafty cold—
Bounced about the fruit with glee foretelling rainbow tales untold.

Suddenly the fleeting moment, sidetracked there as if supine,
Dropped a treasure map while lapsing of a hidden trove to find.

Dauntless near and far I wandered, less the fruit to pass the news;
Plodding through increasing darkness where I sniffed around for clues.

Stage 2: The Animals

Hoards of diverse breathing species, I not knowing every name.
Some I feared and some I didn't; most I wouldn't like the same.

Chipmunk noticed my dilemma, scampered by and bade me well;
He declared, "We're all related. Can't you see or can't you tell?"

Panther crept along with stealth; she startled me beside the pond.
I was frozen in my footsteps, wishing for the great beyond.

Her reflection stirred the water, 'neath a gloomy crescent moon.
"Cherish every hour," she offered, "Dreadful days are coming soon."

Restlessly, I slept in respite rising at the crack of dawn.
Watched a gnat light on my breakfast; reckoned then we shared no bond.

I proceeded thus to squash him. Tumbling to my feet he fell;
Plus rebuked with indignation, "Please resolve, your hate to quell."

While I contemplated reasons, darting forth sir scorpion came.
Scowled, "We're not the enemy. Compared to you we're downright tame."

Stage 3: The Elements

Gulped the water down, exhausted; feeling tired, alone and bored.
"Never quench your thirst for knowledge," endlessly the ocean roared.

Glimmerings of trust abandoned—there besets a vulture's stare;
Once unveiling pure intentions, withering into despair.

Hurricanes and floods were waning; earthquakes and volcanoes, still.
As I paused reverberating, sky cried, "You shall have your fill."

I supposed this meant disaster: I was hungry, angry, sad.
These occurred to me by nightfall: I was nourished, peaceful, glad.

Hypnotized by empty dreams not fathoming what waits in store.
Gasping for my breath I tarried, scarcely closer than before.

Standing 'lone beside myself, I happened thrice to slap the air,
Who urged, "Mustn't venture forward," leaving me to kiss the glare.

So I probed the winds in passing, "Is it luck or is it skill?"
"Benefit from both," they echoed, dealing me a greater will.

Rapidly the clouds were clearing, now revealing good and bad.
This was all I ever needed. This was all I ever had.

Stage 4: The Heart

Wasting ample time carousing, menacing the neighborhood.
Anyplace discovering freedom to possess it if I could.

Wickedness arose to tempt me: pleasure, riches, power, fame.
I presumed to be entitled—only then was I to blame.

Smelling sweet and winking at me, danced the flowers in the breeze.
Frolicking while harmonizing, "Creature hearken to the trees."

Twice I heard, aloft they whispered, "Everywhere a pot of gold."
Sunset shouted at the evening, "Nothing ever grows too old."

Fate was riddled with frustration—comprehending but a glance.
Earth decreed, "The noble deed is done without such petulance."

Sighing, piqued, afraid, bewildered, swaying farther from the goal;
Cosmos yet communicating, "Ever nearer to your soul."

Strolling in the woods I stumbled, as I sought the birds and bees.
Guessing, while approaching Nature, she endured for me to please.

Curious, I reached my hand out and I touched the fiery flame.
Flickering retorts they scorched me, warning, "Love is not a game."

Everything displayed before me, I critiqued and judged as good.
Wondering, was I forgiven? (Looking bleak from where I stood.)

Stage 5: The Mind

Fantasies emerged aplenty, clogging my receptive mind.
I commenced to scale the gate, inventing rules not well-defined.

I spied kingdoms, trophies, fortunes. Ought I gamble and partake?
Anxiously I would pursue them, unconcerned about the stake.

It was next I met the Devil, grinning at the choice I made.
If it wasn't so persuasive, possibly I might have stayed.

Deep inside the walls of wisdom, sat real Truth upon His throne;
Clarifying ancient mysteries; grasping all that could be known.

"Everything," He said, "is precious." "Everyone," He said, "is blind."
"Anywhere is life abounding. Anytime can love be kind."

Oft' I tossed and turned in torment, fighting free and to awake.
Else my brain should lock in conflict, or my promises would break.

I perceived One sacred presence, while I worked and while I played.
And the price of my admission? It already had been paid.

I resumed my quest for meaning; sacrificing what I owned.
Still, relentless evil lurked beneath a ruthless heart of stone.

Stage 6: The Spirit

Marveling at my adventures, puzzled by the will to die.
"Just as life eternal beckons," was the infinite reply.

Passions of the flesh were rampant; brainstorms of the mind intense.
Such experience was shallow to the spirit, so immense.

"Love and faith and hope," His words rang, "Welcome them into your heart."
"When you let them guide your actions, everything to you impart."

Broken by my self-destruction; stricken with my self-beguile.
Searching for the most elusive—that which follows all the while.

Oddly you'll hear no restrictions, but to practice if you're smart.
Bring the proper motivation. Try the earliest to start.

Had I lost the prized possession, might I also lose my sense?
Nothing in this world of value which could hardly recompense.

Finally, I saw that vision isn't merely of the eye.
Further, I discerned that heaven isn't only there on high.

Stage 7: Eternity

Striving for a simple joy, the sort I yearned for since the womb.
Losing focus constantly, inviting nigh the brink of doom.

Pondering to gain an answer rendering my task complete.
Not prepared to work the harvest and divide the chaff from wheat.

Realizing at long last, I begged permission to confess.
Seeking strength of mind and body, I beheld a soul oppressed.

Frequently, the prime objective—hidden by the sight of gloom.
Dreading not the day of judgment—too distracted by the tomb.

Everyone a million chances, to assert or to retreat.
Slave to one's own binding contracts—eager, ill to sound defeat.

Persevere with moral guidance; set a course for righteousness.
Help each other, serve the Master; be the host—become the guest.

Epilogue: The Victory

Saved by Grace through faith unyielding—undeserved, lest we should boast.
Blessed be the everlasting Father, Son, and Holy Ghost!